FABLES, FOLKLORE
& ANCIENT STORIES

AFRICAN

FOLK & FAIRY TALES

FLAME TREE PUBLISHING
6 Melbray Mews, Fulham,
London SW6 3NS, United Kingdom
www.flametreepublishing.com

First published and copyright © 2022
Flame Tree Publishing Ltd

22 24 26 25 23
1 3 5 7 9 10 8 6 4 2

ISBN: 978-1-80417-231-5

Cover and pattern art was created by Flame Tree Studio, with elements courtesy of
Shutterstock.com/takahuli.production/chasiki/svekloid.
Inside decorations courtesy of Shutterstock.com/goodwin_x/svekloid.

Judith John (Glossary) is a writer and editor specializing in literature and history. A former
secondary school English Language and Literature teacher, she has subsequently worked
as an editor on major educational projects, including *English A: Literature* for the Pearson
International Baccalaureate series. Judith's major research interests include Romantic and
Gothic literature, and Renaissance drama.

Original compilers, authors, editors and translators for the stories in this book include:
William H. Barker/Cecilia Sinclair, Rosetta Gage (Harvey) Baskerville, René Basset/
Chauncey C. Starkweather, George W. Bateman, W. H. I. Bleek/L. C. Lloyd, Natalie
Curtis Burlin, Harold Courlander, James A. Honey, Andrew Lang, Mūkūyū, Robert Hamill
Nassau, M. I. Ogumefu, Maalam Shaihua/R. Sutherland Rattray, J. Rivière/Chauncey C.
Starkweather, Henry M. Stanley, C. H. Stigand, Percy Amaury Talbot, Alice Werner.

A copy of the CIP data for this book is available
from the British Library.

Designed and created in the UK | Printed and bound in China

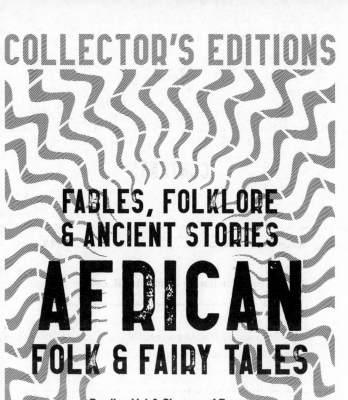

COLLECTOR'S EDITIONS

FABLES, FOLKLORE
& ANCIENT STORIES
AFRICAN
FOLK & FAIRY TALES

Reading List & Glossary of Terms
with a New Introduction by
PROFESSOR LÉRÈ ADÉYẸMÍ

FLAME TREE PUBLISHING

CONTENTS

FABLES, FOLKLORE
& ANCIENT STORIES
AFRICAN
FOLK & FAIRY TALES

SERIES FOREWORD

Stretching back to the oral traditions of thousands of years ago, tales of heroes and disaster, creation and conquest have been told by many different civilizations in many different ways. Their impact sits deep within our culture even though the detail in the tales themselves are a loose mix of historical record, transformed narrative and the distortions of hundreds of storytellers.

Today the language of mythology lives with us: our mood is jovial, our countenance is saturnine, we are narcissistic and our modern life is hermetically sealed from others. The nuances of myths and legends form part of our daily routines and help us navigate the world around us, with its half truths and biased reported facts.

The nature of a myth is that its story is already known by most of those who hear it, or read it. Every generation brings a new emphasis, but the fundamentals remain the same: a desire to understand and describe the events and relationships of the world. Many of the great stories are archetypes that help us find our own place, equipping us with tools for self-understanding, both individually and as part of a broader culture.

For Western societies it is Greek mythology that speaks to us most clearly. It greatly influenced the mythological heritage of the ancient Roman civilization and is the lens through which we still see the Celts, the Norse and many of the other great peoples and religions. The Greeks themselves learned much from their neighbours, the Egyptians, an older culture that became weak with age and incestuous leadership.

It is important to understand that what we perceive now as mythology had its own origins in perceptions of the divine and the rituals of the sacred. The earliest civilizations, in the crucible of the Middle East, in the Sumer of the third millennium BC, are the source to which many of the mythic archetypes can be traced. As humankind collected together in cities for the first time, developed writing and industrial scale agriculture, started to irrigate the rivers and attempted to control rather than be at the mercy of its environment, humanity began to write down its tentative explanations of natural events, of floods and plagues, of disease.

Early stories tell of Gods (or god-like animals in the case of tribal societies such as African, Native American or Aboriginal cultures) who are crafty and use their wits to survive, and it is reasonable to suggest that these were the first rulers of the gathering peoples of the earth, later elevated to god-like status with the distance of time. Such tales became more political as cities vied with each other for supremacy, creating new Gods, new hierarchies for their pantheons. The older Gods took on primordial roles and became the preserve of creation and destruction, leaving the new gods to deal with more current, everyday affairs. Empires rose and fell, with Babylon assuming the mantle from Sumeria in the 1800s BC, then in turn to be swept away by the Assyrians of the 1200s BC; then the Assyrians and the Egyptians were subjugated by the Greeks, the Greeks by the Romans and so on, leading to the spread and assimilation of common themes, ideas and stories throughout the world.

The survival of history is dependent on the telling of good tales, but each one must have the 'feeling' of truth, otherwise it will be ignored. Around the firesides, or embedded in a book or a computer, the myths and legends of the past are still the living materials of retold myth, not restricted to an exploration of origins. Now we have devices and global communications that give us unparalleled access to a diversity of traditions. We can find out about Native American, Indian, Chinese and tribal African mythology in a way that was denied to our ancestors, we can find connections, match the archaeology, religion and the mythologies of the world to build a comprehensive image of the human experience that is endlessly fascinating.

The stories in this book provide an introduction to the themes and concerns of the myths and legends of their respective cultures, with a short introduction to provide a linguistic, geographic and political context. This is where the myths have arrived today, but undoubtedly over the next millennia, they will transform again whilst retaining their essential truths and signs.

Jake Jackson
General Editor

FABLES, FOLKLORE & ANCIENT STORIES

AFRICAN

FOLK & FAIRY TALES

A NEW INTRODUCTION TO
AFRICAN FOLK & FAIRY TALES

INTRODUCTION
& FURTHER READING

A NEW INTRODUCTION TO
AFRICAN FOLK & FAIRY TALES

AFRICA: LAND OF DIVERSITIES

Africa **is a land** of diverse cultures, languages, religions, oral traditions and folklore. The continent is blessed with an incredibly rich variety of people and mineral resources, as well as amazing biodiversity and abundantly diverse agro-ecologies. Linguists have described Africa as a melting pot of over 2000 languages. It contains over 50 countries and spans about 30.37 million square kilometres with a population of 1,225,080,510 people, as reported in 2016 by the UN Department of Economic and Social Affairs. Given the plurality of languages and the multitude of fairy tales in Africa, the call for a symphony that weaves together their folk tales, myths, legends, short stories and other traditional narratives to benefit not only African societies but the global community is frequently heard.

Each country in Africa has a long history of civilization and each culture has its own language, oral traditions, folk tales and other verbal arts. This means that millions of folk tales in Africa have yet to be written down. Unfortunately, indigenous tales are fast fading away in the modern-day continent because most still exist and are dispensed in oral, unwritten forms of expression.

Despite the impact of print culture during colonization, both on people's experience and in the formation of new cultural modes, the oral tradition remains predominant in Africa, with the bulk of literary activities still occurring in oral forms. There is thus an urgent need to document the orally transmitted folk tales and make them accessible to the global community. This will not only avoid total extinction of both the fairy tales and the languages that carry them, but will also reduce negative representation of Africa by those who regard Africa as a dark continent.

NEW REPRESENTATION OF AFRICAN STORIES

Representation, or the act of stating facts in order to influence the actions of others, is currently one of the most debated topics in cultural studies. The term itself has a semiotic meaning in that something is standing for something ('signifier' and 'signified'), and it affects the ways in which individuals are perceived. For example, the representation of Africa in foreign narratives, films and textbooks in the past was biased and confused representation with reality. In fact, such representations are mere constructed images that are not true.

Representation of people or of how a group of people is seen, understood and described depends on who is doing the describing, where they come from, what their interests are and what they stand to gain or lose from such description or representation. The representation of African cultural values by many non-Africanist scholars has been essentially prejudiced and mostly negative. Some of its incorrect perceptions were that African indigenous knowledge systems are obsolete, static and romantic, lacking universal usage because of their localized, community-based nature.

However, by the 1930s several African intellectuals and sincere Africanist researchers began writing novels and short stories to debunk Eurocentric narratives and falsehoods, thus closing the gaps created by many years of marginalization of Africans' knowledge system. Authors such as D.O. Fagúnwà, Amos Tutuola, Chinua Achebe, Ngugi, Soyinka, Pita Nwana and Ngugi wa Thiongo, among many others, have used storytelling to debunk negative narratives about African knowledge-making systems before the coming of a European mode of civilization. In so doing they have deconstructed the stereotypical representation of African cultural heritage. Such deconstruction does not simply consist of reversing existing stereotypes and binary paradigms; rather it creates a process of *alternative* representations and reclaims the right to represent oneself rather than being represented by others. In this book we therefore document African oral traditions, particularly folk tales, through African eyes and for their own sake and that of the world at large – as with other volumes published to provide new representation of African stories.

FAIRY TALES AS COLLECTIVE IDEOLOGY OF AFRICAN SOCIETIES

In pre-colonial, pre-writing African societies with a primarily oral culture, the continent's narrative spirit is embedded in verbal arts – particularly folk tales, myths, legends, short stories and other poetic forms. From Egypt to Uganda, Nigeria, Kenya, Tanzania,

Morocco, Ghana, Benin, Rwanda, Lesotho, Senegal, Tunisia, South Africa and many parts of traditional African societies, there was a time when folk tales, legends and short stories were told around the fire. Younger people listened with rapt attention and great amusement. These stories are still told mostly in the evening for relaxation, amusement and instruction after a day's work. They are often used for mediation and the teaching of relevant lessons, especially to younger listeners. Their amusement is achieved by the way in which the story is narrated, as well as by the humorous episodes they contain. Their didactic purpose is achieved through a careful selection of thematic content. The themes of fairy tales usually exhibit some virtues, vices or general wickedness; they also manipulate the story so that the culprit is punished or the person with good nature and virtue rewarded, as the case may be.

Folk tales have also served not only as sociological tools that transmit oral traditions from one generation to another, but also as people's artistic expressions and memories. They bear – and celebrate – the original marks of African cultural resilience. However, in modern-day African urban centres, lifestyles have changed: routine duties, modern professional life and the new era of information technology leave little room for parents to come back from a day's work and still find time to recount a story or tale. Many generations of African children now find it difficult to experience the tales by moonlight, as they would traditionally have done.

Folk tales are of different kinds: they include stories accompanied by songs and others without; 'why tales', which explain the origin of life and the world, the creation of man and why things exist; tales featuring the tortoise, spider and other animals; dilemma tales, tales of many wives, and moral tales that portray human exploits and follies. Each story in this book has an entertaining overview, which makes the tales easy to read and understand. Here we explain a little more about the essential elements of fairy tales featured in this book to give readers a clear understanding of their meaning.

THE 'WORLD' OF FAIRY TALES

The 'world' of African folk tales is a fairy world in which fact and fiction are blurred and the supernatural is as accepted a presence as the natural. This world of marvellous realism exists not only in African tales, but is also a universal tendency – one which, it may be added, is inherent in human existence. The 'marvellous' narrative depicts a fictitious world totally removed from conventional reality. For example, in 'Sudika-Mbambi the Invincible', Sudika-Mbambi is born a 'wonder-child' who 'spoke before his entrance into the world, and came forth equipped with knife, stick, and his *kilembe*'; there are supernatural beings called *makishi* and *kipalendes*, and the brothers cannot kill each other when they fight since they are both 'endowed with some magical power'.

A sense of the marvellous prevails in most African folk tales and only readers deeply knowledgeable in African culture can fully interpret the stories' significance. In some categories of African folk tales, however, the narratives are marked by magical realism, where two diametrically opposed ontologies coexist on equal terms: the empirical world of reason and logic and the supernatural world of unreason. In contrast to purely romantic or fantastic tales in which the supernatural predominates, in magical realist tales the supernatural serves to disturb the 'coherence' of the systematically empirical world. In such tales it is revealed to be not a universally true or absolute representation of external reality, but rather one of several possible representations.

In the African fairy tales collected in this volume, the 'real' and the 'magical' realms exist side by side on equal terms. Magic and reality may sound like a contradictory pairing, but in literary history the terms seem to exist in oxymoronic or paradoxical cohesion rather than antithesis. Magical realism is an attitude towards reality that can be expressed in popular or cultured forms. In magical realism, the narrator confronts reality and tries to untangle it in order to discover what is mysterious in things, in life and in human acts. Most of the tales concerned with human exploits and follies fall under reality and romantic elements; see, for example, 'The Ogre and the Beautiful Woman', 'The Adventure of Sidi Mahomet', 'The Haunted Garden' and 'The Magic Napkin', all from the Berber people of North Africa. Other illustrations can be seen in the tales of 'Oluronbi', 'Olè and the Ants' and 'Secrets of the Fishing Basket' (Yorùbá, Southern Nigeria), as well as 'The Girl who Married a Lion' (Lamba people of Southern Africa), among many others.

SEEN AND UNSEEN FORCES

The African people believe in both seen and unseen forces, and that these have a real impact on human beings. Those forces that are not seen are believed to be present in space. They also believe that animate and inanimate objects, as well as the seen and unseen forces, can hear words and sounds. In their philosophy everything that exists, whether visible or invisible, human or superhuman, has secret names or epithets. Whoever has the knowledge of the primordial names of things can invoke these names and send them on errands, either for good purposes or for bad. The seen and unseen forces can be manipulated or controlled through rituals, sacrifices and spoken words.

The reaction of African people to this type of mystery and the things that are based on facts as they exist in reality constitutes the importance of the fairy tales in this collection. This juxtaposition of fantasy and reality provides the foundation for the magical realist episodes in traditional folk tales across Africa, especially as documented in this book. The world of African fairy tales is partly a reflection of the continent's world-view, its people's thoughts and beliefs regarding the existence and power of spirits, magic, witches, sorcerers, communication with the departed ancestors and the invisible hidden forces that influence the lives of the living. Such tales have storylines with fantastic actions, unusual characters and the co-existence of human and non-human characters, as seen in sections two and three. The stories in this book reflect what African people believe, what they do, what they think, how they live and have lived, as well as their values, joys and sorrows.

ORIGIN OF THE WORLD

Tales of creation abound everywhere in African societies. These are the tales that explain people's beliefs and their understanding of the mysteries found in nature, including their cosmology, their climate and weather, and the 'why tales' designed to explain natural phenomena or the origin of life and death. Even though the myth of creation varies across different countries in Africa, one element common to African myths of creation as reflected in this book is a belief in the Supreme Being as the creator of the universe. He brings the world into being through his messengers, namely lesser gods and spirits. In the Egyptian creation story, for example, the creation of the world is attributed to different gods: the set of eight primordial divinities called Ogdoad, the self-engendered god Atum and his offspring, the contemplative deity Ptah and the mysterious, transcendent god Amum. In the Yorùbá (Nigeria) version of the myth, it was Olódùmarè (Almighty God) who sent Obatala to create the world. The earth was then full of water with no dry land. The Bantu tribe in Central Africa believed that Bumba was the creator of all things. When the great god Bumba came into being, he was made with darkness; one day he had stomach pain and vomited the sun. The sun dried up the water, leaving the land to live on. Bumba also vomited other things such as the stars, moon and the animals.

In the myth of creation of the Fon people of Benin, Gui – the oldest son of creation twins Mawu (the moon) and Lisa (the sun) – was responsible for the creation of the universe. Among the Gikuyu people of Kenya, Ngai lives on the mountain Kiri Nyaga. He created Gikuyu and instructed him to go to a specific spot on the south of the mountain where fig trees were plentiful. When Gikuyu arrived there he met a woman, Mumbi, who became his wife. Male and female goddess of creation came together and, as the milk essence from Mukuyu entered the earth, Gikuyu and Mumbi brought forth ten daughters; they became the mothers of the ten Gikuyu clans. In the tale of Gikuyu and Mumbi, we observe hierogamy – that is, the union between a god and a goddess – which bears the symbolic representation of fertility and life. The two cosmic phenomena were united and in turn created human beings.

LIFE AND DEATH

In one of the myths of the Mende people of Sierra Leone, God's original plan for mankind was immortality. When God gave a message to a dog and another message to a toad to deliver to human beings, the message given to the dog stated 'Life has come' while that sent through the toad was 'Death has come'. While the dog was coming, he stopped over a plate of food to eat. The toad overtook him and delivered his message of death first, thus bringing death to the world. Another myth about death, that of the Khoi, states that Kaang (the Supreme Being) created the world as a peaceful place with strict instructions on how to live in it, but man flagrantly disobeyed God; as a result Kaang sent death and destruction to them. The tale of the Zulu people of Southern Africa attributes the coming of death to the world to the Chameleon, sent to the world by Ukulunkulu (Supreme Creator) with a message: 'Let not man die!' But the Chameleon loitered on the way, which made the Creator send another message through the Lizard, this time the opposite: 'Let men die!' The lizard delivered the message before the arrival of the slow chameleon, and so humans became subject to the power of life and death. The theme of the tales across Africa is that human beings were originally not designed to die, but that through total human disregard for and disobedience of God death came to the world.

SUPERNATURAL INTERVENTIONS

African fairy tales contain diverse elements of the supernatural, such as the intervention of the deities/gods, demi-gods and spirits in the lives of human beings. In African beliefs God can use anything to intervene and help people in situations of grave danger. For example, when a good person is in danger organized by evil people, or when an innocent person is falsely accused of an offence which he or she has not committed, and is then punished unjustly, the gods can help the person to bear the punishment, later exposing the original culprit and the injustice suffered by the victim. Orphans, widows and people with disabilities often receive supernatural assistance when confronted with dangers. In the folk tale of the Akan people of Ghana entitled 'Why the Moon and the Stars Receive their Light from the Sun', Anansi and his son Kweku Tsin were caught in a terrible famine. With food very scarce, Kweku Tsin went to the forest to hunt. He killed a deer and came back to inform his father Anansi. A ferocious dragon then came, kidnapping both Anansi and Kweku Tsin and taking them to his cave for food. The god from the sky saved Kweku Tsin, bringing him unusual wisdom that helped him to escape, together with the dragon's other victims, into the sky. Through the help of the gods, he became the sun, his father the moon and the other victims (who had become his friends) the stars. They all tap their light from Kweku Tsin because he has been supernaturally empowered to become the sun in the sky, while the moon and stars are dull and powerless.

ANCESTORS

Africans believe in the continued existence of departed souls who have joined the cult of the ancestors. For them, the departed father or mother serves as an intermediary between the living and the dead. The beliefs of African people about those who have died are reflected in several of the folk tales as documented in this book. The Ronga-speaking people of Mozambique and the Zaramo of Tanzania, like other African societies, believe that when a person dies he or she becomes a spirit. They believe that communication exists between the world of living human beings and the world of the dead; although no longer present physically, the dead are available spiritually and can be called upon to intercede for living family members or for society at large.

This belief also resonates in folk tales. Stories relating to departed fathers or mothers and visits to other worlds are recurring themes. For example, 'The Road to Heaven', a story from the Ronga-speaking people of Mozambique, reflects an aspect of African belief in life after death. The story tells how a girl was sent to the river to fetch water. There she broke her pot, of a type that is very hard to find. 'Bukali Bwa Ngoti!' ('Oh! that I had a rope!') she exclaimed – and suddenly a rope descended from heaven. The girl climbed the rope and ascended to heaven. Her moral uprightness made the old woman at the gate of heaven help her, and she later returned to her family with abundant prosperity.

Another tale, that of Kwege and Bahati, comes from the Zaramo people of Tanzania. In this story the intervention comes like a *deus ex machina*, in the shape of dead parents or some form of natural phenomenon. Kwege lost his parents very early in life, but was left with his father's slave Bahati. He went to look for his mother's brother in Mutingu village, all the while bearing a taboo that he must not cross over a log: if he did so, he would die. He begged Bahati to carry him and the slave agreed, on one condition: Kwege must give him his garments in exchange for his help. Kwege agreed, so Bahati collected all his garments and put them on. When they got to Mutingu village, Kwege was taken to be the slave, enabling Bahati to become the master because of his better clothes. Kwege was reduced to undertaking forced labour on the rice farm, where he burst into song. On hearing the emotional song of sorrow, Kwege's dead parents appeared; they changed from birds to human beings and intervened. His parents changed Kwege's clothes from the rags of a slave to royal garments and anointed him with fresh oil. This intervention continued until Kwege regained his rightful position and the disloyal Bahati was killed.

NATURAL PHENOMENA

Africans believe that natural phenomena such as the sun, moon, stars, trees, mountains, hills, streams, rivers and oceans, among others, possess powers that can be tapped for human use. They can be used to benefit people through intervention in the affairs of human beings and for magical resources. Interventions in African folk tales occur through natural phenomena – the sun, moon, rainbow or even thunder, as seen in 'The Thunder's Bride'. In this tale from the Banyarwanda people of Rwanda the thunder of heaven intervened in the story of a woman, the wife of Kwisaba, a warrior. Her husband had gone off to war and she became very sick and cried for help. She shouted for help without seeing anybody, then the thunder of heaven appeared in the shape of a man and assisted her to split firewood. Magic is also deployed in African fairy tales, intervening to demonstrate superiority or one's authority over other characters. It is also used to avoid perils in ordinary life, to escape from grave danger, or even as a way to test a man's patience, as in the magic dwarf of 'Abundance: A Play on the Meaning of a Word' (From the Fang and Bulu peoples, Cameroon).

ANIMALS

In African folk tales, like those from other continents of the world, animals have the power of speech and can communicate with human beings. Both domestic and wild animals are represented in African fairy tales. Wild animals such as deer, lions, snakes and others may possess human features and are able to disguise themselves as human beings. Their disguise is usually known to the elders, especially hunters in the community, who are able to recognize features such as their excessive height; snake-men may be perceived through their smooth skin or tiny eyes, while bird-men are revealed through their diminutive size or sonorous voice.

Not everyone can see through the animals' disguise, however. The stories describe how they can come to towns to transact business on market days and even engage in lovemaking, which may result in marriages with human beings. Such marriages usually end in disaster because the partners are incompatible in both character and world views. In frenzied anger, the animal-wife might return to her forest with vengeance in her heart and later go on to kill many people, including her husband's other wives.

CONCLUSION

The tales in this book are presented in a way that provokes entertainment and gives moral, social, emotional, spiritual, kinetic (through singing, dancing and hand clapping), aesthetic, psychological and intellectual benefits to their readers. The collection of fairy tales in this book constitutes a special gift to humanity. It makes an effective pedagogical tool, which a teacher could utilize in the teaching of any subject – at all levels and in all settings. Individual folk tales can be used to teach moral lessons across cultures; they also serve in building bridges across cultures, especially important since the reality of globalization has turned the world into a 'global village'. This book will help people to appreciate other cultures by recognizing the 'unity in diversity' that exists among the various countries, values and belief systems of the world. The songs of fairy tales also have a cathartic function: Africans believe folk songs to have healing powers which can be used to soothe the nerves of those experiencing issues with mental health. Educators at all levels, as well as school counsellors and clinical psychologists – especially those dealing with children who have emotional and cognitive challenges – can deploy the power of the tales in this volume effectively and to great effect.

This volume will also help many people to discover themselves. They can identify with others portrayed in the selected tales and be able to make sense of their world through fairy tales. The fairy tales collected in this book can be adopted by musicians and artists to recreate and re-enact the traditional past, thus creating something new that can be truly labelled as a product of our own generation. Each story in this book has an entertaining overview which makes the tales easy to read and understand.

It is our hope that the folk tales collected in this volume will assist students and general readers interested in exploring African cultural practices and African folklore. It will also serve researchers whose studies fall within oral literature, folklore and cultural studies. This book has a distinctive edge over existing texts on African fairy tales because it contains folk tales from a cross section of African tribes, including those previously 'invisible'; it is also written in splendid, engaging language spiced with proverbs, idioms, similes, metaphors and other intriguing ornaments. It is thus an invaluable pedagogical tool for teachers of cultural studies across the globe.

Professor Lérè Adéyẹmí

FURTHER READING

Abimbola, Wande, *An Exposition of Ifa Literary Corpus* (Ibadan: Oxford University Press, 1969)

Abimbola, Wande, *Yorùbá Oral Tradition* (Ile-Ifẹ: University of Ife, 1975)

Akinyemi, Akintunde, *Orature and Yorùbá Riddles* (New York: Palgrave Macmillan, 2015)

Akinyemi, A. and Toyin Falola (eds), *The Palgrave Handbook of African Oral Traditions and Folklore*, vols 1 & 2 (Cham, Switzerland: Palgrave Macmillan, 2021)

Ambali, H.I. 'The Functions of Folk tales as a Process of Educating Children in the 21st Century. In *21st Century Academic Forum Conference Proceedings*88–97, IC21CE, 88–97. (Dubai: UAC, 2014)

Bamgbose, Ayo, *The Novels of D.O. Fagunwa – A Commentary*. (Ibadan: Nelson Publishers Ltdd, 2007)

Bavala, S., *The Benefits of Storytelling* (www.storyteller.net/articles/312,2012)

Bivins, Mary, *Telling Stories, Making Histories: Women, Words, and Islam in Nineteenth Century Hausaland and Sokoto Caliphate* (Portsmouth: Heinemann, 2007)

Blavin, Jonathan, *Folklore in Africa. Open Knowledge Network* (Harvard Law School, 2003)

Canonici, N.N., 'Educational Value of Folk tales', *Educamus* xxxi (3) (1985): 13–23

Crapanzano, V., *Tuhami: Portrait of a Morrocan* (Chicago: The University of Chicago Press, 1980)

Curtis, S., *Mainane Tswana Tales* (Botswana: Botswana Book Centre, 1975)

Darah, G.G., 'The Folk tale is Dead: Long Live Storytelling', *Journal of Oral Literatures* 2 (2014): 37–50

Falola, Toyin, Jason Morgan and Bukola A. Oyeniyi, *Culture and Customs of Libya* (Santa Barbara, USA: Greenwood, 2021)

Hall, Stuart (ed.), *Representation: Cultural Representation and Signifying Practices.* (London: Sage, 1997)

Lawuyi, O.B., Ìjàpá and Ìgbín: *A Discursive Meditation on Politics, Public Culture and Moral Imaginings in Nigeria* (Ibadan: Ibadan University Press, 2012)

Lindfords, Bernith, *Folklore in Nigerian Literatures* (Ibadan: Caltop, 2002)

Majasan, J.A., *Folklore as an Instrument of Education Among the Yorùbá* (Ibadan: Ibadan University Press, 1969)

Mbiti, S. John, *African Religions and Philosophy* (London: Heinemann, 1969)

Mdlalose, N. and Mabalane, J., 'Synthesisation of Storytelling and Technology', *Southern African Journal for Folklore Studies* 25 (1) (2015): 573–580

Mhando, J., 'Safeguarding Endangered Oral Traditions in Africa: A Report for UNESCO'. Accessed from www.unesco.org/culture/ich/doc/003474- ENP, 2008

Mtonga, M., *Children's Games and Play in Zambia* (Lusaka: University of Zambia Press, 2012)

Mweti, C., 'The Use of Stories and their Power in the Secondary Curriculum Among the Akamba of Kenya'. Unpublished Ph.D thesis, University of Wisconsin. Madison, WI, 1999

Okpewho, Isidore, *Myth in Africa* (Cambridge: Cambridge University Press, 1983)

Okpewho, Isidore, *African Oral Literature* (Bloomington: Indiana University Press, 1992)

Lérè Adéyẹmí (PhD) is Professor of Yorùbá Literature and Culture in the Department of Linguistics and Nigerian Languages, University of Ilọrin, Nigeria. He obtained his first, second and PhD degrees from the same university between 1988 and 2003 and was head of his department from 2005 to 2006, and 2008 to 2009. His areas of specialization are Yorùbá literature and culture, particularly oral traditions and folklores. He has published scholarly articles and textbooks in the area of Yoruba studies and was the former Associate Editor of *Ilọrin Journal of Linguistics, Literature and Culture* (IJLLC). Adéyẹmí is also a published creative writer. His most recent novel is entitled *Ọba Mẹ́wàá Ìgbà Mẹ́wàá* (2020, Ten Kings Ten Epochs). His other creative works are: *Ọ̀dájú Ni Wọ́n* (2018, They Are Ruthless), *Ìṣèlú Onírèké `Ogè* (2014, The Politics of Sweetness and Bitterness), *Kọ́rọ̀ Tó Dayọ̀* (2011, Before the Dawn of Joy), *Kò Sáyè Láàfin* (2008, No Vacancy in the Palace), *Ọ̀gá Nìyáà Mi* (2005, My Mother is Great) and *Àkùkọ Gàgàrà* (2001, The Overmighty Cock).

ORIGINS, THE HEAVENS, LIFE & DEATH

The fairy tales in this section concentrate on the origin of the world from African perspectives. The creation myth retold at the beginning of this section comes from Egypt in North Africa. Every tribe has its own version of the creation of the world, human beings and other creatures. The belief in the Almighty God is sacrosanct, as well as in divinities as messengers of the Supreme Being. In Egyptian myths of creation, lesser gods or divinities were given the responsibility of creating the earth and human and non-human creatures, a belief shared by other countries in Africa. This informs the act of multiple naming of God, as portrayed in the tales in this section. He is known as Njinyi (Cameroon), Mawu (Ghana), Olódùmarè (Yoruba, Nigeria), Chukwu (Igbo, Nigeria), Ngai (Kenya), Jok (Uganda), Chilenga (Zambia), Inkosi (South Africa) and Mwari (Zimbabwe).

The tales show different stories inherent in each tribe, encompassing such themes as the origin of life and death, light and darkness, the relationship between the living and the dead and what transpires in the Otherworld. However, the general belief is that God is the creator, ruler and owner of the world. Only a selection of such stories is documented in this section.

THE EGYPTIAN STORY OF THE CREATION
(From Ancient Egypt)

If we consider for a moment the vast amount of thought which the Egyptian gave to the problems of the future life, and their deep-seated belief in resurrection and immortality, we cannot fail to conclude that he must have theorised deeply about the constitution of the heaven in which he hoped to live everlastingly, and about its Maker.

The theologians of Egypt were ready enough to describe heaven, and the life led by the blessed there, and the powers and the attributes of the gods, but they appear to have shrunk from writing down in a connected form their beliefs concerning the Creation and the origin of the Creator. The worshippers of each great god proclaimed him to be the Creator of All, and every great town had its own local belief on the subject. According to the Heliopolitans, Atem, or Tem, and at a later period Ra, was the Creator; according to Memphite theology he was Ptah; according to the Hermopolitans he was Thoth; and according to the Thebans he was Amen (Ammon). In only one native Egyptian work up to the present has there been discovered any connected account of the Creation, and the means by which it was effected, namely, the British Museum Papyrus, No. 10,188.

The British Museum Papyrus

This papyrus was written about 305 BC, and is therefore of a comparatively late date, but the subject matter of the works contained in it is thousands of years older, and it is only their *forms* which are of a late date.

The Story of the Creation is found in the last work in the papyrus, which is called the 'Book of overthrowing Aapep, the Enemy of Ra, the Enemy of Un-Nefer' (i.e. Osiris). This work is a liturgy, which was said at certain times of the day and night in the great temple of Amen-Ra at Thebes, with the view of preventing the monster Aapep from obstructing the sunrise.

In the midst of the magical spells of this papyrus we find two copies of the 'Book of knowing how Ra came into being, and of overthrowing Aapep'. One copy is a little fuller than the other, but they agree substantially. The words of this book are said in the opening line to have been spoken by the god Nebertcher, i.e. the 'Lord to the uttermost limit,' or God Himself. The Egyptian Christians, or Copts, in their religious writings use this name as an equivalent of God Almighty, the Lord of All, the God of the Universe. The second version of the book states that the name of Nebertcher is Ausares (Osiris).

How Ra Came Into Being

Nebertcher says: 'I am the creator of what has come into being. I myself came into being under the form of the god Khepera. I came into being under the form of Pautti (or, in primeval time), I formed myself out of the primeval matter, I made myself out of the substance that was in primeval time.' Nothing existed at that time except the great primeval watery mass called Nu, but in this there were the germs of everything that came into being subsequently. There was no heaven, and no earth, and the god found no place on which to stand; nothing, in fact, existed except the god. He says, 'I was alone.'

He first created himself by uttering his own name as a word of power, and when this was uttered his visible form appeared. He then uttered another kind of word of power, and as a result of this his soul (*ba*) came into being, and it worked in connection with his heart or mind (*ab*). Before every act of creation Nebertcher, or his visible form Khepera, thought out what form the thing to be created was to take, and when he had uttered its name the thing itself appeared in heaven or earth. To fill the heaven, or place where he lived, the god next produced from his body and its shadow the two gods Shu and Tefnut. These with Nebertcher, or Khepera, formed the first triad of gods, and the 'one god became three', or, as we should say, the one god had three aspects, each of which was quite distinct from the other. The tradition of the begetting of Shu and Tefnut is as old as the time of the pyramids, for it is mentioned in the text of Pepi I.

The next act of creation resulted in the emerging of the Eye of Nebertcher (later identified with Ra) from the watery mass (*Nu*), and light shone upon its waters. Shu and Tefnut then united and they produced Keb, the Earth-god, and Nut, the Sky-goddess. The text then refers to some calamity which befell the Eye of Nebertcher or of Khepera, but what it was is not clear; at all events the Eye became obscured, and it ceased to give light. This period of darkness is, of course, the night, and to obviate the inconvenience caused by this recurring period of darkness, the god made a second Eye, i.e. the Moon, and set it in the heavens. The greater Eye ruled the day, and the lesser Eye the night. One of the results of the daily darkness was the descent of the Sky-goddess Nut to the Earth-god Keb each evening.

The gods and goddesses next created were five, namely, Osiris, Horus, Set, Isis, and Nephthys. Osiris married Isis, and their son was called Horus; Set married Nephthys, but their son Anpu, or Anubis, is not mentioned in our text. Osiris became the great Ancestor-god of Egypt, and was a reincarnation of his great-grandfather. Men and women were first formed from the tears that fell from the Eye of Khepera, or the Sun-god, upon his body; the old Egyptian word for 'men' very closely resembles in form and sound the word for 'tears'. Plants, vegetables, herbs, and trees owe their origin to the light of the moon falling upon the earth. Our text contains no mention of a special creation of the 'beasts of the field', but the god states distinctly that he created the children of the earth, or creeping things of all kinds, and among this class quadrupeds are probably included. The men and women, and all the other living creatures that were made at that time by Nebertcher, or Khepera, reproduced their species, each in his own way, and thus the earth became filled with their descendants as we see at the present time. The elements of this Creation legend are very, very old, and the form in which they are grouped in our text suggests the influence of the priests of Heliopolis. It is interesting to note that only very ancient gods appear as Powers of creation, and these were certainly worshipped for many centuries before the priests of Heliopolis invented their cult of the Sun-god, and identified their god with the older gods of the country. We may note, too, that gods like Ptah and Amen, whose reputation was so great in later times, and even when our text was copied in 305 BC, find no mention at all.

THE DESTRUCTION OF MANKIND
(From Ancient Egypt)

This legend was cut in hieroglyphs on the walls of a small chamber in the tomb of Seti I, about 1350 BC.

When Ra, the self-begotten and self-formed god, had been ruling gods and men for some time, men began to complain about him, saying, 'His Majesty has become old. His bones have turned into silver, his flesh into gold, and his hair into real lapis-lazuli.' His Majesty heard these murmurings and commanded his followers to summon to his presence his Eye (i.e. the goddess Hathor), Shu, Tefnut, Keb, Nut, and the father and mother gods and goddesses who were with him in the watery abyss of Nu, and also the god of this water, Nu. They were to come to him with all their followers secretly, so that men should not suspect the reason for their coming, and take flight, and they were to assemble in the Great House in Heliopolis, where Ra would take counsel with them.

In due course all the gods assembled in the Great House, and they ranged themselves down the sides of the House, and they bowed down in homage before Ra until their heads touched the ground, and said, 'Speak, for we are listening.' Then Ra, addressing Nu, the father of the first-born gods, told him to give heed to what men were doing, for they whom he had created were murmuring against him. And he said, 'Tell me what you would do. Consider the matter, invent a plan for me, and I will not slay them until I have heard what you shall say concerning this thing.' Nu replied, 'You, Oh my son Ra, are greater than the god who made you (i.e. Nu himself), you are the king of those who were created with you, your throne is established, and the fear of you is great. Let your Eye (Hathor) attack those who blaspheme you.' And Ra said, 'Lo, they have fled to the mountains, for their hearts are afraid because of what they have said.' The gods replied, 'Let your Eye go forth and destroy those who blasphemed you, for no eye can resist you when it goes forth in the form of Hathor.' Thereupon

42

the Eye of Ra, or Hathor, went in pursuit of the blasphemers in the mountains, and slew them all. On her return Ra welcomed her, and the goddess said that the work of vanquishing men was dear to her heart. Ra then said that he would be the master of men as their king, and that he would destroy them. For three nights the goddess Hathor-Sekhmet waded about in the blood of men, the slaughter beginning at Hensu (Herakleopolis Magna).

Then the Majesty of Ra ordered that messengers should be sent to Abu, a town at the foot of the First Cataract, to fetch mandrakes (?), and when they were brought he gave them to the god Sekti to crush. When the women slaves were bruising grain for making beer, the crushed mandrakes (?) were placed in the vessels that were to hold the beer, together with some of the blood of those who had been slain by Hathor. The beer was then made, and seven thousand vessels were filled with it. When Ra saw the beer he ordered it to be taken to the scene of slaughter, and poured out on the meadows of the four quarters of heaven. The object of putting mandrakes (?) in the beer was to make those who drank fall asleep quickly, and when the goddess Hathor came and drank the beer mixed with blood and mandrakes (?) she became very merry, and, the sleepy stage of drunkenness coming on her, she forgot all about men, and slew no more. At every festival of Hathor ever after 'sleepy beer' was made, and it was drunk by those who celebrated the feast.

Now, although the blasphemers of Ra had been put to death, the heart of the god was not satisfied, and he complained to the gods that he was smitten with the 'pain of the fire of sickness'. He said, 'My heart is weary because I have to live with men; I have slain some of them, but worthless men still live, and I did not slay as many as I ought to have done considering my power.' To this the gods replied, 'Trouble not about your lack of action, for your power is in proportion to your will.' Here the text becomes fragmentary, but it seems that the goddess Nut took the form of a cow, and that the other gods lifted Ra on to her back. When men saw that Ra was leaving the earth, they repented of their murmurings, and the next morning they went out with bows and arrows to fight the enemies of the Sun-god. As a reward for this Ra forgave those men their former blasphemies, but persisted in his intention of retiring from the earth. He ascended into the heights of heaven, being still on the back of the Cow-goddess Nut, and he created there Sekhet-hetep and Sekhet-Aaru as abodes for the blessed, and the flowers that blossomed therein he turned into stars. He also created the millions of beings who lived there in order that they might praise him. The height to which Ra had ascended was now so great that the legs of the Cow-goddess on which he was enthroned trembled, and to give her strength he ordained that Nut should be held up in her position by the godhead and upraised arms of the god Shu. This is why we see pictures of the body of Nut being supported by Shu. The legs of the Cow-goddess were supported by the various gods, and thus the seat of the throne of Ra became stable.

When this was done Ra caused the Earth-god Keb to be summoned to his presence, and when he came he spoke to him about the venomous reptiles that lived in the earth and were hostile to him. Then turning to Thoth, he bade him to prepare a series of spells and words of power, which would enable those who knew them to overcome snakes and serpents and deadly reptiles of all kinds. Thoth did so, and the spells which he wrote under the direction of Ra served as a protection of the servants of Ra ever after, and secured for them the help of Keb, who became sole lord of all the beings that lived and moved on and in his body, the earth. Before finally relinquishing his active rule on earth, Ra summoned Thoth and told him of his desire to create a Light-soul in the Tuat and in the Land of the Caves. Over this region he appointed Thoth to rule, and he ordered him to keep a register of those who were there, and to mete out just punishments to them. In fact, Thoth was to be ever after the representative of Ra in the Other World.

WHY THE MOON AND THE STARS RECEIVE THEIR LIGHT FROM THE SUN
(From the Akan peoples, Ghana)

Once upon a time there was great scarcity of food in the land. Father Anansi and his son, Kweku Tsin, being very hungry, set out one morning to hunt in the forest. In a short time Kweku Tsin was fortunate enough to kill a fine deer – which he carried to his father at their resting-place. Anansi was very glad to see such a supply of food, and requested his son to remain there on guard, while he went for a large basket in which to carry it home. An hour or so passed without his return, and Kweku Tsin became anxious. Fearing lest his father had lost his way, he called out loudly, "Father, father!" to guide him to the spot. To his joy he heard a voice reply, "Yes, my son," and immediately he shouted again, thinking it was Anansi. Instead of the latter, however, a terrible dragon appeared. This monster breathed fire from his great nostrils, and was altogether a dreadful sight to behold. Kweku Tsin was terrified at his approach and speedily hid himself in a cave near by.

The dragon arrived at the resting-place, and was much annoyed to find only the deer's body. He vented his anger in blows upon the latter and went away. Soon after, Father Anansi made his appearance. He was greatly interested in his son's tale, and wished to see the dragon for himself. He soon had his desire, for the monster, smelling human flesh, hastily returned to the spot and seized them both. They were carried off by him to his castle, where they found many other unfortunate creatures also awaiting their fate. All were left in charge of the dragon's servant – a fine, white cock – which always crowed to summon his master, if anything unusual happened in the latter's absence. The dragon then went off in search of more prey.

Kweku Tsin now summoned all his fellow-prisoners together, to arrange a way of escape. All feared to run away – because of the wonderful powers of the monster. His eyesight was so keen that he could detect a fly moving miles away. Not only that, but he could move over the ground so swiftly that none could outdistance him. Kweku Tsin, however, being exceedingly clever, soon thought of a plan.

Knowing that the white cock would not crow as long as he has grains of rice to pick up, Kweku scattered on the ground the contents of forty bags of grain which were stored in the great hall. While the cock was thus busily engaged, Kweku Tsin ordered the spinners to spin fine hempen ropes, to make a strong rope ladder. One end of this he intended to throw up to heaven, trusting that the gods would catch it and hold it fast, while he and his fellow-prisoners mounted.

While the ladder was being made, the men killed and ate all the cattle they needed – reserving all the bones for Kweku Tsin at his express desire. When all was ready the young man gathered

46

the bones into a great sack. He also procured the dragon's fiddle and placed it by his side.

Everything was now ready. Kweku Tsin threw one end of the ladder up to the sky. It was caught and held. The dragon's victims began to mount, one after the other, Kweku remaining at the bottom.

By this time, however, the monster's powerful eyesight showed him that something unusual was happening at his abode. He hastened his return. On seeing his approach, Kweku Tsin also mounted the ladder – with the bag of bones on his back, and the fiddle under his arm. The dragon began to climb after him. Each time the monster came too near the young man threw him a bone, with which, being very hungry, he was obliged to descend to the ground to eat.

Kweku Tsin repeated this performance till all the bones were gone, by which time the people were safely up in the heavens. Then he mounted himself, as rapidly as possible, stopping every now and then to play a tune on the wonderful fiddle. Each time he did this, the dragon had to return to earth, to dance – as he could not resist the magic music. When Kweku was quite close to the top, the dragon had very nearly reached him again. The brave youth bent down and cut the ladder away below his own feet. The dragon was dashed to the ground but Kweku was pulled up into safety by the gods.

The latter were so pleased with his wisdom and bravery in giving freedom to his fellowmen, that they made him the sun the source of all light and heat to the world. His father, Anansi, became the moon, and his friends the stars. Thereafter, it was Kweku Tsin's privilege to supply all these with light, each being dull and powerless without him.

HOW MUSHROOMS FIRST GREW
(From the Akan peoples, Ghana)

Long, long ago there dwelt in a town two brothers whose bad habits brought them much trouble. Day by day they got more deeply in debt. Their creditors gave them no peace, so at last they ran away into the woods. They became highway robbers.

But they were not happy. Their minds were troubled by their evil deeds. At last they decided to go home, make a big farm, and pay off their debts gradually.

They accordingly set to work and soon had quite a fine farm prepared for corn. As the soil was good, they hoped the harvest would bring them in much money.

Unfortunately, that very day a bushfowl came along. Being hungry, it scratched up all the newly planted seeds and ate them.

The two poor brothers, on arriving at the field next day, were dismayed to find all their work quite wasted. They put down a trap for the thief. That evening the bushfowl was caught in it. The two brothers, when they came and found the bird, told it that now all their debts would be transferred to it because it had robbed them of the means of paying the debts themselves.

The poor bird – in great trouble at having such a burden thrust upon it made a nest under a silk-cotton tree. There it began to lay eggs, meaning to hatch them and sell the young birds for money to pay off the debts.

A terrible hurricane came, however, and a branch of the tree came down. All the eggs were smashed. As a result, the bushfowl transferred the debts to the tree, as it had broken the eggs.

The silk-cotton tree was in dismay at having such a big sum of

48

money to pay off. It immediately set to work to make as much silk cotton as it possibly could, that it might sell it.

An elephant, not knowing all that had happened, came along. Seeing the silk cotton, he came to the tree and plucked down all its bearings. By this means the debts were transferred to the poor elephant.

The elephant was very sad when he found what he had done. He wandered away into the desert, thinking of a way to make money. He could think of none.

As he stood quietly under a tree, a poor hunter crept up. This man thought he was very lucky to find such a fine elephant standing so still. He at once shot him.

Just before the animal died, he told the hunter that now the debts would have to be paid by him. The hunter was much grieved when he heard this, as he had no money at all.

He walked home wondering what he could do to make enough money to pay the debts. In the darkness he did not see the stump of a tree which the overseers had cut down in the road. He fell and broke his leg. By this means the debts were transferred to the tree-stump.

Not knowing this, a party of white ants came along next morning and began to eat into the tree. When they had broken it nearly to the ground, the tree told them that now the debts were theirs, as they had killed it.

The ants, being very wise, held a council together to find out how best they could make money. They decided each to contribute as much as possible. With the proceeds one of their young men would go to the nearest market and buy pure linen thread. This they would weave and sell and the profits would go to help pay the debts.

This was done. From time to time all the linen in stock was brought and spread out in the sunshine to keep it in good condition. When men see this linen lying out on the ant-hills, they call it "mushroom," and gather it for food.

A STORY ABOUT A GIANT, AND THE CAUSE OF THUNDER
(From the Hausa people, southern Niger and northern Nigeria)

This story is about a forest giant – about him and a man called, A-Man-among-Men. There was a certain man by name, A-Man-among-Men, always when he came from the bush he used to lift up a tree and come and throw it down, and say, "I am A-Man-among-Men." His wife said, "Come now, leave off saying you are a-man-among-men; if you saw a-man-among-men you would run." But he said, "It is a lie."

Now it was always so, if he has brought in wood, then he would throw it down with force and say, "I am A-Man-among-Men." The wife said, "Come now, leave off saying so; if you have seen a man-among-men, you would run." But he said, "It is a lie."

Now one day his wife went to the stream. She came to a certain well; the well bucket, ten men were necessary to draw it up. She came, but had to do without the water, so she turned back. She was going home, when she met another woman who said, "Where are you going with a calabash, with no water?" She said, "I have come and seen a bucket there. I could not draw it; that is what caused me to turn back home." And this second

50

woman, who had a son, said, "Let us return that you may find water." She said, "All right."

So they returned together to the well. This woman, who had the son, told the boy to lift the bucket and draw water. Now the boy was small, not past the age when he was carried on his mother's back. Then he lifted the bucket then and there, and put it in the well, and drew up the water. They filled their large water-pots, they bathed, they washed their clothes, they lifted up the water to go home. This one was astonished.

Then she saw that one who had the boy has turned off the path and was entering the bush. Then the wife of him called A-Man-among-Men said, "Where are you going?" She said to her, "I am going home, where else?" She said, "Is that the way to your home?" She said, "Yes." She said, "Whose home is it?" She said, "The home of A-Man-among-Men." Then she was silent; she did not say anything till she got home. She told her husband. He said that to-morrow she must take him there. She replied, "May Allah give us a to-morrow." Next morning he was the first to get up from sleep. He took the weapons of the chase and slung them over his shoulder. He put his axe on his shoulder and wakened his wife from sleep. He said, "Get up, let us go. Take me that I may see, that I may see the one called A-Man-among-Men."

She got up, lifted her large water-pot, and passed on in front. He was following her until they got to the edge of the well. Now they found what they sought indeed. As they were coming, the wife of A-Man-among-Men came up, both she and her son. They greeted her, and the wife of this one showed him the bucket and said, "Lift it and draw water for me."

So he went and lifted the bucket in a rage and let it down the well; but the bucket pulled him, and he would have fallen into the well, when the little boy seized him, both him and the bucket, and drew out and threw them on one side. Then the boy lifted up the bucket, put it in the well, drew water, and filled their water-pots.

His wife said, "You have said you are going to see him called A-Man-among-Men. You have seen this is his wife and son. If you still want to go you can go together. As for me, I am not going." The boy's mother said, "Oh, what is the matter? You had better not come." But he said he would come; and she said, "Let us be off." They set out.

When they arrived at the house she showed him a place for storing meat, and he got inside. Now he, the master of the house, was not at home; he has gone to the bush. His wife said, "You have seen he has gone to the bush; but you must not stir if he has come." He sat inside till evening came.

The master of the house came. He keeps saying, "I smell the smell of a man." His wife said, "Is there another person here? It is not is not I." Thus, if he said he smelled the smell of a man, then she would say, "Is there another person here. Is it not I? If you want to eat me up, well and good, for there is no one else but I."

Now he was a huge man, his words like a tornado; ten elephants he would eat. When dawn came, he made his morning meal of one; then he went to the bush, and if he should see a person there he would kill him.

Now he (A Man-among-Men) was in the store-house, hidden. The man's wife told him, saying, "You must not move till he is asleep. If you have seen the place dark, he is not asleep; if you have seen the place light, that is a sign he is asleep; come out and fly." Shortly after he saw the place has become light like day, so he came out.

He was running, he was running, until dawn, he was running, till the sun rose he was running, he did not stand. Then that man woke up from sleep and he said, "I smell the smell of a man, I smell the smell of a man." He rose up, he followed where the man had gone. He was running. He also, the other one, was running till he met some people who were clearing the ground for a farm, and they asked what had happened. And he said, "Some one is chasing me." They said, "Stand here till he comes."

A short time passed, and the wind caused by him came; it lifted them and cast them down. And he said, "Yes, that is it, the wind he makes running; he himself has not yet come. If you are able to withstand him tell me. If you are not able, say so." And they said, "Pass on."

So he ran off, and came and met some people hoeing. They said, "What is chasing you?" He replied, "Some one is pursuing me." They said, "What kind of a man is chasing one such as you." He said, "Some one who says he is A-Man-among-Men." They said, "Not a man-among-men, a man-among-women. Stand till he comes."

He stood. Here he was when the wind of him came, it was pushing about the men who were hoeing. So he said, "You have seen, that is the wind he makes; he has not yet come himself If you are a match for him tell me; if not say so." And they said, "Pass on"; and off he ran. He was running. He came across some people sowing; they said, "What are you running for?" He said, "Some one is chasing me." And they said, "What kind of a man is it who is chasing the like of you?" He said, "His name is A-Man-among-Men." They said, "Sit here till he comes." He sat down.

In a short time the wind he made came and it lifted them and cast them down. And they said, "What kind of wind is that?" He, the man who was being pursued, said, "It is his wind." And they said, "Pass on." They threw away the sowing implements, and went into the bush and hid, but that one was running on.

He came and met a certain huge man; he was sitting alone at the foot of a baobab tree. He had killed elephants and was roasting them, as for him, twenty elephants he could eat; in the morning he broke his fast with five. His name was "The Giant of the Forest."

Then he questioned him and said, "Where are you going in all this haste?" And he said, "A-Man-among-Men is chasing me." And the Giant of the Forest said, "Come here, sit down till he comes." He sat down. They waited a little while. Then a wind made by A-Man-among-Men came, and lifted him, and was about to carry him off, when the Giant of the Forest shouted to him to come back. And he said, "It is not I myself who am going off, the wind caused by the man is taking me away." At that the Giant of the Forest got in a rage, he got up and caught his hand, and placed it under his thigh.

He was sitting until A-Man-among-Men came up and said, "You sitting there, are you of the living, or of the dead?" And the Giant of the Forest said, "You are interfering." And A-Man-among-Men said, "If you want to find health give up to me what you are keeping there." And the Giant of the Forest said, "Come and take him." And at that he flew into a rage and sprang and seized him. They were struggling together.

When they had twisted their legs round one another they leaped up into the heavens. Till this day they are wrestling there; when they are tired out they sit down and rest; and if they rise up to struggle that is the thunder you are wont to hear in the sky; it is they struggling.

He also, that other one, escaped, and went home, and told the tale. And his wife said, "That is why I was always telling you whatever you do, make little of it. Whether it be you excel in strength, or in power, or riches, or poverty, and are puffed up with pride, it is all the same; some one is better than you. You said, it was a lie. Behold, your own eyes have seen."

THE KINGDOM OF THE YORUBAS

(From the Yoruba people, southern Nigeria)

The ancient king Oduduwa had a great many grandchildren, and on his death he divided among them all his possessions. But his youngest grandson, Oranyan, was at that time away hunting, and when he returned home he learnt that his brothers and cousins had inherited the old King's money, cattle, beads, native cloths, and crowns, but that to himself nothing was left but twenty-one pieces of iron, a cock, and some soil tied up in a rag.

At that time the whole earth was covered with water, on the surface of which the people lived. The resourceful Oranyan spread upon the water his pieces of iron, and upon the iron he placed the scrap of cloth, and upon the cloth the soil, and on the soil the cock. The cock scratched with his feet and scattered the soil far and wide, so that the ocean was partly filled up and islands appeared everywhere. The pieces of iron became the mineral wealth hidden under the ground.

Now Oranyan's brothers and cousins all desired to live on the land, and Oranyan allowed them to do so on payment of tribute. He thus became King of all the Yorubas, and was rich and prosperous through his grandfather's inheritance.

WHY WOMEN HAVE LONG HAIR

(From the Yoruba people, southern Nigeria)

Two women quarrelled, and one of them went out secretly at night and dug a deep pit in the middle of the path leading from her enemy's house to the village well.

Early next morning, when all were going to the well for water with jars balanced on their heads, this woman fell into the pit and cried loudly for help. Her friends ran to her and, seizing her by the hair, began to pull her out of the pit. To their surprise, her hair stretched as they pulled, and by the time she was safely on the path, her hair was as long as a man's arm.

This made her very much ashamed, and she ran away and hid herself.

But after a while she realized that her long hair was beautiful, and then she felt very proud and scorned all the short-haired women, jeering at them. When they saw this, they were consumed with jealousy, and began to be ashamed of their short hair. "We have men's hair," they said to one another. "How beautiful it would be to have long hair!"

So one by one they jumped into the pit, and their friends pulled them out by the hair.

And in this way they, and all women after them, had long hair.

HOW PALM TREES AND WATER CAME ON EARTH

(From the Ekoi people, Nigeria and Cameroon)

In the beginning of all things Obassi made a man and a woman and brought them down to earth. There for a while he left them, but came again a little later, and asked what they had found to eat and drink. They answered that they neither ate nor drank, so Obassi made a trench in the ground

Then from a fold of his robe he took out a vessel containing water, and poured it into the trench. This became a stream. Afterwards he took a palm kernel, and planted it. He then told the couple to use water for cooking their food, for washing and drinking. He also said they must carefully tend the palm tree which he had planted. When ripe clusters appeared upon it, they should cut these down, and take great care of them, for they would provide food as well as medicine. The outer cover or rind should be used as food, while the kernel makes good medicine.

HOW THE LAME BOY BROUGHT FIRE FROM HEAVEN
(By Okon Asere of Mfamosing; Ekoi people, Nigeria and Cameroon)

In the beginning of the world, Obassi Osaw made everything, but he did not give fire to the people who were on earth. Etim 'Ne said to the Lame Boy, "What is the use of Obassi Osaw sending us here without any fire? Go therefore and ask him to give us some." So the Lame Boy set out.

Obassi Osaw was very angry when he got the message, and sent the boy back quickly to earth to reprove Etim 'Ne for what he had asked. In those days the Lame Boy had not become lame, but could walk like other people.

When Etim 'Ne heard that he had angered Obassi Osaw, he set out himself for the latter's town and said:

"Please forgive me for what I did yesterday. It was by accident."
Obassi would not pardon him, though he stayed for three days
begging forgiveness. Then he went home.

When Etim reached his town the boy laughed at him. "Are you
a chief," said he, "yet could get no fire? I myself will go and bring
it to you. If they will give me none I will steal it."

That very day the lad set out. He reached the house of Obassi
at evening time and found the people preparing food. He helped
with the work, and when Obassi began to eat, knelt down humbly
till the meal was ended.

The master saw that the boy was useful and did not drive him
out of the house. After he had served for several days, Obassi
called to him and said, "Go to the house of my wives and ask them
to send me a lamp."

The boy gladly did as he was bidden, for it was in the house of the
wives that fire was kept. He touched nothing, but waited until the
lamp was given him, then brought it back with all speed. Once, after
he had stayed for many days among the servants, Obassi sent him
again, and this time one of the wives said, "You can light the lamp
at the fire." She went into her house and left him alone.

The boy took a brand and lighted the lamp, then he wrapped
the brand in plantain leaves and tied it up in his cloth, carried
the lamp to his master and said, "I wish to go out for a certain
purpose." Obassi answered, "You can go."

The boy went to the bush outside the town where some dry
wood was lying. He laid the brand amongst it, and blew till it
caught alight. Then he covered it with plantain stems and leaves
to hide the smoke, and went back to the house. Obassi asked,
"Why have you been so long?" and the lad answered, "I did not
feel well."

That night when all the people were sleeping, the thief tied his cloth together and crept to the end of the town where the fire was hidden. He found it burning, and took a glowing brand and some firewood and set out homeward.

When earth was reached once more the lad went to Etim and said:

"Here is the fire which I promised to bring you. Send for some wood, and I will show you what we must do."

So the first fire was made on earth. Obassi Osaw looked down from his house in the sky and saw the smoke rising. He said to his eldest son Akpan Obassi, "Go, ask the boy if it is he who has stolen the fire."

Akpan came down to earth, and asked as his father had bidden him. The lad confessed, "I was the one who stole the fire. The reason why I hid it was because I feared."

Akpan replied, "I bring you a message. Up till now you have been able to walk. From to-day you will not be able to do so any more."

That is the reason why the Lame Boy cannot walk. He it was who first brought fire to earth from Obassi's home in the sky.

HOW HUMAN BEINGS GOT KNEE-CAPS
(From the Ekoi people, Nigeria and Cameroon)

Once, long ago, a woman named Nka Yenge went fishing in the river. With her were many other women. They all went into the water, some down stream and some up. Now deep down in one of the pools a smooth white stone was lying, something like a Nimm stone. As the women went by, several of them said, "What a beautiful stone!" but when Nka Yenge came, she stood looking at it for a long time and said, "I wish I could get that stone!" When she came back she said the same thing, and as she passed a third time she said:

"I must have that stone."

Suddenly the stone sprang out of the water and struck against her knee. There it stayed and she could not loosen it; so she went home weeping with pain. On the way thither, she met a man, who asked, "Why do you weep?"

The woman could not speak for tears, but the stone answered, "I was lying in the water. When the woman passed up and down, she said that she wished to have me. Her wish was so strong that it drew me up out of the water. Now I have joined myself to her, and shall never leave her again."

The man was very sorry, and called to the woman, "Come here. We will go to my house, and I will try what I can do." When they reached his house, he got a strong knife and tried to chop off the stone, but it was no use. The stone had gone inside.

That is the reason why we have knee-caps. Formerly we did not have any.

HOW THE FIRST HIPPOPOTAMI CAME

(From the Ekoi people, Nigeria and Cameroon)

Once, long ago, Elephant had a beautiful daughter, whom all the beasts wished to wed. Now at that time a very great fish named Njokk Mbonn (Elephant fish) dwelt in the river, and one evening he came to Elephant and said, "I should like to marry your daughter."

Next morning Leopard came too, and said, "Do not let anyone marry the girl but me." When he heard that the King of the fishes had also asked her in marriage he was very angry, and went home to call all his family together to fight. Nsun (antelope) happened to pass by while they were arranging the matter, and he went at once and said to Fish:

"Listen to what I have heard to-day. Leopard and all his people are coming to fight you."

When Njokk Mbonn heard this he said nothing, but only took a yam and roasted it. When it was ready he ate part, and put the rest on one side. Just then he heard the sound of his enemies coming in the distance, and close at hand he saw Elephant also with his daughter.

Then Fish went down into the water. By magic he made a big wave rise up and overflow the bank. As this ebbed it drew Elephant and his daughter down to the depths beneath, where Fish lay waiting.

When the other animals saw what had happened they all fled, crying to one another:

"If we try to fight with Njokk Mbonn he will kill us all. Let us go back at once."

Fish thought to himself, "I must kill Leopard, or he will come back again some day."

At dawn, therefore, he came up to the bank, and lay there cleaning his teeth, which were very white and shining.

When Leopard came along he stood looking at his enemy and thought, "My teeth are not so fine as his. What can I do?" So he said, "Will you kindly clean my teeth also?"

When Fish heard this he answered, "Very well, but I cannot do it unless you will lie down. If you are willing to do this I will clean your mouth."

Leopard lay down; Fish sent his wave once more, and swept his enemy down to the depths of the river. Instead of finding a fine house there, as Elephant and his daughter had done, Leopard found only a strong prison, where he soon died.

Njokk Mbonn married the daughter of Elephant, and they lived happily for many years. Their children were the Water-Elephants (i.e., Hippopotami). If Fish had not wedded this wife there would have been no Hippo in our rivers.

THE FLAME TREE
(From Uganda)

Once upon a time there was a little girl who lived in the village of Si. Her parents had no other children, and as she grew older they saw with joy that she was more beautiful every day. People who passed through the village saw her and spoke of her beauty until every one in Kyagwe knew that the most lovely girl in the country lived in the village of Si and every one in the province called her 'the Maiden'.

The Maiden was a gentle, sweet child, and she loved all the animals and birds and butterflies and flowers, and played with them and knew their language. Her parents were very proud of her, and often talked of the time when she should be grown up and marry a great chief with many cows and gardens and people, and bring great wealth to her tribe. When the time came to arrange her marriage, all the Chiefs came and offered many gifts, as the custom of the Baganda is; but the Maiden said, "I will marry none of these rich Chiefs, I will marry Tutu the peasant boy, who has nothing, because I love him." Her parents were very grieved when they heard this, and would have tried to persuade her, but just then a messenger arrived from the Sekibobo to say that the King of Uganda was going to war with Mbubi the chief of the Buvuma Islands, and all. the chiefs went away to collect their people for the King's army. Then the Chief of Si, who is called Kibevu, called all his men together, and Tutu the peasant boy went with them. The army marched down to the Lake shore to fight the Islanders who came across the blue waters in a fleet of war canoes, painted and decorated with horns and feathers and cowry shells and beads. The Maiden was very sad when she said good-bye to Tutu. "Be very brave and win glory," she said, "then my father will let me marry you, for I will never. marry any one else." But when the men had marched away and only the women and children were left in the village with the old people, the Maiden forgot her brave words and only thought how she could bring Tutu safely back.

She called to her friend the hawk. "Come and help me, Double-Eye; fly quickly to the Lake shore and see my peasant boy-tell him I think of him day and night. I cannot be happy till he returns." The hawk knew Tutu well, for often on the hillside he had played with the children. The Baganda called him 'Double Eye', for they say that with one eye he watches the Earth and with the other he sees where he is going.

The Baganda reached the Lake, and there was a great battle, and Tutu the peasant boy was killed by a stone from an Islander's sling; but the Baganda rallied, and drove the enemy back to their canoes, and Mbubi beat the retreat drum, and his men returned to Buvuma. The hawk flies very quickly, and while he was still a long way off he saw Tutu lying where he had fallen on the Lake shore. The soldiers were burying the dead, and the hawk watched to see where they would bury the peasant boy of Si, that he might show the maiden his grave.

The Maiden waited on the hillside for the hawk's return and the moments seemed like hours. She called to a bumble bee who was her friend. "Go quickly to the Lake side and greet my peasant boy, tell him I wait here on the hillside for his return."

The bumble bee flew away quickly, and when he reached the Lake shore he asked the hawk for news. "The Islanders have fled in their canoes, but Tutu the peasant boy is dead, a stone from a sling killed him. I wait to see his grave that I may show it to the Maiden." The bumble bee was afraid to go back with the news, so he stayed near the hawk and watched. Meanwhile the Maiden waited in a fever of impatience, ever gazing at the distant Lake and pacing up and down. She saw a flight of white butterflies playing hide-and-seek round a mimosa bush and called to them.

"Oh, white butterflies, how can you play when my heart is breaking? Go to the Lake shore and see if my peasant boy is well."

So the white butterflies flew away over the green hills to the Lake and arrived on the battle field just as the soldiers were digging Tutu's grave, and they settled sadly down on a tuft of grass, their wings drooping with sorrow, for they loved the Maiden who had often played with them in the sunshine. Far away on the Si hills the Maiden watched in vain for their return. Filled with fear she cried to the Sun, "Oh, Chief of the Cloud Land, help me! Take me on one of your beams to the Lake shore that I may see my peasant boy and tell him of my love." The Sun looked down on her with great pity, for he had seen the battle and knew that Tutu the peasant boy was dead. He stretched out one of his long beams and she caught it in her hands, and he swung her gently round until she rested on the Lake shore. When she saw the soldiers lifting Tutu's body to lay it in the grave she cried to the Sun:

"Oh, Chief of the Cloud Land, do not leave me, burn me with your fire, for how can I live, now that my Love is dead?" Then the Sun was filled with pity and struck her with a hot flame, and the soldiers were very sorry for her too, and they dug a grave for her next to Tutu's.

And when the people of Si visited the graves the next year they found a wonderful thing, for a beautiful tree had grown out of them with large flame-coloured blossoms which ever turned upwards to the sun, and they took the seeds and planted them in their gardens. And now the country is full of these beautiful trees which are called Flame Trees, but the old people call them Kifabakazi, because the stem is as soft as a woman's heart and a woman can cut it down.

THE MPA BANA BIRD
(From Uganda)

The African cuckoo does not sing Cuckoo, Cuckoo; it sings Cuckookoo, Cuckookoo, and it can sing this song for a whole hour, until every one in the neighbourhood is tired of hearing it, then it flies to another tree, clears its throat and begins again. The mother cuckoo is too lazy to build a nest of her own, and to hatch her own eggs. If she finds a nice comfortable looking nest she lays an egg in it and flies away hoping the owner will hatch it for her; but she forgets so soon, that she never returns to see what has happened to her egg.

One day a mother cuckoo found a lovely nest in the forest and laid an egg among the four little eggs which were in it already. Then she flew away and forgot all about it. When the owner of the nest returned, she was too tenderhearted to throw the egg out, so she hatched it with her own. But the young cuckoo was so large and hungry that he soon filled up the nest, and one day when the mother bird was away looking for food he pushed the four little fledglings out of the nest.

A wild cat was passing among the bushes down below and gobbled them up as they fell. When the mother bird returned she found only the cuckoo in her nest, and she searched everywhere for her children crying as she went, "Mpa bana, mpa bana," which means, "Give me children, give me children." She searched under the bushes and all round her nest and then went all through the forest crying all the time, "Mpa bana, mpa bana," till all the other birds and animals knew of her sorrow. When the next nesting season came, she laid four more eggs, and never left the young birds after they were hatched, but she had got into the habit of singing this song:

> I left them safe in the nest, Mpa bana, mpa bana;
> Seeking the food that was best, Mpa bana, mpa bana;
> How did the cruel thief come, Mpa bana, mpa bana;
> Wrecking my joy and my home, Mpa bana, mpa bana.

The young birds heard it all day long and learnt to sing it; and now it has become their tribal song, and they sing it for hours together, and are quite as tiresome as the cuckoo who just sings cuckookoo, cuckookoo, without grumbling about it.

GIKUYU AND MUMBI[1]

(From the Gikuyu people, Kenya)

The Gikuyu myth of origin like other myths of origin relates a garden of Eden scenario where God comes into the picture. According to this myth, the first man, Gikuyu walked with God, *Ngai, Mwene Nyaga, Murungu, Mugai,* or any number of other names given to Him. Call Him *Ngai.*

The scene starts at the top of 'The Mountain of God', *Kiri Nyaga* generally called Mount Kenya. This is where God showed the first Gikuyu man the land below and instructed him to go to a specific spot to the south of the mountain where there was a grove of fig trees, *Mikuyu.* Gikuyu descended the mountain and on arrival at the place found a woman. I suppose he introduced himself and Gikuyu and Mumbi became husband and wife. He was also told that he could make contact with this Ngai at any time by praying to him while facing Mount Kenya or by sacrificing a goat under the *Mukuyu* or another type of fig tree, the *Mugumo.*

The name Gikuyu means a huge fig tree – *Mukuyu,* and Mumbi means Creator. The roots of the *Mukuyu* entered into the Great Mother Earth, each nourishing the other and connecting with God. Man and the Goddess of Creation came together and as the milk essence from the *Mukuyu* entered the earth, the Gikuyu and the Mumbi brought forth the ten daughters who became the mothers of the ten Gikuyu clans. Think of the sun and moon and the ten planets.

When the girls became of age and began to have yearnings for their own husbands, they went to their mother and asked her

---

1   Printed with permission, courtesy of and © Mūkūyū, the Gīkūyū Centre for Cultural Studies (mukuyu.wordpress.com).

where she got hers. She took the problem to her husband Gikuyu. Gikuyu consulted Ngai, God, and Ngai asked him to make a sacrifice of a spotless ram under the fig tree 'Mugumo'. He called his daughters and asked them to go to the Mukuyu and for them to cut for each a straight rod of her own height. Nine of the girls brought the rods and their father placed them on top of the fire as ndara and then placed the sacrifice on them. In the morning nine young men appeared and each of the daughters took a mate her own height. The last born, Wamuyu, was too young to take part in the rods business and thus remained without a husband. The others married young men. Thus, 'Agikuyu' (another name for the Kikuyu/Gikuyu people) means 'of the great Mukuyu tree'.

BATA THE DUCK

(From the Swahili-speaking peoples)

Once upon a time there was a duck called Bata, and she lived with her husband, and they were very happy, for they had never seen the face of man. Till one day there came a man to their home, and he fired his gun and killed Bata's husband.

When she saw that her husband was dead Bata was very unhappy, and flew far, far away to a country where man had never come.

There she met a peahen, and that peahen made friends with her and asked her name. She said, "I am called Bata."

Then she asked her, "Why are you trembling so?"

Bata answered, "Do you know man?"

The peahen said, "No, I have never seen one."

Then said Bata, "I tremble to think of man and how he has made me a widow, for he killed my husband."

Then the peahen said, "I have a husband too, and he is very beautiful."

So she took Bata to her husband the peacock, and when Bata saw him she began to weep.

That peacock said, "Why do you weep?"

Bata answered, "I weep to see how beautiful you are, and to think that if man sees you he will surely kill you."

"What is this creature called man?" asked the peacock.

"He is a creature of great guile," replied Bata.

After that she travelled on till she came to a big river, and she swam up and up the river till she came to a cave.

She looked into the cave and there she saw a lion. The lion asked, "Who are you?"

She replied, "I am Bata the Duck."

Then the lion asked her, "Why are you trembling?"

She answered, "I am trembling to think of man."

The lion asked, "What is this man?"

Bata said, "He is a creature of great cunning, who is even able to kill you."

The lion said, "Then this man must be very big and strong."

"No," said Bata, "he is neither big nor strong, but his guile is great."

Just then a dikdik came running past. When it saw the lion it stopped and greeted him. The lion asked, "What are you running from?"

The dikdik said, "I am running away from man."

"What is this man like?" said the lion.

"Oh, he is very cunning," answered the dikdik, and scampered off.

Presently a bushbuck came running up. When it saw the lion it stopped and greeted him. Then the lion asked, "What are you running from?"

The bushbuck said, "I am running from man."

"What is he like?" said the lion.

"Oh, he is very cunning," answered the bushbuck, and ran off.

Next an eland came galloping up, and when he saw the lion he stopped and greeted him. The lion asked, "And whom are you running away from? Is it also this creature called man?"

The eland answered, "Yes, I am running from man."

The lion said, "This man must be a very big animal, that one of your size should be afraid of him."

"No, he is not big," said the eland, "but his guile is very great."

The eland galloped off, and presently a buffalo came tearing past. When he saw the lion he drew up and greeted him. The lion asked, "And are you also running away from this creature called man?"

The buffalo said, "Yes, it is indeed he from whom I am running."

Then said the lion, "This man must be a great and powerful creature, that one of such a terrifying appearance as you are runs from him."

The buffalo said, "No, he is small, but his guile is exceedingly great."

Then the buffalo rushed off, and presently there came forth a man. Now that man was a carpenter, and he carried planks under his arm and his bag of tools over his shoulder. Suddenly he looked up and saw the lion, and he said to himself, "Now I am indeed lost, for there is a lion, and I have no weapons."

That lion, when he saw the man, asked him, "Who are you who are walking so slowly and carefully? All the animals who have passed here were running away from the creature called man. How is it that you are not afraid of him, that you do not make haste to escape?"

Then that man saw that the lion did not recognise him for a man, so he took heart, and said, "No, it is not man, but the elephant I am afraid of, for I am the servant of the elephant, and he has called me to make a house for him. For the elephant fears this man whom you speak of, so I now go to make him a house, so that when he goes inside it man cannot get him."

The lion said, "First you must make such a house for me."

That man said, "No, I cannot, for I have promised to make it for the elephant."

But that lion insisted on the man making him a house first, so that carpenter put down his load and began making a box like a coffin.

When he had finished it he made a door at one end, and then he said to the lion, "Enter in, my master, and see if the house suits you."

So the lion walked in, and the man shut the door and cried, "Now do you know me? I am that creature called man."

Then he took his axe and rained blows on the lion until he had killed him.

When Bata saw this she flew away, and this was the beginning of her sitting always on the water, even to sleeping on the water in the middle of a pool, for fear of man who killed her husband.

THE 'HADITHI YA LIONGO'
(From the Swahili-speaking peoples)

This poem ('The Story of Liongo') relates how certain Galla [now 'Oromo'] people, coming to Pate to trade, heard of Liongo (hero, warrior and poet of the Swahili people) from the sultan, who dwelt so much on his prowess that their curiosity was aroused, and they expressed a wish to see him. So he sent a letter to Liongo at Shaka, desiring him to come. Liongo replied with respect and courtesy that he would come, and he set out on the following day, fully armed and carrying three trumpets. The journey from Shaka to Pate was reckoned at four days, but Liongo arrived the day after he had started. At the city gate he blew such a blast that the trumpet was split, and the Galla asked, "What is it? Who has raised such a cry?" He answered, "It is Liongo who has come!"

Liongo sounded his second trumpet, and burst it; he then took the third, and the townsfolk all ran together, the Galla among them, to see what this portended. He then sent a messenger to say, "Our lord Liongo asks leave to enter." The gate was thrown open, and he was invited in, all the Galla being struck with astonishment and terror at the sight of him. "This is a lord of war," they said; "he can put a hundred armies to flight."

He sat down, at the same time laying on the ground the wallet which he had been carrying. After resting awhile he took out from it a mortar and pestle, a millstone, cooking pots of no common size, and the three stones used for supporting them over the fire. The Galla stood by, gaping with amazement, and when at last they found speech they said to the sultan, "We want him for a prince, to marry one of our daughters, that a son of his may bring glory to our tribe." The sultan undertook to open the matter to Liongo, who agreed, on certain conditions (what these were we are not told), and the wedding was celebrated with great rejoicing at the Galla kraals. In due course a son was born, who, as he grew up, bade fair to resemble his father in strength and beauty.

It would seem as if Liongo had been living for some time at Pate (for he did not take up his abode permanently with the

Galla) – no doubt as a result of the quarrel with his brother. But now someone – whether an emissary of Mringwari's or some of the Galla whom he had offended – stirred up trouble; enmity arose against him, and, finding that the sultan had determined on his death, he left Pate for the mainland. There he took refuge with the forest folk, the Wasanye and Wadahalo. These soon received a message from Pate, offering them a hundred *reals* (silver dollars) if they would bring in Liongo's head. They were not proof against the temptation, and, unable to face him in fight, planned a treacherous scheme for his destruction. They approached him one day with a suggestion for a *kikoa*, since a regular feast – in their roving forest life – is not to be done. They were to dine off *makoma* (the fruit of the *Hyphaene* palm), each man taking his turn at climbing a tree and gathering for the party, the intention being to shoot Liongo when they had him at a disadvantage. However, when it came to his turn, having chosen the tallest palm, he defeated them by shooting down the nuts, one by one, where he stood. This, by the by, is the only instance recorded of his marksmanship, though his skill with the bow is one of his titles to fame.

Liongo Escapes from Captivity

The Wasanye now gave up in despair, and sent word to the sultan that Liongo was not to be overcome either by force or guile. He, unwilling to trust them any further, left them and went to Shaka, where he met his mother and his son. His Galla wife seems to have remained with her people, and we hear nothing from this authority of any other wives he may have had. Here, at last, he was captured by his brother's men, seized while asleep – one account says: "first having been given wine to drink" (it was probably drugged). He was then secured in the prison in the usual way, his feet chained together with a post between them, and fetters on his hands. He was guarded day and night by warriors. There was much debating as to what should be done with him. There was a general desire to get rid of him, but some of Mringwari's councillors were of opinion that he was too dangerous to be dealt with directly: it would be better to give him the command of the army and let him perish, like Uriah, in the forefront of the battle, Mringwari thought this would be too great a risk, and there could be none in killing him, fettered as he was.

Meanwhile Liongo's mother sent her slave girl Saada every day to the prison with food for her son, which the guards invariably seized, only tossing him the scraps.

Mringwari, when at last he had come to a decision, sent a slave lad to the captive, to tell him that he must die in three days' time, but if he had a last wish it should be granted, "that you may take your leave of the world." Liongo sent word that he wished to have a *gungu* dance performed where he could see and hear it, and this was granted.

He then fell to composing a song, which is known and sung to this day:

> O thou handmaid Saada, list my words today!
> Haste thee to my mother, tell her what I say.
> Bid her bake for me a cake of chaff and bran, I pray,
> And hide therein an iron file to cut my bonds away,
> File to free my fettered feet, swiftly as I may;
> Forth I'll glide like serpent's child, silently to slay.

When Saada came again he sang this over to her several times, till she knew it by heart-the guards either did not understand the words or were too much occupied with the dinner of which they had robbed him to pay any attention to his music. Saada went home and repeated the song to her mistress, who lost no time, but went out at once and bought some files. Next morning she prepared a better meal than usual, and also baked such a loaf as her son asked for, into which she inserted the files, wrapped in a rag.

When Saada arrived at the prison the guards took the food as usual, and, after a glance at the bran loaf, threw it contemptuously to Liongo, who appeared to take it with a look of sullen resignation to his fate.

When the dance was arranged he called the chief performers together and taught them a new song – perhaps one of the 'Gungu Dance Songs' which have been handed down under his name. There was an unusually full orchestra: horns, trumpets, cymbals (*matoazi*), gongs (*tasa*), and the complete set of drums, while Liongo himself led the singing. When the band was playing its loudest he began filing at his fetters, the sound being quite inaudible amid the din; when the performers paused he stopped filing and lifted up his voice again. So he gradually cut through his foot shackles and his handcuffs, and, rising up in his might, like Samson, burst the door, seized two of the guards, knocked their heads together, and threw them down dead. The musicians dropped their instruments and fled, the crowd scattered like a flock of sheep, and Liongo took to the woods, after going outside the town to take leave of his mother, none daring to stay him.

Liongo Undone by Treachery at Last

Here he led an outlaw's life, raiding towns and plundering travellers, and Mringwari was at his wits' end to compass his destruction. At last Liongo's son – or, as some say, his sister's son

– was gained over and induced to ferret out the secret of Liongo's charmed life, since it had been discovered by this time that neither spear nor arrow could wound him. The lad sought out his father, and greeted him with a great show of affection; but Liongo was not deceived. He made no difficulty, however, about revealing the secret – perhaps he felt that his time had come and that it was useless to fight against destiny. When his son said to him, after some hesitation, "My father, it is the desire of my heart – since I fear danger for you – that I might know for certain what it is that can kill you," Liongo replied, "I think, since you ask me this, that you are seeking to kill me." The son, of course, protested: "I swear by the Bountiful One I am not one to do this thing! Father, if you die, to whom shall I go? I shall be utterly destitute."

Liongo answered, "My son, I know how you have been instructed and how you will be deceived in your turn. Those who are making use of you now will laugh you to scorn, and you will bitterly regret your doings! Yet, though it be so, I will tell you! That which can slay me is a copper nail driven into the navel. From any other weapon than this I can take no hurt." The son waited two days, and on the third made an excuse to hasten back to Pate, saying that he was anxious about his mother's health. Mringwari, on receiving the information, at once sent for a craftsman and ordered him to make a copper spike of the kind required. The youth was feasted and made much of for the space of ten days, and then dispatched on his errand, with the promise that a marriage should be arranged for him when he returned successful. On arriving at Shaka he was kindly welcomed by his father (who perhaps thought that, after all, he had been wrong in his suspicions), and remained with him for a month without carrying out his design – either from lack of opportunity or, as one would fain hope, visited by some compunction. As time went on Mringwari grew impatient and wrote, reproaching him in covert terms for the delay. "We, here, have everything ready" – i.e., for the promised wedding festivities, which were to be of the utmost magnificence. It chanced that on the day when this letter arrived Liongo, wearied out with hunting, slept more soundly than usual during the midday heat. The son, seizing his opportunity, screwed his courage to the sticking place, crept up, and stabbed him in the one vulnerable spot.

Liongo started up in the death pang and, seizing his bow and arrows, walked out of the house and out of the town. When he had reached a spot halfway between the city gate and the well at which the folk were wont to draw water his strength failed him: he sank on one knee, fitted an arrow to the string, drew it to the head, and so died, with his face towards the well.

The townsfolk could see him kneeling there, and did not know that he was dead. Then for three days neither man nor woman durst venture near the well. They used the water stored for ablutions in the tank outside the mosque; when that was exhausted there was great distress in the town. The elders of the people went to Liongo's mother and asked her to intercede with her son. "If she goes to him he will be sorry for her." She consented, and went out, accompanied by the principal men, chanting verses (perhaps some of his own poems) with the purpose of soothing him. Gazing at him from a distance, she addressed him with piteous entreaties, but when they came nearer and saw that he was dead she would not believe it. "He cannot be killed; he is angry, and therefore he does not speak; he is brooding over his wrongs in his own mind and refuses to hear me!" So she wailed; but when he fell over they knew that he was dead indeed.

They came near and looked at the body, and drew out the copper needle which had killed him, and carried him into the town, and waked and buried him. And there he lies to this day, near Kipini by the sea.

The Traitor's Doom

The news reached Pate, and Mringwari, privately rejoicing at the removal of his enemy, sent for Mani Liongo, the son (who meanwhile had been sumptuously entertained in the palace), and told him what had happened, professing to be much surprised when he showed no signs of sorrow. When the son replied that, on the contrary, he was very glad Mringwari turned on him. "You are an utterly faithless one! Depart out of my house and from the town; take off the clothes I have given you and wear your own, you enemy of God!" Driven from Pate, he betook himself to his Galla kinsmen, but there he was received coldly, and even his mother cast him off. So, overcome with remorse and grief, he fell into a wasting sickness and died unlamented.

THE THUNDER'S BRIDE
(From the Banyarwanda people, Rwanda)

In this story we find Imana associated with thunder and lightning, so that we may suppose him to be a sky-god, or, at any rate, to have been such in the beginning. In story which follows, the Thunder is treated as a distinct personage, but he is nowhere said to be identical with Imana.

There was a certain woman of Rwanda, the wife of Kwisaba. Her husband went away to the wars, and was absent for many

78

months. One day while she was all alone in the hut she was taken ill, and found herself too weak and wretched to get up and make a fire, which would have been done for her at once had anyone been present. She cried out, talking wildly in her despair: "Oh, what shall I do? If only I had someone to split the kindling wood and build the fire! I shall die of cold if no one comes! Oh, if someone would but come – if it were the very Thunder of heaven himself!"

So the woman spoke, scarcely knowing what she said, and presently a little cloud appeared in the sky. She could not see it, but very soon it spread, other clouds collected, till the sky was quite overcast; it grew dark as night inside the hut, and she heard thunder rumbling in the distance. Then there came a flash of lightning close by, and she saw the Thunder standing before her, in the likeness of a man, with a little bright axe in his hand. He fell to, and had split all the wood in a twinkling; then he built it up and lit it, just with a touch of his hand, as if his fingers had been torches. When the blaze leapt up he turned to the woman and said, "Now, oh wife of Kwisaba, what will you give me?" She was quite paralysed with fright, and could not utter a word. He gave her a little time to recover, and then went on: "When your baby is born, if it is a girl, will you give her to me for a wife?" Trembling all over, the poor woman could only stammer out, "Yes!" and the Thunder vanished.

Not long after this a baby girl was born, who grew into a fine, healthy child, and was given the name of Miseke. When Kwisaba came home from the wars the women met him with the news that he had a little daughter, and he was delighted, partly, perhaps, with the thought of the cattle he would get as her bride-price when she was old enough to be married. But when his wife told him about the Thunder he looked very serious, and said, "When she grows older you must never on any account let her go outside the house, or we shall have the Thunder carrying her off."

So as long as Miseke was quite little she was allowed to play out of doors with the other children, but the time came all too soon when she had to be shut up inside the hut. One day some of the other girls came running to Miseke's mother in great excitement. "Miseke is dropping beads out of her mouth! We thought she had put them in on purpose, but they come dropping out every time she laughs." Sure enough the mother found that it was so, and not only did Miseke produce beads of the kinds most valued, but beautiful brass and copper bangles. Miseke's father was greatly troubled when they told him of this. He said it must be the Thunder, who sent the beads in this extraordinary way as the presents which a man always has to send to his betrothed while she is growing up. So Miseke had always to stay indoors and amuse herself as best she could – when she was not helping in the house work – by plaiting mats and making baskets. Sometimes her old playfellows came to see her, but they too did not care to be shut up for long in a dark, stuffy hut.

One day, when Miseke was about fifteen, a number of the girls made up a party to go and dig *inkwa* (white clay) and they thought it would be good fun to take Miseke along with them. They went to her mother's hut and called her, but of course her parents would not hear of her going, and she had to stay at home. They tried again another day, but with no better success. Some time after this, however, Kwisaba and his wife both went to see to their garden, which was situated a long way off, so that they had to start at daybreak, leaving Miseke alone in the hut. Somehow the girls got to hear of this, and as they had already planned to go for *inkwa* that day they went to fetch her. The temptation was too great, and she slipped out very quietly, and went with them to the watercourse where the white clay was to be found. So many people had gone there at different times for the same purpose that quite a large pit had been dug out. The girls got into it and fell to work, laughing and chattering, when, suddenly, they became aware that it was growing dark, and, looking up, saw a great black cloud gathering overhead. And then, suddenly, they saw the figure of a man standing before them, and he called out in a great voice, "Where is Miseke, daughter of Kwisaba?" One girl came out of the hole, and said, "I am not Miseke, daughter of Kwisaba. When Miseke laughs, beads and bangles drop from her lips." The Thunder said, "Well, then, laugh, and let me see." She laughed, and nothing happened. "No, I see you are not she." So one after another was questioned and sent on her way. Miseke herself came last, and tried to pass, repeating the same words that the others had said; but the Thunder insisted on her laughing, and a shower of beads fell on the ground. The Thunder caught her up and carried her off to the sky and married her.

Of course she was terribly frightened, but the Thunder proved a kind husband, and she settled down quite happily and, in due time, had three children, two boys and a girl. When the baby girl was a few weeks old Miseke told her husband that she would like to go home and see her parents. He not only consented, but provided her with cattle and beer (as provision for the journey and presents on arrival) and carriers for her hammock, and sent her down to earth with this parting advice: "Keep to the high road; do not turn aside into any unfrequented bypath." But, being unacquainted with the country, her carriers soon strayed from the main track. After they had gone for some distance along the wrong road they found the path barred by a strange monster called an *igikoko*, a sort of ogre, who demanded something to eat. Miseke told the servants to give him the beer they were carrying: he drank all the pots dry in no time. Then he seized one of the carriers and ate him, then a second – in short, he devoured them all, as well as the cattle, till no one was left but Miseke and her children. The ogre then demanded a child. Seeing no help for it, Miseke gave him the younger boy, and then, driven to extremity, the baby she was nursing, but while he was thus engaged she contrived to send off the elder boy, whispering to him to run till he came to a house. "If you see an old man sitting on the ash-heap in the front yard that will be your grandfather; if you see some young men shooting arrows at a mark they will be your uncles; the boys herding the cows are your cousins; and you will find your grandmother inside the hut. Tell them to come and help us."

The boy set off, while his mother kept off the ogre as best she could. He arrived at his grandfather's homestead, and told them what had happened, and they started at once, having first tied the bells on their hunting dogs. The boy showed them the way as well as he could, but they nearly missed Miseke just at last; only she heard the dogs' bells and called out. Then the young men rushed in and killed the ogre with their spears. Before he died he said, "If you cut off my big toe you will get back everything belonging to you." They did so, and, behold! out came the carriers and the cattle, the servants and the children, none of them any the worse. Then, first making sure that the ogre was really dead, they set off for Miseke's old home. Her parents were overjoyed to see her and the children, and the time passed all too quickly. At the end of a month she began to think she ought to return, and the old people sent out for cattle and all sorts of presents, as is the custom when a guest is going to leave. Everything was got together outside the village, and her brothers were ready to escort her, when they saw the clouds gathering, and, behold! all of a sudden Miseke, her children, her servants, her cattle, and her porters, with their loads, were all caught up into the air and disappeared. The family were struck dumb with amazement, and they never saw Miseke on earth again. It is to be presumed that she lived happily ever after.

KWEGE AND BAHATI

(From the Zaramo people, Tanzania)

There was once upon a time a man who married a woman of the *Uwingu* clan (*uwingu* means 'sky') who was named Mulamuwingu, and whose brother, Muwingu, lived in her old home a day or two's journey from her husband's.

The couple had a son called Kwege, and lived happily enough till, in course of time, the husband died, leaving his wife with her son and a slave, Bahati, who had belonged to an old friend of theirs and had come to them on that friend's death.

Now the *tabu* of the Sky clan was rain – that is, rain must never be allowed to fall on anyone belonging to it; if this were to happen he or she would die.

One day when the weather looked threatening Mulamuwingu said, "My son Kwege, just go over to the garden and pick some gourds, so that I can cook them for our dinner." Kwege very rudely refused, and his mother re-joined, "I am afraid of my *mwidzilo* (*tabu*). If I go to the garden I shall die." Then Bahati, the slave, said, "I will go," and he went and gathered the gourds and brought them back.

Next day Kwege's mother again asked him to go to the garden, and again he refused. So she said, "Very well; I will go; but if I die it will be your fault." She set out, and when she reached the garden, which was a long way from any shelter, a great cloud gathered, and it began to rain. When the first drops touched her she fell down dead. Kwege had no dinner that evening, and when he found his mother did not come home either that day or the next (it does not seem to have entered into his head that he might go in search of her) he began to cry, saying, "Mother is dead! Mother is dead!" Then he called Bahati, and they set out to go to his uncle's village.

Now Kwege was a handsome lad, but Bahati was very ugly; and Kwege was well dressed, with plenty of cloth, while Bahati had only a bit of rag round his waist.

As they walked along Kwege said to Bahati, "When we come to a log lying across the path you must carry me over. If I step over it I shall die." For Kwege's *mwidzilo* was stepping over a log.

Bahati agreed, but when they came to a fallen tree he refused to lift Kwege over till he had given him a cloth. This went on every time they came to a log, till he had acquired everything Kwege was wearing, down to his leglets and his bead ornaments. And when they arrived at Muwingu's village and were welcomed by the people Bahati sat down on one of the mats brought out for them and told Kwege to sit on the bare ground. He introduced himself to Muwingu as his sister's son, and treated Kwege as his slave, suggesting, after a day or two, that he should be sent out to the rice fields to scare the birds. Kwege, in the ragged kilt which was the only thing Bahati had left him, went out to the fields, looked at the flocks of birds hovering over the rice, and then, sitting down under a tree, wept bitterly. Presently he began to sing:

84

"I, Kwege, weep, I weep!
And my crying is what the birds say.
Oh, you log, my tabu!
I cry in the speech of the birds.
They have taken my clothes,
They have taken my leglets,
They have taken my beads,
I am turned into Bahati.
Bahati is turned into Kwege.
I weep in the speech of the birds."

Now his dead parents had both been turned into birds. They came and perched on the tree above him, listening to his song, and said, "Looo! Muwingu has taken Bahati into his house and is treating him like a free man and Kwege, his nephew, as a slave! How can that be? "

Kwege heard what they said, and told his story. Then his father flapped one wing, and out fell a bundle of cloth; he flapped the other wing and brought out beads, leglets, and a little gourd full of oil. His mother, in the same way, produced a ready-cooked meal of rice and meat. When he had eaten they fetched water (by this time they had been turned back into human beings), washed him and oiled him, and then said, "Never mind the birds – let them eat Muwingu's rice, since he has sent you to scare them while he is treating Bahati as his son!" So they sat down, all three together, and talked till the sun went down.

On the way back Kwege hid all the cloth and beads that his parents had given him in the long grass, and put on his old rag again. But when he reached the house the family were surprised to see him looking so clean and glossy, as if he had just come from a bath, and cried out, "Where did you get this oil you have been rubbing yourself with? Did you run off and leave your work to go after it?" He did not want to say, "Mother gave it me," so he simply denied that he had been anointing himself.

Next day he went back to the rice field and sang his song again. The birds flew down at once, and, seeing him in the same miserable state as before, asked him what he had done with their gifts. He said they had been taken from him, thinking that, while he was about it, he might as well get all he could. They did not question his good faith, but supplied him afresh with everything, and, resuming their own forms, they sat by him while he ate.

Meanwhile Muwingu's son had taken it into his head to go and see how the supposed Bahati was getting on with his job – it is possible that he had begun to be suspicious of the man who called himself Kwege. What was his astonishment to see a good-looking youth, dressed in a clean cloth, with bead necklaces and all the usual ornaments, sitting between two people, whom he recognized as his father's dead sister and her husband. He was terrified, and ran back to tell his father that Kwege was Bahati and Bahati Kwege, and related what he had seen. Muwingu at once went with him to the rice field, and found that it was quite true. They hid and waited for Kwege to come home. Then, as he drew near the place where he had hidden his cloth, his uncle sprang out and seized him. He struggled to get away, but Muwingu pacified him, saying, "So you are my nephew Kwege after all, and that fellow is Bahati! Why did you not tell me before? Never mind; I shall kill him today." And kill him they did; and Kwege was installed in his rightful position. Muwingu made a great feast, inviting all his neighbours, to celebrate the occasion. "Here ends my story," says the narrator.

THE CREATION OF MAN

(From the Basoko people, the Congo)

In the old, old time, all this land, and indeed all the whole earth was covered with sweet water.

But the water dried up or disappeared somewhere, and the grasses, herbs, and plants began to spring up above the ground, and some grew, in the course of many moons, into trees, great and small, and the water was confined into streams and rivers, pools and lakes, and as the rain fell it kept the streams and rivers running, and the pools and lakes always fresh. There was no living thing moving upon the earth, until one day there sat by one of the pools a large Toad. How long he had lived, or how he came to exist, is not known; it is suspected, however, that the water brought him forth out of some virtue that was in it. In the sky there was only the Moon glowing and shining – on the earth there was but this one Toad. It is said that they met and conversed together, and that one day the Moon said to him:

"I have an idea. I propose to make a man and a woman to live on the fruits of the earth, for I believe that there is rich abundance of food on it fit for such creatures."

"Nay," said the Toad, "let me make them, for I can make them fitter for the use of the earth than thou canst, for I belong to the earth, while thou belongest to the sky."

"Verily," replied the Moon, "thou hast the power to create creatures which shall have but a brief existence; but if I make them, they will have something of my own nature; and it is a pity that the creatures of one's own making should suffer and die. Therefore, O Toad, I propose to reserve the power of creation for myself, that the creatures may be endowed with perfection and enduring life."

"Ah, Moon, be not envious of the power which I share with thee, but let me have my way. I will give them forms such as I have often dreamed of. The thought is big within me, and I insist upon realising my ideas."

"An thou be so resolved, observe my words, both thou and they shall die. Thou I shall slay myself and end utterly; and thy creatures can but follow thee, being of such frail material as thou canst give them."

"Ah, thou art angry now, but I heed thee not. I am resolved that the creatures to inhabit this earth shall be of my own creating. Attend thou to thine own empire in the sky."

Then the Moon rose and soared upward, where with his big, shining face he shone upon all the world.

The Toad grew great with his conception, until it ripened and issued out in the shape of twin beings, full-grown male and female. These were the first like our kind that ever trod the earth.

The Moon beheld the event with rage, and left his place in the sky to punish the Toad, who had infringed the privilege that he had thought to reserve for himself. He came direct to Toad's pool, and stood blazingly bright over it.

"Miserable," he cried, "what hast thou done?"

"Patience, Moon, I but exercised my right and power. It was within me to do it, and lo, the deed is done."

"Thou hast exalted thyself to be my equal in thine own esteem. Thy conceit has clouded thy wit, and obscured the memory of the warning I gave thee. Even hadst thou obtained a charter from me to attempt the task, thou couldst have done no better than thou hast done. As much as thou art inferior to me, so these will be inferior to those I could have endowed this earth with. Thy creatures are pitiful things, mere animals without sense, without the gift of perception or self-protection. They see, they breathe, they exist; their lives can be measured by one round journey of mine. Were it not out of pity for them, I would even let them die. Therefore for pity's sake I propose to improve somewhat on what thou hast done: their lives shall be lengthened, and such intelligence as malformed beings as these can contain will I endow them with, that they may have guidance through a life which with all my power must be troubled and sore. But as for thee, whilst thou exist my rage is perilous to them, therefore to save thy kin I end thee."

Saying which the Moon advanced upon Toad, and the fierce sparks from his burning face were shot forth, and fell upon the Toad until he was consumed.

The Moon then bathed in the pool, that the heat of his anger might be moderated, and the water became so heated that it was like that which is in a pot over a fire, and he stayed in it until the hissing and bubbling had subsided.

Then the Moon rose out of the pool, and sought the creatures of Toad: and when he had found them, he called them unto him, but they were afraid and hid themselves.

At this sight the Moon smiled, as you sometimes see him on fine nights, when he is a clear white, and free from stain or blurr, and he was pleased that Toad's creatures were afraid of him. "Poor things," said he, "Toad has left me much to do yet before I can make them fit to be the first of earthly creatures." Saying which he took hold of them, and bore them to the pool wherein he had bathed, and which had been the home of Toad. He held them in the water for some time, tenderly bathing them, and stroking them here and there as a potter does to his earthenware, until he had moulded them into something similar to the shape we men and women possess now. The male became distinguished by breadth of shoulder, depth of chest, larger bones, and more substantial form; the female was slighter in chest, slimmer of waist, and the breadth and fulness of the woman was midmost of the body at the hips. Then the Moon gave them names; the man he called Bateta, the woman Hanna, and he addressed them and said:

"Bateta, see this earth and the trees, and herbs and plants and grasses; the whole is for thee and thy wife Hanna, and for thy children whom Hanna thy wife shall bear unto thee. I have re-made thee greatly, that thou and thine may enjoy such things as thou mayest find needful and fit. In order that thou mayest discover what things are not noxious but beneficial for thee, I have placed the faculty of discernment within thy head, which thou must exercise before thou canst become wise. The more thou prove this, the more wilt thou be able to perceive the abundance of good things the earth possesses for the creatures which are to inhabit it. I have made thee and thy wife as perfect as is necessary for the preservation and enjoyment of the term of life, which by nature of the materials the Toad made thee of must needs be short. It is in thy power to prolong or shorten it. Some things I must teach thee. I give thee first an axe. I make a fire for thee, which thou must feed from time to time with wood, and the first and most necessary utensil for daily use. Observe me while I make it for thee."

The Moon took some dark clay by the pool and mixed it with water, then kneaded it, and twisted it around until its shape was round and hollowed within, and he covered it with the embers of the fire, and baked it; and when it was ready he handed it to them.

"This vessel," continued the Moon, "is for the cooking of food. Thou wilt put water into it, and place whatsoever edible thou desirest to eat in the water. Thou wilt then place the vessel on the fire, which in time will boil the water and cook the edible. All vegetables, such as roots and bulbs, are improved in flavour and give superior nourishment by being thus cooked. It will become a serious matter for thee to know which of all the things pleasant in appearance are also pleasant for the palate. But shouldst thou be long in doubt and fearful of harm, ask and I will answer thee."

Having given the man and woman their first lesson, the Moon ascended to the sky, and from his lofty place shone upon them, and upon all the earth with a pleased expression, which comforted greatly the lonely pair.

Having watched the ascending Moon until he had reached his place in the sky, Bateta and Hanna rose and travelled on by the beautiful light which he gave them, until they came to a very large tree that had fallen. The thickness of the prostrate trunk was about twice their height. At the greater end of it there was a hole, into which they could walk without bending. Feeling a desire for sleep, Bateta laid his fire down outside near the hollowed entrance, cut up dry fuel, and his wife piled it on the fire, while the flames grew brighter and lit the interior. Bateta took Hanna by the hand and entered within the tree, and the two lay down together. But presently both complained of the hardness of their bed, and Bateta, after pondering awhile, rose, and going out, plucked some fresh large leaves of a plant that grew near the fallen tree, and returned laden with it. He spread it about thickly, and Hanna rolled herself on it, and laughed gleefully as she said to Bateta that it was soft and smooth and nice; and opening her arms, she cried, "Come, Bateta, and rest by my side."

Though this was the first day of their lives, the Moon had so perfected the unfinished and poor work of the Toad that they were both mature man and woman. Within a month Hanna bore twins, of whom one was male and the other female, and they were tiny doubles of Bateta and Hanna, which so pleased Bateta that he ministered kindly to his wife who, through her double charge, was prevented from doing anything else.

Thus it was that Bateta, anxious for the comfort of his wife, and for the nourishment of his children, sought to find choice things, but could find little to please the dainty taste which his wife had contracted. Whereupon, looking up to Moon with his hands uplifted, he cried out:

"O Moon, list to thy creature Bateta! My wife lies languishing, and she has a taste strange to me which I cannot satisfy, and the children that have been born unto us feed upon her body, and her strength decreases fast. Come down, O Moon, and show me what fruit or herbs will cure her longing."

The Moon heard Bateta's voice, and coming out from behind the cloud with a white, smiling face, said, "It is well, Bateta; lo! come to help thee."

When the Moon had approached Bateta, he showed the golden fruit of the banana – which was the same plant whose leaves had formed the first bed of himself and wife.

"O Bateta, smell this fruit. How likest thou its fragrance?"

"It is beautiful and sweet. O Moon, if it be as wholesome for the body as it is sweet to smell, my wife will rejoice in it."

Then the Moon peeled the banana and offered it to Bateta, upon which he boldly ate it, and the flavour was so pleasant that he besought permission to take one to his wife. When Hanna had tasted it she also appeared to enjoy it; but she said, "Tell Moon that I need something else, for I have no strength, and I am thinking that this fruit will not give to me what I lose by these children."

Bateta went out and prayed to Moon to listen to Hanna's words – which when he had heard, he said, "It was known to me that this should be, wherefore look round, Bateta, and tell me what thou seest moving yonder."

"Why, that is a buffalo."

"Rightly named," replied Moon. "And what follows it?"

"A goat."

"Good again. And what next?"

"An antelope."

"Excellent, O Bateta; and what may the next be?"

"A sheep."

"Sheep it is, truly. Now look up above the trees, and tell me what thou seest soaring over them."

"I see fowls and pigeons."

"Very well called, indeed," said Moon. "These I give unto thee for meat. The buffalo is strong and fierce, leave him for thy leisure; but the goat, sheep, and fowls, shall live near thee, and shall partake of thy bounty. There are numbers in the woods which will come to thee when they are filled with their grazing and their pecking. Take any of them – either goat, sheep, or fowl – bind it, and chop its head off with thy hatchet. The blood will sink into the soil; the meat underneath the outer skin is good for food, after being boiled or roasted over the fire. Haste now, Bateta; it is meat thy wife craves, and she needs naught else to restore her strength. So prepare instantly and eat."

The Moon floated upward, smiling and benignant, and Bateta hastened to bind a goat, and made it ready as the Moon had advised. Hanna, after eating of the meat which was prepared by boiling, soon recovered her strength, and the children throve, and grew marvellously.

One morning Bateta walked out of his hollowed house, and lo! a change had come over the earth. Right over the tops of the trees a great globe of shining, dazzling light looked out from the sky, and blazed white and bright over all. Things that he had seen dimly before were now more clearly revealed. By the means of the strange light hung up in the sky he saw the difference between that which the Moon gave and that new brightness which now shone out. For, without, the trees and their leaves seemed clad in a luminous coat of light, while underneath it was but a dim reflection of that which was without, and to the sight it seemed like the colder light of the Moon.

And in the cooler light that prevailed below the foliage of the trees there were gathered hosts of new and strange creatures; some large, others of medium, and others of small size.

Astonished at these changes, he cried, "Come out, O Hanna, and see the strange sights without the dwelling, for verily I am amazed, and know not what has happened."

Obedient, Hanna came out with the children and stood by his side, and was equally astonished at the brightness of the light and at the numbers of creatures which in all manner of sizes and forms stood in the shade ranged around them, with their faces towards the place where they stood.

"What may this change portend, O Bateta?" asked his wife.

"Nay, Hanna, I know not. All this has happened since the Moon departed from me."

"Thou must perforce call him again, Bateta, and demand the meaning of it, else I shall fear harm unto thee, and unto these children."

"Thou art right, my wife, for to discover the meaning of all this without other aid than my own wits would keep us here until we perished."

Then he lifted his voice, and cried out aloud upward, and at the sound of his voice all the creatures gathered in the shades looked upward, and cried with their voices; but the meaning of their cry, though there was an infinite variety of sound, from the round, bellowing voice of the lion to the shrill squeak of the mouse, was:

"Come down unto us, O Moon, and explain the meaning of this great change unto us; for thou only who madest us can guide our sense unto the right understanding of it."

When they had ended their entreaty unto the Moon, there came a voice from above, which sounded like distant thunder, saying, "Rest ye where ye stand, until the brightness of this new light shall have faded, and ye distinguish my milder light and that of the many children which have been born unto me, when I shall come unto you and explain."

Thereupon they rested each creature in its own place, until the great brightness, and the warmth which the strange light gave faded and lessened, and it was observed that it disappeared from view on the opposite side to that where it had first been seen, and also immediately after at the place of its disappearance the Moon was seen, and all over the sky were visible the countless little lights which the children of the Moon gave.

Presently, after Bateta had pointed these out to Hanna and the children, the Moon shone out bland, and its face was covered with gladness, and he left the sky smiling, and floated down to the earth, and stood not far off from Bateta, in view of him and his family, and of all the creatures under the shade.

"Hearken, O Bateta, and ye creatures of prey and pasture. A little while ago, ye have seen the beginning of the measurement of time, which shall be divided hereafter into day and night. The time that lapses between the Sun's rising and its setting shall be called day, that which shall lapse between its setting and re-rising shall be called night. The light of the day proceeds from the Sun, but the light of the night proceeds from me and from my children the stars; and as ye are all my creatures, I have chosen that my softer light shall shine during the restful time wherein ye sleep, to recover the strength lost in the waking time, and that ye shall be daily waked for the working time by the stronger light of the Sun. This rule never-ending shall remain.

"And whereas Bateta and his wife are the first of creatures, to them, their families, and kind that shall be born unto them, shall be given pre-eminence over all creatures made, not that they are stronger, or swifter, but because to them only have I given understanding and a gift of speech to transmit it. Perfection and everlasting life had also been given, but the taint of the Toad remains in the system, and the result will be death, – death to all living things, Bateta and Hanna excepted. In the fulness of time, when their limbs refuse to bear the burden of their bodies and their marrow has become dry, my first-born shall return to me, and I shall absorb them. Children shall be born innumerable unto them, until families shall expand into tribes, and from here, as from a spring, mankind will outflow and overspread all lands, which are now but wild and wold, ay, even to the farthest edge of the earth.

"And hearken, O Bateta, the beasts which thou seest, have sprung from the ashes of the Toad. On the day that he measured his power against mine, and he was consumed by my fire, there was one drop of juice left in his head. It was a life-germ which soon grew into another toad. Though not equal in power to the parent toad, thou seest what he has done. Yonder beasts of prey and pasture and fowls are his work. As fast as they were conceived by him, and uncouth and ungainly they were, I dipped them into

Toad's Pool, and perfected them outwardly, according to their uses, and, as thou seest, each specimen has its mate. Whereas, both thou and they alike have the acrid poison of the toad, thou from the parent, they in a greater measure from the child toad, the mortal taint when ripe will end both man and beast. No understanding nor gift of speech has been given to them, and they are as inferior to thyself as the child toad was to the parent toad. Wherefore, such qualities as thou mayst discover in them, thou mayst employ in thy services. Meantime, let them go out each to its own feeding-ground, lair, or covert, and grow and multiply, until the generations descending from thee shall have need for them. Enough for thee with the bounties of the forest, jungle, and plain, are the goats, sheep, and fowls. At thy leisure, Bateta, thou mayst strike and eat such beasts as thou seest akin in custom to these that will feed from thy hand. The waters abound in fish that are thine at thy need, the air swarms with birds which are also thine, as thy understanding will direct thee.

"Thou wilt be wise to plant all such edibles as thou mayest discover pleasing to the palate and agreeable to thy body, but be not rash in assuming that all things pleasant to the eye are grateful to thy inwards.

"So long as thou and Hanna are on the earth, I promise thee my aid and counsel; and what I tell thee and thy wife thou wilt do well to teach thy children, that the memory of useful things be not forgotten – for after I take thee to myself, I come no more to visit man. Enter thy house now, for it is a time, as I have told thee, for rest and sleep. At the shining of the greater light, thou wilt waken for active life and work, and family care and joys. The beasts shall also wander each to his home in the earth, on the tops of the trees, in the bush, or in the cavern. Fare thee well, Bateta, and have kindly care for thy wife Hanna and the children."

The Moon ended his speech, and floated upward, radiant and gracious, until he rested in his place in the sky, and all the children of the Moon twinkled for joy and gladness so brightly, as the parent of the world entered his house, that all the heavens for a short time seemed burning. Then the Moon drew over him his cloudy cloak, and the little children of the Moon seemed to get drowsy, for they twinkled dimly, and then a darkness fell over all the earth, and in the darkness man and beast retired, each to his own place, according as the Moon had directed.

A second time Bateta waked from sleep, and walked out to wonder at the intense brightness of the burning light that made the day. Then he looked around him, and his eyes rested upon a noble flock of goats and sheep, all of whom bleated their morning welcome, while the younglings pranced about in delight, and after curvetting around, expressed in little bleats the joy they felt at seeing their chief, Bateta. His attention was also called to the domestic fowls; there were red and white and spotted cocks, and as many coloured hens, each with its own brood of chicks. The hens trotted up to their master – cluck, cluck, clucking – the tiny chicks, following each its own mother – cheep, cheep, cheeping – while the cocks threw out their breasts and strutted grandly behind, and crowed with their trumpet throats, "All hail, master."

Then the morning wind rose and swayed the trees, plants, and grasses, and their tops bending before it bowed their salutes to the new king of the earth, and thus it was that man knew that his reign over all was acknowledged.

A few months afterwards, another double birth occurred, and a few months later there was still another, and Bateta remembered the number of months that intervened between each event, and knew that it would be a regular custom for all time. At the end of the eighteenth year, he permitted his first-born to choose a wife, and when his other children grew up he likewise allowed them to select their wives. At the end of ninety years, Hanna had born to Bateta two hundred and forty-two children, and there were grandchildren, and great-grandchildren, and countless great-great-grandchildren, and they lived to an age many times the length of the greatest age amongst us now-a-days. When they were so old that it became a trouble to them to live, the Moon came down to the earth as he had promised, and bore them to himself, and soon after the first-born twins died and were buried in the earth, and after that the deaths were many and more frequent. People ceased to live as long as their parents had done, for sickness, dissensions, wars, famines, accidents ended them and cut their days short, until they at last forgot how to live long, and cared not to think how their days might be prolonged. And it has happened after this manner down to us who now live. The whole earth has become filled with mankind, but the dead that are gone and forgotten are far greater in number than those now alive upon the earth.

Ye see now, my friends, what mischief the Toad did unto all mankind. Had his conceit been less, and had he waited a little, the good Moon would have conceived us of a nobler kind than we now are, and the taint of the Toad had not cursed man. Wherefore abandon headstrong ways, and give not way to rashness, but pay good heed to the wise and old, lest ye taint in like manner the people, and cause the innocent, the young, and the weak to suffer. I have spoken my say. If ye have heard aught displeasing, remember I but tell the tale as it was told unto me.

"Taking it as a mere story," said Baraka, "it is very well told, but I should like to know why the Moon did not teach Bateta the value of manioc, since he took the trouble to tell him about the banana."

"For the reason," answered Matageza, "that when he showed him the banana, there was no one but the Moon could have done so. But after the Moon had given goats and sheep and fowls for his companions, his own lively intelligence was sufficient to teach Bateta many things. The goats became great pets of Bateta, and used to follow him about. He observed that there was a certain plant to which the goats flocked with great greed, to feed upon the tops until their bellies became round and large with it. One day the idea came to him that if the goats could feed so freely upon it without harm, it might be also harmless to him. Whereupon he pulled the plant up and earned it home. While he was chopping up the tops for the pot his pet goats tried to eat the tuber which was the root, and he tried that also. He cut up both leaves and root and cooked them, and after tasting them he found them exceedingly good and palatable, and thenceforward manioc became a daily food to him and his family, and from them to his children's children, and so on down to us."

"Verily, that is of great interest. Why did you not put that in the story?"

"Because the story would then have no end. I would have to tell you of the sweet potato, and the tomato, of the pumpkin, of the millet that was discovered by the fowls, and of the palm oil-nut that was discovered by the dog."

"Ah, yes, tell us how a dog could have shown the uses of the palm oil-nut."

"It is very simple. Bateta coaxed a dog to live with him because he found that the dog preferred to sit on his haunches and wait for the bones that his family threw aside after the meal was over, rather than hunt for himself like other flesh-eating beasts. One day Bateta walked out into the woods, and his dog followed him.

After a long walk Bateta rested at the foot of the straight tall tree called the palm, and there were a great many nuts lying on the ground, which perhaps the monkeys or the wind had thrown down. The dog after smelling them lay down and began to eat them, and though Bateta was afraid he would hurt himself, he allowed him to have his own way, and he did not see that they harmed him at all, but that he seemed as fond as ever of them. By thinking of this he conceived that they would be no harm to him; and after cooking them, he found that their fat improved the flavour of his vegetables, hence the custom came down to us. Indeed, the knowledge of most things that we know today as edibles came down to us through the observation of animals by our earliest fathers. What those of old knew not was found out later through stress of hunger, while men were lost in the bushy wilds."

When at last we rose to retire to our tents and huts, the greater number of our party felt the sorrowful conviction that the Toad had imparted to all mankind an incurable taint, and that we poor wayfarers, in particular, were cursed with an excess of it, in consequence of which both Toad and tadpole were heartily abused by all.

THE DAUGHTER OF THE SUN AND MOON
(From the Bantu-speaking peoples, Angola)

Kimanaweze's son, when the time came for him to choose a wife, declared that he would not "marry a woman of the earth," but must have the daughter of the Sun and Moon. He wrote "a letter of marriage" (a modern touch, no doubt added by the narrator) and cast about for a messenger to take it up to the sky. The little duiker (*mbambt*) refused, so did the larger antelope, known as *soko*, the hawk, and the vulture. At last a frog came and offered to carry the letter. The son of Kimanaweze, doubtful of his ability to do this, said, "Begone! Where people of life, who have wings, gave it up dost thou say, 'I will go there'?" But the frog persisted, and was at last sent off, with the threat of a thrashing if he should be unsuccessful. It appears that the Sun and Moon were in the habit of sending their handmaidens down to the earth to draw water, descending and ascending by means of a spider's web. The frog went and hid himself in the well to which they came, and when the first one filled her jar he got into it without being seen, having first placed the letter in his mouth. The girls went up to heaven, carried their water jars into the room, and set them down. When they had gone away he came out, produced the letter, laid it on a table, and hid.

After a while "Lord Sun" (*Kumbi Mwene*) came in, found the letter, and read it. Not knowing what to make of it, he put it away, and said nothing about it. The frog got into an empty water-jar, and was carried down again when the girls went for a fresh supply. The son of Kimanaweze, getting no answer, refused at first to believe that the frog had executed his commission; but, after waiting for some days, he wrote another letter and sent him again. The frog carried it in the same way as before, and the Sun, after reading it, wrote that he would consent, if the suitor came himself, bringing his 'first-present' (the usual gift for opening marriage negotiations). On receiving this the young man wrote another letter, saying that he must wait till told the amount of the 'wooing-present', or bride-price (*kilembu*). He gave this to the frog, along with a sum of money, and it was conveyed as before. This time the Sun consulted his wife, who was quite ready to welcome the mysterious son-in-law.

She solved the question of providing refreshments for the invisible messenger by saying, "We will cook a meal anyhow, and put it on the table where he leaves the letters." This was done, and the frog, when left alone, came out and ate. The letter, which was left along with the food, stated the amount of the bride-price to be "a sack of money." He carried the letter back to the son of Kimanaweze, who spent six days in collecting the necessary amount, and then sent it by the frog with this message: "Soon I shall find a day to bring home my wife." This, however, was more easily said than done, for when his messenger had once more returned he waited twelve days, and then told the frog that he could not find people to fetch the bride. But the frog was equal to the occasion. Again he had himself carried up to the Sun's palace, and, getting out of the water-jar, hid in a corner of the room till after dark, when he came out and went through the house till he found the princess's bedchamber. Seeing that she was fast asleep, he took out one of her eyes without waking her, and then the other. He tied up the eyes in a handkerchief, and went back to his corner in the room where the water jars were kept. In the morning, when the girl did not appear, her parents came to inquire the reason, and found that she was blind. In their distress they sent two men to consult the diviner, who, after casting lots, said (not having heard from them the reason of their coming), "Disease has brought you; the one who is sick is a woman; the sickness that ails her the eyes. You have come, being sent; you have not come of your own will. I have spoken." The Sun's messengers replied, "Truth. Look now what caused the ailment." He told them that a certain suitor had cast a spell over her, and she would die unless she were sent to him.

Therefore they had best hasten on the marriage. The men brought back word to the Sun, who said, "All right. Let us sleep. Tomorrow they shall take her down to the earth." Next day, accordingly, he gave orders for the spider to "weave a large cobweb" for sending his daughter down. Meanwhile the frog had gone down as usual in the water-jar and hidden himself in the bottom of the well. When the water carriers had gone up again he came out and went to the village of the bridegroom and told him that his bride would arrive that day. The young man would not believe him, but he solemnly promised to bring her in the evening, and returned to the well.

After sunset the attendants brought the princess down by way of the stronger cobweb and left her by the well. The frog came out, and told her that he would take her to her husband's house; at the same time he handed back her eyes. They started, and came to the son of Kimanaweze, and the marriage took place. And they lived happy ever after – on earth, for, as the narrator said, "They had all given up going to heaven; who could do it was Mainu the frog."

VASA-GO'RE: LEGEND AND SONG OF THE SKY-MAIDEN
(From the Ndau people, eastern Zimbabwe, Mozambique and Malawi)

There lived in the sky a powerful chief, and he had a beautiful daughter, the Sky-Maiden. Every day with her maiden attendants she came down to earth to bathe in the lake. Each maid bore in her hands a plume which wafted her to the ground and on which she floated up again to the sky. So beautiful was the Sky-Maiden that any man who saw her as she came to earth longed to win her for his wife.

Now, each day when the maid and her attendants flew down to the lake, they laid aside their clothing and left their plumes with their garments on the banks. Often the young men hid in the bush near the lake and tried to steal the plumes, for they well knew that if they could seize these, the maidens could never again fly back to the sky. But the maids, who dreaded to be seen, were quick to hear the approach of any stranger, and at the first faint rustle of a leaf they would rise from the lake, grasp their plumes and vanish into the air. But if a man should succeed in stealing a feather, then the maiden to whom it belonged would shake her 'nthu´zwa' (a soft musical-sounding rattle made of reeds) and sing this song:

Sam'du´mbi-we´-we´, ndekande´,
>   *(Nyalala´!)*

>>   *O youth, I entreat thee, I pray,*
>>   *(Heed her not!)*

Wo chizwa´ nthu´zwa ya´nguyo-we´, ndekande´,
>   *(Nyalala´!)*

>>   *Hearken now to my nthu´zwa, I pray,*
>>   *(Heed her not!)*

Sam'du´mbi-we´-we´, ndekande´,
>   *(Nyalala´!)*

>>   *O youth, I entreat thee, I pray,*
>>   *(Heed her not!)*

Tongo li´ngile-we´, ndekande´,
>   *(Nyalala´!)*

>>   *Look back, look back, I pray,*
>>   *(Heed her not!)*

Sam'du´mbi-we´-we´, ndekande´,
  (Nyalala´!)
                    O youth, I entreat thee, I pray,
                      (Heed her not!)
Mwana-we´ ndo´da ku´pincia-we´, ndekande´,
  (Nyalala´!)
                    Dear Child, I would go, I pray,
                      (Heed her not!)
Sam'du´mbi-we´-we´, ndekande´,
  (Nyalala´!)
                    O youth, I entreat thee, I pray,
                      (Heed her not!)
Mwana-we´ wochi li´ngila-we´, ndekande´,
  (Nyalala´!)
                    Dear Child, look back, I pray,
                      (Heed her not!)
Sam'du´mbi-we´-we´, ndekande´,
  (Nyalala´!)
                    O youth, I entreat thee, I pray,
                      (Heed her not!)
Ndo´da´ kwenda-we´, ndekande´.
  (Nyalala´!)
                    Let me go, let me go, I pray.
                      (Heed her not!)

If the youth heeds her voice and looks back – then the maiden and *nthu´zwa* are gone, and there is nothing to be seen. For at this first backward glance, the plume returns to the maiden and instantly she mounts to the sky.

But the story tells of one youth who stole the plume and, strong of heart, never looked back. And so the maiden had to stay on earth and the youth won her love and took her for his wife. After that the maid shared with her husband her power to fly to the sky, and she took him with her to the sky-land.

This story means that if a man sets out to do a deed he must persevere till the end and never turn back till he has achieved his aim.

THE STORY OF THE HERO MAKOMA FROM THE SENNA
(From Zimbabwe)

Once upon a time, at the town of Senna (Sena) on the banks of the Zambesi, was born a child. He was not like other children, for he was very tall and strong; over his shoulder he carried a big sack, and in his hand an iron hammer. He could also speak like a grown man, but usually he was very silent.

One day his mother said to him: "My child, by what name shall we know you?"

And he answered: "Call all the head men of Senna here to the river's bank." And his mother called the head men of the town, and when they had come he led them down to a deep black pool in the river where all the fierce crocodiles lived.

"O great men!" he said, while they all listened, "which of you will leap into the pool and overcome the crocodiles?" But no one would come forward. So he turned and sprang into the water and disappeared.

The people held their breath, for they thought: "Surely the boy is bewitched and throws away his life, for the crocodiles will eat him!" Then suddenly the ground trembled, and the pool, heaving and swirling, became red with blood, and presently the boy rising to the surface swam on shore.

But he was no longer just a boy! He was stronger than any man and very tall and handsome, so that the people shouted with gladness when they saw him.

"Now, O my people!" he cried, waving his hand, "you know my name – I am Makoma, 'the Greater'; for have I not slain the crocodiles into the pool where none would venture?"

Then he said to his mother: "Rest gently, my mother, for I go to make a home for myself and become a hero." Then, entering his hut he took Nu-endo, his iron hammer, and throwing the sack over his shoulder, he went away.

Makoma crossed the Zambesi, and for many moons he wandered towards the north and west until he came to a very hilly country where, one day, he met a huge giant making mountains.

"Greeting," shouted Makoma, "who are you?"

"I am Chi-eswa-mapiri, who makes the mountains," answered the giant; "and who are you?"

"I am Makoma, which signifies 'greater,'" answered he.

"Greater than who?" asked the giant.

"Greater than you!" answered Makoma.

The giant gave a roar and rushed upon him. Makoma said nothing, but swinging his great hammer, Nu-endo, he struck the giant upon the head.

He struck him so hard a blow that the giant shrank into quite a little man, who fell upon his knees saying: "You are indeed greater than I, O Makoma; take me with you to be your slave!" So Makoma picked him up and dropped him into the sack that he carried upon his back.

He was greater than ever now, for all the giant's strength had gone into him; and he resumed his journey, carrying his burden with as little difficulty as an eagle might carry a hare.

Before long he came to a country broken up with huge stones and immense clods of earth. Looking over one of the heaps he saw a giant wrapped in dust dragging out the very earth and hurling it in handfuls on either side of him.

"Who are you," cried Makoma, "that pulls up the earth in this way?"

"I am Chi-dubula-taka," said he, "and I am making the river-beds."

"Do you know who I am?" said Makoma. "I am he that is called 'greater!'"

"Greater than who?" thundered the giant.

"Greater than you!" answered Makoma.

With a shout, Chi-dubula-taka seized a great clod of earth and launched it at Makoma. But the hero had his sack held over his left arm and the stones and earth fell harmlessly upon it, and, tightly gripping his iron hammer, he rushed in and struck the giant to the ground. Chi-dubula-taka grovelled before him, all the while growing smaller and smaller; and when he had become a convenient size Makoma picked him up and put him into the sack beside Chi-eswa-mapiri.

He went on his way even greater than before, as all the river-maker's power had become his; and at last he came to a forest of baobabs and thorn trees. He was astonished at their size, for every one was full grown and larger than any trees he had ever seen, and close by he saw Chi-gwisa-miti, the giant who was planting the forest.

Chi-gwisa-miti was taller than either of his brothers, but Makoma was not afraid, and called out to him: "Who are you, O Big One?"

"I," said the giant, "am Chi-gwisa-miti, and I am planting these bao-babs and thorns as food for my children the elephants."

"Leave off!" shouted the hero, "for I am Makoma, and would like to exchange a blow with thee!"

The giant, plucking up a monster bao-bab by the roots, struck heavily at Makoma; but the hero sprang aside, and as the weapon sank deep into the soft earth, whirled Nu-endo the hammer round his head and felled the giant with one blow.

So terrible was the stroke that Chi-gwisa-miti shrivelled up as the other giants had done; and when he had got back his breath he begged Makoma to take him as his servant. "For," said he, "it is honourable to serve a man so great as thou."

Makoma, after placing him in his sack, proceeded upon his journey, and travelling for many days he at last reached a country so barren and rocky that not a single living thing grew upon it – everywhere reigned grim desolation. And in the midst of this dead region he found a man eating fire.

"What are you doing?" demanded Makoma.

"I am eating fire," answered the man, laughing; "and my name is Chi-idea-moto, for I am the flame-spirit, and can waste and destroy what I like."

"You are wrong," said Makoma; "for I am Makoma, who is 'greater' than you – and you cannot destroy me!"

The fire-eater laughed again, and blew a flame at Makoma. But the hero sprang behind a rock – just in time, for the ground upon which he had been standing was turned to molten glass, like an overbaked pot, by the heat of the flame-spirit's breath.

Then the hero flung his iron hammer at Chi-idea-moto, and, striking him, it knocked him helpless; so Makoma placed him in the sack, Woro-nowu, with the other great men that he had overcome.

And now, truly, Makoma was a very great hero; for he had the strength to make hills, the industry to lead rivers over dry wastes, foresight and wisdom in planting trees, and the power of producing fire when he wished.

Wandering on he arrived one day at a great plain, well watered and full of game; and in the very middle of it, close to a large river, was a grassy spot, very pleasant to make a home upon.

Makoma was so delighted with the little meadow that he sat down under a large tree and removing the sack from his shoulder, took out all the giants and set them before him. "My friends," said he, "I have travelled far and am weary. Is not this such a place as would suit a hero for his home? Let us then go, to-morrow, to bring in timber to make a kraal."

So the next day Makoma and the giants set out to get poles to build the kraal, leaving only Chi-eswa-mapiri to look after the place and cook some venison which they had killed. In the evening, when they returned, they found the giant helpless and tied to a tree by one enormous hair!

"How is it," said Makoma, astonished, "that we find you thus bound and helpless?"

"O Chief," answered Chi-eswa-mapiri, "at mid-day a man came out of the river; he was of immense statue, and his grey moustaches were of such length that I could not see where they ended! He demanded of me 'Who is thy master?' And I answered: 'Makoma, the greatest of heroes.' Then the man seized me, and pulling a hair from his moustache, tied me to this tree – even as you see me."

Makoma was very wroth, but he said nothing, and drawing his finger-nail across the hair (which was as thick and strong as palm rope) cut it, and set free the mountain-maker.

The three following days exactly the same thing happened, only each time with a different one of the party; and on the fourth day Makoma stayed in camp when the others went to cut poles, saying that he would see for himself what sort of man this was that lived in the river and whose moustaches were so long that they extended beyond men's sight.

So when the giants had gone he swept and tidied the camp and put some venison on the fire to roast. At midday, when the sun was right overhead, he heard a rumbling noise from the river, and looking up he saw the head and shoulders of an enormous man emerging from it. And behold! right down the river-bed and up the river-bed, till they faded into the blue distance, stretched the giant's grey moustaches!

"Who are you?" bellowed the giant, as soon as he was out of the water.

"I am he that is called Makoma," answered the hero; "and, before I slay thee, tell me also what is thy name and what thou doest in the river?"

"My name is Chin-debou Mau-giri," said the giant. "My home is in the river, for my moustache is the grey fever-mist that hangs above the water, and with which I bind all those that come unto me so that they die."

"You cannot bind me!" shouted Makoma, rushing upon him and striking with his hammer. But the river giant was so slimy that the blow slid harmlessly off his green chest, and as Makoma stumbled and tried to regain his balance, the giant swung one of his long hairs around him and tripped him up.

For a moment Makoma was helpless, but remembering the power of the flame-spirit which had entered into him, he breathed a fiery breath upon the giant's hair and cut himself free.

As Chin-debou Mau-giri leaned forward to seize him the hero flung his sack Woronowu over the giant's slippery head, and gripping his iron hammer, struck him again; this time the blow alighted upon the dry sack and Chin-debou Mau-giri fell dead.

When the four giants returned at sunset with the poles, they rejoiced to find that Makoma had overcome the fever-spirit, and they feasted on the roast venison till far into the night; but in the morning, when they awoke, Makoma was already warming his hands to the fire, and his face was gloomy.

"In the darkness of the night, O my friends," he said presently, "the white spirits of my fathers came upon me and spoke, saying: 'Get thee hence, Makoma, for thou shalt have no rest until thou hast found and fought with Sakatirina, who had five heads, and is very great and strong; so take leave of thy friends, for thou must go alone.'"

Then the giants were very sad, and bewailed the loss of their hero; but Makoma comforted them, and gave back to each the gifts he had taken from them. Then bidding them "Farewell," he went on his way.

Makoma travelled far towards the west; over rough mountains and water-logged morasses, fording deep rivers, and tramping for days across dry deserts where most men would have died, until at length he arrived at a hut standing near some large peaks, and inside the hut were two beautiful women.

"Greeting!" said the hero. "Is this the country of Sakatirina of five heads, whom I am seeking?"

"We greet you, O Great One!" answered the women. "We are the wives of Sakatirina; your search is at an end, for there stands he whom you seek!" And they pointed to what Makoma had thought were two tall mountain peaks. "Those are his legs," they said; "his body you cannot see, for it is hidden in the clouds."

Makoma was astonished when he beheld how tall was the giant; but, nothing daunted, he went forward until he reached one of Sakatirina's legs, which he struck heavily with Nu-endo. Nothing happened, so he hit again and then again until, presently, he heard a tired, far-away voice saying: "Who is it that scratches my feet?"

And Makoma shouted as loud as he could, answering: "It is I, Makoma, who is called 'Greater!'" And he listened, but there was no answer.

Then Makoma collected all the dead brushwood and trees that he could find, and making an enormous pile round the giant's legs, set a light to it.

This time the giant spoke; his voice was very terrible, for it was the rumble of thunder in the clouds. "Who is it," he said, "making that fire smoulder around my feet?"

"It is I, Makoma!" shouted the hero. "And I have come from far away to see thee, O Sakatirina, for the spirits of my fathers bade me go seek and fight with thee, lest I should grow fat, and weary of myself."

There was silence for a while, and then the giant spoke softly: "It is good, O Makoma!" he said. "For I too have grown weary. There is no man so great as I, therefore I am all alone. Guard thyself!" and bending suddenly he seized the hero in his hands and dashed him upon the ground. And lo! instead of death, Makoma had found life, for he sprang to his feet mightier in strength and stature than before, and rushing in he gripped the giant by the waist and wrestled with him.

Hour by hour they fought, and mountains rolled beneath their feet like pebbles in a flood; now Makoma would break away, and summoning up his strength, strike the giant with Nu-endo his iron hammer, and Sakatirina would pluck up the mountains and hurl them upon the hero, but neither one could slay the other. At last, upon the second day, they grappled so strongly that they could not break away; but their strength was failing, and, just as the sun was sinking, they fell together to the ground, insensible.

In the morning when they awoke, Mulimo the Great Spirit was standing by them; and he said: "O Makoma and Sakatirina! Ye are heroes so great that no man may come against you. Therefore ye will leave the world and take up your home with me in the clouds." And as he spake the heroes became invisible to the people of the Earth, and were no more seen among them.

HUVEANE PRODUCES A CHILD
(From the Pedi and Venda peoples, South Africa)

Of this legend there are various versions, none apparently complete, but they can be used to supplement each other. One begins in a way which recalls the story of Murile. Only whereas Murile cherishes a *Colocasia* tuber, which magically develops into an infant, Huveane is quite baldly stated to have "had a baby". The narrator seems to see nothing improbable in this (though Huveane's parents and their neighbours did), and no explanation is given of this extraordinary proceeding; but there is a story resembling this in which the result is produced by the boy having swallowed some medicine intended for his mother. Another version has it that Huveane modelled a baby in clay and breathed

life into it. This may possibly have some vague connection with
the idea of his having originated the human race; it may, on the
other hand, be due to some echo of missionary teaching.

Huveane kept his child in a hollow tree, and stole out early
every morning to feed it with milk before it was time for him to
begin herding the sheep and goats. His parents noticed that he
used to take the milk, and could not make out what he did with
it; so one day his father followed him stealthily, saw him feeding
the child, hid till Huveane had one away, and carried the baby
to his wife. They then placed it among the firewood and other
things stacked up under the eaves of the hut. When Huveane
brought the flock home he went straight to his tree and found
no baby there. He went into the courtyard, sat down by the fire,
where his parents were seated, and did not speak, only looking
miserable. His mother asked him what was the matter, and he said
the smoke was hurting his eyes. "Then you had better go out and
sit somewhere else." He did so, but remained gloomy. At last his
mother told him to go and fetch a piece of wood from the pile,
which he did, and found the baby wrapped in a sheepskin and
quite safe. His parents, relieved to find that he had recovered his
spirits, let him have his way, and he went on caring for the child,
whom he called Sememerwane sa Matedi a Telele ('One who
causes much trouble').

Huveane Plays Tricks with the Stock

His parents continued, however, to be uneasy; they could not
understand how the child had been produced, and the neighbours,
when the story leaked out, began to talk of witchcraft. Huveane
did not trouble himself, but went on herding his father's stock and
devising practical jokes to play upon him. When a ewe or goat

had twins, which not infrequently happened, he took one of the lambs or kids and shut it up in a hollow ant-heap. In this way he gradually collected a whole flock. Someone, who had noticed that the ewes, when driven out in the morning, always collected round the ant-heaps, told Huveane's father, and the latter followed his son to the pasture, heard the bleating of the lambs and kids inside the ant-heaps, took away the stones which blocked the entrance, and seized the lambs to take them to their mothers. But as he did not know to which mother each belonged the result was confusion worse confounded. Huveane, exasperated beyond endurance, struck his father with the switch he had in his hand. No doubt this helped to bring matters to a crisis, but for the moment the old man was too much impressed with the sudden increase of the flock to be very angry. In the evening, when the villagers saw the full number being driven home, they were filled with envy, and asked him where he had got all those animals. He told the whole story, which gave rise to endless discussions.

Plans for Huveane's Destruction

It was certain that Huveane could be up to no good; he must have produced those sheep and goats by magic – and how came he to have a child and no mother for it? He certainly ought to be got rid of. They put it to his father that the boy would end by bewitching the whole village. They handed him some poison, and in the evening, when Huveane was squatting by the fire, his mother brought him a bowl of milk. He took it, but, instead of drinking, poured it out on the ground. The neighbours took counsel, and suggested to the father that he should dig a pit close to the fireplace, where Huveane was in the habit of sitting, and cover it over. But Huveane, instead of sitting down in his usual place, forced himself in between his brothers, who were seated by the fire, and in the struggle for a place one of them fell into the pit. Next they dug another pit in the gateway of his father's enclosure, where he would have to pass when he came home with the flocks in the evening. He jumped over the pitfall, and all his sheep and goats did likewise.

This having failed, someone suggested that a man with a spear should be tied up in a bundle of grass, a device adopted, as we have seen, by Kachirambe's mother. This was done, and Huveane's father sent him to fetch the bundle. He took his spear with him to his father's surprise-and, when near enough, threw it with unerring aim. The man inside jumped up and ran away. Huveane returned to his father, saying, "Father, I went to do as you told me, but the grass has run away."

Huveane's Practical Jokes

The villagers were driven to the conclusion that it was quite impossible to compass Huveane's destruction by any stratagem, however cunning, and they were fain to let him be. He knew that he was a match for them, and thenceforth set himself to fool them by pretended stupidity. Whatever tricks he played on them he knew that he was safe.

One day he found a dead zebra, and sat down on it while watching his flock. In the evening, when he returned and was asked where he had been herding that day, he said, "By the striped hill." Three or four days running he gave the same answer, and, his relatives' curiosity being roused, some of them followed him and found the zebra-by this time badly decomposed. They told him, "Why, this is game; if you find an animal like this you should heap branches over it, to keep the hyenas away, and come and call the people from the village to fetch the meat." Next day Huveane found a very small bird lying dead; he heaped branches over it and ran home with the news. Half the village turned out, carrying large baskets; their feelings on beholding the 'game' may be imagined. One of the men informed him that this kind of game should be hung round one's neck; he did this next day, and was set down as a hopeless idiot. Several other tricks of the same kind are told of him; at last, one day, his father, thinking he should no longer be left to himself, went herding with him. When the sun was high he became very thirsty; Huveane showed him a high rock, on the top of which was a pool of water, and knocked in a number of pegs, so that he could climb up. They both went up and drank; then Huveane came down, took away the pegs, one by one, and ran home, where his mother had prepared the evening meal. Huveane ate all that was ready; then he took the empty pots, filled them with cow dung, and ran off to drive in the pegs and let his father come down. The old man came home and sat down to the supper, which, as his graceless son now informed him, had been magically changed, so as to be entirely uneatable. After this the parents and neighbours alike seem to have felt that there was nothing to be done with Huveane, except to put up with him as best they could. We hear nothing more about the child in the hollow tree.

It almost seems as if the trick played by Huveane on his father were a kind of inverted echo of one tradition about the High God, whom some call Huveane. "His abode is in the sky. He created the sky and the earth. He came down from the sky to make the earth and men. When he had finished he returned to the sky. They say he climbed up by pegs, and after he had gone up one step he took away the peg below him, and so on, till he had drawn them all out and disappeared into the sky."

Some say that all the incidents detailed above belong, not to Huveane (whom the narrators call the Great God, Modimo o Moholo), but to his son Hutswane, who, it is believed, will one day come again, bringing happiness and prosperity to mankind – a somewhat unexpected conclusion after all that we have heard about him.

THE GIRL OF THE EARLY RACE, WHO MADE STARS
(From the San people, southern Africa)

My mother was the one who told me that the girl arose; she put her hands into the wood ashes; she threw up the wood ashes into the sky. She said to the wood ashes: "The wood ashes which are here, they must altogether become the Milky Way. They must white lie along in the sky, that the stars may stand outside of the Milky Way, while the Milky Way is the Milky Way, while it used to be wood ashes." They (the ashes) altogether become the Milky Way. The Milky Way must go round with the stars; while the Milky Way feels that, the Milky Way lies going round; while the stars sail along; therefore, the Milky Way, lying, goes along with the stars. The Milky Way, when the Milky Way stands upon the earth, the Milky Way turns across in front, while the Milky Way means to wait(?), While the Milky Way feels that the Stars are turning back; while the Stars feel that the Sun is the one who has turned back; he is upon his path; the Stars turn back; while they go to fetch the daybreak; that they may lie nicely, while the Milky Way lies nicely. The Stars shall also stand nicely around.

They shall sail along upon their footprints, which they, always sailing along, are following. While they feel that, they are the Stars which descend.

The Milky Way lying comes to its place, to which the girl threw up the wood ashes, that it may descend nicely; it had lying gone along, while it felt that it lay upon the sky. It had lying gone round, while it felt that the Stars also turned round. They turning round passed over the sky. The sky lies (still); the Stars are those which go along; while they feel that they sail. They had been setting; they had, again, been coming out; they had, sailing along, been following their footprints. They become white, when the Sun comes out. The Sun sets, they stand around above; while they feel that they did turning follow the Sun.

The darkness comes out; they (the Stars) wax red, while they had at first been white. They feel that they stand brightly around; that they may sail along; while they feel that it is night. Then, the people go by night; while they feel that the ground is made light. While they feel that the Stars shine a little. Darkness is upon the ground. The Milky Way gently glows; while it feels that it is wood ashes. Therefore, it gently glows. While it feels that the girl was the one who said that the Milky Way should give a little light for the people, that they might return home by night, in the middle of the night. For, the earth would not have been a little light, had not the Milky Way been there. It and the Stars.

The girl thought that she would throw up (into the air) roots of the *huing* (a scented root eaten by some Bushmen), in order that the *huing* roots should become Stars; therefore, the Stars are red; while they feel that (they) are *huing* roots.

She first gently threw up wood ashes into the sky, that she might presently throw up *huing* roots; while she felt that she was angry with her mother, because her mother had not given her many *huing* roots, that she might eat abundantly; for, she was in the hut. She did not herself go out to seek food; that she might get(?) *huing* for herself; that she might be bringing it (home) for herself; that she might eat; for, she was hungry; while she lay ill in the hut. Her mothers were those who went out. They were those who sought for food. They were bringing home *huing*, that they might eat. She lay in her little hut, which her mother had made for her. Her stick stood there; because she did not yet dig out food. And, she was still in the hut. Her mother was the one who was bringing her food. That she might be eating, lying in the little hut; while her mother thought that she (the girl) did not eat the young men's game (i.e. game killed by them). For, she ate the game of her father, who was an old man. While she thought that the hands of the young men would become cool. Then, the arrow would become cool. The arrow head which is at the top, it would be cold; while the arrow head felt that the bow was cold; while the bow felt that his (the young man's) hands were cold. While the girl thought of her saliva, which, eating, she had put into the springbok meat; this saliva would go into the bow, the inside of the bow would become cool; she, in this manner, thought. Therefore, she feared the young men's game. Her father was the one from whom she alone ate (game). While she felt that she had worked (i.e. treated) her father's hands: she had worked, taking away her saliva (from them).

SPIDERS, TORTOISES & OTHER
ANIMAL TALES

The stories in this section, just like those from other continents of the world, portray animals as having the power of speech; they can, and do, communicate with human beings. The most prominent characters in animal tales in Africa are the Ìjàpá (tortoise) of the Yorùbá of Nigeria, Anansi (spider) of the Ewe of Ghana, and Leuk or Sango (hare) of the Wolof and the Madinka people of West Africa, respectively. The hare (Hlolo) also features heavily among the Bantu-speaking people of Central and Southern Africa.

The tortoise/spider/hare always engages other bigger animals in contests, surviving all dangers through his intelligence and cunning. In the South African story of elephant and tortoise and the Yorùbá tale of the tortoise, elephant and hippopotamus, the superiority of intelligence over raw strength is clearly shown. The tortoise proposes a tug of war – effectively a contest of power – to the elephant and the hippopotamus. In arranging to meet him, both competitors believe the tortoise will be an easy victim. Yet at the end of the competition, they are left marvelling at his power. The tortoise thus becomes ruler of both the seas and the forest.

This story is replicated in the tale of 'The Hare, the Hyena and the Pot of Beans' by the Bantu-speaking people of Central and Southern Africa. In this story the hare uses his innate intelligence to disgrace the powerful hyena after the latter's initial triumph.

The tortoise/hare/spider may not be physically strong like the elephant, hippopotamus, lion and jackal, yet they display an intelligence that defeats these opponents. The victory of the tortoise, spider or the rabbit in all contests usually represents the victory of intelligence over sheer physical power.

The exploits of the tortoise, spider or rabbit often serve as a metaphor for positive and negative human social relations. So it is in the following tales that appear in this book: 'We shall enthrone the Elephant' (Nigeria), 'The Lion, the Hyena and the Rabbit' (Tanzania), 'Elephant and Tortoise', 'The Name of the Tree', 'The Hare and the Baboon' and 'Jackal and Monkey' (South Africa). The trickster tortoise, the cunning fox, the slow snail, the elephant and lion, which loom large as the leaders of any jungle, as well as the leopard and tiger, ruthless and melancholy with an insatiable will to crush any opposition – all are usually defeated by the wisdom of the tortoise/spider/hare or rabbit. In so doing the smaller creatures harness a weapon more powerful than mere strength. Intelligence is a universal phenomenon, not restricted to the powerful but also wielded by the insignificant people of society. Leaders across the world can thus learn useful lessons from the relationship of the tortoise with other animals, as portrayed in this section.

THE WREN

(From the Kabyle people, Algeria)

A wren had built its nest on the side of a road. When the eggs were hatched, a camel passed that way. The little wrens saw it, and said to their father when he returned from the fields:

"O papa, a gigantic animal passed by."

The wren stretched out his foot. "As big as this, my children?"

"O papa, much bigger."

He stretched out his foot and his wing. "As big as this?"

"O papa, much bigger."

Finally he stretched out fully his feet and legs. "As big as this, then?"

"Much bigger."

"That is a lie; there is no animal bigger than I am."

"Well, wait," said the little ones, "and you will see." The camel came back while browsing the grass of the roadside. The wren stretched himself out near the nest. The camel seized the bird, which passed through its teeth safe and sound.

"Truly," he said to them, "the camel is a gigantic animal, but I am not ashamed of myself."

On the earth it generally happens that the vain are as if they did not exist. But sooner or later a rock falls and crushes them.

THE TURTLE, THE FROG AND THE SERPENT
(From the Berber peoples, North Africa)

Once upon a time the turtle married a frog. One day they quarrelled. The frog escaped and withdrew into a hole. The turtle was troubled and stood in front of his door very much worried. In those days the animals spoke. The griffin came by that way and said: "What is the matter with you? You look worried this morning."

"Nothing ails me," answered the turtle, "except that the frog has left me."

The griffin replied, "I'll bring him back."

"You will do me a great favor."

The griffin took up his journey and arrived at the hole of the frog. He scratched at the door.

The frog heard him and asked, "Who dares to rap at the door of a king's daughter?"

"It is I, the griffin, son of a griffin, who lets no carrion escape him."

"Get out of here, among your corpses. I, a daughter of the King, will not go with you."

He departed immediately.

The next day the vulture came along by the turtle and found it worrying before its door, and asked what was the trouble. It answered: "The frog has gone away."

"I'll bring her back," said the vulture.

"You will do me a great favor."

The vulture started, and reaching the frog's house began to beat its wings.

The frog said: "Who conies to the east to make a noise at the house of the daughter of kings, and will not let her sleep at her ease?"

"It is I, the vulture, son of a vulture, who steals chicks from under her mother."

The frog replied: "Get away from here, father of the dunghill. You are not the one to conduct the daughter of a king."

The vulture was angry and went away much disturbed. He returned to the turtle and said: "The frog refuses to come back with me. Seek someone else who can enter her hole and make her come out. Then I will bring her back even if she won't walk."

The turtle went to seek the serpent, and when he had found him he began to weep. "I'm the one to make her come out," said the serpent. He quickly went before the hole of the frog and scratched at the door.

"What is the name of this other one?" asked the frog.

"It is I, the serpent, son of the serpent. Come out or I'll enter."

"Wait awhile until I put on my best clothes, gird my girdle, rub my lips with nut-shells, put some *koheul* in my eyes; then I will go with you.»

"Hurry up," said the serpent. Then he waited a little while. Finally he got angry, entered her house, and swallowed her. Ever since that time the serpent has been at war with the frog. Whenever he sees one he chases her and eats her.

DJOKHRANE AND THE JAYS
(From the Berber peoples, North Africa)

The ancestor of the grandfather of Mahomet Amokrane was named Djokhrane. He was a Roman of old times, who lived at T'kout at the period of the Romans. One of his countrymen rose against them, and they fought. This Roman had the advantage, until a bird of the kind called jays came to the assistance of Djokhrane, and pecked the Roman in the eyes until he saved his adversary. From that time forth he remained a friend to Djokhrane. The latter said to his children:

"As long as you live, never eat this bird. If you meet anyone who brings one of these birds to eat, buy it and set it free." To this day when anyone brings a jay to one of his descendants, he buys it for silver and gives it liberty. This story is true, and is not a lie.

THE FISHERMAN[2]

(From the Jabo people, Liberia)

Sea gull, the fisherman, lived on the shore of the great ocean. Each day he waited until the tide went out, and then he found many small fish left in little pools along the water's edge.

One day the gull waited patiently for the tide to go down so that he could begin eating. But it seemed to him that the water didn't get lower at all but rose higher and higher. The gull was perplexed. "Formerly at this time of day the sea went down," he said. "Now it is coming up. I wonder what is the matter?"

He decided to consult some other people and make inquiries about the situation. So he flew to the village where the chickens lived. At the gate he met a rooster.

"One moment, my friend," the gull said. "I need your advice. When does the low tide of the ocean generally begin?"

The rooster answered, "Low tide? Just what do you mean by that? And what is this thing, ocean, that you are talking about?"

The gull had no time for explanations. He flew off, and after a while he met a duck swimming in a lake. He said, "One moment, friend. What time does the high tide end and the low tide begin?"

"What are you talking about?" the duck answered. "There is no high tide or low tide. The water here always remains the same."

"I am speaking of the ocean," the gull said. "I don't speak of this miserable little lake."

"Ocean? Whatever is that?" the duck asked.

---

2   From *The King's Drum and Other African Stories* by Harold Courlander. Copyright 1962, 1990 by Harold Courlander. Reprinted by permission of The Emma Courlander Trust.

"What kind of people are these?" the gull said. "They know nothing at all about important things." He flew on toward the bush country and came to a flock of rice birds feeding in a field.

"Friends," he said to them, "what time does the ocean tide go out?"

"Ocean tide go out?" they answered. "We don't know about such things. We are busy getting our rice before the farmer comes to drive us away. We have no time for this kind of conversation."

So the gull flew on. He came to one village, then another, asking he same question and getting no answer. Deep in the bush country, he met a mourning dove who sat in a tree crying over and over, "Neo-o-o balo-o-o! huuu! huuu! huuu!" The gull interrupted, saying, "Excuse me, friend. What time does the sea go down?"

The mourning dove answered: "Don't you see that I am mourning the death of my mother? Why do you bother me with questions at a time like this? Go find the pigeon; he is the one that knows the time of things."

And the gull flew on. Far in the bush country he found the pigeon. He said: "People around here are not helpful. When a question is asked, they known nothing of the answer. But you, you have been highly recommended. Tell me, when does the tide of the ocean fall? This is a matter of great importance, for I eat when the low tide leaves fish in the pools along the ocean's edge."

The pigeon replied: "You live at the ocean's edge, while I live here in the bush country. Isn't it strange that you, a seacoast dweller, come to me, a bush dweller who has never seen the sea, to ask what time the tide falls? Be-gone, you stupid creature. Go back where you came from. The gull should not ask the pigeon about affairs of the ocean."

It is said: "Every man should be the master of his own profession."

HOW WISDOM BECAME THE PROPERTY OF THE HUMAN RACE
(From the Akan peoples, Ghana)

There once lived, in Fanti-land, a man named Father Anansi. He possessed all the wisdom in the world. People came to him daily for advice and help.

One day the men of the country were unfortunate enough to offend Father Anansi, who immediately resolved to punish them. After much thought he decided that the severest penalty he could inflict would be to hide all his wisdom from them. He set to work at once to gather again all that he had already given. When he had succeeded, as he thought, in collecting it, he placed all in one great pot. This he carefully sealed, and determined to put it in a spot where no human being could reach it.

Now, Father Anansi had a son, whose name was Kweku Tsin. This boy began to suspect his father of some secret design, so he made up his mind to watch carefully. Next day he saw his father quietly slip out of the house, with his precious pot hung round his neck. Kweku Tsin followed. Father Anansi went through the forest till he had left the village far behind. Then, selecting the highest and most inaccessible-looking tree, he began to climb. The heavy pot, hanging in front of him, made his ascent almost impossible. Again and again he tried to reach the top of the tree, where he intended to hang the pot. There, he thought, Wisdom would indeed be beyond the reach of every one but himself. He was unable, however, to carry out his desire. At each trial the pot swung in his way.

For some time Kweku Tsin watched his father's vain attempts. At last, unable to contain himself any longer, he cried out: "Father, why do you not hang the pot on your back? Then you could easily climb the tree."

Father Anansi turned and said: "I thought I had all the world's wisdom in this pot. But I find you possess more than I do. All my wisdom was insufficient to show me what to do, yet you have been able to tell me." In his anger he threw the pot down. It struck on a great rock and broke. The wisdom contained in it escaped and spread throughout the world.

ANANSI AND NOTHING
(From the Akan peoples, Ghana)

Near Anansi's miserable little hut there was a fine palace where lived a very rich man called Nothing. Nothing and Anansi proposed, one day, to go to the neighbouring town to get some wives. Accordingly, they set off together.

Nothing, being a rich man, wore a very fine velvet cloth, while Anansi had a ragged cotton one. While they were on their way Anansi persuaded Nothing to change clothes for a little while, promising to give back the fine velvet before they reached the town. He delayed doing this, however, first on one pretext, then on another – till they arrived at their destination.

Anansi, being dressed in such a fine garment, found no difficulty in getting as many wives as he wished. Poor Nothing, with his ragged and miserable cloth, was treated with great contempt. At first he could not get even one wife. At last, however, a woman took pity on him and gave him her daughter. The poor girl was laughed at very heartily by Anansi's wives for choosing such a beggar as Nothing appeared to be. She wisely took no notice of their scorn.

The party set off for home. When they reached the cross-roads leading to their respective houses the women were astonished. The road leading to Anansi's house was only half cleared. The one which led to Nothing's palace was, of course, wide and well made. Not only so, but his servants had strewn it with beautiful skins and carpets, in preparation for his return. Servants were there, awaiting him, with fine clothes for himself and his wife. No one was waiting for Anansi.

Nothing's wife was queen over the whole district and had everything her heart could desire, Anansi's wives could not even get proper food; they had to live on unripe bananas with peppers. The wife of Nothing heard of her friends' miserable state and invited them to a great feast in her palace. They came, and were so pleased with all they saw that they agreed to stay there. Accordingly, they refused to come back to Anansi's hut.

He was very angry, and tried in many ways to kill Nothing, but without success. Finally, however, he persuaded some rat friends to dig a deep tunnel in front of Nothing's door. When the hole was finished Anansi lined it with knives and broken bottles. He then smeared the steps of the palace with okro to make them very slippery, and withdrew to a little distance.

When he thought Nothing's household was safely in bed and asleep, he called to Nothing to come out to the courtyard and see something. Nothing's wife, however, dissuaded him from going. Anansi tried again and again, and each time she bade her husband not to listen. At last Nothing determined to go and see this thing. As he placed his foot on the first step, of course he slipped, and down he fell into the hole. The noise alarmed the household. Lights were fetched and Nothing was found in the ditch, so much wounded by the knives that he soon died. His wife was terribly grieved at his untimely death. She boiled many yams, mashed them, and took a great dishful of them round the district. To every child she met she gave some, so that the child might help her to cry for her husband. This is why, if you find a child crying and ask the cause, you will often be told he is "crying for nothing."

THE STORY ABOUT A BEAUTIFUL MAIDEN, AND HOW THE HARTEBEEST GOT THE MARKS UNDER ITS EYES LIKE TEARDROPS
(From the Hausa people, southern Niger and northern Nigeria)

This is a story about an alliance. A chief begat a beautiful daughter; she had no equal in the town. And he said, "He who hoes on the day the people come together and whose area hoed surpasses every one else's he marries the chief's daughter." So on the day the chief calls his neighbours to hoe (gayaa), "Let the suitors come and hoe for me. But he who hoes and surpasses every one else, to him a wife."

Now of a truth the chameleon had heard about this for a long time past, and he came along. He was eating hoeing medicine. Now when the day of the hoeing came round the chameleon was at home. He did not come out until those hoeing were at work and were far away; then the chameleon came. He struck one blow on the ground with the hoe, then he climbed on the hoe and sat down, and the hoe started to hoe, and fairly flew until it had done as much as the hoers. It passed them, and reached the boundary of the furrow.

The chameleon got off, sat down, and rested, and later on the other hoers got to where he was. Then the chief would not consent, but now said he who ran and passed every one, he should marry his daughter. Then the hartebeest said he surpassed every one in running. So they had a race. But the chameleon turned into a needle; he leaped and stuck fast to the tail of the hartebeest, and the hartebeest ran until he passed every one, until he came to the entrance of the house of the chief. He passed it.

Then the chameleon let go the hartebeest's tail; of a truth the chameleon had seen the maiden. So he embraced her, and when the hartebeest came along he met the chameleon embracing the girl. Thereupon the hartebeest began to shed tears, and that was the origin of what you see like tears in a hartebeest's eyes. From that day he has wept and not dried his tears.

TORTOISE AND MR. FLY

(From the Yoruba people, southern Nigeria)

Once Tortoise and his family fell on hard times and had nothing to eat, but they noticed that their neighbour, Mr. Fly, seemed to be very prosperous and feasted every night.

Tortoise was curious to know how he obtained so much money, and after watching him for some days he discovered that Mr. Fly flew away every morning early with a large empty sack on his back, and returned in the evening with the sack full, and after that his wife would prepare a feast.

One morning Tortoise hid in the sack and waited to see what would happen. Soon Mr. Fly came out of his house, lifted up the sack, and flew away.

He descended at last in the market-place of a large town, where drummers were beating the tones of the dance, and maidens were dancing before a crowd of people.

Mr. Fly laid his sack on the ground, and Tortoise saw him standing beside one of the drummers. When the people threw money, Mr. Fly picked the coins up and hid them in his sack, and by evening he had collected a great quantity. Then he took up the sack again and flew home. Tortoise quickly got out and took most of the money with him, so that poor Mr. Fly was surprised to find the sack almost empty.

This happened several times, until one day as he put money in the sack Mr. Fly caught sight of Tortoise hiding inside it. He was very angry at the trick, and going to the drummer asked him if he had missed any money.

"Yes," said the drummer. "For some days I have been losing coins."

"Look inside this sack," replied Mr. Fly, "and you will see the thief sitting among the money he has stolen."

The drummer peeped inside the sack and saw Tortoise.

"How shall the thief be punished?" he cried angrily.

"Just tie up the sack," said Mr. Fly, "and then beat upon it as if it were a drum."

So the drummer tied up the sack and beat upon it until Tortoise was black and blue, and this is why his back is covered with bruises.

Then Mr. Fly picked up the sack, and flew high up in the air and dropped it. By chance the sack fell down just outside Tortoise's house, and neighbours came to tell Nyanribo, his wife, that someone had left a present outside the door. But when she opened the sack in the presence of a crowd of people, she found only Tortoise inside, more dead than alive. Then Mr. Fly made a song and narrated the whole story, and the drummers also played it, and Tortoise and Nyanribo were so ashamed that they left the place and went to live in another country.

THE VOICES OF BIRDS

(From the Yoruba people, southern Nigeria)

A magician once passed through a grove in the forest where a great many brown birds fluttered from tree to tree and filled the air with songs. For a long time he sat and listened, enraptured by their beautiful melodies, but in the end he became very jealous, for he himself could not sing.

At last he felt that he must by some means or other possess the voices of these singing birds, so he called them all together and said:

"It grieves me that the gods have given you all such poor, ugly brown feathers. How happy you would be if you were brilliantly coloured with red, blue, orange, and green!"

And the birds agreed that it was a great pity to be so ugly.

The magician then suggested that by means of his charms he could give them all beautiful feathers in exchange for their voices

– which were, after all, of very little use to them, since nobody came into the grove to hear them.

The birds thought over his words, and desired very much the beauty he promised them. So they foolishly agreed to give him their voices, which the magician placed all together in a large calabash. He then used his charms to turn the dull brown feathers of the birds into orange and green and red, and they were very pleased.

The magician hurried away, and as soon as he came to a deserted place he opened the calabash and swallowed its contents. From that day he had an exceedingly sweet voice, and people came from far and near to listen to his songs.

But the birds were satisfied with their bright feathers. And this is why the most beautiful birds are quite unable to sing.

HOW LEOPARD GOT HIS SPOTS
(From the Yoruba people, southern Nigeria)

At one time the Leopard was coloured like a lion, and he had no dark markings; but he was pursued by Akiti, the renowned hunter, and feared that he might be slain.

To avoid this he ate the roots of a certain magic plant, which had the effect of making him invulnerable to any of the hunter's weapons.

Soon afterwards Akiti saw him as he slipped through the dense undergrowth of the forest, but though he shot his poisoned arrows, Leopard escaped.

But where each arrow struck him, there appeared a dark mark, and now, though hunters still pursue him, he is rarely caught, but his body is covered with the marks of the arrows, so that as he goes among the trees he looks exactly like the mingling of the sun and shadow.

Another Story of Leopard's Spots

According to another story, Leopard once had a very dark skin. He was prowling one day in a beautiful compound, when he noticed a little hut in which a lady was taking her bath.

Round and round the hut Leopard walked, waiting for an opportunity to spring into the hut and seize his victim, for he was hungry.

But as he passed the opening of the hut, the lady saw him, and, uttering a scream of terror, she threw at him her loofah, which was full of soap.

"She flung it at him and he fled,
But to this day the Leopard still
Is flecked with soap from foot to head!"

HOW OBASSI OSAW PROVED THE WISDOM OF TORTOISE
(By Anjong Ntui Animbun of Nsan, of the Ekoi people, Nigeria and Cameroon)

Obassi Osaw married many wives. Among these was the daughter of Tortoise. She was so proud of her father that she annoyed Obassi by exclaiming, "Oh, my father, you have more sense than any other person!" whenever the least thing happened, even if she only knocked her foot or felt surprised.

Obassi determined to find out for himself if Tortoise was really so very wise. He therefore built a room without doors or windows.

Into this he secretly let down eight persons, and sent to Tortoise to come at once and tell him what was within.

Tortoise sent back a message that he would certainly come next day, but in such a way that no one should see him enter, for he was surely the wisest of men, and none could know how he came. Obassi was still more displeased when he heard this.

Now the daughter went and told Tortoise that her husband was annoyed with her for constantly praising her father's wisdom. "Perhaps," said she, "it is to prove this that he has sent for you." Tortoise answered, "It is well."

Next morning Obassi sent other messengers to bid his father-in-law hasten, but, when the men arrived, Tortoise was nowhere to be found. His wife said that he had gone hunting, so the messengers had better not wait. They agreed to this, and set out once more. The woman ran after them with a parcel and said, "Will you please take this to my daughter?"

This the men promised, and gave the parcel to the girl, not knowing that it was Tortoise whom they carried. She bore the packet before Obassi, set it on the ground and unfastened the tie-tie, when out stepped – what? Tortoise himself.

Obassi was very much surprised, and bade the guest go and stay in his daughter's house till next morning. So they went off together.

At night, when all was quiet, Tortoise made a small hole in the wall of the room which Obassi had built. Then he took a stick and dipped it into some foul-smelling stuff. The men who were inside noticed the bad odour, and began calling to each other by name, asking its cause.

In this way Tortoise heard that there were eight men in the secret room, and also learned their names. He was very careful to fill up the little hole which he had made, and afterwards went back to bed.

Next morning a great company was gathered together to witness the shame of Tortoise when he should fail to answer the question of their Lord.

Obassi stood in the middle of the audience room and said very loudly that Tortoise must now tell him what was hidden in the windowless house, or suffer death if he could not do so.

Then Tortoise rose and said that there were eight men shut up within, and, to the surprise of all the people, he repeated their names, thus proving himself to be wiser than all his fellows, just as his daughter had said.

Obassi was so vexed that he ordered his men to seize Tortoise, sharpen a stick, and drive it through this overwise creature, so as to fasten him to the ground at a place where cross-roads meet. He also ordered that the beast should be fixed upright, so as to look at his judge on high. Obassi decreed further that, whenever a man wished to make him a sacrifice, Tortoise should be offered in this way. That is why we often see Tortoise impaled before Jujus, or at cross-roads.

HOW PYTHONS LOST HANDS AND FEET
(From the Ekoi people, Nigeria and Cameroon)

There was once a Python, whose wife was about to bear him a child. One day, in coming through the bush, he saw some ripe Aju fruits, and plucked them, as he thought, "Perhaps my wife would like these."

The woman ate them with great delight, and from that day on, kept begging her husband to bring her some more. He went out to the bush to search, but could not find any. She, however, threatened that unless more were brought to her, she would break her pregnancy.

In those days Pythons had hands and feet like men, and could walk upright. When therefore he found no fruits in the bush with which to satisfy his wife's desire, Python went to the farm of a man, where an Aju tree stood, and each day plucked some of the fruit.

Now the owner of the tree had a son named Monn-akat-chang-obbaw-chang (Child-feet-not-hands-not), because he had neither hands nor feet. One day he complained to his father that someone was stealing their Aju, and begged that he should be carried to the foot of the tree, so that he might watch for the thief. To this the father consented.

When Nkimm (Python) came next day, he found the tree guarded by a wonderful boy without hands or feet. So soon as the latter saw the snake he called, "Are you the person who steals my father's Aju?" Nkimm denied his guilt, and said that this was the first time he had seen the tree, but begged the boy to give him a few of the fruits for his sick wife.

Akat Chang replied that he would do so with pleasure, had he but hands and feet with which to climb the tree, but, since he had not, this was impossible, as he could not allow any stranger to pluck his father's fruits.

Python offered to take off his own hands and feet and lend them to the boy, that he might be able to climb. This was done and the limbs bound on, after which the boy quickly went up into the tree, and threw down as many of the fruits as the visitor could carry away. He then came down again and returned the limbs to their owner, who thanked him and left with his load. When he reached his house he gave the Aju to his wife, who ate them with great delight.

Before it grew dark, the father of Akat Chang came to the tree to carry the boy home for the night. His son related how he had spent the time with the Aju thief, and enjoyed the advantage of using the latter's hands and feet.

Two days afterwards, Nkimm's wife had finished all the Aju, so told her husband that he must fetch her some more, again threatening to break her pregnancy if he did not do as she asked. So Python was obliged to set out once more for his well-known tree. There again he met his friend, the boy, who had been told by his mother to ask the thief to fix on the hands and feet very firmly. She bade him then climb into the tree, and stay there until his father came.

Once more Python took off his feet and hands and bound them strongly to the boy's body as the latter asked him to do. What a loss to Nkimm!

Off went the boy up the tree, and did not cease from climbing till he reached the topmost branch. Then he began to sing:

> "*Sini sini mokkaw. Sine sine mokkaw*
> *Oro obba*
> *Nta abe Aju, monn akat akpim.*
> *(Lord plant Aju, child feet not get)*
> *Oro obba*
> *Nkimm afonn akat, akaw anam Aju.*
> *(Python has feet, take buy (with) Aju fruit).*

Oro obba
Sini sini mokkaw. Sine sine mokkaw.
Oro obba."

(The narrator repeated the song very carefully as it had been taught him by his grandfather, but he had no idea of the meaning of the refrain. The latter appears to have some similarity to the Efut language.)

When the parents heard the singing, they ran towards their son. In his hands the father bore a great spear. When Nkimm saw this, he rushed off for his life in the opposite direction, throwing himself along the ground in the only way possible to him.

Since then, no man has been born without hands or feet and no Python or other snake with them.

Had it not been for this act of Monn-Akat-Chang, snakes would have continued to be footed animals instead of creepers, and man would sometimes have been born without feet or hands.

TORTOISE COVERS HIS IGNORANCE
(From the Fang and Bulu peoples, Cameroon)

Tortoise (kudu) arose and went to the town of his father-in-law Leopard (Njĕ). Leopard sent him on an errand, saying, "Go, and cut for me utamba-mwa-Ivâtâ." (The fiber of a vine is used for making nets.)

Then he went. But, while he still remembered the object, he forgot the name of the kind of Vine that was used for that purpose. And he was ashamed to confess his ignorance. So, he came back

144

to call the people of the town, and said, "Come ye and help me! I have enclosed Ihĕli (Gazelle) in a thicket."

The people came, and at once they made a circle around the spot. But when they closed in, they saw no beasts there.

Then Tortoise called out, "Let someone of you cut for me, utamba-mwa-Ivâtâ." (As if that was the only thing needed to catch the animal which he had said was there.)

Thereupon, his brother-in-law cut for him a vine which he brought to him, saying, "Here is an Ihenga vine which we use for making nets." Whereupon Tortoise exclaimed, "Is it possible that it was the Ihenga vine that I mistook?"

A LESSON IN EVOLUTION

(From the Fang and Bulu peoples, Cameroon)

Shrew (unyunge) and Lemur (Po) were neighbors in the town of Beasts. At that time, the Animals did not possess fire. Lemur said to Shrew, "Go! and take for us fire from the town of Mankind." Shrew consented, but said, "If I go, do not look, while I am gone, toward any other place except the path on which I go. Do not even wink. Watch for me."

So Shrew went, and came to a Town of Men; and found that the people had all emigrated from that town. Yet, he went on, and on, seeking for fire; and for a long time found none. But, as he continued moving forward from house to house, he at last found a very little fire on a hearth. He began blowing it; and kept on blowing, and blowing; for, the fire did not soon ignite into a flame. He continued so long at this that his mouth extended forward permanently, with the blowing.

Then he went back, and found Lemur faithfully watching with his eyes standing very wide open. Shrew asked him, "What has made your eyes so big?" In return, Lemur asked him, "What has so lengthened your mouth to a snout?"

WHICH IS THE BETTER HUNTER, AN EAGLE OR A LEOPARD?
(From the Fang and Bulu peoples, Cameroon)

Eagle (mbela) and Leopard (Njě) had a discussion about obtaining prey. Eagle said, "I am the one who can surpass you in preying." Leopard said, "Not so! Is it not I?"

Then Eagle said, "Wait; see whether you are the one to surpass me in preying." Thereupon he descended from above, seized a child of Leopard, and flew up with it to his nest.

Leopard exclaimed, "Alas! what shall I do?" And he went, and went, walking about, coming to one place, and going to another, wishing to fly in order to go to the rescue of his child. He could not fly, for want of wings; therefore it was the other one who flew up and away.

So it was that the eagle proved that he surpassed the leopard in seeking prey.

THE FAMINE
(From Uganda)

A long time ago a terrible drought visited the countries round the Great Lake. The spring rains failed, every day the sun rose like a copper ball and made his burning way across a cloudless sky. No flowers bloomed that spring, and the grass dried upon the hillsides. The banana trees in the shady gardens looked desolate and sad, their leaves hung down limp and brown and no heavy bunches of golden fruit filled the air with sweetness. The potato patches had been baked hard and dry, and no Indian corn had been able to struggle through the hard ground.

At last the people began to dig up the banana roots, and to eat the great coarse bulbs to keep themselves from starving. The lake sank lower and lower till the tall papyrus stood high above the water, and the marshy ground was seen for miles among the shallows round the shore. Great rocks stood out round the falls at Jinja, and the water trickled in small rivulets over them where every spring the waters of the Great Lake rush and tumble and roar into the river Nile. Famine and want spread over the land, but the part of the country that suffered most was Busoga. There was a large herd of elephants which lived in Zibondo's country, and they wandered from place to place seeking fresh grass and leaves and roots and finding nothing. At last the chief of the herd spoke.

"When I was a calf in the herd, ninety years ago, I remember a famine like this, and I remember that the Nile was so low that we found a ford and crossed into the Mabira Forest and found food there; let us go now, and seek this ford, for the waters of the river are low.

So the herd moved off towards the Nile, and as they went they passed through deserted villages and wasted country and saw the thin starving animals dragging themselves to the river. The chief of the herd led them straight to the spot he remembered, and there they saw rocky ground gleaming through shallow water and knew they had found a ford. There was one cow elephant who was walking with her calf and cheering him on.

"Courage, my child," she said, "we are nearly there. Think of the cool green glades we shall find in the Mabira Forest, for this pitiless sun can never strike through the thick creepers on the trees, and the water pools are deep and dark."

As she said this her small eyes fell on a pitiful sight. A mother monkey had carried her baby down to the river to drink, but she was too weak to lift it. The cow elephant lifted them both with her trunk and carried them across the ford into the Mabira Forest.

The King of the Cloud Land had seen the distress on the Earth, and as he looked down on Uganda he saw what the cow elephant did. And his heart was filled with pity for the starving people and animals, and he called all his clouds together, a great army, and they poured rain on the sunbaked Earth. And where there had only been hard ground, gardens and fields sprang up, the hillsides became green with grass and brilliant with flowers, and the Great Lake rose and poured its waters over the falls, and where the shallows had been round the lake shore, the water was so deep that it reached to the feathery heads of the papyrus, and the ford across the river was lost under the tumbling rushing waters.

From that time the monkeys have always been the friends of the elephants, for though they are small they can help them. From their homes in the tree-tops they can see the hunters coming and they warn the herd. They see the hunters setting traps and they tell the elephants where they are. And this is why men prefer to hunt elephants on the plains and hillsides and fear to hunt them in the forests, for they never know whether the monkeys have seen their plans and have told the herd their secrets.

THE DOG AND THE LEOPARD
(From Uganda)

Once upon a time a leopard who had several cubs hired a dog to be nurse to them, but she was very unkind to the dog, who was miserable, The dog was always thin and hungry, she only ate what was left over when the leopard and her cubs had finished a meal, and *that* was never much.

One day when the leopard was out visiting, and the dog was left at home with the cubs, she found some bones in a corner and fell upon them ravenously. One of the cubs crept up to look, and a bone hit him in the eye and put the eye out. When the dog saw what she had done she was very frightened and ran away into the forest. She ran on until she came to the house of the old wizard, and then she thought, "I will go and have my fortune told."

So she went into the house and told the wizard what had happened. Now, the old wizard told fortunes by cards, and his cards were bits of buffalo hide, sewn over with cowry shells and beads. He got them out of his goatskin bag and was just going to tell the dog's fortune when he saw the leopard coming down the forest path, and he whispered to the dog:

"There is the leopard coming here, climb up into that basket which hangs from the roof and lie very still."

So the dog climbed up to the basket in which the wizard kept the bananas he was ripening for beer, and lay quietly down. In a few minutes the leopard arrived, and poured out her story to the wizard. "Tell my fortune," she said, "that I may know if I shall catch my enemy." The wizard took out his cards and spoke. "You will catch your enemy in the spring rains, if she goes out in the rain you will catch her. In the sunshine she will be safe, the rain will be her downfall. I speak to those that are above, I speak to those that are below, let her who has ears hear, let her who hears understand." The leopard thanked the wizard and gave him a beautiful white hen as a present, and went away home to her cubs. When the dog came down from the basket the wizard asked:

"Did you understand my warning?"

And the dog said, "I understood, sir; I will never go out in the rain."

The months passed, and one day when the dog was out in the forest a heavy shower came on. The spring rains had begun. The dog ran in the direction of home, but suddenly she saw an anthill by the road side from which the ants were beginning to fly. The dog stopped for a moment to eat a few, and then, as the succulent creatures poured out of the anthill, she lapped them up with her tongue and forgot all about the wizard's warning, and did not see the leopard creeping down the path. The leopard sprang upon the dog and killed her.

And from that day leopards and dogs are enemies, and a constant battle rages between the tribes, for the leopards remember how a dog blinded a cub, and the dogs remember the vengeance of the mother leopard in the spring rains.

THE STORY OF KIBARAKA AND THE BIRD
(From the Swahili-speaking peoples)

Once upon a time there was a Sultan, and he had one son, a very handsome youth, called Hasani. Every day at noon the Sultan and his son used to go to the mosque to pray. After they had gone the Sultan's wife used to sort out the seeds of every kind of grain in the Sultan's store. Those that needed drying she gave to a slave, called Kibaraka, to put out in the sun to dry.

One day, after the Sultan and his son had gone to prayer, she called to the slave, "Kibaraka, take these seeds and put them out in the sun." Kibaraka took the grain and spread it out to dry, each kind by itself.

Suddenly a wondrously fine bird came and sat down by the grain and called out –

"Kibaraka! Kibaraka!"

He answered, "Here, lady, here."

Then the bird sang –

> Bird: *"Shall I eat of this wheat?*
> *Or shall I not eat?*
> *Or shall I eat millet?"*
> Kibaraka: *"Eat, Lady, I will it."*
> Bird: *"Shall I eat rape instead?*
> *Or must I not be fed?*
> *Shall I eat maize today?"*
> Kibaraka: *"Eat, Lady, eat, I pray."*
> Bird: *"Shall I eat all the grain?*
> *Or must I now refrain?*
> *Shall I eat rice today?"*
> Kibaraka: *"Eat, Lady, eat, I pray."*
> Bird: *"Where has your master gone today?"*
> Kibaraka: *"Gone to the mosque to read and pray."*
> Bird: *"My greetings to the Sultan give*
> *When he returns. Long may he live."*

At that it flew away.

On the next day and the day after the bird came again and sung the same song.

Till one day Kibaraka told his young master Hasani, "Master, every day at one o'clock, when you are at the mosque, a lovely bird comes here."

Hasani asked, "What kind of bird is this?"

Kibaraka said, "All ordinary wonders are surpassed by this bird, for it sings a very beautiful song," and he told his master of the song.

At these words the Sultan's son perceived that this bird was of the daughters of the Jins, and he fell in love with her.

Then he said to Kibaraka, "See here, I have given you your freedom, you are no longer a slave, and now you must catch this bird for me."

After that Hasani was seized with a grievous illness because of his longing for that bird till, on the third day at one o'clock, the Sultan went out to look for all the wisest of the medicine men to attend to his son.

Whilst he was gone that bird came and sat by the grain and called, "Kibaraka! Kibaraka!"

Kibaraka cut a thin pole and made a noose at the end and set it near the bullrush millet, the grain the bird loved best.

When it had finished eating all the seeds it wished to fly away, but one of its wings caught in the noose.

Then it said to Kibaraka, "Please let me go and do not touch me, for you will injure me. Take this feather of mine and carry it to your master, and let it be my salaams to him."

So Kibaraka brought the feather to the Sultan's son. Hasani was very pleased. Then he said to him, "Kibaraka, my brother, why did not you catch the owner of this feather?"

Kibaraka said, "I was not able to catch it. When I saw it I fell down seven times because of its light, and my wisdom forsook me."

When the Sultan returned, his son said to him, "My father, you must sound the pallaver-horn, that all the people may come before the palace." The Sultan loved his son exceedingly, so he gathered all his people together. Then Hasani said, "Tell the people that they must look for this bird and bring it to me, and if they do not bring it I shall die."

So the Sultan gave out the order, "There is no leave to weave or spin, to grind corn or pound grain, until this bird has been brought."

At once all the people of that country went out into the jungles and deserts to look for that bird. Everyone who found a fine bird would seize it and bring it to the Sultan's son, but to each he said, "This is not the one."

Till one day, as people were sitting in the Sultan's court holding a pallaver, just after one o'clock had struck, they looked up and saw a dust cloud coming like rain.

Behold, it was that bird coming, and Kibaraka recognised its coming.

When it came it sat down by the grain and ate all the seeds till, as it came to the last, Kibaraka caught it and brought it to his master. When Hasani looked on that bird, behold, it was a beautiful woman.

He said, "Kibaraka, run quickly, go your way to the audience chamber and tell my father that he must fire the cannons, for the thing I desired has come to pass, and the request I made of Allah has been granted."

So Kibaraka came and told the Sultan, and the cannons were fired, and wedding festivities and feastings were held for nine years.

After that Hasani and the fair Jin had a child, a boy like pearls and precious stones.

And Hasani loved his wife exceedingly, and the people of that country saw wonders come to pass, for the second son was like the stars and the moon.

The house of that Sultan was greatly blessed, and the story ends here.

THE HARE DECIDES A CASE
(From the Bantu-speaking people of southeastern Kenya)

There was a man who lived by hunting. One day, just as he was about to take a pig and an antelope out of his traps, a lion sprang upon him, and threatened to kill him unless he gave him a share of the meat. In fear of his life, he agreed, and allowed the lion to take out the hearts, livers, and such other titbits as he chose, while he himself carried the rest home.

This happened every day, and the man's wife was consumed with curiosity, when she found that there was neither heart nor liver in any of the animals he brought home. She insisted, in spite of his denial, that he had given these to some other woman, and so, one day, started early to look at his traps, and was herself caught in one of them. Presently the man and the lion arrived on the scene, and the latter demanded his share of the game. The man refused to kill his wife; the lion insisted on holding him to his bargain. The wretched man, driven to desperation, was about to give in, and the woman would have paid dearly for her suspicions, had the hare not happened to pass by. The husband saw him, and called on him to help; Mwakatsoo (the hare) said at first that it was no business of his, but, yielding at last to the man's entreaties, he stopped, and heard both sides of the story. He then ordered the man to release his wife, and set the trap again. This having been done, he asked the lion to show him how the woman had got into it. The lion fell into the trap and got caught by the hand and foot. "So, this is the way it caught her. Now let me go!" But Mwakatsoo turned to the man and said, "You were a great fool to make such a promise. Now be off, you and your wife!" They did not wait to be told so twice, but hastened home, while the lion called on Mwakatsoo to release him, and received for answer: "I shall do no such thing. You are the enemy!"

A Zimbabwean Version

The husband begged the hare for help. The hare said he could not hear what they were saying for the wind, and they had better all come into a cave, the woman being released for the purpose. Then he called out that the cave was about to fall in, and they must hold up the roof. All four being so engaged, he sent off the man and his wife to get logs for propping it: he and the lion would hold it up till their return. The couple, of course, took the hint and made their escape. The hare ran away, and the lion, in terror lest the rock should fall, went on supporting it till he was tired, and then made a desperate leap to the mouth of the cave, hit his head against a rock, and crawled away half stunned. Since that day lions have hunted their own game.

THE LION, THE HYENA AND THE RABBIT
(From Zanzibar, Tanzanian coast)

Once upon a time Simba, the lion, Feesee, the hyena, and Keeteetee, the rabbit, made up their minds to go in for a little farming. So they went into the country, made a garden, planted all kinds of seeds, and then came home and rested quite a while.

Then, when the time came when their crops should be about ripe and ready for harvesting, they began to say to each other, "Let's go over to the farm, and see how our crops are coming along."

So one morning, early, they started, and, as the garden was a long way off, Keeteetee, the rabbit, made this proposition: "While we are going to the farm, let us not stop on the road; and if anyone does stop, let him be eaten." His companions, not being so cunning as he, and knowing they could outwalk him, readily consented to this arrangement.

Well, off they went; but they had not gone very far when the rabbit stopped.

"Hullo!" said Feesee, the hyena; "Keeteetee has stopped. He must be eaten."

"That's the bargain," agreed Simba, the lion.

"Well," said the rabbit, "I happened to be thinking."

"What about?" cried his partners, with great curiosity.

"I'm thinking," said he, with a grave, philosophical air, "about those two stones, one big and one little; the little one does not go up, nor does the big one go down."

The lion and the hyena, having stopped to look at the stones, could only say, "Why, really, it's singular; but it's just as you say;" and they all resumed their journey, the rabbit being by this time well rested.

When they had gone some distance the rabbit stopped again.

"Aha!" said Feesee; "Keeteetee has stopped again. Now he *must* be eaten."

"I rather think so," assented Simba.

"Well," said the rabbit, "I was thinking again."

Their curiosity once more aroused, his comrades begged him to tell them his think.

"Why," said he, "I was thinking this: When people like us put on new coats, where do the old ones go to?"

Both Simba and Feesee, having stopped a moment to consider the matter, exclaimed together, "Well, I wonder!" and the three went on, the rabbit having again had a good rest.

After a little while the hyena, thinking it about time to show off a little of *his* philosophy, suddenly stopped.

"Here," growled Simba, "this won't do; I guess we'll have to eat you, Feesee."

"Oh, no," said the hyena; "I'm thinking."

"What are you thinking about?" they inquired.

"I'm thinking about nothing at all," said he, imagining himself very smart and witty.

"Ah, pshaw!" cried Keeteetee; "we won't be fooled that way."

So he and Simba ate the hyena.

When they had finished eating their friend, the lion and the rabbit proceeded on their way, and presently came to a place where there was a cave, and here the rabbit stopped.

"H'm!" ejaculated Simba; "I'm not so hungry as I was this morning, but I guess I'll have to find room for you, little Keeteetee."

"Oh, I believe not," replied Keeteetee; "I'm thinking again."

"Well," said the lion, "what is it this time?"

Said the rabbit: "I'm thinking about that cave. In olden times our ancestors used to go in here, and go out there, and I think I'll try and follow in their footsteps."

So he went in at one end and out at the other end several times.

Then he said to the lion, "Simba, old fellow, let's see *you* try to do that;" and the lion went into the cave, but he stuck fast, and could neither go forward nor back out.

In a moment Keeteetee was on Simba's back, and began eating him.

After a little time the lion cried, "Oh, brother, be impartial; come and eat some of the front part of me."

But the rabbit replied, "Indeed, I can't come around in front; I'm ashamed to look you in the face."

So, having eaten all he was able to, he left the lion there, and went and became sole owner of the farm and its crops.

THE SHREW-MOUSE HELPS THE MAN
(From the Swahili-speaking peoples)

A Namwanga man one day went hunting with his dogs, and came upon a shrew (*umulumba*) by the roadside. It said to him, "Master, help me across this swollen stream" (i.e., the path, which for him was just as impassable). He refused, and was going on, but the little creature entreated him again: "Do help me across this swollen stream, and I will help you across yours." The man turned back, picked it up, and carried it across, very reluctantly. It then disappeared from his sight, and he went on with his dogs and killed some guinea fowl.

Then, as it came on to rain, he took refuge in one of the little watch-huts put up in the gardens for those whose business it is to drive away monkeys by day and wild pigs by night. The shrew, which had followed him unseen, was hidden in the thatch.

Presently a lion came along, and thus addressed the hunter: "Give your guinea fowl to the dogs, let them eat them, you eat the dogs, and then I'll eat you!"

The man was terrified, and could neither speak nor move. The lion roared out the same words a second time. Then came a little voice out of the thatch.

"Just so. Give the guinea fowl to the dogs, let them eat them, you eat the dogs, the lion will eat you, and I'll eat the lion."

The lion ran away without looking behind him.

THE TORTOISE AND THE MONITOR LIZARD
(From the Nyanja-speaking people)

The tortoise made friendship with the *ng'anzi* lizard. One day the tortoise was in need of salt and set out to beg some from his friend. Having reached the *ng'anzi's* abode and got his salt, he next asked to have it tied up with string in a piece of bark-cloth. He passed the string over his shoulder, so that the parcel hung under his other arm, and started for home, dragging the salt after him – *gubudu gubudu!* The *ng'anzi* came up behind him and seized the salt; the tortoise, pulled up short – *njutu njutu!* – turned back to see what had caught his load. He found that the *ng'anzi* had seized the bundle of salt in the middle, and said to him, "Don't seize my salt. I have just brought it from my friend's house." The *ng'anzi* replied, "I've just picked it up in the path." "But you can see the string passing round my neck as we tied it. I, the tortoise, am the owner." But the *ng'anzi* insisted that he had found the parcel, and, as the tortoise would not give in, said, "Let us go to the smithy, that the elders may decide our case." The tortoise agreed, and they went to the smithy, where they found eight old men.

The *ng'anzi* opened the case in proper form: "I have a suit against the tortoise." The elders said, "What is your suit with which you have come hither to us?" He stated his case, and they asked, "How did you pick up the tortoise's salt?" The tortoise replied, "Because I am short as to the legs I tied the salt round my neck, and it went bumping along, and then the *ng'anzi* took hold of it, and I turned back to see what had caught it, and there was my friend the *ng'anzi*, and he said, 'Let us go to the smithy,' and therefore we have come here." The elders suggested that they should compromise the case by cutting the bag of salt in two. The tortoise consented, though unwillingly, seeing that he had no chance, since the judges were all relatives of the *ng'anzi*, as he perceived too late. "Perhaps I have been wrong in taking to the road alone," was his reflection on finding that he had fallen among thieves. The bag was cut, and, of course, a great deal of salt fell out on the ground. The tortoise gathered up what he could, but it was only a little, because his fingers were so short, and he failed to tie it up satisfactorily in the piece of bark cloth left to him. The *ng'anzi*, on the contrary, had his full half, and the elders scraped up what had been spilt, earth and all. So the tortoise went away, crying, "my salt is spoilt," and reached his home with one or two tiny screws done up in leaves. His wife asked him what had become of the salt, and he told her the whole story, adding that he would go again to his friend and get a fresh supply. He rested four days, and then started once more.

On reaching the ng'anzi's burrow he found that the owner had entered it and was enjoying a meal of lumwe (the winged males of the termites). The tortoise came walking very softly, nyang'anyang'a, looked carefully about him, spied the ng'anzi, crept up to him without being seen, and seized him by the middle of his body. Thereupon he cried out "Who has seized me by the waist? As for me, I am just eating white ants." The tortoise replied, "I have picked up. Yes, I have picked up. The other day you picked up my salt, and today I have picked you up! Well, let us go to the smithy, as we did the other day." The ng'anzi said, "Do you insist?" The tortoise answered, "Yes." So they came out of the burrow and went to the smithy, where they found nine old men. Having heard the case stated, these elders said, "You should do what you did the other day: you cut the salt in two." The tortoise cried in triumph, "Ha! ha! ha! ha! – it is good so," and rejoiced with his whole heart; but the ng'anzi said, "Are you absolutely resolved on killing me?" "You formerly destroyed my salt, and I, for my part, am going to do the same to you!" "Ha! This is the end of me! To want to cut me in half! ... Well, do what you want to do. It's all over with me, the ng'anzi!" The tortoise leapt up, tu! and took a knife and cut the ng'anzi through the middle, and he cried, "Mother! Mother! I am dead today through picking up!" and died.

The tortoise took the tail and two legs and went on his way, and when he came to his wife's house he said, "We have settled the score: the ng'anzi ate that salt of mine, and today I have paid him back in his own coin, and he is dead."

THE BOY KINNENEH AND THE GORILLA
(From the Congo and central Africa)

In the early days of Uganda, there was a small village situate on the other side of the Katonga, in Buddu, and its people had planted bananas and plantains which in time grew to be quite a large grove, and produced abundant and very fine fruit. From a grove of bananas when its fruit is ripe there comes a very pleasant odour, and when a puff of wind blows over it, and bears the fragrance towards you, I know of nothing so well calculated to excite the appetite, unless it be the smell of roasted meat. Anyhow, such must have been the feeling of a mighty big gorilla, who one day, while roaming about alone in the woods searching for nuts to eat, stopped suddenly and stood up and sniffed for some time, with his nose well out in the direction of the village. After a while he shook his head and fell on all fours again to resume his search for food. Again there came with a whiff of wind a strong smell of ripe bananas, and he stood on his feet once more, and with his nose shot out thus he drew in a greedy breath and then struck himself over the stomach, and said:

"I thought it was so. There are bananas that way, and I must get some."

Down he fell on all fours, and put out his arms with long stretches, just as a fisherman draws in a heavy net, and is eager to prevent the escape of the fish.

In a little while he came to the edge of the grove, and stood and looked gloatingly on the beautiful fruit hanging in great bunches. Presently he saw something move. It was a woman bent double over a basket, and packing the fruit neatly in it, so that she could carry a large quantity at one journey.

The gorilla did not stay long thinking, but crawled up secretly to her; and then with open arms rushed forward and seized her. Before the woman could utter her alarm he had lifted her and her basket and trotted away with them into the deepest bush. On reaching his den he flung the woman on the ground, as you would fling dead meat, and bringing the banana basket close to him, his two legs hugging it close to his round paunch, he began to gorge himself, muttering while he peeled the fruit strange sounds. By-and-by the woman came to her senses, but instead of keeping quiet, she screamed and tried to run away. If it were not for that movement and noise, she perhaps might have been able to creep away unseen, but animals of all kinds never like to be disturbed while eating, so Gorilla gave one roar of rage, and gave her such a squeeze that the breath was clean driven out of her. When she was still he fell to again, and tore the peeling off the bananas, and tossed one after another down his wide throat, until there was not one of the fruit left in the basket, and the big paunch was swollen to twice its first size. Then, after laying his paw on the body to see if there was any life left in it, he climbed up to his nest above, and curled himself into a ball for a sleep.

When he woke he shook himself and yawned, and looking below he saw the body of the woman, and her empty basket, and he remembered what had happened. He descended the tree, lifted the body and let it fall, then took up the basket, looked inside and outside of it, raked over the peelings of the bananas, but could not find anything left to eat.

He began to think, scratching the fur on his head, on his sides, and his paunch, picking up one thing and then another in an absent-minded way. And then he appeared to have made up a plan.

Whatever it was, this is what he did. It was still early morning, and as there was no sign of a sun, it was cold, and human beings must have been finishing their last sleep. He got up and went straight for the plantation. On the edge of the banana-grove he heard a cock crow; he stopped and listened to it; he became angry.

"Someone," he said to himself, "is stealing my bananas," and with that he marched in the direction where the cock was crowing.

He came to the open place in front of the village, and saw several tall houses much larger than his own nest; and while he was looking at them, the door of one of them was opened, and a man came out. He crept towards him, and before he could cry out the gorilla had squeezed him until his ribs had cracked, and he was dead; he flung him down, and entered into the hut. He there saw a woman, who was blowing a fire on the hearth, and he took hold of her and squeezed her until there was no life left in her body. There were three children inside, and a bed on the floor. He treated them also in the same way, and they were all dead. Then he went into another house, and slew all the people in it, one with a squeeze, another with a squeeze and a bite with his great teeth, and there was not one left alive. In this way he entered into five houses and killed all the people in them, but in the sixth house lived the boy Kinneneh and his old mother.

Kinneneh had fancied that he heard an unusual sound, and he had stood inside with his eyes close to a chink in the reed door for some time when he saw something that resembled what might be said to be half animal and half man. He walked like a man, but had the fur of a beast. His arms were long, and his body was twice the breadth and thickness of a full-grown man. He did not know what it was, and when he saw it go into his neighbours' houses, and heard those strange sounds, he grew afraid, and turned and woke his mother, saying,

"Mother, wake up! there is a strange big beast in our village killing our people. So wake up quickly and follow me."

"But whither shall we fly, my son?" she whispered anxiously.

"Up to the loft, and lie low in the darkest place," replied Kinneneh, and he set her the example and assisted his mother.

Now those Uganda houses are not low-roofed like these of Congo-land, but are very high, as high as a tree, and they rise to a point, and near the top there is a loft where we stow our nets, and pots, and where our spear-shafts and bows are kept to season, and where our corn is kept to dry, and green bananas are stored to ripen. It was in this dark lofty place that Kinneneh hid himself and his mother, and waited in silence.

In a short time the gorilla put his head into their house and listened, and stepping inside he stood awhile, and looked searchingly around. He could see no one and heard nothing stir. He peered under the bed-grass, into the black pots and baskets, but there was no living being to be found.

"Ha, ha," he cried, thumping his chest like a man when he has got the big head. "I am the boss of this place now, and the tallest of these human nests shall be my own, and I shall feast every day on ripe bananas and plantains, and there is no one who can molest me – ha, ha!"

"Ha, ha!" echoed a shrill, piping voice after his great bass.

The gorilla looked around once more, among the pots, and the baskets, but finding nothing walked out. Kinneneh, after a while skipped down the ladder and watched between the open cane-work of the door, and saw him enter the banana-grove, and waited there until he returned with a mighty load of the fruit. He then saw him go out again into the grove, and bidding his mother lie still and patient, Kinneneh slipped out and ascended into the loft of the house chosen by the gorilla for his nest, where he hid himself and waited.

Presently the gorilla returned with another load of the fruit, and, squatting on his haunches, commenced to peel the fruit, and fill his throat and mouth with it, mumbling and chuckling, and saying,

"Ha, ha! This is grand! Plenty of bananas to eat, and all – all my own. None to say, 'Give me some,' but all my very own. Ho, ho! I shall feast every day. Ha, ha!"

"Ha, ha," echoed the piping voice again.

The gorilla stopped eating and made an ugly frown as he listened. Then he said:

"That is the second time I have heard a thin voice saying, 'Ha, ha!' If I only knew who he was that cried 'Ha, ha!' I would squeeze him, and squeeze him until he cried, 'Ugh, ugh!'"

"Ugh, ugh!" echoed the little voice again.

The gorilla leaped to his feet and rummaged around the pots and the baskets, took hold of the bodies one after another and dashed them against the floor, then went to every house and searched, but could not discover who it was that mocked him.

In a short time he returned and ate a pile of bananas that would have satisfied twenty men, and afterwards he went out, saying to himself that it would be a good thing to fill the nest with food, as it was a bore to leave the warm nest each time he felt a desire to eat.

No sooner had he departed than Kinneneh slipped down, and carried every bunch that had been left away to his own house, where they were stowed in the loft for his mother, and after enjoining his mother to remain still, he waited, peering through the chinks of the door.

He soon saw Gorilla bearing a pile of bunches that would have required ten men to carry, and after flinging them into the chief's house, return to the plantation for another supply. While Gorilla was tearing down the plants and plucking at the bunches, Kinneneh was actively engaged in transferring what he brought into the loft by his mother's side. Gorilla made many trips in this manner, and brought in great heaps, but somehow his stock appeared to be very small. At last his strength was exhausted, and feeling that he could do no more that day, he commenced to feed on what he had last brought, promising to himself that he would do better in the morning.

At dawn the gorilla hastened out to obtain a supply of fruit for his breakfast, and Kinneneh took advantage of his absence to hide himself overhead.

He was not long in his place before Gorilla came in with a huge lot of ripe fruit, and after making himself comfortable on his haunches with a great bunch before him he rocked himself to and fro, saying while he munched:

"Ha, ha! Now I have plenty again, and I shall eat it all myself. Ha, ha!"

"Ha, ha," echoed a thin voice again, so close and clear it seemed to him, that leaping up he made sure to catch it. As there appeared to be no one in the house, he rushed out raging, champing his teeth, and searched the other houses, but meantime Kinneneh carried the bananas to the loft of the gorilla's house, and covered them with bark-cloth.

In a short time Gorilla returned furious and disappointed, and sat down to finish the breakfast he had only begun, but on putting out his hands he found only the withered peelings of yesterday's bananas. He looked and rummaged about, but there was positively nothing left to eat. He was now terribly hungry and angry, and he bounded out to obtain another supply, which he brought in and flung on the floor, saying,

"Ha, ha! I will now eat the whole at once – all to myself, and that other thing which says, 'Ha, ha!' after me, I will hunt and mash him like this," and he seized a ripe banana and squeezed it with his paw with so much force that the pulp was squirted all over him. "Ha, ha!" he cried.

"Ha, ha!" mocked the shrill voice, so clear that it appeared to come from behind his ear.

This was too much to bear; Gorilla bounded up and vented a roar of rage. He tossed the pots, the baskets, the bodies, and bed grass about – bellowing so loudly and funnily in his fury that Kinneneh, away up in the loft, could scarcely forbear imitating him. But the mocker could not be found, and Gorilla roared loudly in the open place before the village, and tore in and out of each house, looking for him.

Kinneneh descended swiftly from his hiding-place, and bore every banana into the loft as before.

Gorilla hastened to the plantation again, and so angry was he that he uprooted the banana-stalks by the root, and snapped off the clusters with one stroke of his great dogteeth, and having got together a large stock, he bore it in his arms to the house.

"There," said he, "ha, ha! Now I shall eat in comfort and have a long sleep afterwards, and if that fellow who mocks me comes near – ah! I would" – and he crushed a big bunch in his arms and cried, "ha, ha!"

"Ha, ha! Ha, ha!" cried the mocking voice; and again it seemed to be at the back of his head. Whereupon Gorilla flung his arms behind in the hope of catching him, but there was nothing but his own back, which sounded like a damp drum with the stroke.

"Ha, ha! Ha, ha!" repeated the voice, at which Gorilla shot out of the door, and raced round the house, thinking that the owner was flying before him, but he never could overtake the flyer. Then he went around outside of the other houses, and flew round and round the village, but he could discover naught. But meanwhile Kinneneh had borne all the stock of bananas up into the loft above, and when Gorilla returned there was not one banana of all the great pile he had brought left on the floor.

When, after he was certain that there was not a single bit of a banana left for him to eat, he scratched his sides and his legs, and putting his hand on the top of his head, he uttered a great cry just like a great, stupid child, but the crying did not fill his tummy. No, he must have bananas for that – and he rose up after awhile and went to procure some more fruit.

But when he had brought a great pile of it and had sat down with his nice-smelling bunch before him, he would exclaim, "Ha, ha! Now – now I shall eat and be satisfied. I shall fill myself with the sweet fruit, and then lie down and sleep. Ha, ha!"

Then instantly the mocking voice would cry out after him, "Ha, ha!" and sometimes it sounded close to his ears, and then behind his head, sometimes it appeared to come from under the bananas and sometimes from the doorway: – that Gorilla would roar in fury, and he would grind his teeth just like two grinding-stones, and chatter to himself, and race about the village, trying to discover whence the voice came, but in his absence the fruit would be swept away by his invisible enemy, and when he would come in to finish his meal, lo! there were only blackened and stained banana peelings – the refuse of his first feast.

Gorilla would then cry like a whipped child, and would go again into the plantation, to bring some more fruit into the house, but when he returned with it he would always boast of what he was going to do, and cry out "Ha, ha!" and instantly his unseen enemy would mock him and cry "Ha, ha!" and he would start up raving and screaming in rage, and search for him, and in his absence his bananas would be whisked away. And Gorilla's hunger grew on him, until his paunch became like an empty sack, and what with his hunger and grief and rage, and furious raving and racing about, his strength was at last quite exhausted, and the end of him was that on the fifth day he fell from weakness across the threshold of the chief's house, which he had chosen to make his nest, and there died.

When the people of the next village heard of how Kinneneh, a little boy, had conquered the man-killing gorilla, they brought him and his mother away, and they gave him a fine new house and a plantation, and male and female slaves to tend it, and when their old king died, and the period of mourning for him was over, they elected wise Kinneneh to be king over them.

"Ah, friends," said Safeni to his companions, after Kadu had concluded his story, "there is no doubt that the cunning of a son of man prevails over the strongest brute, and it is well for us, Mashallah! that it should be so; for if the elephant, or the lion, or the gorilla possessed but cunning equal to their strength, what would become of us!"

And each man retired to his hut, congratulating himself that he was born a man-child, and not a thick, muddle-headed beast.

THE HARE AND THE BABOON
(From the Ndau people, eastern Zimbabwe, Mozambique and Malawi)

Shu'lo, the Hare, thought he would play a trick on Zinhede, the Baboon. So he said one day: "Baboon, I have a fine plan. Let us do something new for fun! Let us kill our mothers!"

Then the Hare went home, and he took an old hide and whacked it with a stick and cried out and made a great noise, as if he were beating some one to death. And the Baboon heard it and said to himself, "Yes, there is the Hare in his kraal, beating his mother to death. I will do the same."

So the Baboon took up a stick and killed his mother.

Then the Hare and the Baboon went out hunting. But when the Baboon came home, there was no one to cook for him nor to tend him in any way – only his mother's body lay dead on the ground. He was very lonely and hungry and sad. And he wept beside his dead mother.

But the Hare came home leaping and chuckling. For his mother was there in the kraal, and soon his supper was cooking. Together they ate and laughed at the stupid Baboon, who had no more sense than to kill his best friend for fun!

THE JACKAL AND THE ROOSTER
(From the Ndau people, eastern Zimbabwe, Mozambique and Malawi)

One day Mu'hwe, the Jackal, found Jo'ngwe, the Rooster, sitting up in a tree. "Come down, Jo'ngwe," said the Jackal, "today is a holiday. Mpho´ntholo, the King, the Lion, has declared that this day all animals shall be at peace and no one shall eat the other. Come down, and let us play together as friends."

But Jo´ngwe, the Rooster, only kept his eyes on the horizon and did not move.

"Come down, Jo´ngwe," said Mu´hwe, the Jackal, "I tell you the King has said that this day shall be a holiday."

Then Jo´ngwe, still looking off afar said, "Yes, I see that today must be a holiday because of the cloud of dust that is coming nearer." It was in reality only a mist on the horizon, but the Jackal asked anxiously of Jo´ngwe, up in the tree,

"What do you see in the cloud of dust?" "Men and dogs," answered Jo´ngwe.

"Then farewell, Jo´ngwe," said Mu´hwe, the Jackal, "I had better be going now, for dogs and I are not friends."

"But you said that today is a holiday," said Jo´ngwe, the Rooster, "King Mpho´ntholo, the Lion, has declared that all animals shall be friends and that no one shall eat the other. This you told me. You need not fear the dogs; don't go."

But Mu´hwe, the Jackal, ran away.

"You have proved yourself," called after him Jo´ngwe, the Rooster, "You only wanted to eat me!"

HOW ISURO THE RABBIT TRICKED GUDU
(From the Mashona people, Zimbabwe)

Far away in a hot country, where the forests are very thick and dark, and the rivers very swift and strong, there once lived a strange pair of friends. Now one of the friends was a big white rabbit named Isuro, and the other was a tall baboon called Gudu, and so fond were they of each other that they were seldom seen apart.

One day, when the sun was hotter even than usual, the rabbit awoke from his midday sleep, and saw Gudu the baboon standing beside him.

"Get up," said Gudu; "I am going courting, and you must come with me. So put some food in a bag, and sling it round your neck, for we may not be able to find anything to eat for a long while."

Then the rabbit rubbed his eyes, and gathered a store of fresh green things from under the bushes, and told Gudu that he was ready for the journey.

They went on quite happily for some distance, and at last they came to a river with rocks scattered here and there across the stream.

"We can never jump those wide spaces if we are burdened with food," said Gudu, "we must throw it into the river, unless we wish to fall in ourselves." And stooping down, unseen by Isuro, who was in front of him, Gudu picked up a big stone, and threw it into the water with a loud splash.

"It is your turn now," he cried to Isuro. And with a heavy sigh, the rabbit unfastened his bag of food, which fell into the river.

The road on the other side led down an avenue of trees, and before they had gone very far Gudu opened the bag that lay hidden in the thick hair about his neck, and began to eat some delicious-looking fruit.

"Where did you get that from?" asked Isuro enviously.

"Oh, I found after all that I could get across the rocks quite easily, so it seemed a pity not to keep my bag," answered Gudu.

"Well, as you tricked me into throwing away mine, you ought to let me share with you," said Isuro. But Gudu pretended not to hear him, and strode along the path.

By-and-bye they entered a wood, and right in front of them was a tree so laden with fruit that its branches swept the ground. And some of the fruit was still green, and some yellow. The rabbit hopped forward with joy, for he was very hungry; but Gudu said to him: "Pluck the green fruit, you will find it much the best. I will leave it all for you, as you have had no dinner, and take the yellow for myself." So the rabbit took one of the green oranges and began to bite it, but its skin was so hard that he could hardly get his teeth through the rind.

"It does not taste at all nice," he cried, screwing up his face; "I would rather have one of the yellow ones."

"No! no! I really could not allow that," answered Gudu. "They would only make you ill. Be content with the green fruit." And as they were all he could get, Isuro was forced to put up with them.

After this had happened two or three times, Isuro at last had his eyes opened, and made up his mind that, whatever Gudu told him, he would do exactly the opposite. However, by this time they had reached the village where dwelt Gudu's future wife, and as they entered Gudu pointed to a clump of bushes, and said to Isuro: "Whenever I am eating, and you hear me call out that my food has burnt me, run as fast as you can and gather some of those leaves that they may heal my mouth."

The rabbit would have liked to ask him why he ate food that he knew would burn him, only he was afraid, and just nodded in reply; but when they had gone on a little further, he said to Gudu:

"I have dropped my needle; wait here a moment while I go and fetch it."

"Be quick then," answered Gudu, climbing into a tree. And the rabbit hastened back to the bushes, and gathered a quantity of the leaves, which he hid among his fur, "For," thought he, "if I get them now I shall save myself the trouble of a walk by-and-by."

When he had plucked as many as he wanted he returned to Gudu, and they went on together.

The sun was almost setting by the time they reached their journey's end and being very tired they gladly sat down by a well. Then Gudu's betrothed, who had been watching for him, brought out a pitcher of water – which she poured over them to wash off the dust of the road – and two portions of food. But once again the rabbit's hopes were dashed to the ground, for Gudu said hastily:

"The custom of the village forbids you to eat till I have finished." And Isuro did not know that Gudu was lying, and that he only wanted more food. So he saw hungrily looking on, waiting till his friend had had enough.

In a little while Gudu screamed loudly: "I am burnt! I am burnt!" though he was not burnt at all. Now, though Isuro had the leaves about him, he did not dare to produce them at the last moment lest the baboon should guess why he had stayed behind. So he just went round a corner for a short time, and then came hopping back in a great hurry. But, quick though he was, Gudu had been quicker still, and nothing remained but some drops of water.

"How unlucky you are," said Gudu, snatching the leaves; "no sooner had you gone than ever so many people arrived, and washed their hands, as you see, and ate your portion." But, though Isuro knew better than to believe him, he said nothing, and went to bed hungrier than he had ever been in his life.

Early next morning they started for another village, and passed on the way a large garden where people were very busy gathering monkey-nuts.

"You can have a good breakfast at last," said Gudu, pointing to a heap of empty shells; never doubting but that Isuro would meekly take the portion shown him, and leave the real nuts for himself. But what was his surprise when Isuro answered:

"Thank you; I think I should prefer these." And, turning to the kernels, never stopped as long as there was one left. And the worst of it was that, with so many people about, Gudu could not take the nuts from him.

It was night when they reached the village where dwelt the mother of Gudu's betrothed, who laid meat and millet porridge before them.

"I think you told me you were fond of porridge," said Gudu; but Isuro answered: "You are mistaking me for somebody else, as I always eat meat when I can get it." And again Gudu was forced to be content with the porridge, which he hated.

While he was eating it, however a sudden thought darted into his mind, and he managed to knock over a great pot of water which was hanging in front of the fire, and put it quite out.

"Now," said the cunning creature to himself, "I shall be able in the dark to steal his meat!" But the rabbit had grown as cunning as he, and standing in a corner hid the meat behind him, so that the baboon could not find it.

"O Gudu!" he cried, laughing aloud, "it is you who have taught me to be clever." And calling to the people of the house, he bade them kindle the fire, for Gudu would sleep by it, but that he would pass the night with some friends in another hut.

It was still quite dark when Isuro heard his name called very softly, and, on opening his eyes, beheld Gudu standing by him. Laying his finger on his nose, in token of silence, he signed to Isuro to get up and follow him, and it was not until they were some distance from the hut that Gudu spoke.

"I am hungry and want something to eat better than that nasty porridge that I had for supper. So I am going to kill one of those goats, and as you are a good cook you must boil the flesh for me." The rabbit nodded, and Gudu disappeared behind a rock, but soon returned dragging the dead goat with him. The two then set about skinning it, after which they stuffed the skin with dried leaves, so that no one would have guessed it was not alive, and set it up in the middle of a lump of bushes, which kept it firm on its feet. While he was doing this, Isuro collected sticks for a fire, and when it was kindled, Gudu hastened to another hut to steal a pot which he filled with water from the river, and, planting two branches in the ground, they hung the pot with the meat in it over the fire.

"It will not be fit to eat for two hours at least," said Gudu, "so we can both have a nap." And he stretched himself out on the ground, and pretended to fall fast asleep, but, in reality, he was only waiting till it was safe to take all the meat for himself. "Surely I hear him snore," he thought; and he stole to the place where Isuro was lying on a pile of wood, but the rabbit's eyes were wide open.

"How tiresome," muttered Gudu, as he went back to his place; and after waiting a little longer he got up, and peeped again, but still the rabbit's pink eyes stared widely. If Gudu had only known, Isuro was asleep all the time; but this he never guessed, and by-and-bye he grew so tired with watching that he went to sleep himself. Soon after, Isuro woke up, and he too felt hungry, so he crept softly to the pot and ate all the meat, while he tied the bones together and hung them in Gudu's fur. After that he went back to the wood-pile and slept again.

In the morning the mother of Gudu's betrothed came out to milk her goats, and on going to the bushes where the largest one seemed entangled, she found out the trick. She made such lament that the people of the village came running, and Gudu and Isuro jumped up also, and pretended to be as surprised and interested as the rest. But they must have looked guilty after all, for suddenly an old man pointed to them, and cried:

"Those are thieves." And at the sound of his voice the big Gudu trembled all over.

"How dare you say such things? I defy you to prove it," answered Isuro boldly. And he danced forward, and turned head over heels, and shook himself before them all.

"I spoke hastily; you are innocent," said the old man; 'but now let the baboon do likewise." And when Gudu began to jump the goat's bones rattled and the people cried: "It is Gudu who is the goat-slayer!" But Gudu answered:

"Nay, I did not kill your goat; it was Isuro, and he ate the meat, and hung the bones round my neck. So it is he who should die!" And the people looked at each other, for they knew not what to believe. At length one man said:

"Let them both die, but they may choose their own deaths."

Then Isuro answered:

"If we must die, put us in the place where the wood is cut, and heap it up all round us, so that we cannot escape, and set fire to the wood; and if one is burned and the other is not, then he that is burned is the goat-slayer."

And the people did as Isuro had said. But Isuro knew of a hole under the wood-pile, and when the fire was kindled he ran into the hole, but Gudu died there.

When the fire had burned itself out and only ashes were left where the wood had been, Isuro came out of his hole, and said to the people:

"Lo! did I not speak well? He who killed your goat is among those ashes."

THE HARE, THE HYENA AND THE POT OF BEANS
(From the Bantu-speaking peoples, central and southern Africa)

One day, the hare and the hyena, being in want of food, they went to the chief of a certain village and offered to cultivate his garden. He agreed, and gave them a pot of beans as their food supply for the day. When they reached the garden they made a fire and put the beans on to boil. By the time they knocked off for the midday rest the beans were done, and the hyena, saying that he wanted to wash before eating, went to the stream and left the hare to watch the pot. No sooner was he out of sight than he stripped off his skin and ran back. The hare, thinking this was some strange and terrible beast, lost his head and ran away; the hyena sat down by the fire, finished the whole pot full of beans, returned to the stream, resumed his skin, and came back at his leisure. The hare, as all seemed quiet, ventured back, found the pot empty and the hyena clamorously demanding his food. The hare explained that he had been frightened away by an unknown monster, which had evidently eaten up the beans. The hyena refused to accept this excuse, and accused the hare of having eaten the beans himself. The unfortunate hare had to go hungry; but, finding denial useless, contented himself with remarking that if that beast came again he meant to shoot it; so he set to work making a bow. The hyena watched him till the bow was finished, and then said. "You have not made it right. Give it here!" And, taking it from him, he pretended to trim it into shape, but all the while he was cutting away the wood so as to weaken it in one spot. The hare so far suspected nothing, and kept his bow handy against the lunch hour on the following day. When the 'wild beast' appeared, he fitted an arrow to the string and bent the bow, but it broke in his hand, and once more he fled.

By this time his suspicions were awakened, and when he had made himself a new bow he hid it in the grass when the hyena was not looking. On the next occasion when the hyena appeared he shot at him and wounded him, but not seriously, so that he ran back to get into his skin and returned to find the hare calmly eating beans.

THE NAME OF THE TREE
(From the Lamba people, southern Africa)

In a time of famine all the animals gathered near a tree full of wonderful fruit, which could not be gathered unless the right name of the tree was menrtioned, and built their huts there. When the fruit ripened Wakalulu ('Mr Little Hare') went to the chief of the tree and asked him its name. The chief answered, "When you arrive just stand still and say *Uwungelema*." The hare started on his way back, but when he had reached the outskirts of his village he tripped, and the name went out of his head. Trying to recover it, he kept saying to himself, "*Uwungelenyense, Uwuntuluntumba*, Uwu-what?"

When he arrived the animals asked, "What is the name, Little Hare, of these things?" But he could only stammer the wrong words, and not a fruit fell. Next morning two buffaloes arose and tried their luck-it seems to have been considered safer to send two-but on their return both tripped and forgot the word. In answer to their eager questioners they said, "He said, *Uwumbilakanwa, Uwuntuluntumba*, or what?" – which, of course, could not help matters.

Then two elands were sent, with the same result.

Then the lion went, and, though he took care to repeat the word. over and over again on the way home, he too tripped against the obstacle and forgot it. Then all the animals, the roans and the sables, and the mongooses, all came to an end going there. They all just returned in vain.

Then the tortoise went to the chief and asked for the name. He had it repeated more than once, to make sure, and then set out on his slow and cautious journey.

He travelled a great distance and then said, "*Uwungelema*." Again he reached the outskirts of the village, again he said, "*Uwungelema*." Then he arrived in the village and reached his house and had a smoke. When he had finished smoking, the people arrived and said, "What is it, Tortoise?" Mr Tortoise went out and said, "*Uwungelema!*" The fruit pelted down. The people just covered the place, all the animals picking up. They sat down again: in the morning they said, "Go to Mr Tortoise." And Mr Tortoise came out and said, "*Uwungelema!*" Again numberless fruits pelted down. Then they began praising Mr Tortoise, saying,

"Mr Tortoise is chief, because he knows the name of these fruits."

This happened again and again, till the fruit came to an end, and the animals dispersed, to seek subsistence elsewhere.

So in the Benga country the grateful beasts proclaimed Kudu, the tortoise, as their second chief, the python, Mbama, having been their sole ruler hitherto. "We shall have two kings, Kudu and Mbama, each at his end of the country. For the one, with his wisdom, told what was fit to be eaten, and the other, with his skill, brought the news."

THE MASON WASP AND HIS WIFE
(From the San people, southern Africa)

The Mason Wasp formerly did thus as he walked along, while (his) wife walked behind him, the wife said: "O my husband! Shoot for me that hare!" And the Mason Wasp laid down his quiver; the Mason Wasp said: "Where is the hare?" And (his) wife said: "The hare lies there."

And the Mason Wasp took out an arrow; the Mason Wasp in this manner went stooping along. And the wife said: "Put down (thy) kaross! Why is it that thou art not willing to put down (thy) kaross?" Therefore, the Mason Wasp, walking along, unloosened the strings of the kaross; he put down the kaross. Therefore the wife said: "Canst thou be like this? This must have been why thou wert not willing to lay down the kaross." (She mocked the man on account of the middle of his body, which was slender.)

Therefore, the Mason Wasp walked, turning to one side; he aimed at (his) wife, he shot, hitting the (head of) the arrow on (his) wife's breast (bone).

And (his) wife fell down dead on account of it. Then he exclaimed: "*Yi ü hihi!* O my wife *hi!*" (crying) as if he had not been the one to shoot (his) wife. He cried, that he should have done thus, have shot his wife; his wife died.

THE VULTURES, THEIR ELDER SISTER AND HER HUSBAND
(From the San people, southern Africa)

The Vultures formerly made their elder sister of a person; they lived with her.

They, when their elder sister's husband brought (home) a springbok, they ate up the springbok. And their elder sister's husband cursed them, he scolded at them.

And their elder sister took up the skin of the springbok, she singed it. Their elder sister boiled the skin of the springbok, their elder sister took it out (of the pot).

And they were taking hold of the pieces of skin, they swallowed them down. Their elder sister's husband scolded them, because they again, they ate with their elder sister, of the springbok's skin, when they had just eaten the body of the springbok, they again, they ate with their elder sister of the springbok's skin.

And they were afraid of their elder sister's husband, they went away, they went in all directions, they, in this manner, sat down. And they looked at their elder sister's husband, they were looking furtively at their elder sister's husband.

Their elder sister's husband went hunting. He again, he went (and) killed a springbok; he brought the springbok home, slung upon his back. They again, they came (and) ate up the springbok.

Their elder sister's husband scolded them. And they moved away, they sat down.

Their elder sister singed the springbok's skin she boiled the springbok's skin. Their elder sister was giving to them pieces of the skin, they were swallowing them down.

Therefore, on the morrow, their elder sister's husband said that his wife must go with him; she should altogether eat on the hunting ground; for, his younger sisters-in-law were in the habit of eating up the springbok. Therefore, the wife should go with him. Then, the wife went with him.

Therefore, they, when their elder sister had gone, they went out of the house, they sat down opposite to the house, and they conspired together about it. They said, this other one said: "Thou shalt ascend, and then thou must come to tell us what the place seems to be like." And another said: "Little sister shall be the one to try; and then, she must tell us." And then, a Vulture who was a little Vulture girl, she arose, she ascended.

They said: "Allow us, that we may see what little sister will do." Then, she went, disappearing in the sky, they no longer perceived her.

They sat; they were awaiting the time at which their younger sister should descend. Then, their younger sister descended (lit. fell) from above out of the sky, she (came and) sat in the midst of them.

And they exclaimed "Ah! What is the place like?" And their younger sister said: "Our mate (the elder sister) who is here shall ascend, that she may look. For, the place seems as if we should perceive a thing, when we are above there."

Then, her elder sister who was a grownup girl, she arose, she ascended, she went, disappearing in the sky. She descended from above, she sat in the midst of the other people.

And the other people said: "What is the place like?" And she said: "There is nothing the matter with the place; for, the place is clear. The place is very beautiful; for, I do behold the whole place; the stems of the trees, I do behold them; the place seems as if we should perceive a springbok, if a springbok were lying under a tree; for the place is very beautiful."

Then, they altogether arose, all of them, they ascended into the sky, while they wished that their elder sister should eat; for, their elder sister's husband scolded them.

Therefore, they used, when they espied their elder sister's husband coming, they ate in great haste. They said: "Ye must eat! Ye must eat! ye must eat in great haste! for, that accursed man who comes yonder, he could not endure us." And, they finished the springbok, they flew away, flew heavily away, they thus, they yonder alighted; while their elder sister's husband came to pick up the bones.

They, when they perceived a springbok, they descended, and their elder sister perceived them, their elder sister followed them up. They ate, (they) ate, they were looking around; they said: "Ye must eat; ye should look around; ye shall leave some meat for (our) elder sister; ye shall leave for (our) elder sister the undercut, when ye see that (our) elder sister is the one who comes." And they perceived their older sister coming, they exclaimed: "Elder sister really seems to be coming yonder, ye must leave the meat which is in the springbok's skin." And, they left (it). And, when they beheld that their elder sister drew near to them, they went away, they went in all directions.

Their elder sister said: "Fie! how can ye act in this manner towards me? as if I had been the one who scolded you!"

And their elder sister came up to the springbok, she took up the springbok, she returned home; while the Vultures went forward (?), they went to fly about, while they sought for another springbok, which they intended again to eat.

THE JACKAL AND THE SPRING
(From southern Africa)

Once upon a time all the streams and rivers ran so dry that the animals did not know how to get water. After a very long search, which had been quite in vain, they found a tiny spring, which only wanted to be dug deeper so as to yield plenty of water. So the beasts said to each other, "Let us dig a well, and then we shall not fear to die of thirst;" and they all consented except the jackal, who hated work of any kind, and generally got somebody to do it for him.

When they had finished their well, they held a council as to who should be made the guardian of the well, so that the jackal might not come near it, for, they said, "he would not work, therefore he shall not drink."

After some talk it was decided that the rabbit should be left in charge; then all the other beasts went back to their homes.

When they were out of sight the jackal arrived. "Good morning! Good morning, rabbit!" and the rabbit politely said, "Good morning!" Then the jackal unfastened the little bag that hung at his side, and pulled out of it a piece of honeycomb which he began to eat, and turning to the rabbit he remarked:

"As you see, rabbit, I am not thirsty in the least, and this is nicer than any water."

"Give me a bit," asked the rabbit. So the jackal handed him a very little morsel.

"Oh, how good it is!" cried the rabbit; "give me a little more, dear friend!"

But the jackal answered, "If you really want me to give you some more, you must have your paws tied behind you, and lie on your back, so that I can pour it into your mouth."

The rabbit did as he was bid, and when he was tied tight and popped on his back, the jackal ran to the spring and drank as much as he wanted. When he had quite finished he returned to his den.

In the evening the animals all came back, and when they saw the rabbit lying with his paws tied, they said to him: "Rabbit, how did you let yourself be taken in like this?"

"It was all the fault of the jackal," replied the rabbit; "he tied me up like this, and told me he would give me something nice to eat. It was all a trick just to get at our water."

"Rabbit, you are no better than an idiot to have let the jackal drink our water when he would not help to find it. Who shall be our next watchman? We must have somebody a little sharper than you!" and the little hare called out, "I will be the watchman."

The following morning the animals all went their various ways, leaving the little hare to guard the spring. When they were out of sight the jackal came back. "Good morning! good morning, little hare," and the little hare politely said, "Good morning."

"Can you give me a pinch of snuff?" said the jackal.

"I am so sorry, but I have none," answered the little hare.

The jackal then came and sat down by the little hare, and unfastened his little bag, pulling out of it a piece of honeycomb. He licked his lips and exclaimed, "Oh, little hare, if you only knew how good it is!"

"What is it?" asked the little hare.

"It is something that moistens my throat so deliciously," answered the jackal, "that after I have eaten it I don't feel thirsty anymore, while I am sure that all you other beasts are forever wanting water."

"Give me a bit, dear friend," asked the little hare.

"Not so fast," replied the jackal. "If you really wish to enjoy what you are eating, you must have your paws tied behind you, and lie on your back, so that I can pour it into your mouth."

"You can tie them, only be quick," said the little hare, and when he was tied tight and popped on his back, the jackal went quietly down to the well, and drank as much as he wanted. When he had quite finished he returned to his den.

In the evening the animals all came back; and when they saw the little hare with his paws tied, they said to him: "Little hare, how did you let yourself be taken in like this? Didn't you boast you were very sharp? You undertook to guard our water; now show us how much is left for us to drink!"

"It is all the fault of the jackal," replied the little hare, "He told me he would give me something nice to eat if I would just let him tie my hands behind my back."

Then the animals said, "Who can we trust to mount guard now?" And the panther answered, "Let it be the tortoise."

The following morning the animals all went their various ways, leaving the tortoise to guard the spring. When they were out of sight the jackal came back. "Good morning, tortoise; good morning."

But the tortoise took no notice.

"Good morning, tortoise; good morning." But still the tortoise pretended not to hear.

Then the jackal said to himself, "Well, today I have only got to manage a bigger idiot than before. I shall just kick him on one side, and then go and have a drink." So he went up to the tortoise and said to him in a soft voice, "Tortoise! tortoise!" but the tortoise took no notice. Then the jackal kicked him out of the way, and went to the well and began to drink, but scarcely had he touched the water, than the tortoise seized him by the leg. The jackal shrieked out: "Oh, you will break my leg!" but the tortoise only held on the tighter. The jackal then took his bag and tried to make the tortoise smell the honeycomb he had inside; but the tortoise turned away his head and smelt nothing. At last the jackal said to the tortoise, "I should like to give you my bag and everything in it," but the only answer the tortoise made was to grasp the jackal's leg tighter still.

So matters stood when the other animals came back. The moment he saw them, the jackal gave a violent tug, and managed to free his leg, and then took to his heels as fast as he could. And the animals all said to the tortoise:

"Well done, tortoise, you have proved your courage; now we can drink from our well in peace, as you have got the better of that thieving jackal!"

ELEPHANT AND TORTOISE
(From South Africa)

Two powers, Elephant and Rain, had a dispute. Elephant said, "If you say that you nourish me, in what way is it that you say so?" Rain answered, "If you say that I do not nourish you, when I go away, will you not die?" And Rain then departed.

Elephant said, "Vulture! cast lots to make rain for me."

Vulture said, "I will not cast lots."

Then Elephant said to Crow, "Cast lots!" who answered, "Give the things with which I may cast lots." Crow cast lots and rain fell. It rained at the lagoons, but they dried up, and only one lagoon remained.

Elephant went a-hunting. There was, however, Tortoise, to whom Elephant said, "Tortoise, remain at the water!" Thus Tortoise was left behind when Elephant went a-hunting.

There came Giraffe, and said to Tortoise, "Give me water!" Tortoise answered, "The water belongs to Elephant."

There came Zebra, who said to Tortoise, "Give me water!" Tortoise answered, "The water belongs to Elephant."

There came Gemsbok, and said to Tortoise, "Give me water!" Tortoise answered, "The water belongs to Elephant."

There came Wildebeest, and said, "Give me water!" Tortoise said, "The water belongs to Elephant."

There came Roodebok, and said to Tortoise, "Give me water!" Tortoise answered, "The water belongs to Elephant."

There came Springbok, and said to Tortoise, "Give me water!" Tortoise said, "The water belongs to Elephant."

There came Jackal, and said to Tortoise, "Give me water!" Tortoise said, "The water belongs to Elephant."

There came Lion, and said, "Little Tortoise, give me water!" When little Tortoise was about to say something, Lion got hold of him and beat him; Lion drank of the water, and since then the animals drink water.

When Elephant came back from the hunting, he said, "Little Tortoise, is there water?" Tortoise answered, "The animals have drunk the water." Elephant asked, "Little Tortoise, shall I chew you or swallow you down?" Little Tortoise said, "Swallow me, if you please!" and Elephant swallowed him whole.

After Elephant had swallowed Little Tortoise, and he had entered his body, he tore off his liver, heart, and kidneys. Elephant said, "Little Tortoise, you kill me."

So Elephant died; but little Tortoise came out of his dead body, and went wherever he liked.

THE HUNT OF LION AND JACKAL
(From South Africa)

Lion and Jackal, it is said, were one day lying in wait for Eland. Lion shot (with a bow) and missed, but Jackal hit and sang out, "Hah! hah!"

Lion said, "No, you did not shoot anything. It was I who hit."

Jackal answered, "Yea, my father, thou hast hit."

Then they went home in order to return when the eland was dead, and cut it up. Jackal, however, turned back, unknown to Lion, hit his nose so that the blood ran on the spoor of the eland, and followed their track thus, in order to cheat Lion. When he had gone some distance, he returned by another way to the dead eland, and creeping into its carcass, cut out all the fat.

Meanwhile Lion followed the blood-stained spoor of Jackal, thinking that it was eland blood, and only when he had gone some distance did he find out that he had been deceived. He then returned on Jackal's spoor, and reached the dead eland, where, finding Jackal in its carcass, he seized him by his tail and drew him out with a swing.

Lion upbraided Jackal with these words: "Why do you cheat me?"

Jackal answered: "No, my father, I do not cheat you; you may know it, I think. I prepared this fat for you, father."

Lion said: "Then take the fat and carry it to your mother" (the lioness); and he gave him the lungs to take to his own wife and children.

When Jackal arrived, he did not give the fat to Lion's wife, but to his own wife and children; he gave, however, the lungs to Lion's wife, and he pelted Lion's little children with the lungs, saying:

> *"You children of the big-pawed one!*
> *You big-pawed ones!"*

He said to Lioness, "I go to help my father" (the lion); but he went far away with his wife and children.

JACKAL AND MONKEY
(From South Africa)

Every evening Jackal went to the Boer's kraal. He crept through the sliding door and stole a fat young lamb. This, clever Jackal did several times in succession. Boer set a wip for him at the door. Jackal went again and zip – there he was caught around the body by the noose. He swung and swayed high in the air and couldn't touch ground. The day began to dawn and Jackal became uneasy.

On a stone kopje, Monkey sat. When it became light he could see the whole affair, and descended hastily for the purpose of mocking Jackal. He went and sat on the wall. "Ha, ha, good morning. So there you are hanging now, eventually caught."

"What? I caught? I am simply swinging for my pleasure; it is enjoyable."

"You fibber. You are caught in the wip."

"If you but realized how nice it was to swing and sway like this, you wouldn't hesitate. Come, try it a little. You feel so healthy and strong for the day, and you never tire afterwards."

"No, I won't. You are caught."

After a while Jackal convinced Monkey. He sprang from the kraal wall, and freeing Jackal, adjusted the noose around his own body. Jackal quickly let go and began to laugh, as Monkey was now swinging high in the air.

"Ha, ha, ha," he laughed. "Now Monkey is in the wip."

"Jackal, free me," he screamed.

"There, Boer is coming," shouted Jackal.

"Jackal, free me of this, or I'll break your playthings."

"No, there Boer is coming with his gun; you rest a while in the noose."

"Jackal, quickly make me free."

"No, here's Boer already, and he's got his gun. Good morning." And with these parting words he ran away as fast as he could. Boer came and saw Monkey in the wip.

"So, so, Monkey, now you are caught. You are the fellow who has been stealing my lambs, hey?"

"No, Boer, no," screamed Monkey, "not I, but Jackal."

"No, I know you; you aren't too good for that."

"No, Boer, no, not I, but Jackal," Monkey stammered.

"Oh, I know you. Just wait a little," and Boer, raising his gun, aimed and shot poor Monkey dead.

HUMAN EXPLOITS & FOLLIES

The last section of this book concentrates on moral tales selected from different parts of Africa. They are concerned with human exploits, especially the strengths and weaknesses in our day-to-day relationships with other human beings. The plot of the moral tales is generally simple. It is told in straightforward language decorated with engaging aesthetic ornaments: repetitions, similes, hyperbole, rhetorical questions, folk songs and proverbs.

Many of the tales in this section such as 'The Two Friends from Kabyle' from the people of Algeria, 'The Ogre and the Beautiful Woman' from North Africa, 'The Death of Abu Nowas and his Wife' from Tunisia, 'Sanba the Coward' from Sudan and 'Olúrónbi' from the Yorùbá people in Nigeria, along with many other stories, take their main themes from the exhibition of some vice or wickedness: treachery, envy, rebellion, theft, greed, cruelty, ingratitude, lust, the drunkenness and/or weaknesses of humans and man's inhumanity to man, among others. The stories are mainly concerned with the condemnation of vice and exaltation of virtues such as love, helpfulness, honesty, bravery, kindness, perseverance and fear of God. Goodness and virtue are encouraged in the tales as ways of promoting peace and harmonious living. Wickedness is condemned, as recounted in the tale from the Ekon people of Cameroon and Nigeria, titled 'Why a Murderer must Die'; here justice functions as a mechanism of a social control.

ALI AND OU ALI (THE TWO FRIENDS)
(Kabyle people, Algeria)

Ali and Ou Ali were two friends. One day they met at the market. One of them bore ashes and the other carried dust. The first one had covered his goods with a little flour. The other had concealed his merchandise under some black figs. "Come, I will sell you some flour," said Ali.

"Come, I will sell you some black figs," answered Ou Ali.

Each regained his own horse. Ali, who thought he was carrying flour, found, on opening his sack, that it was only ashes. Ou Ali, who thought he was bearing black figs, found on opening his sack that it was nothing but dust. Another day they again greeted each other in the market. Ali smiled. Ou Ali smiled, and said to his friend:

"For the love of God, what is your name?"

"Ali; and yours?"

"Ou Ali."

Another time they were walking together, and said to each other:

"Let us go and steal."

One of them stole a mule and the other stole a rug. They passed the night in the forest. Now, as the snow was falling, Ali said to Ou Ali:

"Give me a little of your rug to cover me."

Ou Ali refused. "You remember," he added, "that I asked you to put my rug on your mule, and you would not do it." An instant afterward Ali cut off a piece of the rug, for he was dying of cold. Ou Ali got up and cut the lips of the mule. The next morning, when they awaked, Ou Ali said to Ali:

"O my dear friend, your mule is grinning."

"O my dear friend," replied Ali, "the rats have gnawed your rug."

And they separated. Some time afterward they met anew. Ali said to Ou Ali:

"Let us go and steal."

They saw a peasant, who was working. One of them went to the brook to wash his cloak there, and found it dry. He laid the blade of his sabre so that it would reflect the rays of the sun, and began to beat his cloak with his hands as if to wash it. The laborer came to the brook also, and found the man who was washing his cloak without water.

"May God exterminate you," said he, "who wash without water."

"May God exterminate you," answered the washer, "who work without a single ox."

The other robber watched the laborer, and had already stolen one of his oxen. The laborer went back to his plough, and said to the washer, "Keep this ox for me while I go and hunt for the other." As soon as he was out of sight the robber took away the ox left in his charge. The laborer returned, and seizing the goad by one end he gave a great blow on the plough-handle, crying:

"Break, now. It matters little."

The robbers met in a wood and killed the oxen. As they lacked salt, they went to purchase it. They salted the meat, roasted it, and ate it. Ali discovered a spring. Ou Ali not being able to find water, was dying of thirst.

"Show me your spring," he said to Ali, "and I will drink."

"Eat some salt, my dear friend," answered Ali. What could he do? Some days afterward Ou Ali put ashes on the shoes of Ali. The next day he followed the traces of the ashes, found the spring, and discovered thus the water that his friend was drinking. He took the skin of one of the oxen and carried it to the fountain. He planted two sticks above the water, hung the skin on the sticks, and placed the horns of the ox opposite the road. During the night his friend went to the spring. At the sight of the skin thus stretched out, fear seized him, and he fled.

"I am thirsty," said Ou Ali.

"Eat some salt, my dear friend," answered Ali, "for salt removes thirst."

Ali retired, and, after having eaten, ran to examine the skin that he had stretched out. Ou Ali ate the salt, and was dying of thirst.

"For the love of God," he said finally, "show me where you drink."

Ali was avenged. "Come, Jew-face, and I will show you the water." He made him drink at the spring, and said to him: "See what you were afraid of." The meat being finished, they started away. Ou Ali went to the house of Ali, and said to him:

"Come, we will marry you to the daughter of an old woman."

Now, the old woman had a herd of oxen. She said to Ali: "Take this drove to the fields and mount one of the animals." Ali mounted one of the oxen. He fell to the ground; the oxen began to run and trample on him. Ou Ali, who was at the house, said to the old woman:

"O my old woman, give me your daughter in marriage."

She called her daughter. "Take a club," she said to her, "and we will give it to him until he cries for mercy."

The daughter brought a club and gave Ou Ali a good beating. Ali, who was watching the herd, came at nightfall and met his friend.

"Did the old woman accept you?" he asked him.

"She accepted me," answered Ali. "And is the herd easy to watch?"

"From morning till night I have nothing to do but to repose. Take my place to-morrow, and mount one of the oxen."

The next day Ou Ali said to the old woman, "To-day I will take care of the herd." And, on starting, he recommended Ali to ask the old woman for her daughter's hand.

"It is well," answered Ali. Ou Ali arrived in the fields; one of the oxen seized him with his horns and tossed him into the air. All the others did the same thing. He regained the horse half dead. Ali, who had remained at the house, asked the old woman for her daughter's hand. "You ask me again?" said she. She took a club and gave it to him till he had had enough. Ou Ali said to Ali: "You have played me a trick." Ali answered him: "Without doubt they gave me the stick so hard that I did not hear the last blow."

"It is well, my dear friend. Ali owes nothing to Ou Ali."

They went away. The old woman possessed a treasure. Ou Ali therefore said to Ali: "I will put you in a basket, for you know that we saw that treasure in a hole." They returned to the old woman's house. Ali goes down into the hole, takes the treasure, and puts it into the basket. Ou Ali draws up the basket, takes it, abandons his friend, now a prisoner, and runs to hide the treasure in the forest. Ali was in trouble, for he knew not how to get out. What could he do? He climbed up the sides of the hole. When he found himself in the house, he opened the door and fled. Arriving at the edge of the forest he began to bleat. Ou Ali, thinking it was a ewe, ran up. It was his friend.

"O my dear," cried Ali, "I have found you at last."

"God be praised. Now, let us carry our treasure."

They started on the way. Ou Ali, who had a sister, said to Ali: "Let us go to my sister's house." They arrived at nightfall. She received them with joy. Her brother said to her:

"Prepare some pancakes and some eggs for us."

She prepared the pancakes and the eggs and served them with the food.

"O my sister," cried Ou Ali, "my friend does not like eggs; bring us some water." She went to get the water. As soon as she had gone, Ali took an egg and put it into his mouth. When the woman returned, he made such efforts to give it up that he was all out of breath. The repast was finished, and Ali had not eaten anything. Ou Ali said to his sister: "O my sister, my friend is ill; bring me a skewer." She brought him a skewer, which he put into the fire. When the skewer was red with the heat, Ou Ali seized it and applied it to the cheek of Ali. The latter uttered a cry, and rejected the egg. "Truly," said the woman, "you do not like eggs."

The two friends started and arrived at a village.

"Let us go to my sister's house," said Ali to his friend. She received them with open arms.

Ali said to her: "O my sister, prepare a good stew for us."

They placed themselves at the table at nightfall, and she served them with food.

"O my sister," cried Ali, "my friend does not like stew."

Ali ate alone. When he was satisfied, the two friends started, without forgetting the treasure. On the way Ali said to Ou Ali: "Give it to me to-day and I will deposit it in my house." He took it and gave it to his wife. "Bury me," he said to her. "And if Ou Ali comes tell him that his old friend is dead, and receive him with tears." Ou Ali arrived, and asked the woman in tears to see the tomb of his dead friend. He took an ox-horn and began to dig in the earth that covered the body.

"Behind! behind!" cried the pretended dead man.

"Get up, there, you liar," answered Ali.

They went away together. "Give me the treasure," asked Ou Ali; "to-day I will take it to my house." He took it to his house, and said to his wife: "Take this treasure. I am going to stretch myself out as if I were dead. When Ali comes receive him weeping, and say to him: 'Your friend is dead. He is stretched out in the bedroom.'"

Ali went and said to the woman: "Get me some boiling water, for your husband told me to wash him when he should die." When the water was ready the woman brought it. Ali seized the kettle and poured it on the stomach of Ou Ali, who sprang up with a bound. Thus he got even for the trick of his friend. The two friends divided the treasure then, and Ali went home.

THADHELLALA

(From the Kabyle people, Algeria)

A woman had seven daughters and no son. She went to the city, and there saw a rich shop. A little farther on she perceived at the door of a house a young girl of great beauty. She called her parents, and said:

"I have my son to marry; let me have your daughter for him."

They let her take the girl away. She came back to the shop and said to the man in charge of it:

"I will gladly give you my daughter; but go first and consult your father."

The young man left a servant in his place and departed. Thadhellala (that was her name) sent the servant to buy some bread in another part of the city. Along came a caravan of mules. Thadhellala packed all the contents of the shop on their backs and said to the muleteer:

"I will go on ahead; my son will come in a moment. Wait for him--he will pay you."

She went off with the mules and the treasures which she had packed upon them. The servant came back soon.

"Where is your mother?" cried the muleteer; "hurry and, pay me."

"You tell me where she is and I will make her give me back what she has stolen." And they went before the justice.

Thadhellala pursued her way, and met seven young students. She said to one of them, "A hundred francs and I will marry you." The student gave them to her. She made the same offer to the others, and each one took her word.

Arriving at a fork in the road, the first one said, "I will take you," the second one said, "I will take you," and so on to the last.

Thadhellala answered: "You shall have a race as far as that ridge over there, and the one that gets there first shall marry me."

The young men started. Just then a horseman came passing by. "Lend me your horse," she said to him. The horseman jumped off. Thadhellala mounted the horse and said:

"You see that ridge? I will rejoin you there."

The scholars perceived the man. "Have you not seen a woman?" they asked him. "She has stolen 700 francs from us."

"Haven't you others seen her? She has stolen my horse?"

They went to complain to the Sultan, who gave the command to arrest Thadhellala. A man promised to seize her. He secured a comrade, and they both pursued Thadhellala, who had taken flight. Nearly overtaken by the man, she met a negro who pulled teeth, and said to him:

"You see my son coming down there; pull out his teeth." When the other passed the negro pulled out his teeth. The poor toothless one seized the negro and led him before the Sultan to have him punished. The negro said to the Sultan: "It was his mother that told me to pull them out for him."

"Sidi," said the accuser, "I was pursuing Thadhellala."

The Sultan then sent soldiers in pursuit of the woman, who seized her and hung her up at the gates of the city. Seeing herself arrested, she sent a messenger to her relatives.

Then there came by a man who led a mule. Seeing her he said, "How has this woman deserved to be hanged in this way?"

"Take pity on me," said Thadhellala; "give me your mule and I will show you a treasure." She sent him to a certain place where the pretended treasure was supposed to be hidden. At this the brother-in-law of Thadhellala had arrived.

"Take away this mule," she said to him. The searcher for treasures dug in the earth at many places and found nothing. He came back to Thadhellala and demanded his mule.

She began to weep and cry. The sentinel ran up, and Thadhellala brought complaint against this man. She was released, and he was hanged in her place.

She fled to a far city, of which the Sultan had just then died. Now, according to the custom of that country, they took as king the person who happened to be at the gates of the city when the King died. Fate took Thadhellala there at the right time. They conducted her to the palace, and she was proclaimed Queen.

MAHOMET-BEN-SOLTAN

(From the Kabyle people, Algeria)

A certain sultan had a son who rode his horse through the city where his father reigned, and killed everyone he met. The inhabitants united and promised a flock to him who should make him leave the city. An old woman took it upon herself to realize the wishes of her fellow-citizens. She procured some bladders and went to the fountain to fill them with the cup of an acorn. The old man came to water his horse and said to the old woman:

"Get out of my way."

She would not move. The young man rode his horse over the bladders and burst them.

"If you had married Thithbirth, a cavalier," cried the old woman, "you would not have done this damage. But I predict that you will never marry her, for already seventy cavaliers have met death on her account."

The young man, pricked to the quick, regained his horse, took provisions, and set out for the place where he should find the young girl. On the way he met a man. They journeyed together. Soon they perceived an ogress with a dead man at her side.

"Place him in the earth," said the ogress to them; "it is my son; the Sultan hanged him and cut off his foot with a sword."

They took one of the rings of the dead man and went on their way. Soon they entered a village and offered the ring to the governor, who asked them for another like it. They went away from there, returned through the country which they had traversed, and met a pilgrim who had made the tour of the world. They had visited every place except the sea. They turned toward the sea. At the moment of embarking, a whale barred their passage. They retraced their steps, and met the ogress, took a second ring from the dead man, and departed. At a place they found sixty corpses. A singing bird was guarding them. The travellers stopped and heard the bird say:

"He who shall speak here shall be changed into a rock and shall die. Mahomet-ben-Soltan, you shall never wed the young girl. Ninety-nine cavaliers have already met death on her account."

Mahomet stayed till morning without saying one word. Then he departed with his companion for the city where Thithbirth dwelt. When they arrived they were pressed with hunger. Mahomet's companion said to him:

"Sing that which you heard the bird sing." He began to sing. The young girl, whom they meant to buy, heard him and asked him from whom he had got that song.

"From my head," he answered.

Mahomet's companion said: "We learned it in the fields from a singing bird."

"Bring me that bird," she said, "or I'll have your head cut off."

Mahomet took a lantern and a cage which he placed upon the branch of the tree where the bird was perching.

"Do you think to catch me?" cried the bird. The next day it entered the cage and the young man took it away. When they were in the presence of the young girl the bird said to her:

"We have come to buy you."

The father of the young girl said to Mahomet: "If you find her you may have her. But if not, I will kill you. Ninety-nine cavaliers have already met death thus. You will be the hundredth."

The bird flew toward the woman.

"Where shall I find you?" it asked her.

She answered: "You see that door at which I am sitting; it is the usual place of my father. I shall be hidden underneath."

The next day Mahomet presented himself before the Sultan: "Arise," he said, "your daughter is hidden there."

The Sultan imposed this new condition: "My daughter resembles ninety-nine others of her age. She is the hundredth. If you recognize her in the group I will give her to you. But if not, I will kill you."

The young girl said to Mahomet, "I will ride a lame horse." Mahomet recognized her, and the Sultan gave her to him, with a serving-maid, a female slave, and another woman.

Mahomet and his companion departed. Arriving at a certain road they separated. Mahomet retained for himself his wife and the slave woman, and gave to his companion the two other women. He gained the desert and left for a moment his wife and the slave woman. In his absence an ogre took away his wife. He ran in search of her and met some shepherds.

"O shepherds," he said, "can you tell me where the ogre lives?"

They pointed out the place. Arriving, he saw his wife. Soon the ogre appeared, and Mahomet asked where he should find his destiny.

"My destiny is far from here," answered the ogre. "My destiny is in an egg, the egg in a pigeon, the pigeon in a camel, the camel in the sea."

Mahomet arose, ran to dig a hole at the shore of the sea, stretched a mat over the hole; a camel sprang from the water and fell into the hole. He killed it and took out an egg, crushed the egg in his hands, and the ogre died. Mahomet took his wife and came to his father's city, where he built himself a palace. The father promised a flock to him who should kill his son. As no one offered, he sent an army of soldiers to besiege him. He called one of them in particular and said to him:

"Kill Mahomet and I will enrich you."

The soldiers managed to get near the young prince, put out his eyes, and left him in the field. An eagle passed and said to Mahomet: "Don't do any good to your parents, but since your father has made you blind take the bark of this tree, apply it to your eyes, and you will be cured."

The young man was healed.

A short time after his father said to him, "I will wed your wife."

"You cannot," he answered. The Sultan convoked the Marabout, who refused him the dispensation he demanded. Soon Mahomet killed his father and celebrated his wedding-feast for seven days and seven nights.

THE OGRE AND THE BEAUTIFUL WOMAN
(From the Berber peoples, North Africa)

Some hunters set out with their camels. When they came to the hunting-ground they loosed their camels to let them graze, and hunted until the setting of the sun, and then came back to their camp. One day while one of them was going along he saw the marks of an ogre, each one three feet wide, and began to follow them. He proceeded and found the place where the ogre had lately made his lair. He returned and said to his companions:

"I've found the traces of an ogre. Come, let us seek him."

"No," they answered, "we will not go to seek him, because we are not stronger than he is."

"Grant me fourteen days," said the huntsman. "If I return, you shall see. If not, take back my camel with the game."

The next day he set out and began to follow the traces of the ogre. He walked for four days, when he discovered a cave, into which he entered. Within he found a beautiful woman, who said to him:

"What brings thee here, where thou wilt be devoured by this ogre?"

"But thou," answered the hunter, "what is thy story and how did the ogre bring thee here?"

"Three days ago he stole me," she replied. "I was betrothed to the son of my uncle, then the ogre took me. I have stayed in the cavern. He often brings me food. I stay here, and he does not kill me."

"Where does he enter," asked the hunter, "when he comes back here?"

"This is the way," she answered. The hunter went in to the middle of the cave, loaded his gun, and waited. At sunset the ogre arrived. The hunter took aim and fired, hitting the ogre between the eyes as he was sitting down. Approaching him he saw that he had brought with him two men to cook and eat them. In the morning he employed the day in collecting the hidden silver, took what he could, and set out on the return. On the fourteenth day he arrived at the place where he had left his comrades, and found them there.

"Leave the game you have secured and return with me to the cave," he said to them. When they arrived they took all the arms and clothing, loaded it upon their camels, and set out to return to their village. Half way home they fought to see which one should marry the woman. The powder spoke between them. Our man killed four, and took the woman home and married her.

ADVENTURE OF SIDI MAHOMET
(From the Berber peoples, North Africa)

One day Mouley Mahomet summoned Sidi Adjille to come to Morocco, or he would put him in prison. The saint refused to go to the city until the prince had sent him his chaplit and his "dalil" as pledges of safety. Then he started on the way and arrived at Morocco, where he neither ate nor drank until three days had passed. The Sultan said to him:

"What do you want at my palace? I will give it to you, whatever it may be."

Sidi Adjille answered, "I ask of you only one thing, that is, to fill with wheat the feed-bag of my mule."

The prince called the guardian, and said to him, "Fill the feed-bag of his mule." The guardian went and opened the door of the first granary and put wheat in the feed-bag until the first granary was entirely empty. He opened another granary, which was soon equally exhausted, then a third, and so on in this fashion until all the granaries of the King were emptied. Then he wanted to open the silos, but their guardian went and spoke to the Sultan, together with the guardian of the granaries.

"Lord," they said, "the royal granaries are all empty, and yet we have not been able to fill the feed-bag of the saint's mule."

The donkey-drivers came from Fas and from all countries, bringing wheat on mules and camels. The people asked them,

"Why do you bring this wheat?"

"It is the wheat of Sidi Mahomet Adjille that we are taking."
The news came to the King, who said to the saint, "Why do you
act so, now that the royal granaries are empty?" Then he called
together the members of his council and wanted to have Sidi
Mahomet's head cut off. "Go out," he said to him.

"Wait till I make my ablutions" [for prayer], answered the saint.

The people of the makhzen who surrounded him watched him
among them, waiting until he had finished his ablutions, to take
him to the council of the King and cut off his head. When Sidi
Mahomet had finished washing, he lifted his eyes to heaven, got
into the tub where was washing, and vanished completely from
sight. When the guardians saw that he was no longer there, they
went vainly to continue the search at his house at Tagountaft.

THE HAUNTED GARDEN
(From the Berber peoples, North Africa)

A man who possessed much money had two daughters. The son
of the caliph of the King asked for one of them, and the son of
the cadi asked for the other, but their father would not let them
marry, although they desired it. He had a garden near his house.
When it was night, the young girls went there, the young men
came to meet them, and they passed the night in conversation.
One night their father saw them. The next morning he killed his
daughters, buried them in his garden, and went on a pilgrimage.

That lasted so until one night the son of the cadi and the son
of the caliph went to a young man who knew how to play on the
flute and the rebab. "Come with us," they said to him, "into the

garden of the man who will not give us his daughters in marriage. You shall play for us on your instruments." They agreed to meet there that night. The musician went to the garden, but the two young men did not go. The musician remained and played his music alone. In the middle of the night two lamps appeared, and the two young girls came out of the ground under the lamps. They said to the musician: "We are two sisters, daughters of the owner of the garden. Our father killed us and buried us here. You, you are our brother for this night. We will give you the money which our father has hidden in three pots. Dig here," they added. He obeyed, found the three pots, took them away, and became rich, while the two girls returned to their graves.

THE MAGIC NAPKIN

(From the Berber peoples, North Africa)

A taleb made a proclamation in these terms: "Is there anyone who will sell himself for 100 mitquals?" A man agreed to sell himself. The stranger took him to the cadi, who wrote out the bill of sale. He took the 100 mitquals and gave them to his mother and departed with the taleb. They went to a place where the latter began to repeat certain formulas. The earth opened and the man entered it. The other said to him, "Bring me the candlestick of reed and the box." He took this and came out keeping it in his pocket.

"Where is the box?" asked the taleb.

"I did not find it."

"By the Lord, let us go." He took him to the mountains, cast a stone at him, and went away. He lay on the ground for three days. Then he came to himself, went back to his own country, and rented a house. He opened the box, found inside a silk napkin, which he opened, and in which he found seven folds. He unfolded one. Genii came around the chamber, and a young girl danced until the day dawned. The man stayed there all that day until night. The King came out that night, and, hearing the noise of the dance, he knocked at the door, with his vezir. They received him with a red *h'aik*. He amused himself until the day dawned. Then he went home with his vezir. The latter sent for the man and said, "Give me the box which you have at home." He brought it to the King, who said to him: "Give me the box which you have so that I may amuse myself with it, and I will marry you to my daughter." The man obeyed and married the Sultan's daughter. The Sultan amused himself with the box, and after his death his son-in-law succeeded him.

THE DEATH OF ABU NOWAS AND OF HIS WIFE
(From Tunisia)

Once upon a time there lived a man whose name was Abu Nowas, and he was a great favourite with the Sultan of the country, who had a palace in the same town where Abu Nowas dwelt.

One day Abu Nowas came weeping into the hall of the palace where the Sultan was sitting, and said to him: "Oh, mighty Sultan, my wife is dead."

"That is bad news," replied the Sultan; "I must get you another wife." And he bade his Grand Vizir send for the Sultana.

"This poor Abu Nowas has lost his wife," said he, when she entered the hall.

"Oh, then we must get him another," answered the Sultana; "I have a girl that will suit him exactly," and clapped her hands loudly. At this signal a maiden appeared and stood before her.

"I have got a husband for you," said the Sultana.

"Who is he?" asked the girl.

"Abu Nowas, the jester," replied the Sultana.

"I will take him," answered the maiden; and as Abu Nowas made no objection, it was all arranged. The Sultana had the most beautiful clothes made for the bride, and the Sultan gave the bridegroom his wedding suit, and a thousand gold pieces into the bargain, and soft carpets for the house.

So Abu Nowas took his wife home, and for some time they were very happy, and spent the money freely which the Sultan had given them, never thinking what they should do for more when that was gone. But come to an end it did, and they had to sell their fine things one by one, till at length nothing was left but a cloak apiece, and one blanket to cover them. "We have run through our fortune," said Abu Nowas, "what are we to do now? I am afraid to go back to the Sultan, for he will command his servants to turn me from the door. But you shall return to your mistress, and throw yourself at her feet and weep, and perhaps she will help us."

"Oh, you had much better go," said the wife. "I shall not know what to say."

"Well, then, stay at home, if you like," answered Abu Nowas, "and I will ask to be admitted to the Sultan's presence, and will tell him, with sobs, that my wife is dead, and that I have no money for her burial. When he hears that perhaps he will give us something."

"Yes, that is a good plan," said the wife; and Abu Nowas set out.

The Sultan was sitting in the hall of justice when Abu Nowas entered, his eyes streaming with tears, for he had rubbed some pepper into them. They smarted dreadfully, and he could hardly see to walk straight, and everyone wondered what was the matter with him.

"Abu Nowas! What has happened?" cried the Sultan.

"Oh, noble Sultan, my wife is dead," wept he.

"We must all die," answered the Sultan; but this was not the reply for which Abu Nowas had hoped.

"True, O Sultan, but I have neither shroud to wrap her in, nor money to bury her with," went on Abu Nowas, in no wise abashed by the way the Sultan had received his news.

"Well, give him a hundred pieces of gold," said the Sultan, turning to the Grand Vizir. And when the money was counted out Abu Nowas bowed low, and left the hall, his tears still flowing, but with joy in his heart.

"Have you got anything?" cried his wife, who was waiting for him anxiously.

"Yes, a hundred gold pieces," said he, throwing down the bag, 'but that will not last us any time. Now you must go to the Sultana, clothed in sackcloth and robes of mourning, and tell her that your husband, Abu Nowas, is dead, and you have no money for his burial. When she hears that, she will be sure to ask you what has become of the money and the fine clothes she gave us on our marriage, and you will answer, 'before he died he sold everything.'"

The wife did as she was told, and wrapping herself in sackcloth went up to the Sultana's own palace, and as she was known to have been one of Subida's favourite attendants, she was taken without difficulty into the private apartments.

"What is the matter?" inquired the Sultana, at the sight of the dismal figure.

"My husband lies dead at home, and he has spent all our money, and sold everything, and I have nothing left to bury him with," sobbed the wife.

Then Subida took up a purse containing two hundred gold pieces, and said: "Your husband served us long and faithfully. You must see that he has a fine funeral."

The wife took the money, and, kissing the feet of the Sultana, she joyfully hastened home. They spent some happy hours planning how they should spend it, and thinking how clever they had been. "When the Sultan goes this evening to Subida's palace," said Abu Nowas, "she will be sure to tell him that Abu Nowas is dead. 'Not Abu Nowas, it is his wife,' he will reply, and they will quarrel over it, and all the time we shall be sitting here enjoying ourselves. Oh, if they only knew, how angry they would be!"

As Abu Nowas had foreseen, the Sultan went, in the evening after his business was over, to pay his usual visit to the Sultana.

"Poor Abu Nowas is dead!" said Subida when he entered the room.

"It is not Abu Nowas, but his wife who is dead," answered the Sultan.

"No; really you are quite wrong. She came to tell me herself only a couple of hours ago," replied Subida, "and as he had spent all their money, I gave her something to bury him with."

"You must be dreaming," exclaimed the Sultan. "Soon after midday Abu Nowas came into the hall, his eyes streaming with tears, and when I asked him the reason he answered that his wife was dead, and they had sold everything they had, and he had nothing left, not so much as would buy her a shroud, far less for her burial."

For a long time they talked, and neither would listen to the other, till the Sultan sent for the door-keeper and bade him go instantly to the house of Abu Nowas and see if it was the man or his wife who was dead. But Abu Nowas happened to be sitting with his wife behind the latticed window, which looked on the street, and he saw the man coming, and sprang up at once. "There is the Sultan's door-keeper! They have sent him here to find out the truth. Quick! throw yourself on the bed and pretend that you are dead." And in a moment the wife was stretched out stiffly, with a linen sheet spread across her, like a corpse.

She was only just in time, for the sheet was hardly drawn across her when the door opened and the porter came in. "Has anything happened?" asked he.

"My poor wife is dead," replied Abu Nowas. "Look! she is laid out here." And the porter approached the bed, which was in a corner of the room, and saw the stiff form lying underneath.

"We must all die," said he, and went back to the Sultan.

"Well, have you found out which of them is dead?" asked the Sultan.

"Yes, noble Sultan; it is the wife," replied the porter.

"He only says that to please you," cried Subida in a rage; and calling to her chamberlain, she ordered him to go at once to the dwelling of Abu Nowas and see which of the two was dead. "And be sure you tell the truth about it," added she, "or it will be the worse for you."

As her chamberlain drew near the house, Abu Nowas caught sight of him. "There is the Sultana's chamberlain," he exclaimed in a fright. "Now it is my turn to die. Be quick and spread the sheet over me." And he laid himself on the bed, and held his breath when the chamberlain came in. "What are you weeping for?" asked the man, finding the wife in tears.

"My husband is dead," answered she, pointing to the bed; and the chamberlain drew back the sheet and beheld Abu Nowas lying stiff and motionless. Then he gently replaced the sheet and returned to the palace.

"Well, have you found out this time?" asked the Sultan.

"My lord, it is the husband who is dead."

"But I tell you he was with me only a few hours ago," cried the Sultan angrily. "I must get to the bottom of this before I sleep! Let my golden coach be brought round at once."

The coach was before the door in another five minutes, and the Sultan and Sultana both got in. Abu Nowas had ceased being a dead man, and was looking into the street when he saw the coach coming. "Quick! quick!" he called to his wife. "The Sultan will be here directly, and we must both be dead to receive him." So they laid themselves down, and spread the sheet over them, and held their breath. At that instant the Sultan entered, followed by the Sultana and the chamberlain, and he went up to the bed and found the corpses stiff and motionless. "I would give a thousand gold pieces to anyone who would tell me the truth about this," cried he, and at the words Abu Nowas sat up. "Give them to me, then," said he, holding out his hand. "You cannot give them to anyone who needs them more."

"Oh, Abu Nowas, you impudent dog!" exclaimed the Sultan, bursting into a laugh, in which the Sultana joined. "I might have known it was one of your tricks!" But he sent Abu Nowas the gold he had promised, and let us hope that it did not fly so fast as the last had done.

THE DAUGHTER OF BUK ETTEMSUCH
(From Libya)

Once upon a time there lived a man who had seven daughters. For a long time they dwelt quite happily at home together, then one morning the father called them all before him and said:

"Your mother and I are going on a journey, and as we do not know how long we may be away, you will find enough provisions in the house to last you three years. But see you do not open the door to anyone till we come home again."

"Very well, dear father," replied the girls.

For two years they never left the house or unlocked the door; but one day, when they had washed their clothes, and were spreading them out on the roof to dry, the girls looked down into the street where people were walking to and fro, and across to the market, with its stalls of fresh meat, vegetables, and other nice things.

"Come here," cried one. "It makes me quite hungry! Why should not we have our share? Let one of us go to the market, and buy meat and vegetables."

"Oh, we mustn't do that!" said the youngest. "You know our father forbade us to open the door till he came home again."

Then the eldest sister sprang at her and struck her, the second spit at her, the third abused her, the fourth pushed her, the fifth flung her to the ground, and the sixth tore her clothes. Then they left her lying on the floor, and went out with a basket.

In about an hour they came back with the basket full of meat and vegetables, which they put in a pot, and set on the fire, quite forgetting that the house door stood wide open. The youngest sister, however, took no part in all this, and when dinner was ready and the table laid, she stole softly out to the entrance hall, and hid herself behind a great cask which stood in one corner.

Now, while the other sisters were enjoying their feast, a witch passed by, and catching sight of the open door, she walked in. She went up to the eldest girl, and said: "Where shall I begin on you, you fat bolster?"

"You must begin," answered she, "with the hand which struck my little sister."

So the witch gobbled her up, and when the last scrap had disappeared, she came to the second and asked: "Where shall I begin on you, my fat bolster?"

And the second answered, "You must begin on my mouth, which spat on my sister."

And so on to the rest; and very soon the whole six had disappeared. And as the witch was eating the last mouthful of the last sister, the youngest, who had been crouching, frozen with horror, behind the barrel, ran out through the open door into the street. Without looking behind her, she hastened on and on, as fast as her feet would carry her, till she saw an ogre's castle standing in front of her. In a corner near the door she spied a large pot, and she crept softly up to it and pulled the cover over it, and went to sleep.

By-and-by the ogre came home. "Fee, Fo, Fum," cried he, "I smell the smell of a man. What ill fate has brought him here?" And he looked through all the rooms, and found nobody. "Where are you?" he called. "Do not be afraid, I will do you no harm."

But the girl was still silent.

"Come out, I tell you," repeated the ogre. "Your life is quite safe. If you are an old man, you shall be my father. If you are a boy, you shall be my son. If your years are as many as mine, you shall be my brother. If you are an old woman, you shall be my mother. If you are a young one, you shall be my daughter. If you are middle-aged, you shall be my wife. So come out, and fear nothing."

Then the maiden came out of her hiding-place, and stood before him.

"Fear nothing," said the ogre again; and when he went away to hunt he left her to look after the house. In the evening he returned, bringing with him hares, partridges, and gazelles, for the girl's supper; for himself he only cared for the flesh of men, which she cooked for him. He also gave into her charge the keys of six rooms, but the key of the seventh he kept himself.

And time passed on, and the girl and the ogre still lived together.

She called him "Father," and he called her "Daughter," and never once did he speak roughly to her.

One day the maiden said to him, "Father, give me the key of the upper chamber."

"No, my daughter," replied the ogre. "There is nothing there that is any use to you."

"But I want the key," she repeated again.

However the ogre took no notice, and pretended not to hear. The girl began to cry, and said to herself: "To-night, when he thinks I am asleep, I will watch and see where he hides it;" and after she and the ogre had supped, she bade him good-night, and left the room. In a few minutes she stole quietly back, and watched from behind a curtain. In a little while she saw the ogre take the key from his pocket, and hide it in a hole in the ground before he went to bed. And when all was still she took out the key, and went back to the house.

The next morning the ogre awoke with the first ray of light, and the first thing he did was to look for the key. It was gone, and he guessed at once what had become of it.

But instead of getting into a great rage, as most ogres would have done, he said to himself, "If I wake the maiden up I shall only frighten her. For to-day she shall keep the key, and when I return to-night it will be time enough to take it from her." So he went off to hunt.

The moment he was safe out of the way, the girl ran upstairs and opened the door of the room, which was quite bare. The one window was closed, and she threw back the lattice and looked out. Beneath lay a garden which belonged to the prince, and in the garden was an ox, who was drawing up water from the well all by himself – for there was nobody to be seen anywhere. The ox raised his head at the noise the girl made in opening the lattice, and said to her, "Good morning, O daughter of Buk Ettemsuch! Your father is feeding you up till you are nice and fat, and then he will put you on a spit and cook you."

These words so frightened the maiden that she burst into tears and ran out of the room. All day she wept, and when the ogre came home at night, no supper was ready for him.

"What are you crying for?' said he. "Where is my supper, and is it you who have opened the upper chamber?"

"Yes, I opened it," answered she.

"And what did the ox say to you?"

"He said, 'Good morning, O daughter of Buk Ettemsuch. Your father is feeding you up till you are nice and fat, and then he will put you on a spit and cook you.'"

"Well, to-morrow you can go to the window and say, 'My father is feeding me up till I am nice and fat, but he does not mean to eat me. If I had one of your eyes I would use it for a mirror, and look at myself before and behind; and your girths should be loosened, and you should be blind – seven days and seven nights.'"

"All right," replied the girl, and the next morning, when the ox spoke to her, she answered him as she had been told, and he fell down straight upon the ground, and lay there seven days and seven nights. But the flowers in the garden withered, for there was no one to water them.

When the prince came into his garden he found nothing but yellow stalks; in the midst of them the ox was lying. With a blow from his sword he killed the animal, and, turning to his attendants, he said, "Go and fetch another ox!" And they brought in a great beast, and he drew the water out of the well, and the flowers revived, and the grass grew green again. Then the prince called his attendants and went away.

The next morning the girl heard the noise of the waterwheel, and she opened the lattice and looked out of the window.

"Good morning, O daughter of Buk Ettemsuch!" said the new ox. "Your father is feeding you up till you are nice and fat, and then he will put you on a spit and cook you."

And the maiden answered: "My father is feeding me up till I am nice and fat, but he does not mean to eat me. If I had one of your eyes I would use it for a mirror, and look at myself before and behind; and your girths should be loosened, and you should be blind – seven days and seven nights."

Directly she uttered these words the ox fell to the ground and lay there, seven days and seven nights. Then he arose and began to draw the water from the well. He had only turned the wheel once or twice, when the prince took it into his head to visit his garden and see how the new ox was getting on. When he entered the ox was working busily; but in spite of that the flowers and grass were dried up. And the prince drew his sword, and rushed at the ox to slay him, as he had done the other. But the ox fell on his knees and said:

"My lord, only spare my life, and let me tell you how it happened."

"How what happened?" asked the prince.

"My lord, a girl looked out of that window and spoke a few words to me, and I fell to the ground. For seven days and seven nights I lay there, unable to move. But, O my lord, it is not given to us twice to behold beauty such as hers."

"It is a lie," said the prince. "An ogre dwells there. Is it likely that he keeps a maiden in his upper chamber?"

"Why not?" replied the ox. "But if you come here at dawn to-morrow, and hide behind that tree, you will see for yourself."

"So I will," said the prince; "and if I find that you have not spoken truth, I will kill you."

The prince left the garden, and the ox went on with his work. Next morning the prince came early to the garden, and found the ox busy with the waterwheel.

"Has the girl appeared yet?" he asked.

"Not yet; but she will not be long. Hide yourself in the branches of that tree, and you will soon see her."

The prince did as he was told, and scarcely was he seated when the maiden threw open the lattice.

"Good morning, O daughter of Buk Ettemsuch!" said the ox. "Your father is feeding you up till you are nice and fat, and then he will put you on a spit and cook you."

"My father is feeding me up till I am nice and fat, but he does not mean to eat me. If I had one of your eyes I would use it for a mirror, and look at myself before and behind; and your girths should be loosened, and you should be blind – seven days and seven nights." And hardly had she spoken when the ox fell on the ground, and the maiden shut the lattice and went away. But the prince knew that what the ox had said was true, and that she had not her equal in the whole world. And he came down from the tree, his heart burning with love.

"Why has the ogre not eaten her?" thought he. "This night I will invite him to supper in my palace and question him about the maiden, and find out if she is his wife."

So the prince ordered a great ox to be slain and roasted whole, and two huge tanks to be made, one filled with water and the other with wine. And towards evening he called his attendants and went to the ogre's house to wait in the courtyard till he came back from hunting. The ogre was surprised to see so many people assembled in front of his house; but he bowed politely and said, "Good morning, dear neighbours! To what do I owe the pleasure of this visit? I have not offended you, I hope?"

"Oh, certainly not!" answered the prince.

"Then," continued the ogre, "What has brought you to my house to-day for the first time?"

"We should like to have supper with you," said the prince.

"Well, supper is ready, and you are welcome," replied the ogre, leading the way into the house, for he had had a good day, and there was plenty of game in the bag over his shoulder.

A table was quickly prepared, and the prince had already taken his place, when he suddenly exclaimed, "After all, Buk Ettemsuch, suppose you come to supper with me?"

"Where?" asked the ogre.

"In my house. I know it is all ready."

"But it is so far off – why not stay here?"

"Oh, I will come another day; but this evening I must be your host."

So the ogre accompanied the prince and his attendants back to the palace. After a while the prince turned to the ogre and said:

"It is as a wooer that I appear before you. I seek a wife from an honourable family."

"But I have no daughter," replied the ogre.

"Oh, yes you have, I saw her at the window."

"Well, you can marry her if you wish," said he.

So the prince's heart was glad as he and his attendants rode back with the ogre to his house. And as they parted, the prince said to his guest, "You will not forget the bargain we have made?"

"I am not a young man, and never break my promises," said the ogre, and went in and shut the door.

Upstairs he found the maiden, waiting till he returned to have her supper, for she did not like eating by herself.

"I have had my supper," said the ogre, "for I have been spending the evening with the prince."

"Where did you meet him?" asked the girl.

"Oh, we are neighbours, and grew up together, and to-night I promised that you should be his wife."

"I don't want to be any man's wife," answered she; but this was only pretence, for her heart too was glad.

Next morning early came the prince, bringing with him bridal gifts, and splendid wedding garments, to carry the maiden back to his palace.

But before he let her go the ogre called her to him, and said, "Be careful, girl, never to speak to the prince; and when he speaks to you, you must be dumb, unless he swears 'by the head of Buk Ettemsuch.' Then you may speak."

"Very well," answered the girl.

They set out; and when they reached the palace, the prince led his bride to the room he had prepared for her, and said "Speak to me, my wife," but she was silent; and by-and-by he left her, thinking that perhaps she was shy. The next day the same thing happened, and the next.

At last he said, "Well, if you won't speak, I shall go and get another wife who will." And he did.

Now when the new wife was brought to the palace the daughter of Buk Ettemsuch rose, and spoke to the ladies who had come to attend on the second bride. "Go and sit down. I will make ready the feast." And the ladies sat down as they were told, and waited.

The maiden sat down too, and called out, "Come here, firewood," and the firewood came. "Come here, fire," and the fire came and kindled the wood. "Come here, pot. Come here, oil;" and the pot and the oil came. "Get into the pot, oil!" said she, and the oil did it. When the oil was boiling, the maiden dipped all her fingers in it, and they became ten fried fishes. "Come here, oven," she cried next, and the oven came. "Fire, heat the oven." And the fire heated it. When it was hot enough, the maiden jumped in, just as she was, with her beautiful silver and gold dress, and all her jewels. In a minute or two she had turned into a snow-white loaf, that made your mouth water.

Said the loaf to the ladies, "You can eat now; do not stand so far off;" but they only stared at each other, speechless with surprise.

"What are you staring at?" asked the new bride.

"At all these wonders," replied the ladies.

"Do you call these wonders?" said she scornfully; "I can do that too," and she jumped straight into the oven, and was burnt up in a moment.

Then they ran to the prince and said: "Come quickly, your wife is dead!"

"Bury her, then!" returned he. "But why did she do it? I am sure I said nothing to make her throw herself into the oven."

Accordingly the burnt woman was buried, but the prince would not go to the funeral as all his thoughts were still with the wife who would not speak to him. The next night he said to her, "Dear wife, are you afraid that something dreadful will happen if you speak to me? If you still persist in being dumb, I shall be forced to get another wife." The poor girl longed to speak, but dread of the ogre kept her silent, and the prince did as he had said, and brought a fresh bride into the palace. And when she and her ladies were seated in state, the maiden planted a sharp stake in the ground, and sat herself down comfortably on it, and began to spin.

"What are you staring at so?" said the new bride to her ladies. "Do you think that is anything wonderful? Why, I can do as much myself!"

"I am sure you can't," said they, much too surprised to be polite.

Then the maid sprang off the stake and left the room, and instantly the new wife took her place. But the sharp stake ran through, and she was dead in a moment. So they sent to the prince and said, "Come quickly, and bury your wife."

"Bury her yourselves," he answered. "What did she do it for? It was not by my orders that she impaled herself on the stake."

So they buried her; and in the evening the prince came to the daughter of Buk Ettemsuch, and said to her, "Speak to me, or I shall have to take another wife." But she was afraid to speak to him.

The following day the prince hid himself in the room and watched. And soon the maiden woke, and said to the pitcher and to the water-jug, "Quick! go down to the spring and bring me some water; I am thirsty."

And they went. But as they were filling themselves at the spring, the water-jug knocked against the pitcher and broke off its spout. And the pitcher burst into tears, and ran to the maiden, and said: "Mistress, beat the water-jug, for he has broken my spout!"

"By the head of Buk Ettemsuch, I implore you not to beat me!"

"Ah," she replied, "if only my husband had sworn by that oath, I could have spoken to him from the beginning, and he need never have taken another wife. But now he will never say it, and he will have to go on marrying fresh ones."

And the prince, from his hiding-place, heard her words, and he jumped up and ran to her and said, "By the head of Buk Ettemsuch, speak to me."

So she spoke to him, and they lived happily to the end of their days, because the girl kept the promise she had made to the ogre.

[Fairy tales and poems from the city of Tripoli. By Hans Stumme.]

MOHAMMED WITH THE MAGIC FINGER
(From Tripoli, Libya)

Once upon a time, there lived a woman who had a son and a daughter. One morning she said to them: "I have heard of a town where there is no such thing as death: let us go and dwell there." So she broke up her house, and went away with her son and daughter.

When she reached the city, the first thing she did was to look about and see if there was any churchyard, and when she found none, she exclaimed, "This is a delightful spot. We will stay here for ever."

By-and-by, her son grew to be a man, and he took for a wife a girl who had been born in the town. But after a little while he grew restless, and went away on his travels, leaving his mother, his wife, and his sister behind him.

He had not been gone many weeks when one evening his mother said, "I am not well, my head aches dreadfully."

"What did you say?" inquired her daughter-in-law.

"My head feels ready to split," replied the old woman.

The daughter-in-law asked no more questions, but left the house, and went in haste to some butchers in the next street.

"I have got a woman to sell; what will you give me for her?" said she.

The butchers answered that they must see the woman first, and they all returned together.

Then the butchers took the woman and told her they must kill her.

"But why?" she asked.

"Because," they said, "it is always our custom that when persons are ill and complain of their head they should be killed at once. It is a much better way than leaving them to die a natural death."

"Very well," replied the woman. "But leave, I pray you, my lungs and my liver untouched, till my son comes back. Then give both to him."

But the men took them out at once, and gave them to the daughter-in-law, saying: "Put away these things till your husband returns." And the daughter-in-law took them, and hid them in a secret place.

When the old woman's daughter, who had been in the woods, heard that her mother had been killed while she was out, she was filled with fright, and ran away as fast as she could. At last she reached a lonely spot far from the town, where she thought she was safe, and sat down on a stone, and wept bitterly. As she was sitting, sobbing, a man passed by.

"What is the matter, little girl? Answer me! I will be your friend."

"Ah, sir, they have killed my mother; my brother is far away, and I have nobody."

"Will you come with me?" asked the man.

"Thankfully," said she, and he led her down, down, under the earth, till they reached a great city. Then he married her, and in course of time she had a son. And the baby was known throughout the city as "Mohammed with the magic finger," because, whenever he stuck out his little finger, he was able to see anything that was happening for as far as two days' distance.

By-and-by, as the boy was growing bigger, his uncle returned from his long journey, and went straight to his wife.

"Where are my mother and sister?" he asked; but his wife answered: "Have something to eat first, and then I will tell you."

But he replied: "How can I eat till I know what has become of them?"

Then she fetched, from the upper chamber, a box full of money, which she laid before him, saying, "That is the price of your mother. She sold well."

"What do you mean?" he gasped.

"Oh, your mother complained one day that her head was aching, so I got in two butchers and they agreed to take her.

However, I have got her lungs and liver hidden, till you came back, in a safe place."

"And my sister?"

"Well, while the people were chopping up your mother she ran away, and I heard no more of her."

"Give me my mother's liver and lungs," said the young man. And she gave them to him. Then he put them in his pocket, and went away, saying: "I can stay no longer in this horrible town. I go to seek my sister."

Now, one day, the little boy stretched out his finger and said to his mother, "My uncle is coming!"

"Where is he?" she asked.

"He is still two days' journey off: looking for us; but he will soon be here." And in two days, as the boy had foretold, the uncle had found the hole in the earth, and arrived at the gate of the city. All his money was spent, and not knowing where his sister lived, he began to beg of all the people he saw.

"Here comes my uncle," called out the little boy. "Where?" asked his mother. "Here at the house door;" and the woman ran out and embraced him, and wept over him. When they could both speak, he said: "My sister, were you by when they killed my mother?"

"I was absent when they slew her," replied she, "and as I could do nothing, I ran away. But you, my brother, how did you get here?"

"By chance," he said, "after I had wandered far; but I did not know I should find you!"

"My little boy told me you were coming," she explained, "when you were yet two days distant; he alone of all men has that great gift."

But she did not tell him that her husband could change himself into a serpent, a dog, or a monster, whenever he pleased. He was a very rich man, and possessed large herds of camels, goats, sheep, cattle, horses and asses; all the best of their kind. And the next morning, the sister said: "Dear brother, go and watch our sheep, and when you are thirsty, drink their milk!"

"Very well," answered he, and he went.

Soon after, she said again, "Dear brother, go and watch our goats."

"But why? I like tending sheep better!"

"Oh, it is much nicer to be a goatherd," she said; so he took the goats out.

When he was gone, she said to her husband, "You must kill my brother, for I cannot have him living here with me."

"But, my dear, why should I? He has done me no harm."

"I wish you to kill him," she answered, "or if not I will leave."

"Oh, all right, then," said he; "to-morrow I will change myself into a serpent, and hide myself in the date barrel; and when he comes to fetch dates I will sting him in the hand."

"That will do very well," said she.

When the sun was up next day, she called to her brother, "Go and mind the goats."

"Yes, of course," he replied; but the little boy called out: "Uncle, I want to come with you."

"Delighted," said the uncle, and they started together.

After they had got out of sight of the house the boy said to him, "Dear uncle, my father is going to kill you. He has changed himself into a serpent, and has hidden himself in the date barrel. My mother has told him to do it."

"And what am I to do?" asked the uncle.

"I will tell you. When we bring the goats back to the house, and my mother says to you, 'I am sure you must be hungry: get a few dates out of the cask,' just say to me, 'I am not feeling very well, Mohammed, you go and get them for me.'"

So, when they reached the house the sister came out to meet them, saying, "Dear brother, you must certainly be hungry: go and get a few dates."

But he answered, "I am not feeling very well. Mohammed, you go and get them for me."

"Of course I will," replied the little boy, and ran at once to the cask.

"No, no," his mother called after him; "come here directly! Let your uncle fetch them himself!"

But the boy would not listen, and crying out to her "I would rather get them," thrust his hand into the date cask.

Instead of the fruit, it struck against something cold and slimy, and he whispered softly, "Keep still; it is I, your son!"

Then he picked up his dates and went away to his uncle.

"Here they are, dear uncle; eat as many as you want."

And his uncle ate them.

When he saw that the uncle did not mean to come near the cask, the serpent crawled out and regained his proper shape.

"I am thankful I did not kill him," he said to his wife; "for, after all, he is my brother-in-law, and it would have been a great sin!"

"Either you kill him or I leave you," said she.

"Well, well!" sighed the man, "to-morrow I will do it."

The woman let that night go by without doing anything further, but at daybreak she said to her brother, "Get up, brother; it is time to take the goats to pasture!"

"All right," cried he.

"I will come with you, uncle," called out the little boy.

"Yes, come along," replied he.

But the mother ran up, saying, "The child must not go out in this cold or he will be ill;" to which he only answered, "Nonsense! I am going, so it is no use your talking! I am going! I am! I am!"

"Then go!" she said.

And so they started, driving the goats in front of them.

When they reached the pasture the boy said to his uncle: "Dear uncle, this night my father means to kill you. While we are away he will creep into your room and hide in the straw. Directly we get home my mother will say to you, 'Take that straw and give it to the sheep,' and, if you do, he will bite you."

"Then what am I to do?" asked the man.

"Oh, do not be afraid, dear uncle! I will kill my father myself."

"All right," replied the uncle.

As they drove back the goats towards the house, the sister cried: "Be quick, dear brother, go and get me some straw for the sheep."

"Let me go," said the boy.

"You are not big enough; your uncle will get it," replied she.

"We will both get it," answered the boy; "come, uncle, let us go and fetch that straw!"

"All right," replied the uncle, and they went to the door of the room.

"It seems very dark," said the boy; "I must go and get a light;" and when he came back with one, he set fire to the straw, and the serpent was burnt.

Then the mother broke into sobs and tears. "Oh, you wretched boy! What have you done? Your father was in that straw, and you have killed him!"

"Now, how was I to know that my father was lying in that straw, instead of in the kitchen?" said the boy.

But his mother only wept the more, and sobbed out, "From this day you have no father. You must do without him as best you can!"

"Why did you marry a serpent?" asked the boy. "I thought he was a man! How did he learn those odd tricks?"

As the sun rose, she woke her brother, and said, "Go and take the goats to pasture!"

"I will come too," said the little boy.

"Go then!" said his mother, and they went together.

On the way the boy began: "Dear uncle, this night my mother means to kill both of us, by poisoning us with the bones of the serpent, which she will grind to powder and sprinkle in our food."

"And what are we to do?" asked the uncle.

"I will kill her, dear uncle. I do not want either a father or a mother like that!"

When they came home in the evening they saw the woman preparing supper, and secretly scattering the powdered bones of the serpent on one side of the dish. On the other, where she meant to eat herself, there was no poison.

And the boy whispered to his uncle, "Dear uncle, be sure you eat from the same side of the dish as I do!"

"All right," said the uncle.

So they all three sat down to the table, but before they helped themselves the boy said, "I am thirsty, mother; will you get me some milk?"

"Very well," said she, "but you had better begin your supper."

And when she came back with the milk they were both eating busily.

"Sit down and have something too," said the boy, and she sat down and helped herself from the dish, but at the very first moment she sank dead upon the ground.

"She has got what she meant for us," observed the boy; "and now we will sell all the sheep and cattle."

So the sheep and cattle were sold, and the uncle and nephew took the money and went to see the world.

For ten days they travelled through the desert, and then they came to a place where the road parted in two.

"Uncle!" said the boy.

"Well, what is it?" replied he.

"You see these two roads? You must take one, and I the other; for the time has come when we must part."

But the uncle cried, "No, no, my boy, we will keep together always."

"Alas! that cannot be," said the boy; "so tell me which way you will go."

"I will go to the west," said the uncle.

"One word before I leave you," continued the boy. "Beware of any man who has red hair and blue eyes. Take no service under him."

"All right," replied the uncle, and they parted.

For three days the man wandered on without any food, till he was very hungry. Then, when he was almost fainting, a stranger met him and said, "Will you work for me?"

"By contract?" asked the man.

"Yes, by contract," replied the stranger, "and whichever of us breaks it, shall have a strip of skin taken from his body."

"All right," replied the man; "what shall I have to do?"

"Every day you must take the sheep out to pasture, and carry my old mother on your shoulders, taking great care her feet shall never touch the ground. And, besides that, you must catch, every evening, seven singing birds for my seven sons."

"That is easily done," said the man.

Then they went back together, and the stranger said, "Here are your sheep; and now stoop down, and let my mother climb on your back."

"Very good," answered Mohammed's uncle.

The new shepherd did as he was told, and returned in the evening with the old woman on his back, and the seven singing birds in his pocket, which he gave to the seven boys, when they came to meet him. So the days passed, each one exactly like the other.

At last, one night, he began to weep, and cried: "Oh, what have I done, that I should have to perform such hateful tasks?"

And his nephew Mohammed saw him from afar, and thought to himself, "My uncle is in trouble – I must go and help him;" and the next morning he went to his master and said: "Dear master, I must go to my uncle, and I wish to send him here instead of myself, while I serve under his master. And that you may know it is he and no other man, I will give him my staff, and put my mantle on him."

"All right," said the master.

Mohammed set out on his journey, and in two days he arrived at the place where his uncle was standing with the old woman on his back trying to catch the birds as they flew past. And Mohammed touched him on the arm, and spoke: "Dear uncle, did I not warn you never to take service under any blue-eyed red-haired man!"

"But what could I do?" asked the uncle. "I was hungry, and he passed, and we signed a contract."

"Give the contract to me!" said the young man.

"Here it is," replied the uncle, holding it out.

"Now," continued Mohammed, "let the old woman get down from your back."

"Oh no, I mustn't do that!" cried he.

But the nephew paid no attention, and went on talking: "Do not worry yourself about the future. I see my way out of it all. And, first, you must take my stick and my mantle, and leave this place. After two days' journey, straight before you, you will come to some tents which are inhabited by shepherds. Go in there, and wait."

"All right!" answered the uncle.

Then Mohammed with the Magic Finger picked up a stick and struck the old woman with it, saying, "Get down, and look after the sheep; I want to go to sleep."

"Oh, certainly!" replied she.

So Mohammed lay down comfortably under a tree and slept till evening. Towards sunset he woke up and said to the old woman: "Where are the singing birds which you have got to catch?"

"You never told me anything about that," replied she.

"Oh, didn't I?" he answered. "Well, it is part of your business, and if you don't do it, I shall just kill you."

"Of course I will catch them!" cried she in a hurry, and ran about the bushes after the birds, till thorns pierced her foot, and she shrieked from pain and exclaimed, "Oh dear, how unlucky I am! and how abominably this man is treating me!" However, at last she managed to catch the seven birds, and brought them to Mohammed, saying, "Here they are!"

"Then now we will go back to the house," said he.

When they had gone some way he turned to her sharply:

"Be quick and drive the sheep home, for I do not know where their fold is." And she drove them before her. By-and-by the young man spoke:

"Look here, old hag; if you say anything to your son about my having struck you, or about my not being the old shepherd, I'll kill you!"

"Oh, no, of course I won't say anything!"

When they got back, the son said to his mother: "That is a good shepherd I've got, isn't he?"

"Oh, a splendid shepherd!" answered she. "Why, look how fat the sheep are, and how much milk they give!"

"Yes, indeed!" replied the son, as he rose to get supper for his mother and the shepherd.

In the time of Mohammed's uncle, the shepherd had had nothing to eat but the scraps left by the old woman; but the new shepherd was not going to be content with that.

"You will not touch the food till I have had as much as I want," whispered he.

"Very good!" replied she. And when he had had enough, he said:

"Now, eat!" But she wept, and cried: "That was not written in your contract. You were only to have what I left!"

"If you say a word more, I will kill you!" said he.

The next day he took the old woman on his back, and drove the sheep in front of him till he was some distance from the house, when he let her fall, and said: "Quick! go and mind the sheep!"

Then he took a ram, and killed it. He lit a fire and broiled some of its flesh, and called to the old woman:

"Come and eat with me!" and she came. But instead of letting her eat quietly, he took a large lump of the meat and rammed it down her throat with his crook, so that she died. And when he saw she was dead, he said: "That is what you have got for tormenting my uncle!" and left her lying where she was, while he went after the singing birds. It took him a long time to catch them; but at length he had the whole seven hidden in the pockets of his tunic, and then he threw the old woman's body into some bushes, and drove the sheep before him, back to their fold. And when they drew near the house the seven boys came to meet him, and he gave a bird to each.

"Why are you weeping?" asked the boys, as they took their birds.

"Because your grandmother is dead!" And they ran and told their father. Then the man came up and said to Mohammed: "What was the matter? How did she die?"

And Mohammed answered: "I was tending the sheep when she said to me, 'Kill me that ram; I am hungry!' So I killed it, and gave her the meat. But she had no teeth, and it choked her."

"But why did you kill the ram, instead of one of the sheep?" asked the man.

"What was I to do?" said Mohammed. "I had to obey orders!"

"Well, I must see to her burial!" said the man; and the next morning Mohammed drove out the sheep as usual, thinking to himself, "Thank goodness I've got rid of the old woman! Now for the boys!"

All day long he looked after the sheep, and towards evening he began to dig some little holes in the ground, out of which he took six scorpions. These he put in his pockets, together with one bird which he caught. After this he drove his flock home.

When he approached the house the boys came out to meet him as before, saying: "Give me my bird!" and he put a scorpion into the hand of each, and it stung him, and he died. But to the youngest only he gave a bird.

As soon as he saw the boys lying dead on the ground, Mohammed lifted up his voice and cried loudly: "Help, help! the children are dead!"

And the people came running fast, saying: "What has happened? How have they died?"

And Mohammed answered: "It was your own fault! The boys had been accustomed to birds, and in this bitter cold their fingers grew stiff, and could hold nothing, so that the birds flew away, and their spirits flew with them. Only the youngest, who managed to keep tight hold of his bird, is still alive."

And the father groaned, and said, "I have borne enough! Bring no more birds, lest I lose the youngest also!"

"All right," said Mohammed. As he was driving the sheep out to grass he said to his master: "Out there is a splendid pasture, and I will keep the sheep there for two or, perhaps, three days, so do not be surprised at our absence."

"Very good!" said the man; and Mohammed started. For two days he drove them on and on, till he reached his uncle, and said to him, "Dear uncle, take these sheep and look after them. I have killed the old woman and the boys, and the flock I have brought to you!"

Then Mohammed returned to his master; and on the way he took a stone and beat his own head with it till it bled, and bound his hands tight, and began to scream. The master came running and asked, "What is the matter?"

And Mohammed answered: "While the sheep were grazing, robbers came and drove them away, and because I tried to prevent them, they struck me on the head and bound my hands. See how bloody I am!"

"What shall we do?" said the master; "are the animals far off?"

"So far that you are not likely ever to see them again," replied Mohammed. "This is the fourth day since the robbers came down. How should you be able to overtake them?"

"Then go and herd the cows!" said the man.

"All right!" replied Mohammed, and for two days he went. But on the third day he drove the cows to his uncle, first cutting off their tails. Only one cow he left behind him.

"Take these cows, dear uncle," said he. "I am going to teach that man a lesson."

"Well, I suppose you know your own business best," said the uncle. "And certainly he almost worried me to death."

So Mohammed returned to his master, carrying the cows' tails tied up in a bundle on his back. When he came to the sea-shore, he stuck all the tails in the sand, and went and buried the one cow, whose tail he had not cut off, up to her neck, leaving the tail projecting. After he had got everything ready, he began to shriek and scream as before, till his master and all the other servants came running to see what was the matter.

"What in the world has happened?" they cried

"The sea has swallowed up the cows," said Mohammed, "and nothing remains but their tails. But if you are quick and pull hard, perhaps you may get them out again!"

The master ordered each man instantly to take hold of a tail, but at the first pull they nearly tumbled backwards, and the tails were left in their hands.

"Stop," cried Mohammed, "you are doing it all wrong. You have just pulled off their tails, and the cows have sunk to the bottom of the sea."

"See if you can do it any better," said they; and Mohammed ran to the cow which he had buried in the rough grass, and took hold of her tail and dragged the animal out at once.

"There! that is the way to do it!" said he, "I told you you knew nothing about it!"

The men slunk away, much ashamed of themselves; but the master came up to Mohammed. "Get you gone!" he said, "there is nothing more for you to do! You have killed my mother, you have slain my children, you have stolen my sheep, you have drowned my cows; I have now no work to give you."

"First give me the strip of your skin which belongs to me of right, as you have broken your contract!"

"That a judge shall decide," said the master; "we will go before him."

"Yes, we will," replied Mohammed. And they went before the judge.

"What is your case?" asked the judge of the master.

"My lord," said the man, bowing low, "my shepherd here has robbed me of everything. He has killed my children and my old mother; he has stolen my sheep, he has drowned my cows in the sea."

The shepherd answered: "He must pay me what he owes me, and then I will go."

"Yes, that is the law," said the judge.

"Very well," returned the master, "let him reckon up how long he has been in my service."

"That won't do," replied Mohammed, "I want my strip of skin, as we agreed in the contract."

Seeing there was no help for it, the master cut a bit of skin, and gave it to Mohammed, who went off at once to his uncle.

"Now we are rich, dear uncle," cried he; "we will sell our cows and sheep and go to a new country. This one is no longer the place for us."

The sheep were soon sold, and the two comrades started on their travels. That night they reached some Bedouin tents, where they had supper with the Arabs. Before they lay down to sleep, Mohammed called the owner of the tent aside. "Your greyhound will eat my strip of leather," he said to the Arab.

"No; do not fear."

"But supposing he does?"

"Well, then, I will give him to you in exchange," replied the Arab.

Mohammed waited till everyone was fast asleep, then he rose softly, and tearing the bit of skin in pieces, threw it down before the greyhound, setting up wild shrieks as he did so.

"Oh, master, said I not well that your dog would eat my thong?"

"Be quiet, don't make such a noise, and you shall have the dog."

So Mohammed put a leash round his neck, and led him away.

In the evening they arrived at the tents of some more Bedouin, and asked for shelter. After supper Mohammed said to the owner of the tent, 'Your ram will kill my greyhound.'

"Oh, no, he won't."

"And supposing he does?"

"Then you can take him in exchange."

So in the night Mohammed killed the greyhound, and laid his body across the horns of the ram. Then he set up shrieks and yells, till he roused the Arab, who said: "Take the ram and go away."

Mohammed did not need to be told twice, and at sunset he reached another Bedouin encampment. He was received kindly, as usual, and after supper he said to his host: "Your daughter will kill my ram."

"Be silent, she will do nothing of the sort; my daughter does not need to steal meat, she has some every day."

"Very well, I will go to sleep; but if anything happens to my ram I will call out."

"If my daughter touches anything belonging to my guest I will kill her," said the Arab, and went to his bed.

When everybody was asleep, Mohammed got up, killed the ram, and took out his liver, which he broiled on the fire. He placed a piece of it in the girl's hands, and laid some more on her night-dress while she slept and knew nothing about it. After this he began to cry out loudly.

"What is the matter? be silent at once!" called the Arab.

"How can I be silent, when my ram, which I loved like a child, has been slain by your daughter?"

"But my daughter is asleep," said the Arab.

"Well, go and see if she has not some of the flesh about her."

"If she has, you may take her in exchange for the ram;" and as they found the flesh exactly as Mohammed had foretold, the Arab gave his daughter a good beating, and then told her to get out of sight, for she was now the property of this stranger.

They wandered in the desert till, at nightfall, they came to a Bedouin encampment, where they were hospitably bidden to enter. Before lying down to sleep, Mohammed said to the owner of the tent: "Your mare will kill my wife."

"Certainly not."

"And if she does?"

"Then you shall take the mare in exchange."

When everyone was asleep, Mohammed said softly to his wife: "Maiden, I have got such a clever plan! I am going to bring in the mare and put it at your feet, and I will cut you, just a few little flesh wounds, so that you may be covered with blood, and everybody will suppose you to be dead. But remember that you must not make a sound, or we shall both be lost."

This was done, and then Mohammed wept and wailed louder than ever.

The Arab hastened to the spot and cried, "Oh, cease making that terrible noise! Take the mare and go; but carry off the dead girl with you. She can lie quite easily across the mare's back."

Then Mohammed and his uncle picked up the girl, and, placing her on the mare's back, led it away, being very careful to walk one on each side, so that she might not slip down and hurt herself. After the Arab tents could be seen no longer, the girl sat up on the saddle and looked about her, and as they were all hungry they tied up the mare, and took out some dates to eat. When they had finished, Mohammed said to his uncle: "Dear uncle, the maiden shall be your wife; I give her to you. But the money we got from the sheep and cows we will divide between us. You shall have two-thirds and I will have one. For you will have a wife, but I never mean to marry. And now, go in peace, for never more will you see me. The bond of bread and salt is at an end between us."

So they wept, and fell on each other's necks, and asked forgiveness for any wrongs in the past. Then they parted and went their ways.

UBAANER AND THE WAX CROCODILE
(From Egypt)

The first story describes an event that happened during the reign of Nebka, a king of the third dynasty. It was told by Prince Khafra to King Khufu (Cheops). The tale tells of a magician named Ubaaner (meaning 'splitter of stones'), who was the chief Kher-heb in the temple of Ptah of Memphis, and a very learned man. He was a married man, but unfortunately his wife had fallen in love with a young man who worked in the fields.

One day, the wife sent one of her maids to deliver a box containing a supply of very fine clothes to the young man. Soon after receiving this gift, the young man suggested to the magician's wife that they should meet and talk in a certain lodge in her garden. So she instructed the steward to have the lodge made ready for her to receive her friend. When this was done, she went to the lodge and she sat there with the young man and drank beer with him until the evening, when he went on his way.

The steward, knowing what had happened, made up his mind to report the matter to his master, and as soon as morning came, he went to Ubaaner and informed him that his wife had spent the previous day drinking beer with the young man. Ubaaner then told the steward to bring him his casket made of ebony, silver and gold, which contained materials and instruments used for working magic. When it was brought him, Ubaaner took out some wax and fashioned a figure of a crocodile seven spans long. He then recited certain magical words over the crocodile and said to it, 'When the young man comes to bathe in my lake you shall seize him.' Then giving the wax crocodile to the steward, Ubaaner said to him, 'When the young man goes down to the lake to bathe according to his daily habit, you shall throw the crocodile into the water after him.' Having taken the crocodile from his master, the steward departed.

A little later the wife of Ubaaner told the steward to set the little lodge in the garden in order, because she was going to spend some time there. When the steward had furnished the lodge, she went there and the young man paid her a visit. After leaving the lodge he went and bathed in the lake. So the steward followed him and threw the wax crocodile into the water; it immediately turned into a large crocodile 7 cubits (about 3.5 metres/11 feet) long. It seized the young man and swallowed him up.

As this was unfolding, Ubaaner was visiting the king and he remained with him for seven days, during which time the young man was in the lake with no air to breathe. When the seven days were almost up, King Nebka suggested taking a walk with the magician. Whilst they were walking Ubaaner asked the king if he would like to see a wonderful thing that had happened to a young peasant. The king said he would and the pair immediately set off walking towards the lake. When they arrived Ubaaner uttered a spell over the crocodile and commanded it to come up out of the water bringing the young man with him; and the crocodile did so. When the king saw the beast he exclaimed at its hideousness and seemed to be afraid of it, but the magician stooped down fearlessly and took the crocodile up in his hand. Amazingly the living crocodile had disappeared and only a wax crocodile remained in its place.

Then Ubaaner told King Nebka the story of how this young man had spent days in the lodge of his garden talking and drinking beer with his wife. His Majesty said to the wax crocodile, 'Be gone and take what is yours with you.' The wax crocodile leaped out of the magician's hand into the lake and once more became a large, living crocodile. It swam away with the young man and no one ever knew what became of it afterwards. Then the king commanded his servants to seize Ubaaner's wife. They carried her off to the grounds on the north side of the royal palace, where they burned her and scattered her ashes in the river.

Once King Khufu had heard the story of Ubaaner and the wax crocodile he ordered many offerings to be made in the tomb of his predecessor Nebka and gifts to be presented to the magician.

THE STORY OF THE SHIPWRECKED TRAVELLER
(From Egypt)

Prefixed to the narrative of the shipwrecked traveller is the following: "A certain servant of wise understanding has said, Let your heart be of good cheer, Oh prince. Verily we have arrived at [our] homes. The mallet has been grasped, and the anchor-post has been driven into the ground, and the bow of the boat has grounded on the bank. Thanksgivings have been offered up to God, and every man has embraced his neighbour. Our sailors have returned in peace and safety, and our fighting men have lost none of their comrades, even though we travelled to the uttermost parts of Uauat (Nubia), and through the country of Senmut (Northern Nubia). Verily we have arrived in peace, and we have reached our own land [again]. Hearken, Oh prince, to me, even though I be a poor man. Wash yourself, and let water run over your fingers. I would that you should be ready to return an answer to the man who addresses you, and to speak to the King [from] your heart, and assuredly you must give your answer promptly and without hesitation. The mouth of a man delivers him, and his words provide a covering for [his] face. Act you according to the promptings of your heart, and when you have spoken [you will have made him] be at rest."

The shipwrecked traveller then narrates his experiences in the following words: I will now speak and give you a description of the things that [once] happened to me myself [when] I was journeying to the copper mines of the king. I went down into the sea in a ship that was one hundred and fifty cubits in length, and forty cubits in breadth, and it was manned by one hundred and fifty sailors who were chosen from among the best sailors of Egypt. They had looked upon the sky, they had looked upon the land, and their hearts were more understanding than the hearts of lions. Now although they were able to say beforehand when a tempest was coming, and could tell when a squall was going to rise before it broke upon them, a storm actually overtook us when we were still on the sea. Before we could make the land the wind blew with redoubled violence, and it drove before it upon us a wave that was eight cubits [high]. A plank was driven towards me by it, and I seized it; and as for the ship, those who were therein perished, and not one of them escaped.

Then a wave of the sea bore me along and cast me up upon an island, and I passed three days there by myself, with none but mine own heart for a companion; I laid me down and slept in a hollow in a thicket, and I hugged the shade. And I lifted up my legs (i.e. I walked about), so that I might find out what to put in my mouth, and I found there figs and grapes, and all kinds of fine large berries; and there were there gourds, and melons, and pumpkins as large as barrels (?), and there were also there fish and water-fowl. There was no [food] of any sort or kind that did not grow in this island.

And when I had eaten all I could eat, I laid the remainder of the food upon the ground, for it was too much for me [to carry] in my arms. I then dug a hole in the ground and made a fire, and I prepared pieces of wood and a burnt-offering for the gods.

And I heard a sound [as of] thunder, which I thought to be [caused by] a wave of the sea, and the trees rocked and the earth quaked, and I covered my face. And I found [that the sound was caused by] a serpent that was coming towards me. It was thirty cubits in length, and its beard was more than two cubits in length, and its body was covered with [scales of] gold, and the two ridges over its eyes were of pure lapis-lazuli (i.e. they were blue); and it coiled its whole length up before me. And it opened its mouth to me, now I was lying flat on my stomach in front of it, and it said to me, "Who has brought you here? Who has brought you here, Oh miserable one? Who has brought you here? If you do not immediately declare to me who has brought you to this island, I will make you know what it is to be burnt with fire, and you will become a thing that is invisible. You speak to me, but I cannot hear what you say; I am before you, do you not know me?" Then the serpent took me in its mouth, and carried me off to the place where it was wont to rest, and it set me down there, having done me no harm whatsoever; I was sound and whole, and it had not carried away any portion of my body. And it opened its mouth to me whilst I was lying flat on my stomach, and it said to me, 'Who has brought you here? Who has brought you here, Oh miserable one? Who has brought you to this island of the sea, the two sides of which are in the waves?'

Then I made answer to the serpent, my two hands being folded humbly before it, and I said to it, "I am one who was travelling to the mines on a mission of the king in a ship that was one hundred and fifty cubits long, and fifty cubits in breadth, and it was manned by a crew of one hundred and fifty men, who were chosen from among the best sailors of Egypt. They had looked upon the sky, they had looked upon the earth, and their hearts were more understanding than the hearts of lions. They were able to say beforehand when a tempest was coming, and to tell when a squall was about to rise before it broke. The heart of every man among them was wiser than that of his neighbour, and the arm of each was stronger than that of his neighbour; there was not one weak man among them. Nevertheless it blew a gale of wind whilst we were still on the sea and before we could make the land. A gale rose, which continued to increase in violence, and with it there came upon [us] a wave eight cubits [high]. A plank of wood was driven towards me by this wave, and I seized it; and as for the ship, those who were therein perished and not one of them escaped alive [except] myself. And now behold me by your side! It was a wave of the sea that brought me to this island."

And the serpent said to me, "Have no fear, have no fear, Oh little one, and let not your face be sad, now that you have arrived at the place where I am. Verily, God has spared your life, and you have been brought to this island where there is food. There is no kind of food that is not here, and it is filled with good things of every kind. Verily, you shall pass month after month on this island, until you have come to the end of four months, and then a ship shall come, and there shall be therein sailors who are acquaintances of thine, and you shall go with them to your country, and you shall die in your native town." [And the serpent continued,] "What a joyful thing it is for the man who has experienced evil fortunes, and has passed safely through them, to declare them! I will now describe to you some of the things that have happened to me on this island. I used to live here with my brethren, and with my children who dwelt among them; now my children and my brethren together numbered seventy-five. I do not make mention of a little maiden who had been brought to me by fate. And a star fell [from heaven], and these (i.e. his children, and his brethren, and the maiden) came into the fire which fell with it. I myself was not with those who were burnt in the fire, and I was not in their midst, but I [well-nigh] died [of grief] for them. And I found a place wherein I buried them all together. Now, if you are strong, and your heart flourishes, you shall fill both your arms (i.e. embrace) with your children, and you shall kiss your wife, and you shall see your own house, which is the most beautiful thing of all, and you shall reach your country, and you shall live therein again together with your brethren, and dwell therein."

Then I cast myself down flat upon my stomach, and I pressed the ground before the serpent with my forehead, saying, "I will describe your power to the King, and I will make him understand your greatness. I will cause to be brought to you the unguent and spices called *aba*, and *hekenu*, and *inteneb*, and *khasait*, and the incense that is offered up in the temples, whereby every god is propitiated. I will relate [to him] the things that have happened to me, and declare the things that have been seen by me through your power, and praise and thanksgiving shall be made to you in my city in the presence of all the nobles of the country. I will slaughter bulls for you, and will offer them up as burnt-offerings, and I will pluck feathered fowl in your [honour]. And I will cause to come to you boats laden with all the most costly products of the land of Egypt, even according to what is done for a god who is beloved by men and women in a land far away, whom they know not." Then the serpent smiled at me, and the things which I had said to it were regarded by it in its heart as nonsense, for it said to me, "You have not a very great store of myrrh [in Egypt], and all that you have is incense. Behold, I am the Prince of Punt, and the myrrh which is therein belongs to me. And as for the *heken* which you have said you will cause to be brought to me, is it not one of the chief [products] of this island? And behold, it shall come to pass that when you have once departed from this place, you shall never more see this island, for it shall disappear into the waves."

And in due course, even as the serpent had predicted, a ship arrived, and I climbed up to the top of a high tree, and I recognised those who were in it. Then I went to announce the matter to the serpent, but I found that it had knowledge thereof already. And the serpent said to me, "A safe [journey], a safe [journey], Oh little one, to your house. You shall see your children [again]. I beseech you that my name may be held in fair repute in your city, for verily this is the thing which I desire of you."

Then I threw myself flat upon my stomach, and my two hands were folded humbly before the serpent. And the serpent gave me a [ship-] load of things, namely, myrrh, *heken*, *inteneb*, *khasait*, *thsheps* and *shaas* spices, eye-paint (antimony), skins of panthers, great balls of incense, tusks of elephants, greyhounds, apes, monkeys, and beautiful and costly products of all sorts and kinds. And when I had loaded these things into the ship, and had thrown myself flat upon my stomach in order to give thanks to it for the same, it spoke to me, saying, "Verily you shall travel to [your] country in two months, and you shall fill both your arms with your children, and you shall renew your youth in your coffin." Then I went down to the place on the sea-shore where the ship was, and I hailed the bowmen who were in the ship, and I spoke words of thanksgiving to the lord of this island, and those who were in the ship did the same. Then we set sail, and we journeyed on and returned to the country of the King, and we arrived there at the end of two months, according to all that the serpent had said. And I entered into the presence of the King, and I took with me for him the offerings which I had brought out of the island. And the King praised me and thanked me in the presence of the nobles of all his country, and he appointed me to be one of his bodyguard, and I received my wages along with those who were his [regular] servants.

Cast you your glance then upon me [Oh Prince], now that I have set my feet on my native land once more, having seen and experienced what I have seen and experienced. Listen to me, for verily it is a good thing to listen to men. And the Prince said to me, "Make not yourself out to be perfect, my friend! Does a man give water to a fowl at daybreak which he is going to kill during the day?"

Here ends [The Story of the Shipwrecked Traveller], which has been written from the beginning to the end thereof according to the text that has been found written in an [ancient] book. It has been written (i.e. copied) by Ameni-Amen-aa, a scribe with skilful fingers. Life, strength, and health be to him!

SAMBA THE COWARD
(From Sudan)

In the great country far away south, through which flows the river Nile, there lived a king who had an only child called Samba.

Now, from the time that Samba could walk he showed signs of being afraid of everything, and as he grew bigger he became more and more frightened. At first his father's friends made light of it, and said to each other:

"It is strange to see a boy of our race running into a hut at the trumpeting of an elephant, and trembling with fear if a lion cub half his size comes near him; but, after all, he is only a baby, and when he is older he will be as brave as the rest."

"Yes, he is only a baby," answered the king who overheard them, "it will be all right by-and-by." But, somehow, he sighed as he said it, and the men looked at him and made no reply.

The years passed away, and Samba had become a tall and strong youth. He was good-natured and pleasant, and was liked by all, and if during his father's hunting parties he was seldom to be seen in any place of danger, he was too great a favourite for much to be said.

"When the king holds the feast and declares him to be his heir, he will cease to be a child," murmured the rest of the people, as they had done before; and on the day of the ceremony their hearts beat gladly, and they cried to each other:

"It is Samba, Samba, whose chin is above the heads of other men, who will defend us against the tribes of the robbers!"

* * *

Not many weeks after, the dwellers in the village awoke to find that during the night their herds had been driven away, and their herdsmen carried off into slavery by their enemies. Now was the time for Samba to show the brave spirit that had come to him with his manhood, and to ride forth at the head of the warriors of his race. But Samba could nowhere be found, and a party of the avengers went on their way without him.

It was many days later before he came back, with his head held high, and a tale of a lion which he had tracked to its lair and killed, at the risk of his own life. A little while earlier and his people would have welcomed his story, and believed it all, but now it was too late.

"Samba the Coward," cried a voice from the crowd; and the name stuck to him, even the very children shouted it at him, and his father did not spare him. At length he could bear it no longer, and made up his mind to leave his own land for another where peace had reigned since the memory of man. So, early next morning, he slipped out to the king's stables, and choosing the quietest horse he could find, he rode away northwards.

Never as long as he lived did Samba forget the terrors of that journey. He could hardly sleep at night for dread of the wild beasts that might be lurking behind every rock or bush, while, by day, the distant roar of a lion would cause him to start so violently, that he almost fell from his horse. A dozen times he was on the point of turning back, and it was not the terror of the mocking words and scornful laughs that kept him from doing so, but the terror lest he should be forced to take part in their wars. Therefore he held on, and deeply thankful he felt when the walls of a city, larger than he had ever dreamed of, rose before him.

Drawing himself up to his full height, he rode proudly through the gate and past the palace, where, as was her custom, the princess was sitting on the terrace roof, watching the bustle in the street below.

"That is a gallant figure," thought she, as Samba, mounted on his big black horse, steered his way skilfully among the crowds; and, beckoning to a slave, she ordered him to go and meet the stranger, and ask him who he was and whence he came.

"Oh, princess, he is the son of a king, and heir to a country which lies near the Great River," answered the slave, when he had returned from questioning Samba. And the princess on hearing this news summoned her father, and told him that if she was not allowed to wed the stranger she would die unmarried.

Like many other fathers, the king could refuse his daughter nothing, and besides, she had rejected so many suitors already that he was quite alarmed lest no man should be good enough for her. Therefore, after a talk with Samba, who charmed him by his good humour and pleasant ways, he gave his consent, and three days later the wedding feast was celebrated with the utmost splendour.

The princess was very proud of her tall handsome husband, and for some time she was quite content that he should pass the days with her under the palm trees, telling her the stories that she loved, or amusing her with tales of the manners and customs of his country, which were so different to those of her own. But, by-and-by, this was not enough; she wanted other people to be proud of him too, and one day she said:

"I really almost wish that those Moorish thieves from the north would come on one of their robbing expeditions. I should love so to see you ride out at the head of our men, to chase them home again. Ah, how happy I should be when the city rang with your noble deeds!"

She looked lovingly at him as she spoke; but, to her surprise, his face grew dark, and he answered hastily:

"Never speak to me again of the Moors or of war. It was to escape from them that I fled from my own land, and at the first word of invasion I should leave you for ever."

"How funny you are," cried she, breaking into a laugh. "The idea of anyone as big as you being afraid of a Moor! But still, you mustn't say those things to anyone except me, or they might think you were in earnest."

* * *

Not very long after this, when the people of the city were holding a great feast outside the walls of the town, a body of Moors, who had been in hiding for days, drove off all the sheep and goats which were peacefully feeding on the slopes of a hill. Directly the loss was discovered, which was not for some hours, the king gave orders that the war drum should be beaten, and the warriors assembled in the great square before the palace, trembling with fury at the insult which had been put upon them. Loud were the cries for instant vengeance, and for Samba, son-in-law of the king, to lead them to battle. But shout as they might, Samba never came.

And where was he? No further than in a cool, dark cellar of the palace, crouching among huge earthenware pots of grain. With a rush of pain at her heart, there his wife found him, and she tried with all her strength to kindle in him a sense of shame, but in vain. Even the thought of the future danger he might run from the contempt of his subjects was as nothing when compared with the risks of the present.

"Take off your tunic of mail," said the princess at last; and her voice was so stern and cold that none would have known it. "Give it to me, and hand me besides your helmet, your sword and your spear." And with many fearful glances to right and to left, Samba stripped off the armour inlaid with gold, the property of the king's son-in-law. Silently his wife took, one by one, the pieces from him, and fastened them on her with firm hands, never even glancing at the tall form of her husband who had slunk back to his corner. When she had fastened the last buckle, and lowered her vizor, she went out, and mounting Samba's horse, gave the signal to the warriors to follow.

Now, although the princess was much shorter than her husband, she was a tall woman, and the horse which she rode was likewise higher than the rest, so that when the men caught sight of the gold-inlaid suit of chain armour, they did not doubt that Samba was taking his rightful place, and cheered him loudly. The princess bowed in answer to their greeting, but kept her vizor down; and touching her horse with the spur, she galloped at the head of her troops to charge the enemy. The Moors, who had not expected to be so quickly pursued, had scarcely time to form themselves into battle array, and were speedily put to flight. Then the little troop of horsemen returned to the city, where all sung the praises of Samba their leader.

The instant they reached the palace the princess flung her reins to a groom, and disappeared up a side staircase, by which she could, unseen, enter her own rooms. Here she found Samba lying idly on a heap of mats; but he raised his head uneasily as the door opened and looked at his wife, not feeling sure how she might act towards him. However, he need not have been afraid of harsh words: she merely unbuttoned her armour as fast as possible, and bade him put it on with all speed. Samba obeyed, not daring to ask any questions; and when he had finished the princess told him to follow her, and led him on to the flat roof of the house, below which a crowd had gathered, cheering lustily.

"Samba, the king's son-in-law! Samba, the bravest of the brave! Where is he? Let him show himself!" And when Samba did show himself the shouts and applause became louder than ever.

"See how modest he is! He leaves the glory to others!" cried they. And Samba only smiled and waved his hand, and said nothing.

Out of all the mass of people assembled there to do honour to Samba, one alone there was who did not shout and praise with the rest. This was the princess's youngest brother, whose sharp eyes had noted certain things during the fight which recalled his sister much more than they did her husband. Under promise of secrecy, he told his suspicions to the other princes, but only got laughed at, and was bidden to carry his dreams elsewhere.

"Well, well," answered the boy, "we shall see who is right; but the next time we give battle to the Moors I will take care to place a private mark on our commander."

In spite of their defeat, not many days after the Moors sent a fresh body of troops to steal some cattle, and again Samba's wife dressed herself in her husband's armour, and rode out at the head of the avenging column. This time the combat was fiercer than before, and in the thick of it her youngest brother drew near, and gave his sister a slight wound on the leg. At the moment she paid no heed to the pain, which, indeed, she scarcely felt; but when the enemy had been put to flight and the little band returned to the palace, faintness suddenly overtook her, and she could hardly stagger up the staircase to her own apartments.

"I am wounded," she cried, sinking down on the mats where he had been lying, "but do not be anxious; it is really nothing. You have only got to wound yourself slightly in the same spot and no one will guess that it was I and not you who were fighting."

"What!" cried Samba, his eyes nearly starting from his head in surprise and terror. "Can you possibly imagine that I should agree to anything so useless and painful? Why, I might as well have gone to fight myself!"

"Ah, I ought to have known better, indeed," answered the princess, in a voice that seemed to come from a long way off; but, quick as thought, the moment Samba turned his back she pierced one of his bare legs with a spear.

He gave a loud scream and staggered backwards, from astonishment, much more than from pain. But before he could speak his wife had left the room and had gone to seek the medicine man of the palace.

"My husband has been wounded," said she, when she had found him, "come and tend him with speed, for he is faint from loss of blood." And she took care that more than one person heard her words, so that all that day the people pressed up to the gate of the palace, asking for news of their brave champion.

"You see," observed the king's eldest sons, who had visited the room where Samba lay groaning, "you see, O wise young brother, that we were right and you were wrong about Samba, and that he really *did* go into the battle." But the boy answered nothing, and only shook his head doubtfully.

It was only two days later that the Moors appeared for the third time, and though the herds had been tethered in a new and safer place, they were promptly carried off as before. "For," said the Moors to each other, "the tribe will never think of our coming back so soon when they have beaten us so badly."

When the drum sounded to assemble all the fighting men, the princess rose and sought her husband.

"Samba," cried she, "my wound is worse than I thought. I can scarcely walk, and could not mount my horse without help. For to-day, then, I cannot do your work, so you must go instead of me."

"What nonsense," exclaimed Samba, "I never heard of such a thing. Why, I might be wounded, or even killed! You have three brothers. The king can choose one of them."

"They are all too young," replied his wife; "the men would not obey them. But if, indeed, you will not go, at least you can help me harness my horse." And to this Samba, who was always ready to do anything he was asked when there was no danger about it, agreed readily.

So the horse was quickly harnessed, and when it was done the princess said:

"Now ride the horse to the place of meeting outside the gates, and I will join you by a shorter way, and will change places with you." Samba, who loved riding in times of peace, mounted as she had told him, and when he was safe in the saddle, his wife dealt the horse a sharp cut with her whip, and he dashed off through the town and through the ranks of the warriors who were waiting for him. Instantly the whole place was in motion. Samba tried to check his steed, but he might as well have sought to stop the wind, and it seemed no more than a few minutes before they were grappling hand to hand with the Moors.

Then a miracle happened. Samba the coward, the skulker, the terrified, no sooner found himself pressed hard, unable to escape, than something sprang into life within him, and he fought with all his might. And when a man of his size and strength begins to fight he generally fights well.

That day the victory was really owing to Samba, and the shouts of the people were louder than ever. When he returned, bearing with him the sword of the Moorish chief, the old king pressed him in his arms and said:

"Oh, my son, how can I ever show you how grateful I am for this splendid service?"

But Samba, who was good and loyal when fear did not possess him, answered straightly:

"My father, it is to your daughter and not to me to whom thanks are due, for it is she who has turned the coward that I was into a brave man."

THE KING OF SEDO[3]

(From the Wolof people, Senegal)

In the town of Sedo, it is said, there was a King named Sabar. Sabar's armies were powerful. They conquered many towns, and many people paid tribute to him. If a neighbouring Chief passed through Sedo, he came to Sabar's house, touched his forehead to the ground, and presented gifts to the King. As the King grew old, he grew proud. His word was law in Sedo. And if his word was heard in other places, it was law there too. Sabar said to himself, "I am indeed great, for who is there to contradict me? And who is my master?"

There came to Sedo one day a minstrel, and he was called on to entertain the King. He sang a song of praise to Sabar and to Sabar's ancestors. He danced. And then he sang:

> "The dog is great among dogs,
>   Yet he serves man.

3   From *The King's Drum and Other African Stories* by Harold Courlander. Copyright 1962, 1990 by Harold Courlander. Reprinted by permission of The Emma Courlander Trust.

> *The woman is great among women,*
> *Yet she waits upon her children.*
> *The hunter is great among hunters,*
> *Yet he serves the village.*
> *Minstrels are great among minstrels,*
> *Yet they sing for the King and his slaves."*

When the song was finished, Sabar said to the minstrel, "What is the meaning of this song?"

The minstrel replied, "The meaning is that all men serve, whatever their station."

And Sabar said to him, "Not all men. The King of Sedo does not serve. It is others who serve him."

The minstrel was silent, and Sabar asked, "Is this not the truth?"

The minstrel answered, "Who am I to say the King of Sedo speaks what is not true?"

At this moment a wandering holy man came through the crowd and asked for some food. The minstrel said to the King. "Allow me to give this unfortunate man a little of the food which you have not eaten."

Sabar said, "Give it, and let us get on with the discussion."

The minstrel said, "Here is my harp until I have finished feeding him." He placed his harp in the King's hands, took a little food from the King's bowl, and gave it to the holy man. Then he came back and stood before Sabar.

"O King of Sedo," he said, "you have spoken what I could not say, for who contradicts a king? You have said that all men serve the King of Sedo and that he does not serve. Yet you have given a wandering holy man food from your bowl, and you have held the harp for a mere minstrel while he reserved another. How then can one say a king does not serve? It is said, 'The head and the body must serve each other.'"

And the minstrel picked up his harp from the hands of the King and sang:

> "The soldier is great among soldiers,
>   Yet he serves the clan.
> The King is great among kings,
>   Yet he serves his people."

THREE FAST MEN[4]
(From the Mende people, Ivory Coast)

Three young men went out to their fields to harvest millet. It began to rain. One of the men carried a basket of millet on his head. The earth was wet form the rain, and the man slipped. His foot skidded from the city of Bamako to the town of Kati. The basket of millet on his head began to fall. The man reached into a house as he slid by and picked up a knife. He cut the tall reed grass that grew along the path, wove a mat out of it, and laid it on the ground beneath him. Spilling from the falling basket, the millet fell upon the mat. The man arose, shook the millet from the mat back into the basket, and said: "If I had not had the presence of mind to make a mat and put it beneath me, I would have lost my grain."

---

4   From *The King's Drum and Other African Stories* by Harold Courlander. Copyright 1962, 1990 by Harold Courlander. Reprinted by permission of The Emma Courlander Trust.

The second young man had forty chickens in fifteen baskets, and on the way to his millet field he took the chickens from the baskets to let them feed. Suddenly a hawk swooped down, its talons ready to seize one of the chickens. The man ran swiftly among his chickens, picked them up, put each one in its proper basket, covered the baskets, and caught the swooping hawk by its talons. He said, "What do you think you are doing – trying to steal my chickens?"

The third young man and the first young man went hunting together. The first man shot an arrow at an antelope. The other man leaped forward at the same instant, caught the antelope, killed it, skinned it, cut up the meat, stretched the skin out to dry, and placed the meat in his knapsack. Then he reached out his hand and caught the first man's arrow as it arrived. He said, "What do you think you are doing – trying to shoot holes in my knapsack?"

HONOURABLE MINU
(From the Akan peoples, Ghana)

It happened one day that a poor Akim-man had to travel from his own little village to Accra – one of the big towns on the coast. This man could only speak the language of his own village – which was not understood by the men of the town. As he approached Accra he met a great herd of cows. He was surprised at the number of them, and wondered to whom they could belong. Seeing a man with them he asked him, "To whom do these cows belong?" The man did not know the language of the Akim-man, so he replied, "Minu" (I do not understand). The traveller, however, thought that Minu was the name of the owner of the cows and exclaimed, "Mr. Minu must be very rich."

He then entered the town. Very soon he saw a fine large building, and wondered to whom it might belong. The man he asked could not understand his question, so he also answered, "Minu." "Dear me! What a rich fellow Mr. Minu must be!" cried the Akim-man.

Coming to a still finer building with beautiful gardens round it, he again asked the owner's name. Again came the answer, "Minu." "How wealthy Mr. Minu is!" said our wondering traveller.

Next he came to the beach. There he saw a magnificent steamer being loaded in the harbour. He was surprised at the great cargo which was being put on board and inquired of a bystander, "To whom does this fine vessel belong?"

"Minu," replied the man. "To the Honourable Minu also! He is the richest man I ever heard of!" cried the Akim-man.

Having finished his business, the Akim-man set out for home. As he passed down one of the streets of the town he met men carrying a coffin, and followed by a long procession, all dressed in black. He asked the name of the dead person, and received the usual reply, "Minu." "Poor Mr. Minu!" cried the Akim-man. "So he has had to leave all his wealth and beautiful houses and die just as a poor person would do! Well, well – in future I will be content with my tiny house and little money." And the Akim-man went home quite pleased to his own hut.

KWOFI AND THE GODS

(From the Akan peoples, Ghana)

Kwofi was the eldest son of a farmer who had two wives. Kwofi's mother had no other children. When the boy was three years old his mother died. Kwofi was given to his stepmother to mind. After this she had many children. Kwofi, of course, was the eldest of all.

When he was about ten years old his father also died. Kwofi had now no relative but his stepmother, for whom he had to work.

As he grew older, she saw how much more clever and handsome he was than her own children, and grew very jealous of him. He was such a good hunter that day after day he came home laden with meat or with fish.

Every day she treated him in the same way. She cooked the meat, then portioned it out. She gave to each a large helping, but when it came to Kwofi's turn she would say, "Oh, my son Kwofi, there is none left for you! You must go to the field and get some ripe paw-paw." Kwofi never complained. Never once did he taste any of the meat he had hunted. At every meal the others were served, but there was never enough for him.

One evening, when the usual thing had happened, Kwofi was preparing to go to the field to fetch some paw-paw for his supper. All at once one of the gods appeared in the village, carrying a great bag over his shoulder. He summoned all the villagers together with these words: "Oh, my villagers, I come with a bag of death for you!"

Thereupon he began to distribute the contents of his bag among them. When he came to Kwofi he said: "Oh, my son Kwofi, there was never sufficient meat for you, neither is there any death."

As he said these words every one in the village died except Kwofi. He was left to reign there in peace, which he did very happily.

A STORY ABOUT MISS SALT, MISS PEPPER, ETC.
(From the Hausa people, southern Niger and northern Nigeria)

This story is about Salt, and Daudawa (sauce), and Nari (spice), and Onion-leaves, and Pepper, and Daudawar-batso (a sauce). A story, a story! Let it go, let it come.

Salt, and Daudawa, and Ground-nut, and Onion-leaves, and Pepper, and Daudawar-batso heard a report of a certain youth, by name Daskandarini. Now he was a beautiful youth, the son of the evil spirit. They all rose up, and turned into beautiful maidens, and they set off. As they (Salt, Onion-leaves, etc.) were going along, Daudawar-batso followed them.

They drove her off, telling her she stank. But she crouched down until they had gone on. She kept following them behind, until they reached a certain stream. There they came across an old woman; she was bathing. She said they must rub down her back for her, but this one said, "May Allah save me that I should lift my hand to touch an old woman's back." And the old woman did not say anything more.

They passed on, and soon Daudawar-batso came, and met her washing. She greeted her, and she answered and said, "Maiden, where are you going?" She replied, "I am going to where a certain youth is." And the old woman said, "Rub my back for me!" She said, "All right." She stopped, and rubbed her back well for her. The old woman said, "May Allah bless you." And she said, "This youth to whom you are all going to, have you known his name?" She said, "No, we do not know his name."

Then the old woman said, "He is my son, his name is Daskandarini, but you must not tell them." Then she ceased. She was following them far behind till they got to the place where the boy was. They were about to enter, but he said, "Go back, and enter one at a time." They said, "It is well," and returned. And then Salt came forward, and was about to enter, "little girl, go back." She turned back. So Daudawa came forward.

When she was about to enter, she was asked, "Who are you?" She said,"It is I." "Who are you? What is your name?" "My name is Daudawa, who makes the soup sweet." And he said, "What is my name?" She said, "I do not know your name, little boy, I do not know your name." He said, "Turn back, little girl, turn back." She turned back, and sat down.

Then Nari (spice) rose up and came forward, and she was about to enter when she was asked, "Who is this little girl? Who is this?" She said, "It is I who greet you, little boy, it is I who greet you." "What is your name, little girl, what is your name?" "My name is Nari, who makes the soup savoury." "I have heard your name, little girl, I have heard your name. Speak my name." She said, "I do not know your name, little boy, I do not know your name." "Turn back, little girl, turn back." So she turned back, and sat down.

Then Onion-leaves rose and came up, and she stuck her head into the room and was asked, "Who is this little girl, who is this?" "It is I who salute you, little boy, it is I who salute you." "What is your name, little girl, what is your name?" "My name is Onion-leaves, who makes the soup smell nicely." He said, "I have heard your name, little girl. What is my name?" She said, "I do not know your name, little boy, I do not know your name." "Turn back, little girl, turn back." So she turned back.

Now Pepper came along; she said, "Your pardon, little boy, your pardon." She was asked who was there. She said, "It is I, Pepper, little boy, it is I, Pepper, who make the soup hot." "I have heard your name, little girl, I have heard your name. Tell me my name, little girl, tell me my name." "I do not know your name, little boy, I do not know your name." He said, "Turn back, little maid, turn back."

There was only left Daudawar-batso, and they said, "Are not you coming?" She said, "Can I enter the house where such good people as you have gone, and been driven away? Would not they the sooner drive me out who stink?" They said, "Rise up and go." So she got up and went. He asked her, "Who is there, little girl, who is there?" And she said, "It is I who am greeting you, little boy, it is I who am greeting you." "What is your name, little girl, what is your name?" "My name is Batso, little boy, my name is Batso, which makes the soup smell." He said, "I have heard your name, little girl, I have heard your name. There remains my name to be told." She said, "Daskandarini, little boy, Daskandarini." And he said, "Enter."

A rug was spread for her, clothes were given to her, and slippers of gold; and then of these who had driven her away one said, "I will always sweep for you"; another, "I will pound for you."

Another said, "I will see about drawing water for you"; and another, "I will pound the ingredients of the soup"; and another, "I will stir the food." They all became her handmaids.

And the moral of all this is, if you see a man is poor do not despise him; you do not know but that some day he may be better than you.

OLURONBI

(From the Yoruba people, southern Nigeria)

In a certain village no children had been born for many years, and the people were greatly distressed. At last all the women of the village went together into the forest, to the magic tree, the Iroko, and implored the spirit of the tree to help them.

The Iroko-man asked what gifts they would bring if he consented to help them, and the women eagerly promised him corn, yams, fruit, goats, and sheep; but Oluronbi, the young wife of a wood-carver, promised to bring her first child.

In due course children came to the village, and the most beautiful of all the children was the one born to Oluronbi. She and her husband so greatly loved their child that they could not consent to give it up to the Iroko-man.

The other women took their promised gifts of corn, yams, fruit, goats, and sheep; but Oluronbi took nothing to propitiate. the tree.

Alas! one day as Oluronbi passed through the forest, the Iroko-man seized her and changed her into a small brown bird, which sat on the branches of the tree and plaintively sang:

"One promised a sheep, One promised a goat, One promised fruit, But Oluronbi promised her child."

When the wood-carver heard the bird's song, he realized what had happened, and tried to find some means of regaining his wife.

After thinking for many days, he began to carve a large wooden doll, like a real child in size and appearance, and with a small gold chain round its neck. Covering it with a beautiful native cloth, he laid it at the foot of the tree. The Iroko-man thought that this was Oluronbi's child, so he transformed the little bird once more into a woman and snatched up the child into the branches.

Oluronbi joyfully returned home, and was careful never to stray into the forest again.

OLE AND THE ANTS

(From the Yoruba people, southern Nigeria)

There was a certain lazy and disagreeable man whom everyone called "Ole," or "Lazy one." He liked to profit by the work of others, and was also very inquisitive about other people's affairs.

Once he saw that the ants had begun building a pillar in the compound of his house. But though the ants destroyed all the plants in the compound, and stripped all the trees, Ole would not trouble to kill them, or to break down their pillar.

Instead, he thought to himself: "When the ants have made this pillar very high, I will sit on the top of it, and then I shall be able to see all that my neighbours are doing without leaving my compound."

This thought pleased him, and he was glad that the ants swarmed in his compound. Each day the pillar grew higher, and at last the ants ceased their building and began again elsewhere. Ole then climbed up on to the pillar and spent the whole day observing the doings of his neighbours, and laughing at their activity.

> *"Here sit I like a great Chief,*
> *And I see all things!"*

sang Ole.

But while he sat on the pillar, the ants began to demolish his house and all that it contained, and in a short time there was nothing left of all his food and possessions.

Ole thus became the laughing-stock of the village, and everyone who saw him cried: "Ku ijoko!" or "Greetings to you on your sitting!"

Soon afterwards he died, and it is not known to this day whether he died of shame or of laziness.

THE SECRET OF THE FISHING-BASKETS
(From the Yoruba people, southern Nigeria)

Across a certain river a poor fisherman set a row of stakes, and on each stake was fastened a basket in which he hoped to trap the fishes as they swam down the river.

But his luck was very bad, and every evening, as he went from basket to basket in his canoe, he was disappointed to find that no fishes, or only a few very small ones, had been caught.

This made him very sad, and he was forced to live frugally.

One day he found a stranger lying asleep on the river-bank. Instead of killing the stranger, the fisherman spoke kindly to him, and invited him to share his evening meal.

The stranger appeared very pleased and ate and drank, but spoke no word at all, The fisherman thought: "He speaks another language."

Quite suddenly the stranger vanished, and only the remains of the meal convinced the fisherman that he had not been dreaming.

The next evening when he went to empty his baskets, he was astonished to find them overflowing with fish. He could not account for his good fortune, and his surprise was even greater when the same thing occurred the next day. On the third day the baskets were again quite full, and when the fisherman came to the last basket he saw that it contained a single monstrous fish.

"Do you not know me?" said the fish.

"Indeed no, Mr. Fish. I have never seen you before!" declared the fisherman, nearly upsetting the canoe in his astonishment.

"Have you forgotten the stranger whom you treated so courteously?" went on the fish. "It was I, and I am the King of the fishes. I am grateful for your kindness and intend to reward you."

Then the fish jumped into the river with a great splash. But ever afterwards the fishing-baskets were full every evening, and the fisherman became rich and prosperous.

WHY A MURDERER MUST DIE

(From the Ekoi people, Nigeria and Cameroon)

There was once a woman named Ukpong Ma, who had only one daughter. Just before it was time to put the girl into the fatting-house the mother died.

One day the husband, whose name was Uponnsoraw, set out for market. On his way he passed through a neighbouring town, where he saw a beautiful woman, and persuaded her to return with him as his wife.

When the couple reached the man's house, his daughter came out to salute them, and the new wife saw that in a little while her step-daughter would be more beautiful than she. So she hated the girl, and thought how she might destroy her.

One day, therefore, when the husband went out to hunt, the new wife called to her step-child and said, "Take the great water-pot, and go to the far river for water. Do not bring home any from the streams near by."

So soon as the girl had set out, the new wife killed a goat, ate the best part of the meat herself, and hid what was left over.

As the girl came back from the river it began to grow dark. Rain fell and she felt cold. When she reached home she went to the fireside to warm herself. Some water fell down on her, and she said to the new wife, "Where does it come from?" and the latter answered, "The roof leaks."

When Uponnsoraw came back from the hunt, he could not see the goat, so he called to his daughter and asked where it was. She answered, "Your new wife sent me to the river for water. I have only just come back, and do not know what has been happening at home."

At this the cruel step-mother came out of her room and said, "Let us practise the charm to find who has stolen the goat."

They sent for the Diviner, and he came with a very long rope and said, "We will go down to the river where the girl filled the jar."

Now the new wife was a great witch, so she secretly made a strong charm. Then, when they came to the river and threw the rope across, she stood on the brink and called, "If I have stolen the goat may the rope break and let me fall into the river. If I am guiltless may I walk over safely."

She put her foot upon the rope, but the charm held, and she crossed without mishap.

The young girl stood by the river-side and said the same words. Then she walked on the rope as far as mid-stream. There the charm which the witch had made caused it to break, and the girl fell into the water. A great crocodile came up to the surface and caught her as she fell. Then all the people said, "She it was who stole the goat." Only her father said, "My daughter never stole anything. I must find out the reason of her death."

A palm tree grew by the river-side, just by the place where the girl was lost, and one day a man climbed up this to collect palm wine.

Now beneath the water was the house of a were-crocodile, and she it was who had seized the girl, and kept her all this while as a slave. When the man began to climb the palm tree the crocodile was angry. So she took an axe and put it into the girl's hand and said, "Go up to the top of the water and throw this axe at the man, that he may leave my palm tree and go back whence he came."

The girl did as she was bidden, but threw the axe so as not to hit the man. As it struck the tree the climber looked down and saw her. He therefore went back to his town with all haste, and told her father what had happened.

The latter wondered, and went before the chief and said, "This man says that he saw my daughter who died two years ago in the great river."

The chief was angry because he thought that the man was lying. So he ordered that chains should be brought and put upon him. The man, however, begged that they would take him to the place where he had seen the girl, and watch while he climbed the palm tree. To this the chief consented, and sent him, with three men, to the river. With them also went Uponnsoraw. The man climbed the tree and struck it with his matchet. No sooner did the girl hear than she rose to the surface, covered with ornaments, but sank down again almost at once. On this all the men ran back to the chief to tell him that the man had spoken truth, for they also had seen the girl.

The whole town set forth to fetch the Diviner, and asked him to practise the charm. This he did, and told them they must bring a black cock, an egg, a piece of white cloth, a ball of red cam wood dye, and some of the yellow 'ogokk' powder; also they must bring the great nets which are used in hunting. All these things, save the red powder, they must sacrifice to the crocodile, but the nets they must hold ready in their hands.

As soon as they threw the offering into the river the girl rose to the surface. When she appeared they cast the nets and caught her like a fish. Then they drew her to land and washed her with the red powder and with sand, and carried her in triumph to the house of the chief.

The cruel witch-wife came out to salute her, but no sooner did the girl hear her voice than she said:

"I will not see her at all. Crocodile told me a story about her. It was she who stole the goat." Then she said to her father, "Call all the people. I wish to say something."

When the townsfolk had come together they carried the girl before the Egbo house, where she stood up and said:

"Here I am. It was the new wife of my father who stole the goat that she might destroy me, lest I should be counted more beautiful than herself. Then she made a strong magic, so that the rope might bear her across the river, but break when I tried to pass over. Therefore all the people thought that I was guilty of the theft. Judge now, oh ye people, between her and me."

Then the Head Chief said, "Let the town give judgment"; and they cried in a great shout:

"The witch shall die for her crime." Then they set up two great posts, and from these hanged the woman by the very cord which by her magic she had caused to break beneath the feet of the innocent girl. Thus died the witch in the sight of all men.

From that day forward a law was made, "If anyone is proved guilty of the death of another, he shall surely die."

That is the reason why if anyone kills another they must hang.

ABUNDANCE: A PLAY ON THE MEANING OF A WORD
(From the Fang and Bulu peoples, Cameroon)

There was a certain Man who was very poor; he had no goods with which to buy a wife. He went one day into the forest to set snares. On the morrow, he went off to examine them; and found a Wild-Goat caught in the snares. He rejoiced and said, "I must eat Mbindi today!"

But the Wild-Goat said to that Man, "Let me alone, Bwinge is coming after awhile."

So, the Man, thinking that 'Bwinge' was the name of some other and more desirable animal, at once let the Wild-Goat loose, and went off to his town. On the next day, the Man went to examine the snare, to see whether Bwinge was there, and found Hog caught fast in the net. And he exclaimed, "I must eat Ngweya today!"

But the Hog said, "Let me go. Bwinge is coming." The man at once left the Hog, (still thinking that many more were coming); and it went away.

The Man wondered, and said to himself, "What Thing is it that is named 'Bwinge'?"

On another day, he went to set his snare. He found there a dwarf child of a Human Being; and, in anger, he said, "You are the one who has caused me to send away the beasts? Is it possible that you are he who is 'Bwinge'? I shall kill you." But the dwarf said, "No! don't kill me. I will call Ungumba for you." So, the Man said, "Call in a hurry!"

The Dwarf ordered, "Let guns come!" And they at once came. (This was done by the Dwarf's Magic-Power.) The Man again said, "Call, in a hurry!" The Dwarf called for women; and they came. The Man again said to him, "Call for Goats, in a hurry!" And they came, with abundance of other things.

Then the Man freed him, and said to him, "Go!"

The Man also went his way with his riches. And he became a great man. This was because of his patient waiting.

THE SEARCH FOR THE HOME OF THE SUN
(From the Songora people, central Africa)

Master and friends. We have an old phrase among us which is very common. It is said that he who waits and waits for his turn, may wait too long, and lose his chance. My tongue is not nimble like some, and my words do not flow like the deep river. I am rather like the brook which is fretted by the stones in its bed, and I hope after this explanation you will not be too impatient with me.

My tale is about King Masama and his tribe, the Balira, who dwelt far in the inmost region, behind (east) us, who throng the banks of the great river. They were formerly very numerous, and many of them came to live among us, but one day King Masama and the rest of the tribe left their country and went eastward, and they have never been heard of since, but those who chose to stay with us explained their disappearance in this way.

A woman, one cold night, after making up her fire on the hearth, went to sleep. In the middle of the night the fire had spread, and spread, and began to lick up the litter on the floor, and from the litter it crept to her bed of dry banana-leaves, and in a little time shot up into flames. When the woman and her husband were at last awakened by the heat, the flames had already mounted into the roof, and were burning furiously. Soon they broke through the top and leaped up into the night, and a gust of wind came and carried the long flames like a stream of fire towards the neighbouring huts, and in a short time the fire had caught hold of every house, and the village was entirely burned. It was soon known that besides burning up their houses and much property, several old people and infants had been destroyed by the fire, and the people were horror-struck and angry.

Then one voice said, "We all know in whose house the fire began, and the owner of it must make our losses good to us."

The woman's husband heard this, and was alarmed, and guiltily fled into the woods.

In the morning a council of the elders was held, and it was agreed that the man in whose house the fire commenced should be made to pay for his carelessness, and they forthwith searched for him. But when they sought for him he could not be found. Then all the young warriors who were cunning in wood-craft, girded and armed themselves, and searched for the trail, and when one of them had found it, he cried out, and the others gathered themselves about him and took it up, and when many eyes were set upon it, the trail could not be lost.

They soon came up to the man, for he was seated under a tree, bitterly weeping.

Without a word they took hold of him by the arms and bore him along with them, and brought him before the village fathers. He was not a common man by any means. He was known as one of Masama's principal men, and one whose advice had been often followed.

"Oh," said everybody, "he is a rich man, and well able to pay; yet, if he gives all he has got, it will not be equal to our loss."

The fathers talked a long time over the matter, and at last decided that to save his forfeited life he should freely turn over to them all his property. And he did so. His plantation of bananas and plantains, his plots of beans, yams, manioc, potatoes, ground-nuts, his slaves, spears, shields, knives, paddles and canoes. When he had given up all, the hearts of the people became softened towards him, and they forgave him the rest.

After the elder's property had been equally divided among the sufferers by the fire, the people gained new courage, and set about rebuilding their homes, and before long they had a new village, and they had made themselves as comfortable as ever.

Then King Masama made a law, a very severe law – to the effect that, in future, no fire should be lit in the houses during the day or night; and the people, who were now much alarmed about fire, with one heart agreed to keep the law. But it was soon felt that the cure for the evil was as cruel as the fire had been. For the houses had been thatched with green banana-leaves, the timbers were green and wet with their sap, the floor was damp and cold, the air was deadly, and the people began to suffer from joint aches, and their knees were stiff, and the pains travelled from one place to another through their bodies. The village was filled with groaning.

Masama suffered more than all, for he was old. He shivered night and day, and his teeth chattered sometimes so that he could not talk, and after that his head would burn, and the hot sweat would pour from him, so that he knew no rest.

Then the king gathered his chiefs and principal men together, and said:

"Oh, my people, this is unendurable, for life is with me now but one continuous ague. Let us leave this country, for it is bewitched, and if I stay longer there will be nothing left of me. Lo, my joints are stiffened with my disease, and my muscles are withering. The only time I feel a little ease is when I lie on the hot ashes without the house, but when the rains fall I must needs withdraw indoors, and there I find no comfort, for the mould spreads everywhere. Let us hence at once to seek a warmer clime. Behold whence the sun issues daily in the morning, hot and glowing; there, where his home is, must be warmth, and we shall need no fire. What say you?"

Masama's words revived their drooping spirits. They looked towards the sun as they saw him mount the sky, and felt his cheering glow on their naked breasts and shoulders, and they cried with one accord: "Let us hence, and seek the place whence he comes."

And the people got ready and piled their belongings in the canoes, and on a certain day they left their village and ascended their broad river, the Lira. Day after day they paddled up the stream, and we heard of them from the Bafanya as they passed by their country, and the Bafanya heard of them for a long distance up – from the next tribe – the Bamoru – and the Bamoru heard about them arriving near the Mountain Land beyond.

Not until a long time afterwards did we hear what became of Masama and his people.

It was said that the Balira, when the river had become shallow and small, left their canoes and travelled by land among little hills, and after winding in and out amongst them they came to the foot of the tall mountain which stands like a grandsire amongst the smaller mountains. Up the sides of the big mountain they straggled, the stronger and more active of them ahead, and as the days passed, they saw that the world was cold and dark until the sun showed himself over the edge of the big mountain, when the day became more agreeable, for the heat pierced into their very marrows, and made their hearts rejoice. The greater the heat became, the more certain were they that they were drawing near the home of the sun. And so they pressed on and on, day after day, winding along one side of the mountain, and then turning to wind again still higher. Each day, as they advanced towards the top, the heat became greater and greater. Between them and the sun there was now not the smallest shrub or leaf, and it became so fiercely hot that finally not a drop of sweat was left in their bodies. One day, when not a cloud was in the sky, and the world was all below them – far down like a great buffalo hide – the sun came out over the rim of the mountain like a ball of fire, and the nearest of them to the top were dried like a leaf over a flame, and those who were behind were amazed at its burning force, and felt, as he sailed over their heads, that it was too late for them to escape. Their skins began to shrivel up and crackle, and fall off, and none of those who were high up on the mountain side were left alive. But a few of those who were nearest the bottom, and the forest belts, managed to take shelter, and remaining there until night, they took advantage of the darkness, when the sun sleeps, to fly from the home of the sun. Except a few poor old people and toddling children, there was none left of the once populous tribe of the Balira.

That is my story. We who live by the great river have taken the lesson, which the end of this tribe has been to us, close to our hearts, and it is this. Kings who insist that their wills should be followed, and never care to take counsel with their people, are as little to be heeded as children who babble of what they cannot know, and therefore in our villages we have many elders who take all matters from the chief and turn them over in their minds, and when they are agreed, they give the doing of them to the chief, who can act only as the elders decree.

SUDIKA-MBAMBI THE INVINCIBLE

(From the Bantu-speaking people, Angola)

Sudika-Mbambi was the son of Nzua dia Kimanaweze, who married the daughter of the Sun and Moon. The young couple were living with Nzua's parents, when one day Kimanaweze sent his son away to Loanda to trade. The son demurred, but the father insisted, so he went. While he was gone certain cannibal monsters, called *makishi*, descended on the village and sacked it – all the people who were not killed fled. Nzua, when he returned, found no houses and no people; searching over the cultivated ground, he at last came across his wife, but she was so changed that he did not recognize her at first. "The *makishi* have destroyed us," was her explanation of what had happened.

They seem to have camped and cultivated as best they could; and in due course Sudika-Mbambi ('the Thunderbolt') was born. He was a wonder-child, who spoke before his entrance into the world, and came forth equipped with knife, stick, and his *kilembe* (a 'mythic plant', explained as 'life-tree'), which he requested his mother to plant at the back of the house. Scarcely had he made his appearance when another voice was heard, and his twin brother Kabundungulu was born. The first thing they did was to cut down poles and build a house for their parents. Soon after this, Sudika-Mbambi announced that he was going to fight the *makishi*. He told Kabundungulu to stay at home and to keep an eye on the *kilembe*: if it withered he would know that his brother was dead; he then set out. On his way he was joined by four beings who called themselves *kipalendes* and boasted various accomplishments – building a house on the bare rock (a sheer impossibility under local conditions), carving ten clubs a day, and other more recondite operations, none of which, however, as the event proved, they could accomplish successfully. When they had gone a certain distance through the bush Sudika Mbambi directed them to halt and build a house, in order to fight the *makishi*. As soon as he had cut one pole all the others needed cut themselves. He ordered the kipalende who had said he could erect a house on a rock to begin building, but as fast as a pole was set up it fell down again. The leader then took the work in hand, and it was speedily finished.

Next day he set out to fight the *makishi*, with three *kipalendes*, leaving the fourth in the house. To him soon after appeared an old woman, who told him that he might marry her granddaughter if he would fight her (the grandmother) and overcome her. They wrestled, but the old woman soon threw the *kipalende*, placed a large stone on top of him as he lay on the ground, and left him there, unable to move.

Sudika-Mbambi, who had the gift of second-sight, at once knew what had happened, returned with the other three, and released the *kipalende*. He told his story, and the others derided him for being beaten by a woman. Next day he accompanied the rest, the second *kipalende* remaining in the house. No details are given of the fighting with the *makishi*, beyond the statement that "they are firing." The second *kipalende* met with the same fate as his brother, and again Sudika-Mbambi was immediately aware of it. The incident was repeated on the third and on the fourth day. On the fifth Sudika-Mbambi sent the *kipalendes* to the war, and stayed behind himself. The old woman challenged him; he fought her and killed her – she seems to have been a peculiarly malignant kind of witch, who had kept her granddaughter shut up in a stone house, presumably as a lure for unwary strangers. It is not stated what she intended to do with the captives whom she secured under heavy stones, but, judging from what takes place in other stories of this kind, one may conclude that they were kept to be eaten in due course.

Sudika-Mbambi married the old witch's granddaughter, and they settled down in the stone house. The *kipalendes* returned with the news that the *makishi* were completely defeated, and all went well for a time.

Treachery of the Kipalendes

The *kipalendes*, however, became envious of their leader's good fortune, and plotted to kill him. They dug a hole in the place where he usually rested and covered it with mats; when he came in tired they pressed him to sit down, which he did, and immediately fell into the hole. They covered it up, and thought they had made an end of him. His younger brother, at home, went to look at the 'life-tree', and found that it had withered. Thinking that, perhaps, there was still some hope, he poured water on it, and it grew green again.

Sudika-Mbambi was not killed by the fall; when he reached the bottom of the pit he looked round and saw an opening. Entering this, he found himself in a road – the road, in fact, which leads to the country of the dead. When he had gone some distance he came upon an old woman, or, rather, the upper half of one (half-beings are very common in African folklore, but they are usually split lengthways, having one eye, one arm, one leg, and so on), hoeing her garden by the wayside. He greeted her, and she returned his greeting. He then asked her to show him the way, and she said she would do so if he would hoe a little for her, which he did. She set him on the road, and told him to take the narrow path, not the broad one, and before arriving at Kalunga-ngombe's house he must carry a jug of red pepper and a jug of wisdom. It is not explained how he was to procure these, though it is evident from the sequel that he did so, nor how they were to be used, except that Kalunga-ngombe makes it a condition that anyone who wants to marry his daughter must bring them with him. We have not previously been told that this was Sudika-Mbambi's intention. On arriving at the house a fierce dog barked at him; he scolded it, and it let him pass. He entered, and was courteously welcomed by people who showed him into the guest house and spread a mat for him. He then announced that he had come to marry the daughter of Kalunga-ngombe. Kalunga answered that he consented if Sudika-Mbambi had fulfilled the conditions. He then retired for the night, and a meal was sent in to him-a live cock and a bowl of the local porridge (*Junji*). He ate the porridge, with some meat which he had brought with him; instead of killing the cock he kept him under his bed. Evidently it was thought he would assume that the fowl was meant for him to eat (perhaps we have here a remnant of the belief, not known to or not understood by the narrator of the story, that the living must not eat of the food of the dead), and a trick was intended, to prevent his return to the upper world. In the middle of the night he heard people inquiring who had killed Kalunga's cock; but the cock crowed from under the bed, and Sudika-Mbambi was not trapped. Next morning, when he reminded Kalunga of his promise, he was told that the daughter had been carried off by the huge serpent called Kinyoka kya Tumba, and that if he wanted to marry her he must rescue her.

Sudika-Mbambi started for Kinyoka's abode, and asked for him. Kinyoka's wife said, "He has gone shooting." Sudika-Mbambi waited awhile, and presently saw driver ants approaching – the dreaded ants which would consume any living thing left helpless in their path. He stood his ground and beat them off; they were followed by red ants, these by a swarm of bees, and these by wasps, but none of them harmed him. Then Kinyoka's five heads appeared, one after the other. Sudika-Mbambi cut off each as it came, and when the fifth fell the snake was dead. He went into the house, found Kalunga's daughter there, and took her home to her father.

But Kalunga was not yet satisfied. There was a giant fish, Kimbiji, which kept catching his goats and pigs. Sudika-Mbambi baited a large hook with a sucking-pig and caught Kimbiji, but even he was not strong enough to pull the monster to land. He fell into the water, and Kimbiji swallowed him.

Kabundungulu, far away at their home, saw that his brother's life-tree had withered once more, and set out to find him. He reached the house where the *kipalendes* were keeping Sudika-Mbambi's wife captive, and asked where he was. They denied all knowledge of him, but he felt certain there had been foul play. "You have killed him. Uncover the grave." They opened up the pit, and Kabundungulu descended into it. He met with the old woman, and was directed to Kalunga-ngombe's dwelling. On inquiring for his brother he was told, "Kimbiji has swallowed him." Kabundungulu asked for a pig, baited his hook, and called the people to his help. Between them they landed the fish, and Kabundungulu cut it open. He found his brother's bones inside it, and took them out. Then he said, "My elder, arise!" and the bones came to life. Sudika-Mbambi married Kalunga-ngombe's daughter, and set out for home with her and his brother. They reached the pit, which had been filled in, and the ground cracked and they got out. They drove away the four *kipalendes* and, having got rid of them, settled down to a happy life.

Kabundungulu felt that he was being unfairly treated, since his brother had two wives, while he had none, and asked for one of them to be handed over to him. Sudika-Mbambi pointed out that this was impossible, as he was already married to both of them, and no more was said for the time being. But some time later, when Sudika-Mbambi returned from hunting, his wife complained to him that Kabundungulu was persecuting them both with his attentions. This led to a desperate quarrel between the brothers, and they fought with swords, but could not kill each other. Both were endowed with some magical power, so that the swords would not cut, and neither could be wounded. At last they got tired of fighting and separated, the elder going east and the younger west.

THE ABSENT-MINDED BRIDEGROOM
(From Uganda)

Once upon a time there was a man called Nagamba, who was very absent-minded. Everybody laughed at him, but he did not mind. He had many friends and was quite a good fellow. At last the time came for his marriage, and he paid the dowry and arranged the feast, and married his sweetheart, and they started on the journey to his house. But as they walked along they came to a place called Nakuse, and Nagamba remembered that a friend of his lived there; so he said to his bride:

"Sit here and rest in the shade for a little while, and I will fetch you a cooling drink."

When he got to his friend's house he found a feast going on and many people he knew were there, and he sat down with them and forgot the poor little bride sitting in the shade waiting for a cooling drink. And the sun went down, and night fell, and still he sat on and talked and joked and sang, and the dawn broke in the east and suddenly the cocks crowed. Nagamba sprang to his feet:

"My friends," he cried, "I am married, and my bride sits in the shade waiting for a cooling drink."

They all went to find her; but the girl had become tired of waiting and had returned to her father's house, and refused to go back to Nagamba, and as no one else would marry him he remained a bachelor all his life. And now in Uganda this has become a proverb; if a man is absent-minded and forgetful, his friends say: "You will never get a wife; you will have the fate of Nagamba, the absent-minded bridegroom.

THE QUITS OF GOMBA
(From Uganda)

There was a battle going on round the village of Gomba. In the village there was a lame man who had never walked. Every morning he was carried out into the sunny courtyard and every evening he was carried back to his house; but the battle was raging, and no one remembered the lame man. As he lay in his house he saw a blind man passing by, and a sudden thought struck him. He called to the blind man:

"Come here, my friend, I have something important to tell you." The blind man groped his way with his long stick till he stood before the lame man, who said:

"Listen, my friend, no one has remembered us during the battle, and assuredly we shall die, you who are blind, and I who am lame; but I have a plan. Take me on your back, and we will escape from the village. I will be eyes to you, and you shall be feet to me."

The blind man agreed to the plan and hoisted the lame man on his back, and they escaped from Gomba. When they reached safety the blind man said: "Give me a reward, for I have saved your life."

But the lame man said, "Not so, it was I who saved yours." They spoke hot and angry words to each other, and at last they decided to take the case to the Chief's Council. But when the Chief heard it, he said: "There is no case; the lame man was eyes to the blind, and. the blind man was feet to the lame, both have saved their lives, which in itself is a great reward. The words are finished."

And now this has become a proverb in Uganda. When two men quarrel and both of them are in the right (or in the wrong) the people say, "It is a case of the Quits of Gomba."

THE STORY OF THE FROG
(From Uganda)

If a frog comes into a house in Uganda and you call a boy and say, "Drive that frog away," he will not do so, but he goes and calls a married man who drives the frog into the garden, and if you ask the boy:

"Are you afraid of frogs?" he will say, "No; but it is our custom to call a married man to drive one out of the house."

Now I will tell you how this became a custom. Long ago there was a widow who had a beautiful daughter, and they lived in a round hut in a banana garden. One day the girl saw a frog in the road. The poor creature was panting along in the sun, for it was midday and there was no shade. Every moment it grew weaker, and soon it would have fainted, but the girl picked it up and carried it into her shady banana garden and put it down in a pool of water where it soon revived. The next day as the girl was peeling bananas in the kitchen she heard a croak at the door and there was the frog.

"Good morning," he said, "I have come to thank you for saving my life. Some day I may be able to repay your kindness."

They became great friends, and the frog came every day to the kitchen and told the girl many stories about the animals. One day he noticed that she looked sad. "What is your sorrow?" he said. "Cannot you tell your friend?" So the girl told him. "My guardians are arranging for my marriage, and there are four men who want to marry me, and I do not know which to choose."

The frog said, "Now, I will give you some advice. Choose a man who has a kind heart: that is greater wealth than flocks and herds and a great chieftainship."

But the girl said, "How am I to know which one has a kind heart?"

Then the frog said, "We will make a little plan and find out. I know that *you* have a kind heart because you saved my life. I will help you to choose a man who is kind to animals. If he is kind to animals he will be kind to you."

So they arranged a plan, and the girl went to her guardian, and said, "I want to choose my husband for myself. I want the four men to come one by one, on an appointed day, and I will choose."

The guardian consented, and they arranged a day, and laid freshly cut grass down in the house, and the girl dressed herself in a beautiful bark cloth, and sat on a new mat, and three old ladies of her father's tribe sat near her to see that everything was done properly and in order. But they knew nothing about the frog.

As the first lover entered the porch the frog hopped out in front of him and croaked. He drove it away angrily, and went into the house, and the girl refused him at once. This happened to three young men and as the fourth entered the porch he stepped carefully over the frog, and when he had greeted the girl and the old ladies, he said, "There is a frog in the porch, does the croaking annoy you?"

"Not at all," said the girl; "I like frogs."

"I am glad of that," said the young man, "for I like frogs too." Then they both burst out laughing, which was a very improper thing to do, and shocked the old ladies very much; but it made them friends, and the girl decided to marry him, and they lived happy ever after.

That is why a boy will never drive away a frog. He thinks that if he does so the girl he wants to marry will refuse him.

THE CHILDREN AND THE ZIMWI
(From the Swahili-speaking peoples)

Some little girls went out to look for shells on the seashore. One of them found a very beautiful shell and, fearing to lose it, laid it on a rock, so that she could pick it up on the way home. However, as they were returning she forgot it till they had passed the place, and then, suddenly remembering it, asked her companions to go back with her. They refused, and she went alone, singing to keep up her courage, and found a *zimwi* sitting on the rock. He said, "What do you want?" and she sang her song over again. He said, "I can't hear you. Come closer!" And when she had done so he seized her and put her into a barrel (*pipa*) which he was carrying.

He then set off on his travels, and when he came to a village made for the place of meeting and announced that he was prepared to give a musical entertainment in return for a meal. "I have this drum of mine. I should like a fowl and rice." He beat the drum, and the imprisoned child sang in time to the rhythm, to the delight of everyone. He was given plenty of food, but gave none to the girl. He went on and repeated his performance at the next village, which happened to be the girl's own home. The report of his music seems to have preceded him, for the people said, "We have heard, Oh *zimwi*, that you have a most beautiful drum; now, please, play to us!" He asked for *pombe* (native beer), and, being promised that he should have some, began to beat the drum, and the girl sang. Her parents at once recognized her voice, and when the performance was over supplied the drummer with all the liquid refreshment he required. He soon went to sleep, and they opened the drum, released their daughter, and hid her in the inner compartment of the hut. They then put into the drum a snake and a swarm of bees and some biting ants, and fastened it up again.

In the Sesuto and Xosa versions the parents, instead of making the ogre drunk, induce him to go to the stream for water, and give him a leaky pot in order to delay his return as long as possible. In one case they put in a dog as well as the venomous ants, in the other snakes and toads, the latter being supposed poisonous.

After a while they awakened him, saying, "Ogre, wake up! Some strangers have arrived, and they want to hear your music." So he lifted his drum and began to beat it, but the voice was silent. He went on beating, but no other sound was heard, and at last he took his leave, and was not pressed to stay.

When he had gone a certain distance and was no longer in sight of the village he stopped and opened his drum. Immediately the snake shot out and bit him, the bees stung him, and he died.

The Baleful Pumpkin

But that was not the end of him. On the spot where he died there sprang up a pumpkin-vine, which bore pumpkins of unusual size. One day some small boys passing by stopped to admire them, and, prompted by the destructive instinct which seems to be inherent in the very young of all climes, exclaimed, "Jolly fine pumpkins, these! Let's get father's sword and have a slash at them!"

The largest of the pumpkins waxed wroth and chased the children – breaking off its stem and rolling over and over, one must suppose – and they took to their heels. In their headlong flight they came to a river, and saw the old ferryman sitting on the bank by his canoe.

"You, Daddy, ferry us over! Take us to the other side! We are running away from a pumpkin."

The old man, without waiting for explanations, took them across, and they ran on till they came to a village, and found all the men sitting in the *baraza*, to whom they appealed: "Hide us from that pumpkin! The *zimwi* has turned into a pumpkin. You will just have to take it and burn it with fire."

No doubt this version has lost some particulars in transmission; the whole neighbourhood must have known the story, and been aware that the pumpkin-plant had grown out of the *zimwi's* remains; one may guess that the boys had, over and over again, been told not to go near it, and, boylike, were all the more attracted to the forbidden thing.

The men seem at once to have appreciated the danger; they hurried the boys off into a hut and told them to keep quiet behind the partition at the back. Presently the pumpkin arrived. It is not explained how it had crossed the river, but in such a case one marvel the more is easily taken for granted. It spoke with a human voice, saying, "Have you seen my people [i.e., my slaves] who are running away?"

The village elders, who by this time had returned to their seats and were deliberately taking snuff, asked, "What are your people like? We don't know anything about them." But the pumpkin was not to be put off. "You have them shut up inside the hut!"

Then the old headman gave the word, two or three strong men seized the pumpkin, chopped it to pieces, and built a roaring fire, in which it was consumed to ashes. They scattered the ashes, and then released the boys, who went home to their mothers.

THE OGRE HUSBAND
(From the Duruma people, Kenya)

There was a girl named Mbodze, who had a younger sister, Matsezi, and a brother, Nyange. She went one day, with six other girls, to dig clay – either for plastering the huts or for making pots, which is usually women's work. There was a stone in the path, against which one after the other stubbed her toes; Mbodze, coming last, picked up the stone and threw it away. It must be supposed that the stone was an ogre who had assumed this shape for purposes of his own; for when the girls came back with their loads of clay they found that the stone had become a huge rock, so large that it shut out the view of their village, and they could not even see where it ended. When they found that they could not get past it the foremost in the line began to sing:

> "Stone, let me pass, O stone! It is not I
> who threw you away, O stone!
> She who threw you away is Mbodze, Matsezi's sister,
> And Nyange is her brother."

The rock moved aside just enough to let one person pass through, and then closed again. The second girl sang the same words, and was allowed to pass, and so did the rest, till it came to Mbodze's turn. She, too, sang till she was tired, but the rock did not move. At last the rock turned into a *zimwi* (ogre) – or, rather, we may suppose, he resumed his proper shape – seized hold of Mbodze, and asked her, "What shall I do with you? Will you be my child, or my wife, or my sister, or my aunt?" She answered, "You may do what you like with me." So he said, "I will make you my wife"; and he carried her off to his house.

There was a wild fig tree growing in front of the *zimwi's* house. Mbodze climbed up into it, and sang:

> "Matsezi, come, come! Nyange, come, come!"

But Matsezi and Nyange could not hear her.

She lived there for days and months, and the *zimwi* kept her well supplied with food, till he thought she was plump enough to be eaten. Then he set out to call the other ogres, who lived a long way off and were expected to bring their own firewood with them. No sooner had he gone than there appeared a *chitsimbakazi* (sprite), who, by some magic art, put Mbodze into a hollow bamboo and stopped up the opening with wax. She then collected everything in the house except a cock, which she was careful to leave behind, spat in every room, including the kitchen, and on both the doorposts, and started.

Before she had gone very far she met the ogres, coming along the path in single file, each one carrying his log of wood on his head. The first one stopped her, and asked, "Are you Marimira's wife?" – Marimira being the ogre, Mbodze's husband.

She sang in answer, "I am not Marimira's wife: Marimira's wife has not a swollen mouth [like me]. *Ndi ndi!* This great bamboo!"

At each *ndi* she struck the bamboo on the ground, to show that it was hollow, and the ogre, seeing that the upper end was closed with wax, suspected nothing and passed on.

The other ogres now passed her, one after another. The second was less easily satisfied than the first had been, and insisted on having the bamboo unstopped, but when he heard a great buzzing of bees he said hastily, "Close it! Close it!" The same happened with all the rest, except the last, who was Marimira himself. He asked the same question as the others, and was answered in the same way, and then said, "What are you carrying in that stick? Unstop it and let me see!" The sprite, recognizing him, said to herself, "Now this is the end! It is Marimira; I must be very cunning," and she sang:

> "I am carrying honey, ka-ya-ya!
> I am carrying honey, brother, ka-ya-ya!
> Ndi ndi! This great bamboo!"

But he kept on insisting that he must see, and at last she took out the wax: the bees swarmed out and began to settle upon him, and he cried in a panic, *"Funikia! Funikia!* Shut them up!"

So he passed on with his guests, and the sprite went on her way.

The ogres reached Marimira's house, and he called out, *"Mbodze!"* The spittle by the doorposts answered, "He-e!" He then cried, "Bring some water!" and a voice from inside answered, "Presently!" He got angry, and, leaving the others seated on the mats, went in and searched through the whole house, finding no one there and hearing nothing but the buzzing of flies. Terrified at the thought of the guests who would feel themselves to have been brought on false pretences, he dug a hole to hide in and covered himself with earth – but his one long tooth projected above the soil.

It will be remembered that a cock had been left in the house when everything else was removed; and this cock now began to crow, *"Kokoi koko-o-o!* Father's tooth is outside!"

The guests, waiting outside, wondered. "Hallo! Listen to that cock. What is he saying? "Come! Go in and see what Marimira is doing in there, for the sun is setting, and we have far to go!" So they searched the house, and, coming upon the tooth, dug him up and dragged him outside, where they killed, roasted, and ate him – all but his head. While doing so they sang:

> *"Him who shall eat the head, we will eat him too."*

After a while one of them bit off a piece from the head; the others at once fell upon him and ate him. This went on till only one was left. He fixed up a rope to make a swing and climbed into it, but the rope was not strong enough; it broke, and he fell into the fire. And he began to cry out, "*Maye! Maye!* [Mother!] I'm dying!" And he started to chew himself there in the fire, and so perished.

Meanwhile the *chitsimbakazi* had reached Mbodze's home. A little bird flew on ahead, perched outside the house, and sang:

> "*Mother, sweep the yard! Mbodze is coming!*"

The mother said, "Just listen to that bird! What does it say? It is telling us to sweep the yard, because Mbodze is coming." So she set to work at once, and presently the sprite arrived and said, "Let me have a bath, and then I will give you your daughter."

She gave her a bath and rubbed her with oil and cooked gruel for her. The sprite said, "Don't pour it into a big dish for me; put it into a coconut shell," which the woman did. When the *chitsimbakazi* had eaten she unstopped the bamboo and let Mbodze out, to the great joy of the whole family, who could not do enough to show their gratitude.

RYANGOMBE AND BINEGO

(From the Banyarwanda people, Rwanda)

Ryangombe's father was Babinga, described as the 'king of the ghosts (*imandwa*)'; his mother, originally called Kalimulore, was an uncomfortable sort of person, who had the power of turning herself into a lioness, and took to killing her father's cattle, till he forbade her to herd them, and sent someone else in her place. She so frightened her first husband that he took her home to her parents and would have no more to do with her. After her second marriage, to Babinga, there seems to have been no further trouble.

When Babinga died, his son, Ryangombe, announced that he was going to take his father's place. This was disputed by one of Babinga's followers named Mpumutimuchuni, and the two agreed to decide the question by a game of *kisoro*, which Ryangombe lost.

Ryangombe passed some time in exile. He went out hunting, and heard a prophecy from some herd-lads which led to his marriage. After some difficulties with his parentsin-law he settled down with his wife, and had a son, Binego, but soon left them and returned to his own home.

As soon as Binego was old enough, his mother's brother set him to herd the cattle; he speared a heifer the first day, a cow and her calf the next, and when his uncle objected he speared him too. He then called his mother, and they set out for Ryangombe's place, which they reached in due course, Binego having, on the way, killed two men who refused to leave their work and guide him, and a baby, for no particular reason.

When he arrived, he found his father playing the final game with Mpumutimuchuni. The decision had been allowed to stand over during the interval, and Ryangombe, if he lost this game, was not only to hand over the kingdom, but to let his opponent shave his head – that is, deprive him of the crest of hair which marked his royal rank. Binego went and stood behind his father to watch the game, suggested a move which enabled him to win, and when Mpumutimuchuni protested, stabbed him. Thus he secured his father in the kingship, which, apparently, was so far counted to him for righteousness as to outweigh all the murders he had committed. Ryangombe named him, first as his second-in-command and afterwards as his successor, and Binego, as will be seen, avenged his death. Like all the *imandwa*, with the exception of Ryangombe himself, who is uniformly kind and beneficent, Binego is mischievous and cruel.

Ryangombe's Death

The story of his death is as follows.

Ryangombe one day went hunting, accompanied by his sons, Kagoro and Ruhanga, two of his sisters, and several other *imandwa*. His mother tried to dissuade him from going, as during the previous night she had had four strange dreams, which seemed to her prophetic of evil. She had seen, first, a small beast without a tail; then an animal all of one colour; thirdly, a stream running two ways at once; and, fourthly, an immature girl carrying a baby without a *ngobe* (the skin in which an African woman carries a baby on her back; the Zulus call it *imbeleko*). She was very uneasy about these dreams, and begged her son to stay at home, but, unlike most Africans, who attach great importance to such things, he paid no attention to her words, and set out. Before he had gone very far he killed a hare, which, when examined, was found to have no tail. His personal attendant at once exclaimed that this was the fulfilment of Nyiraryangombe's dream, but Ryangombe only said, "Don't repeat a woman's words while we are after game."

Soon after this they encountered the second and third portents (the "animal all of one colour" was a black hyena), but Ryangombe still refused to be impressed. Then they met a young girl carrying a baby, without the usual skin in which it is supported. She stopped Ryangombe and asked him to give her a *ngobe*. He offered her the skin of one animal after another; but she refused them all, till he produced a buffalo hide. Then she said she must have it properly dressed, which he did, and also gave her the thongs to tie it with. Thereupon she said, "Take up the child." He objected, but gave in when she repeated her demand, and even, at her request, gave the infant a name. Finally, weary of her importunity, he said, "Leave me alone!" and the girl rushed away, was lost to sight among the bushes, and became a buffalo. Ryangombe's dogs, scenting the beast, gave chase, one after the other, and when they did not return he sent his man, Nyarwambali, to see what had become of them. Nyarwambali came back and reported: "There is a beast here which has killed the dogs." Ryangombe followed him, found the buffalo, speared it, and thought he had killed it, but just as he was shouting his song of triumph it sprang up, charged, and gored him. He staggered back and leaned against a tree; the buffalo changed into a woman, picked up the child, and went away.

At the very moment when he fell, a bloodstained leaf dropped out of the air on his mother's breast. She knew then that her dream had in fact been a warning of disaster; but it was not till a night and a day had passed that she heard what had happened. Ryangombe, as soon as he knew he had got his death-wound, called all the *imandwa* together, and told first one and, on his refusal, another to go and call his mother and Binego. One after another all refused, except the maidservant, Nkonzo, who set off at once, travelling night and day, till she came to Nyiraryangombe's house and gave her the news. She came at once with Binego, and found her son still living. Binego, when he had heard the whole story, asked his father in which direction the buffalo had gone; having had it pointed out, he rushed off, overtook the woman, brought her back, and killed her, with the child, cutting both in pieces. So he avenged his father.

Ryangombe then gave directions for the honours to be paid him after his death; these are, so to speak, the charter of the Kubandwa society which practises the cult of the *imandwa*. He specially insisted that Nkonzo, as a reward for her services, should have a place in these rites. Then at the moment when his throat tightened, he named Binego as his successor, and so died.

MKAAAH JEECHONEE, THE BOY HUNTER
(From Zanzibar, Tanzanian coast)

Sultan Maajnoon had seven sons and a big cat, of all of whom he was very proud. Everything went well until one day the cat went and caught a calf. When they told the sultan he said, "Well, the cat is mine, and the calf is mine." So they said, "Oh, all right, master," and let the matter drop.

A few days later the cat caught a goat; and when they told the sultan he said, "The cat is mine, and the goat is mine;" and so that settled it again.

Two days more passed, and the cat caught a cow. They told the sultan, and he shut them up with "My cat, and my cow."

After another two days the cat caught a donkey; same result.

Next it caught a horse; same result.

The next victim was a camel; and when they told the sultan he said: "What's the matter with you folks? It was my cat, and my camel. I believe you don't like my cat, and want it killed, bringing me tales about it every day. Let it eat whatever it wants to."

In a very short time it caught a child, and then a full-grown man; but each time the sultan remarked that both the cat and its victim were his, and thought no more of it.

Meantime the cat grew bolder, and hung around a low, open place near the town, pouncing on people going for water, or animals out at pasture, and eating them.

At last some of the people plucked up courage; and, going to the sultan, said: "How is this, master? As you are our sultan you are our protector, – or ought to be, – yet you have allowed this cat to do as it pleases, and now it lives just out of town there, and kills everything living that goes that way, while at night it comes into town and does the same thing. Now, what on earth are we to do?"

But Maajnoon only replied: "I really believe you hate my cat. I suppose you want me to kill it; but I shall do no such thing. Everything it eats is mine."

Of course the folks were astonished at this result of the interview, and, as no one dared to kill the cat, they all had to remove from the vicinity where it lived. But this did not mend matters, because, when it found no one came that way, it shifted its quarters likewise.

So complaints continued to pour in, until at last Sultan Maajnoon gave orders that if anyone came to make accusations against the cat, he was to be informed that the master could not be seen.

When things got so that people neither let their animals out nor went out themselves, the cat went farther into the country, killing and eating cattle, and fowls, and everything that came its way.

One day the sultan said to six of his sons, "I'm going to look at the country today; come along with me."

The seventh son was considered too young to go around anywhere, and was always left at home with the women folk, being called by his brothers Mkaa'ah Jeecho'nee, which means Mr. Sit-in-the-kitchen.

Well, they went, and presently came to a thicket. The father was in front and the six sons following him, when the cat jumped out and killed three of the latter.

The attendants shouted, "The cat! the cat!" and the soldiers asked permission to search for and kill it, which the sultan readily granted, saying: "This is not a cat, it is a noon'dah. It has taken from me my own sons."

Now, nobody had ever seen a noondah, but they all knew it was a terrible beast that could kill and eat all other living things.

When the sultan began to bemoan the loss of his sons, some of those who heard him said: "Ah, master, this noondah does not select his prey. He doesn't say: 'This is my master's son, I'll leave him alone,' or, 'This is my master's wife, I won't eat her.' When we told you what the cat had done, you always said it was your cat, and what it ate was yours, and now it has killed your sons, and we don't believe it would hesitate to eat even you."

And he said, "I fear you are right."

As for the soldiers who tried to get the cat, some were killed and the remainder ran away, and the sultan and his living sons took the dead bodies home and buried them.

Now when Mkaaah Jeechonee, the seventh son, heard that his brothers had been killed by the noondah, he said to his mother, "I, too, will go, that it may kill me as well as my brothers, or I will kill it."

But his mother said: "My son, I do not like to have you go. Those three are already dead; and if you are killed also, will not that be one wound upon another to my heart?"

"Nevertheless," said he, "I cannot help going; but do not tell my father."

So his mother made him some cakes, and sent some attendants with him; and he took a great spear, as sharp as a razor, and a sword, bade her farewell, and departed.

As he had always been left at home, he had no very clear idea what he was going to hunt for; so he had not gone far beyond the suburbs, when, seeing a very large dog, he concluded that this was the animal he was after; so he killed it, tied a rope to it, and dragged it home, singing,

> *"Oh, mother, I have killed*
> *The noondah, eater of the people."*

When his mother, who was upstairs, heard him, she looked out of the window, and, seeing what he had brought, said, "My son, this is not the noondah, eater of the people."

So he left the carcass outside and went in to talk about it, and his mother said, "My dear boy, the noondah is a much larger animal than that; but if I were you, I'd give the business up and stay at home."

"No, indeed," he exclaimed; "no staying at home for me until I have met and fought the noondah."

So he set out again, and went a great deal farther than he had gone on the former day. Presently he saw a civet cat, and, believing it to be the animal he was in search of, he killed it, bound it, and dragged it home, singing,

> *"Oh, mother, I have killed*
> *The noondah, eater of the people."*

When his mother saw the civet cat, she said, "My son, this is not the noondah, eater of the people." And he threw it away.

Again his mother entreated him to stay at home, but he would not listen to her, and started off again.

This time he went away off into the forest, and seeing a bigger cat than the last one, he killed it, bound it, and dragged it home, singing,

> *"Oh, mother, I have killed*
> *The noondah, eater of the people."*

But directly his mother saw it, she had to tell him, as before, "My son, this is not the noondah, eater of the people."

He was, of course, very much troubled at this; and his mother said, "Now, where do you expect to find this noondah? You don't know where it is, and you don't know what it looks like. You'll get sick over this; you're not looking so well now as you did. Come, stay at home."

But he said: "There are three things, one of which I shall do: I shall die; I shall find the noondah and kill it; or I shall return home unsuccessful. In any case, I'm off again."

This time he went farther than before, saw a zebra, killed it, bound it, and dragged it home, singing,

> *"Oh, mother, I have killed*
> *The noondah, eater of the people."*

Of course his mother had to tell him, once again, "My son, this is not the noondah, eater of the people."

After a good deal of argument, in which his mother's persuasion, as usual, was of no avail, he went off again, going farther than ever, when he caught a giraffe; and when he had killed it he said: "Well, this time I've been successful. This must be the noondah." So he dragged it home, singing,

> "Oh, mother, I have killed
> The noondah, eater of the people."

Again his mother had to assure him, "My son, this is not the noondah, eater of the people." She then pointed out to him that his brothers were not running about hunting for the noondah, but staying at home attending to their own business. But, remarking that all brothers were not alike, he expressed his determination to stick to his task until it came to a successful termination, and went off again, a still greater distance than before.

While going through the wilderness he espied a rhinoceros asleep under a tree, and turning to his attendants he exclaimed, "At last I see the noondah."

"Where, master?" they all cried, eagerly.

"There, under the tree."

"Oh-h! What shall we do?" they asked.

And he answered: "First of all, let us eat our fill, then we will attack it. We have found it in a good place, though if it kills us, we can't help it."

So they all took out their arrowroot cakes and ate till they were satisfied.

Then Mkaaah Jeechonee said, "Each of you take two guns; lay one beside you and take the other in your hands, and at the proper time let us all fire at once."

And they said, "All right, master."

So they crept cautiously through the bushes and got around to the other side of the tree, at the back of the rhinoceros; then they closed up till they were quite near it, and all fired together. The beast jumped up, ran a little way, and then fell down dead.

They bound it, and dragged it for two whole days, until they reached the town, when Mkaaah Jeechonee began singing,

> "Oh, mother, I have killed
> The noondah, eater of the people."

But he received the same answer from his mother: "My son, this is not the noondah, eater of the people."

And many persons came and looked at the rhinoceros, and felt very sorry for the young man. As for his father and mother, they both begged of him to give up, his father offering to give him anything he possessed if he would only stay at home. But he said, "I don't hear what you are saying; goodbye," and was off again.

This time he still further increased the distance from his home, and at last he saw an elephant asleep at noon in the forest. Thereupon he said to his attendants, "Now we *have* found the noondah."

"Ah, where is he?" said they.

"Yonder, in the shade. Do you see it?"

"Oh, yes, master; shall we march up to it?"

"If we march up to it, and it is looking this way, it will come at us, and if it does that, some of us will be killed. I think we had best let one man steal up close and see which way its face is turned."

As everyone thought this was a good idea, a slave named Keerobo'to crept on his hands and knees, and had a good look at it. When he returned in the same manner, his master asked: "Well, what's the news? Is it the noondah?"

"I do not know," replied Keeroboto; "but I think there is very little doubt that it is. It is broad, with a very big head, and, goodness, I never saw such large ears!"

"All right," said Mkaaah Jeechonee; "let us eat, and then go for it."

So they took their arrowroot cakes, and their molasses cakes, and ate until they were quite full.

Then the youth said to them: "My people, today is perhaps the last we shall ever see; so we will take leave of each other. Those who are to escape will escape, and those who are to die will die; but if I die, let those who escape tell my mother and father not to grieve for me."

But his attendants said, "Oh, come along, master; none of us will die, please God."

So they went on their hands and knees till they were close up, and then they said to Mkaaah Jeechonee, "Give us your plan, master;" but he said, "There is no plan, only let all fire at once."

Well, they fired all at once, and immediately the elephant jumped up and charged at them. Then such a helter-skelter flight as there was! They threw away their guns and everything they carried, and made for the trees, which they climbed with surprising alacrity.

As to the elephant, he kept straight ahead until he fell down some distance away.

They all remained in the trees from three until six o'clock in the morning, without food and without clothing.

The young man sat in his tree and wept bitterly, saying, "I don't exactly know what death is, but it seems to me this must be very like it." As no one could see anyone else, he did not know where his attendants were, and though he wished to come down from the tree, he thought, "Maybe the noondah is down below there, and will eat me."

Each attendant was in exactly the same fix, wishing to come down, but afraid the noondah was waiting to eat him.

Keeroboto had seen the elephant fall, but was afraid to get down by himself, saying, "Perhaps, though it has fallen down, it is not dead." But presently he saw a dog go up to it and smell it, and then he was sure it was dead. Then he got down from the tree as fast as he could and gave a signal cry, which was answered; but not being sure from whence the answer came, he repeated the cry, listening intently. When it was answered he went straight to the place from which the sound proceeded, and found two of his companions in one tree. To them he said, "Come on; get down; the noondah is dead." So they got down quickly and hunted around until they found their master. When they told him the news, he came down also; and after a little the attendants had all gathered together and had picked up their guns and their clothes, and were all right again. But they were all weak and hungry, so they rested and ate some food, after which they went to examine their prize.

As soon as Mkaaah Jeechonee saw it he said, "Ah, this *is* the noondah! This is it! This is it!" And they all agreed that it was *it*.

So they dragged the elephant three days to their town, and then the youth began singing,

> *"Oh, mother, this is he,*
> *The noondah, eater of the people."*

He was, naturally, quite upset when his mother replied, "My son, this is not the noondah, eater of the people." She further said: "Poor boy! what trouble you have been through. All the people are astonished that one so young should have such a great understanding!"

Then his father and mother began their entreaties again, and finally it was agreed that this next trip should be his last, whatever the result might be.

Well, they started off again, and went on and on, past the forest, until they came to a very high mountain, at the foot of which they camped for the night.

In the morning they cooked their rice and ate it, and then Mkaaah Jeechonee said: "Let us now climb the mountain, and look all over the country from its peak." And they went and they went, until after a long, weary while, they reached the top, where they sat down to rest and form their plans.

Now, one of the attendants, named Shindaa′no, while walking about, cast his eyes down the side of the mountain, and suddenly saw a great beast about half way down; but he could not make out its appearance distinctly, on account of the distance and the trees. Calling his master, he pointed it out to him, and something in Mkaaah Jeechonee's heart told him that it was the noondah. To make sure, however, he took his gun and his spear and went partly down the mountain to get a better view.

"Ah," said he, "this must be the noondah. My mother told me its ears were small, and those are small; she told me the noondah is broad and short, and so is this; she said it has two blotches, like a civet cat, and there are the blotches; she told me the tail is thick, and there is a thick tail. It must be the noondah."

Then he went back to his attendants and bade them eat heartily, which they did. Next he told them to leave every unnecessary thing behind, because if they had to run they would be better without encumbrance, and if they were victorious they could return for their goods.

When they had made all their arrangements they started down the mountain, but when they had got about half way down Keeroboto and Shindaano were afraid. Then the youth said to them: "Oh, let's go on; don't be afraid. We all have to live and die. What are you frightened about?" So, thus encouraged, they went on.

When they came near the place, Mkaaah Jeechonee ordered them to take off all their clothing except one piece, and to place that tightly on their bodies, so that if they had to run they would not be caught by thorns or branches.

So when they came close to the beast, they saw that it was asleep, and all agreed that it was the noondah.

Then the young man said, "Now the sun is setting, shall we fire at it, or let be till morning?"

And they all wished to fire at once, and see what the result would be without further tax on their nerves; therefore they arranged that they should all fire together.

They all crept up close, and when the master gave the word, they discharged their guns together. The noondah did not move; that one dose had been sufficient. Nevertheless, they all turned and scampered up to the top of the mountain. There they ate and rested for the night.

In the morning they ate their rice, and then went down to see how matters were, when they found the beast lying dead.

After resting and eating, they started homeward, dragging the dead beast with them. On the fourth day it began to give indications of decay, and the attendants wished to abandon it; but Mkaaah Jeechonee said they would continue to drag it if there was only one bone left.

When they came near the town he began to sing,

> "Mother, mother, I have come
> From the evil spirits, home.
> Mother, listen while I sing;
> While I tell you what I bring.
> Oh, mother, I have killed
> The noondah, eater of the people."

And when his mother looked out, she cried, "My son, this *is* the noondah, eater of the people."

Then all the people came out to welcome him, and his father was overcome with joy, and loaded him with honours, and procured him a rich and beautiful wife; and when he died Mkaaah Jeechonee became sultan, and lived long and happily, beloved by all the people.

THE WERE-WOLF HUSBAND
(From the Chaga people, Tanzania)

There was once a girl who refused to marry. Her parents, too, discouraged all wooers who presented themselves, as they said they would not give their daughter to any common man.

On a certain day the sword dance was going on at this girl's village, and men came from the whole countryside to take part in it. Among the dancers there appeared a tall and handsome young man, wearing a broad ring like a halo round his head, who drew all eyes by his grace and noble bearing. The maiden fell in love with him at first sight, and her parents also approved of him. The dancing went on for several days, during which time she scarcely took her eyes off him. But one day, as he happened to turn his back, she caught sight of a second mouth behind his head, and said to her mother, "That man is a *rimu!*" They would not believe it. "That fine fellow a *rimu!* Nonsense! Just you go with him and let him eat you, that's all!"

The suitor presented himself in due course, and the marriage took place. After spending some days with the bride's parents the couple left for their home. But her brothers, knowing the husband to be a *rimu*, felt uneasy, and followed them, without their knowledge, keeping in the bushes alongside the path. When they had gone some distance the husband stopped and said, "Look back and tell me if you can still see the smoke from your father's hut." She looked, and said that she could. They went on for another hour or two, and then he asked her if she could see the hills behind her home. She said yes, and again they went on. At last he asked her again if she could see the hills, and when he found that she could not said, "What will you do now? I am a *rimu*. Climb up into this tree and weep your last tears, for you must die!"

But her brothers, watching their chance, shot him with poisoned arrows, and he died. She came down from the tree, and the brothers took her home.

THE HYENA BRIDEGROOM
(From Malawi)

There was a girl in a certain village who refused all suitors, though several very decent young men had presented themselves. Her parents remonstrated in vain; she only said, "I don't like the young men of our neighbourhood; if one came from a distance I might look at him!" So they left off asking for her, and she remained unmarried for an unusually long time.

One day a handsome stranger arrived at the village and presented himself to the girl's parents. He had all the appearance of a rich man; he was wearing a good cloth, had ivory bracelets on his arms, and carried a gun and a powder-horn curiously ornamented with brass wire. The maiden exclaimed, on seeing him, "This is the one I like!" Her father and mother were more doubtful, as was natural, since no one knew anything about him; but in spite of all they could say she insisted on accepting him. He was, in fact, a hyena, who had assumed human shape for the time being. The usual marriage ceremonies took place, and the husband, in accordance with Yao and Nyanja custom, settled down at the village of his parents-in-law, and made himself useful in the gardens for the space of several months. At the end of that time he said that he had a great wish to visit his own people. His wife, whom he had purposely refrained from asking, begged him to let her accompany him. When all was ready for the journey her little brother, who was suffering from sore eyes, said he wanted to go too; but his sister, ashamed to be seen in company with such an object, refused him sharply. He waited till they had started, and then followed, keeping out of sight, till he was too far from home to be sent back.

They went on for many days, and at last arrived at the hyenas' village, where the bride was duly welcomed by her husband's relations. She was assigned a hut to sleep in, but, to keep her brother out of the way, she sent him into the hen house.

In the middle of the night, when she was asleep, the people of the village took their proper shape and, called together by the hyena husband, marched round the hut, chanting:

"Let us eat the game, but it is not fat yet."

The little boy in the hen-house was awake and heard them; his worst fears were confirmed. In the morning he told his sister what he had heard, but she would not believe him. So he told her to tie a string to her toe and put the end outside where he could get it. This he drew into the hen house, and that night, when the hyenas began their march, he pulled the string, and awakened his sister. She was now thoroughly frightened, and when he asked her next morning, "Did you hear them, sister?" she had nothing more to say.

The boy then went to his brother-in-law and asked him for the loan of an axe and an adze. The man (as he appeared to be), who had no notion that he was detected and every reason to show himself good-natured, consented at once, and watched him going off into the bush, well pleased that the child should amuse himself.

The latter soon found and cut down a tree such as he needed, and then began to shape a thing which he called *nguli* – something in the nature of a small boat. When he had finished it he got into it and sang:

"My boat! swing! swing!"

And the *nguli* began to rise up from the earth. As he went on singing it rose higher and higher, till it floated above the tops of the tallest trees. The hyena-villagers all rushed out to gaze at this wonder, and the boy's sister came with them. Then he sang once more:

"My boat! come down! down, de-de! come down!"

And it floated gently down to the ground. The people were delighted, and cried out to him to go up again. He made some excuse for a little delay, and whispered to his sister to get her bundle (which, no doubt, she had ready) and climb in. She did so, and when both were safely stowed he sang his first song once more. Again the vessel rose, and this time did not come down again. The spectators, after waiting in vain, began to suspect that their prey was escaping, and shouted to the boy to come back, but no attention was paid to them, and the *nguli* quickly passed out of sight. Before the day was out they found themselves above the courtyard of their home, and the boy sang the words which caused them to descend, so that they alighted on their mother's grain mortar. The whole family came running out and overwhelmed them with questions; the girl could not speak for crying with joy and relief, and her brother told the whole story, winding up with: "Look here, sister, you thought I was no good, because I had sore eyes – but who was it heard them singing, 'Let us eat her!' and told you about it?" The parents, too, while praising the boy, did not fail to point the moral for the benefit of their foolish daughter, who, some say, had to remain unmarried to the end of her days.

THE DEVOURING PUMPKIN

(From the Yao people, Malawi, northern Mozambique and southern Tanzania)

Some little boys, playing in the gardens outside their village, noticed a very large gourd, and said, "Just see how big that gourd is getting!" Then the gourd spoke and said, "If you pluck me I'll pluck you!" They went home and told what they had heard, and their mother refused to believe them, saying, "Children, you lie!" But their sisters asked to be shown the place where the boys had seen the talking gourd. It was pointed out to them, and they at once went there by themselves, and said, as their brothers had done, "Just see how big that gourd is getting!" But nothing happened. They went home, and, of course, said that the boys had been making fun of them. Then the boys went again and heard the gourd speak as before. But when the girls went it was silent.

The gourd continued to grow: it became as big as a house, and began swallowing all the people in the village. Only one woman escaped – we are not told how. Having swallowed everyone within reach, the gourd made its way into a lake and stayed there.

In a short time, the woman bore a boy, and, apparently, they lived on together on the site of the ruined village. When the boy had grown older he asked his mother one day where his father was. She said, "He was swallowed up by a gourd which has gone into the lake." So he went forth, and when he came to a lake he called out, "Gourd, come out! Gourd, come out!" There was no answer, and he went on to another lake and repeated his command. He saw one ear of the gourd come out

322

of the water (by which it would appear that the gourd had by this time assumed some sort of animal shape), and climbed a tree, where he kept on shouting, "Gourd, come out!" At last the gourd came out and set off in pursuit of him; but he ran home and asked his mother for his bow and quiver. He hastened back, and when he came in sight of the monster, loosed an arrow and hit it. He shot again and again, till, wounded by the tenth arrow, it died, roaring so that it could be heard from here to Vuga. The boy then called to his mother to bring a knife, cut open the gourd and liberated all the people.

KACHIRAMBE OF THE ANYANJA
(From the Nyanja/Chewa people, southern Africa)

Some little girls had gone out into the bush to gather herbs. While they were thus busied one of them found a hyena's egg and put it into her basket. Apparently none of the others saw it; she told them, somewhat to their surprise, that she had now picked enough, and hastened home. After she was gone the hyena came and asked them, "Who has taken my egg?" They said they did not know, but perhaps their companion who had gone home had carried it off. Meanwhile the girl's mother, on finding the egg in her basket, had put it on the fire. The hyena arrived and demanded the egg; the woman said it was burnt, but offered to give him the next child she had to eat. Apparently this callous suggestion was quite spontaneous on her part; but as there was no child in prospect just then she probably thought that the promise was quite a safe one, and that by the time its fulfilment became possible some way out could be found. The hyena, however, left her no peace, waylaid her every day when she went to the stream for water, and kept asking her when the child was to be produced. At last he said, "If you do not have that child quickly I will eat you yourself." She went home in great trouble, and soon after noticed a boil on her shin-bone, which swelled and swelled, till it burst, and out came a child. He was fully armed, with bow, arrows, and quiver, had his little gourd of charms slung round his neck, and was followed by his dogs! He announced himself in these words: "I, Kachirambe, have come forth, the child of the shin-bone!" The mother was struck with astonishment, but it does not seem to have occurred to her to go back on her promise. When next she went to draw water and the hyena met her with the usual question she replied, "Yes, I have borne a child, but he is very clever; you will never be able to catch him, but I myself will beguile him for you. I will tie you up in a bundle of grass, and tell Kachirambe to go and fetch it." So she tied up the hyena in a bundle of the long grass used for thatching, and left it lying beside the path. Kachirambe, when sent to fetch it, stood still a little way off, and said, "You, bundle, get up, that I may lift you the better!" And the bundle of grass rose up of itself. Kachirambe said, "What sort of bundle is this that gets up by itself? I have never seen the like, and I am not going to lift it, not I!" So he went home.

The hyena, after releasing himself from the grass, came back and said to the woman, "Yes, truly, that youngster of yours is a sharp one!" She told him to go in the evening and wait in a certain place; then she called Kachirambe and said, "I want you to set a trap in such and such a place for the rats; they have been destroying all my baskets." Kachirambe went and chose out a large, flat stone; then he cut a forked stick, and whittled the cross-piece and the little stick for the catch, and twisted some bark-string, and made a falling trap, of the kind called *diwa*, and set and baited it. In the evening his mother said to him, "The trap has fallen. Go and see what it has caught!" He said, "You, trap, fall again, so that I may know whether you have caught a rat!" The hyena, waiting beside the trap, heard him, lifted up the stone, and let it fall with a bang. Kachirambe said, "What sort of trap is it that falls twice? I have never seen such a one."

Next the mother told the hyena that she would send Kachirambe to pick beans. The boy took the basket and went to the field, but then he turned himself into a fly, and the hyena waited in vain. Kachirambe returned home with a full basket, to his mother's astonishment. She was nearly at her wits' end, but thought of one last expedient; she sent him into the bush to cut wood. The night before he had a dream, which warned him that he was in great danger, so he took with him his bow, and his quiver full of arrows, and his 'medicine-gourd', as well as a large knife. He climbed up into a tree which had dead branches, and began to cut. Presently he saw the hyena below, who said, "You are dead today; you shall not escape. Come down quickly, and I will eat you!" He answered, "I am coming down, but just open your mouth wide!" The hyena, with his usual stupidity, did as he was told, and Kachirambe threw down a sharp stick which he had just cut – it entered the hyena's mouth and killed him. Kachirambe then came down and went home; when drawing near the house he shot an arrow towards it, to frighten his mother, and said, "What have I done to you, that you should send wild beasts after me to eat me?" She, thoroughly scared, begged his pardon.

UNTOMBINDE AND THE SQUATTING MONSTER
(From the Zulu people, southern Africa)

A chief's daughter, Untombinde, goes, with a number of other
girls, to bathe in the Ilulange, against the warnings of her
parents: "To the Ilulange nothing goes and returns again; it
goes there forever." The girls found, on coming out of the water,
that the clothes and ornaments they had left on the bank had
disappeared; they knew that the *isiququmadevu* must have
taken them, and one after another petitioned politely for their
return. Untombinde, however, said, "I will never beseech the
isiququmadevu," and was immediately seized by the monster and
dragged down into the water.

Her companions went home and reported what had happened.
The chief, though he evidently despaired of recovering her
("Behold, she goes there forever!"), sent a troop of young men
to fetch the *isiququmadevu*, which has killed Untombinde. The
warriors found the monster squatting on the riverbank, and were
swallowed up, everyone, before they could attack her. She then
went on to the chiefs kraal, swallowed up all the inhabitants,
with their dogs and their cattle, as well as all the people in the
surrounding country.

Among the victims were two beautiful children, much
beloved. Their father, however, escaped, took his two clubs and
his large spear, and went his way, saying, "It is I who will kill
the *isiququmadevu*."

By this time the monster had left the neighbourhood, and
the man went on seeking her till he met with some buffaloes,
whom he asked, "Whither has Usiququmadevu gone? She has
gone away with my children!" The buffaloes directed him on his

way, and he then came across some leopards, of whom he asked the same question, and who also told him to go forward. He next met an elephant, who likewise sent him on, and so at last he came upon the monster herself, and announced, "I am seeking Usiququmadevu, who is taking away my children!" Apparently she hoped to escape recognition, for she directed him, like the rest, to go forward. But the man was not to be deceived by so transparent a device: he came and stabbed the lump, and so the *isiququmadevu* died."

Then all the people, cattle, and dogs, and, lastly, Untombinde herself, came out unharmed, and she returned to her father.

THE GIRL WHO MARRIED A LION
(From the Lamba people, southern Africa)

A lion went to a village of human beings and married. And the people thought that maybe it was but a man and not a wild creature.

In due course the couple had a child. Some time after this the husband proposed that they should visit his parents, and they set out, accompanied by the wife's brother. In several parallel stories a younger brother or sister of the bride desires to go with her, and when she refuses follows the party by stealth, but there is no indication of this here.

At the end of the first day's journey they all camped in the forest, and the husband cut down thorn bushes and made a kraal (*mutanda*), after which he went away, saying that he was going to catch some fish in the river. When he was gone the brother said to his sister, "He has built this kraal very badly," and he took his axe and cut down many branches, with which to strengthen the weak places.

Meanwhile the husband had gone to seek out his lion relations, and when they asked him, "How many animals have you killed?" he replied, "Two and a young one." When darkness fell he had become a huge male lion, and led the whole clan (with a contingent of hyenas) to attack his camp. Those inside heard the stealthy footfalls and sat listening. The lions hurled themselves on the barrier, trying to break through, but it was too strong, and they fell back, wounded with the thorns. He who by day had been the husband growled: "M . . .," and the baby inside the kraal responded: "M . . .". Then the mother sang:

> "The child has bothered me with crying; watch the dance!
> Walk with a stoop; watch the dance!"

The were-lion's father, quite disgusted, said, "You have brought us to a man who has built a strong kraal; we cannot eat him." And as day was beginning to break they all retired to the forest.

When it was light the husband came back with his fish, and said that he had been detained, adding, "You were nearly eaten," meaning that his absence had left them exposed to danger. It seems to be implied that the others were taken in by his excuses, but the brother, at any rate, must have had his suspicions. When the husband had gone off again, ostensibly to fish, he said, "See, it was that husband of yours who wanted to eat us last night." So he went and walked about, thinking over the position. Presently he saw the head of a gnome (*akachekulu*) projecting from a cleft in a tree; it asked him why he had come, and, on being told, said, "You are already done for; your brother-in-law is an ogre that has finished off all the people in this district." The creature then asked him to sweep out the midden inside his house – and after he had done so told him to cut down the tree, which it then hollowed out and made into a drum, stretching two prepared skins over the ends. It then slung the drum round the man's waist, and said, "Do as if you were going to do this" – that is, raise himself from the ground. And, behold, he found himself rising into the air, and he reached the top of a tree. The gnome told him to jump down, and he did so quite easily. Then it said, "Put your sister in the drum and go home." So he called her, and, having stowed her in it, with the baby, rose up and sat in the tree-top, where he began to beat the drum. The lion, hearing the sound, followed it, and when he saw the young man in the tree said, "Brother-in-law, just beat a little"; so the man beat the drum and sang:

> "Boom, boom sounds the little drum
> Of the sounding drum, sounds the little drum!
> Ogre, dance, sounds the little drum
> Of the sounding drum, sounds the little drum!"

The lion began to dance, and the skins he was wearing fell off and were blown away by the wind, and he had to go back and pick them up. Meanwhile the drum carried the fugitives on, and the lion pursued them as soon as he had recovered his skins. Having overtaken them, he called up into the tree, "Brother-in-law, show me my child!" and the following dialogue took place:

"What, you lion, am I going to show you a relation of mine?"

"Would I eat my child?" conveniently ignoring the fact that he had himself announced the killing of the young one.

"How about the night you came? You would have eaten us!"

Again the brother-in-law beat the drum, and the lion danced (apparently unable to help himself), and as before lost his skins, stopped to pick them up, and began the chase again, while the man went springing along the tree-tops like a monkey. At last he reached his own village, and his mother saw as it were a swallow settle in the courtyard of his home. She said, "Well, I never! Greeting, my child!" and asked where his sister was. He frightened her at first by telling her that she had been eaten by her husband, who was really a lion, but afterwards relented and told her to open the drum. Her daughter came out with the baby, safe and sound, and the mother said, praising her son, "You have grown up; you have saved your sister!" She gave him five slave girls.

The lion had kept up the pursuit, and reached the outskirts of the village, but, finding that his intended victims were safe within the stockade, he gave up and returned to the forest.

KHODUMODUMO, OR KAMMAPA, THE SWALLOWING MONSTER
(From Lesotho, southern Africa)

Once upon a time there appeared in our country a huge, shapeless thing called Khodumodumo (but some people call it Kammapa). It swallowed every living creature that came in its way. At last it came through a pass in the mountains into a valley where there were several villages; it went to one after another, and swallowed the people, the cattle, the goats, the dogs, and the fowls. In the last village was a woman who had just happened to sit down on the ash-heap. She saw the monster coming, smeared herself all over with ashes, and ran into the calves' pen, where she crouched on the ground. Khodumodumo, having finished all the people and animals, came and looked into the place, but could see nothing moving, for, the woman being smeared with ashes and keeping quite still, it took her for a stone. It then turned and went away, but when it reached the narrow pass (or *nek*) at the entrance to the valley it had swelled to such a size that it could not get through, and was forced to stay where it was.

Meanwhile the woman in the calves' pen, who had been expecting a baby shortly, gave birth to a boy. She laid him down on the ground and left him for a minute or two, while she looked for something to make a bed for him. When she came back she found a grown man sitting there, with two or three spears in his hand and a string of divining bones (*ditaola*) round his neck. She said, "Hallo, man! Where is my child?" and he answered, "It is I, Mother!" Then he asked what had become of the people, and the cattle, and the dogs, and she told him.

"Where is this thing, Mother?"

"Come out and see, my child."

So they both went out and climbed to the top of the wall surrounding the calves' kraal, and she pointed to the pass, saying, "That object which is filling the *nek*, as big as a mountain, that is Khodumodumo."

Ditaolane got down from the wall, fetched his spears, sharpened them on a stone, and set off to the end of the valley, where Khodumodumo lay. The beast saw him, and opened its mouth to swallow him, but he dodged and went round its side – it was too unwieldy to turn and seize him – and drove one of his spears into it. Then he stabbed it again with his second spear, and it sank down and died.

He took his knife, and had already begun to cut it open, when he heard a man's voice crying out, "Do not cut me!" So he tried in another place, and another man cried out, but the knife had already slashed his leg. Ditaolane then began cutting in a third place, and a cow lowed, and someone called out, "Don't stab the cow!" Then he heard a goat bleat, a dog bark, and a hen cackle, but he managed to avoid them all, as he went on cutting, and so, in time, released all the inhabitants of the valley.

There was great rejoicing as the people collected their belongings, and all returned to their several villages praising their young deliverer, and saying, "This young man must be our chief." They brought him gifts of cattle, so that, between one and another, he soon had a large herd, and he had his choice of wives among their daughters. So he built himself a fine kraal and married and settled down, and all went well for a time.

But the unintentionally wounded man never forgot his grudge, and long after his leg was healed began, when he noticed signs of discontent among the people, to drop a cunning word here and there and encourage those who were secretly envious of Ditaolane's good fortune, as well as those who suspected him because, as they said, he could not be a normal human being, to give voice to their feelings.

So before long they were making plans to get rid of their chief. They dug a pit and covered it with dry grass – just as the Bapedi did in order to trap Huveane – but he avoided it. They kindled a great fire in the courtyard, intending to throw him into it, but a kind of madness seized them; they began to struggle with each other, and at last threw in one of their own party. The same thing happened when they tried to push him over a precipice; in this case he restored to life the man who was thrown over and killed.

Next they got up a big hunt, which meant an absence of several days from the village. One night when the party were sleeping in a cave they induced the chief to take the place farthest from the entrance, and when they thought he was asleep stole out and built a great fire in the cave mouth. But when they looked round they saw him standing among them.

After this, feeling that nothing would soften their inveterate hatred, he grew weary of defeating their stratagems, and allowed them to kill him without offering any resistance. Some of the Basuto, when relating this story, add, "It is said that his heart went out and escaped and became a bird."

HLAKANYANA'S PRECOCIOUS DEVELOPMENT AND MISCHIEVOUS PRANKS
(From the Pedi and Venda peoples, South Africa)

They said that "Uhlakanyana is a very cunning man; he is also very small, of the size of a weasel", "it is as though he really was of that genus; he resembles it in all respects" – hence his other name *icakide*.

Hlakanyana was a chief's son. Like Ryangombe, he spoke before he was born; in fact, he repeatedly declared his impatience to enter the world. No sooner had he made his appearance than he walked out to the cattle kraal, where his father had just slaughtered some oxen, and the men were sitting round, ready for a feast of meat. Scared by this portent – for they had been waiting for the birth to be announced – they all ran away, and Hlakanyana sat down by the fire and began to eat a strip of meat which was roasting there. They came back, and asked the mother whether this was really the expected baby. She answered, "It is he"; whereupon they said, "Oh, we thank you, our queen. You have brought forth for us a child who is wise as soon as he is born. We never saw a child like this child. This child is fit to be the great one among all the king's children, for he has made us wonder by his wisdom."

But Hlakanyana, thinking that his father did not take this view, but looked upon him as a mere infant, asked him to take a leg of beef and throw it downhill, over the kraal fence (the gateway being on the upper side). All the boys and men present were to race for it, and "he shall be the man who gets the leg." They all rushed to the higher opening, but Hlakanyana wormed his way between the stakes at the lower end of the kraal, picked up the leg, and carried it in triumph to meet the others, who were coming round from the farther side. He handed it over to his mother, and then returned to the kraal, where his father was distributing the rest of the meat. He offered to carry each man's share to his hut for him, which he did, smeared some blood on the mat (on which meat is laid to be cut up), and then carried the joint to his mother. He did this to each one in turn, so that by the evening no house had any meat except that of the chiefs wife, which was overstocked. No wonder that the women cried out, "What is this that has been born today? He is a prodigy, a real prodigy!" His next feat was to take out all the birds which had been caught in the traps set by the boys, and bring them home, telling his mother to cook them and cover the pots, fastening down the lids. He then went off to sleep in the boys' house (*ilau*), which he would not ordinarily have entered for several years to come, and overbore their objections, saying, "Since you say this I shall sleep here, just to show you!" He rose early in the morning, went to his mother's house, got in without waking her, opened the pots, and ate all the birds, leaving only the heads, which he put back, after filling the lower half of the pots with cow dung, and fastened down the lids. Then he went away for a time, and came back to play Huveane's trick on his mother. He pretended to have come in for the first time, and told her that the sun had risen, and that she had slept too long – for if the birds were not taken out of the pot before the sun was up they would turn into dung. So he washed himself and sat down to his breakfast, and when he opened the pots it was even as he had said, and his mother believed him. He finished up the heads, saying that, as she had spoilt his food she should not have even these, and then announced that he did not consider himself her child at all, and that his father was a mere man, one of the people and nothing more. He would not stay with them, but would go on his travels. So he picked up his stick and walked out, still grumbling about the loss of his birds.

He Goes on His Travels

When he had gone some distance and was beginning to get hungry he came upon some traps with birds in them and, beginning to take them out, found himself stuck fast. The owner of the traps was a 'cannibal' – or, rather, an ogre – who, finding that birds had more than once disappeared from his traps, had put sticks smeared with birdlime in front of them. Now he came along to look at them, and found Hlakanyana, who, quite undisturbed, addressed him thus: "Don't beat me, and I will tell you. Take me out and cleanse me from the birdlime and take me home with you. Have you a mother?" The ogre said he had. Hlakanyana, evidently assuming that he was to be eaten, said that if he were beaten and killed at once his flesh would be ruined for the pot. "I shall not be nice; I shall be bitter. Cleanse me and take me home with you, that you may put me in your house, that I may be cooked by your mother. And do you go away and just leave me at your home. I cannot be cooked if you are there; I shall be bad; I cannot be nice."

The ogre, a credulous person, like most of his kind, did as he was asked, and handed Hlakanyana over to his mother, to be cooked next morning.

When the ogre and his younger brother were safely out of the way, Hlakanyana proposed to the old woman that they should "play at boiling each other." He got her to put on a large pot of water, made up the fire under it, and when it was beginning to get warm he said, "Let us begin with me." She put him in and covered the pot. Presently he asked to be taken out, and then, saying that the fire was not hot enough, made it up to a blaze and began, very rudely, to unfasten the old woman's skin petticoat. When she objected he said: "What does it matter if I have unfastened your dress, I who am mere game, which is about to be eaten by your sons and you?" He thrust her in and put on the lid. No sooner had he done so than she shrieked that she was being scalded; but he told her that could not be, or she would not be able to cry out. He kept the lid on till the poor creature's cries ceased, and then put on her clothes and lay down in her sleeping place. When the sons came home he told them to take their 'game' and eat; he had already eaten, and did not mean to get up. While they were eating he slipped out at the door, threw off the clothes, and ran away as fast as he could. When he had reached a safe distance he called out to them, "You are eating your mother, you cannibals!" They pursued him hot-foot; he came to a swollen river and changed himself into a piece of wood. They came up, saw his footprints on the ground, and, as he was nowhere in sight, concluded he had crossed the river and flung the piece of wood after him. Safe on the other bank, he resumed his own shape and jeered at the ogres, who gave up the pursuit and turned back.

He Kills a Hare, Gets a Whistle and Is Robbed of It

Hlakanyana went on his way, and before very long he spied a hare. Being hungry, he tried to entice it within reach by offering to tell a tale, but the hare would not be beguiled. At last, however (this part of the story is not very clear, and the hare must have been a different creature from the usual Bantu hare!), he caught it, killed it, and roasted it, and, after eating the flesh, made one of the bones into a whistle. He went on, playing his whistle and singing:

> "I met Hloya's mother,
> And we cooked each other.
> I did not burn;
> She was done to a turn."

In time he came to a large tree on the bank of a river, overhanging a deep pool. On a branch of the tree lay an iguana, who greeted him, and Hlakanyana responded politely. The iguana said, "Lend me your whistle, so that I can hear if it will sound." Hlakanyana refused, but the iguana insisted, promising to give it back. Hlakanyana said, "Come away from the pool, then, and come out here on to the open ground; I am afraid near a pool. I say you might run into the pool with my whistle, for you are a person that lives in deep water." The iguana came down from his tree, and when Hlakanyana thought that he was at a safe distance from the river he handed him the whistle. The iguana tried the whistle, approved the sound, and wanted to take it away with him. Hlakanyana would not hear of this, and laid hold of the iguana as he was trying to make off, but received such a blow from the powerful tail that he had to let go, and the iguana dived into the river, carrying the whistle with him.

Hlakanyana again went on till he came to a place where a certain old man had hidden some bread. He ran off with it, but not before the owner had seen him; the old man evidently knew him, for he called out, "Put down my bread, Hlakanyana." Hlakanyana only ran the faster, the old man after him, till, finding that the latter was gaining on him, he crawled into a snake's hole. The old man put in his hand and caught him by the leg. Hlakanyana cried, laughing, "He! He! you've caught hold of a root!" So the old man let go, and, feeling about for the leg, caught a root, at which Hlakanyana yelled, "Oh! oh! you're killing me!" The old man kept pulling at the root till he was tired out and went away. Hlakanyana ate the bread in comfort, and then crawled out and went on his way once more.

He Nurses the Leopard's Cubs

In the course of his wanderings he came upon a leopard's den, where he found four cubs and sat down beside them till the mother leopard came home, carrying a buck with which to feed her little ones. She was very angry when she saw Hlakanyana, and was about to attack him, but he disarmed her by his flattering tongue, and finally persuaded her to let him stay and take care of the cubs, while she went out to hunt. "I will take care of them, and I will build a beautiful house, that you may lie here at the foot of the rock with your children." He also told her he could cook – a somewhat unnecessary accomplishment, one would think, in this case; but it would seem that he had his reasons. The leopard having agreed, Hlakanyana brought the cubs, one by one, for her to suckle. She objected, wanting them all brought at once, but the little cunning fellow persisted and got his way. When they had all been fed she called on him to make good his promise and skin the buck and cook it, which he did. So they both ate, and all went to sleep. In the morning, when the leopard had gone to hunt, Hlakanyana set to work building the house. He made the usual round Zulu hut, but with a very small doorway; then, inside, he dug a burrow, leading to the back of the hut, with an opening a long way off. Then he took four assagais which he had carried with him on his travels, broke them off short to rather less than the width of the doorway, and hid them in a convenient place. Having finished, he ate one of the cubs. When the mother came home he brought them out as before, one by one, taking the third twice, so that she never missed any of them. He did the same the next day, and the next.

On the fourth day he brought out the last cub four times, and at length it refused to drink. The mother was naturally surprised at this, but Hlakanyana said he thought it was not well. She said, "Take care of it, then," and when he had carried it into the house called him to prepare supper. When she had eaten Hlakanyana went into the house, and the leopard called out that she was coming in to look after the child. Hlakanyana said, "Come in, then," knowing that she would take some time squeezing herself through the narrow entrance, and at once made his escape through the burrow. Meanwhile she had got in, found only one cub, concluded that he must have eaten the rest, and followed him into the burrow. By this time Hlakanyana was out at the other end; he ran round to the front of the house, took his assagais from the hiding place, and fixed them in the ground at the doorway, the points sloping inward. The leopard found she could not get very far in the burrow, so she came back into the hut, and, squeezing through the doorway to pursue Hlakanyana into the open, was pierced by the assagais and killed.

Hlakanyana and the Ogre

Hlakanyana now sat down and ate the cub; then he skinned the leopard, and gradually – for he remained on the spot for some time – ate most of the flesh, keeping, however, one leg, with which he set out once more on his travels, "for he was a man who did not stay long in one place." Soon after he met a hungry ogre, with whom he easily made friends by giving him some meat, and they went on together. They came across two cows, which the *izimu* said belonged to him. Hlakanyana suggested that they should build a hut, so that they could slaughter the cows and eat them in peace and comfort. The ogre agreed; they killed the cows and started to build. As rain was threatening Hlakanyana said they had better get on with the thatching.

This is done by two people, one inside the hut and the other on the roof, passing the string with which the grass is tied backward and forward between them, pushing it through by means of a pointed stick. Hlakanyana went inside, while the ogre climbed on the roof. The latter had very long hair (a distinguishing feature of the *amazimu*), and Hlakanyana managed to knit it, lock by lock, into the thatch, so firmly that he would not be able to get off. He then sat down and ate the beef which was boiling on the fire. A hailstorm came on, Hlakanyana went into the house with his joint, and the ogre (who seems to have been a harmless creature enough) was left to perish. "He was struck with the hailstones, and died there on the house" – as anyone who has seen an African hailstorm can readily believe.

Having caused the death of another *izimu* in a way which need not be related here, Hlakanyana took up his abode for a time with yet another, who seems to have had no reason to complain of him. As usual, when no ill fortune befell him he became restless, and took the road once more, directing his steps towards the place on the river where the iguana had robbed him of his whistle. He found the iguana on his tree, called him down, killed him, and recovered the whistle. Then he went back to the ogre's hut, but the owner had gone away, and the hut was burned down. So he said, "I will now go back to my mother, for, behold, I am in trouble."

He Goes Home

But his return was by no means in the spirit of the Prodigal Son, for he professed to have come back purely out of affection for her, saying, "Oh, now I have returned, my mother, for I remembered you!" and calmly omitting all mention of his exploits during his absence. She believed this, being only too ready to welcome him back, and he seems to have behaved himself for a time. Nothing is said of his father's attitude, or of that of the clansmen.

The day after his return home Hlakanyana went to a wedding, and as he came over a hill on the way back he found some *umdiandiane* – a kind of edible tuber, of which he was very fond. He dug it up and took it home to his mother, asking her to cook it for him, as he was now going to milk the cow. She did so, and, tasting one to see if it was done, liked it so much that she ate the whole. When he asked for it she said, "I have eaten it, my child," and he answered, "Give me my *umdiandiane*, for I dug it up on a very little knoll, as I was coming from a wedding." His mother gave him a milk pail by way of compensation, and he went off. Soon he came upon some boys herding sheep, who were milking the ewes into old, broken potsherds. He said, "Why are you milking into potsherds? You had better use my milk pail, but you must give me a drink out of it." They used his milk pail, but the last boy who had it broke it. Hlakanyana said, "Give me my milk pail, my milk pail my mother gave me, my mother having eaten my *umdiandiane*" and so on, as before. The boys gave him an assagai, which he lent to some other boys, who were trying to cut slices of liver with splinters of sugar cane. They broke his assagai, and gave him an axe instead. Then he met some old women gathering firewood, who had nothing to cut it with, so he offered them the use of his axe, which again got broken. They gave him a blanket, and he went on his way till nightfall, when he found two young men sleeping out on the hillside, with nothing to cover them. He said, "Ah, friends, do you sleep without covering? Have you no blanket?" They said, "No." He said, "Take this of mine," which they did, but it was rather small for two, and as each one kept dragging it from the other it soon got torn. Then he demanded it back. "Give me my blanket, my blanket which the women gave me," and so on. The young men gave him a shield. Then he came upon some men fighting with a leopard, who had no shields. He questioned them as he had done the other people, and lent one of them his shield. It must have been efficient as a protection, for they killed the leopard, but the hand loop by which the man was holding it broke, and of course it was rendered useless. So Hlakanyana said:

> "Give me my shield, my shield the young men gave me,
>> The young men having torn my blanket,
>> My blanket the women gave me,
>> The women having broken my axe,
>> My axe the boys gave me,
>> The boys having broken my assagai,
>> My assagai the boys gave me,
>> The boys having broken my milk pail,
>> My milk pail my mother gave me,
>> My mother having eaten my umdiandiane,
>> My umdiandiane I dug up on a very little knoll,
>> As I was coming from a wedding."

They gave him a war assagai (isinkemba). What he did with that perhaps I may tell you on another occasion.

A GLOSSARY OF MYTH & FOLKLORE

Aaru Heavenly paradise where the blessed went after death.

Ab Heart or mind.

Abiku (Yoruba) Person predestined to die. Also known as ogbanje.

Absál Nurse to Salámán, who died after their brief love affair.

Achilles The son of Peleus and the sea-nymph Thetis, who distinguished himself in the Trojan War. He was made almost immortal by his mother, who dipped him in the River Styx, and he was invincible except for a portion of his heel which remained out of the water.

Acropolis Citadel in a Greek city.

Adad-Ea Ferryman to Ut-Napishtim, who carried Gilgamesh to visit his ancestor.

Adapa Son of Ea and a wise sage.

Adar God of the sun, who is worshipped primarily in Nippur.

Aditi Sky goddess and mother of the gods.

Adityas Vishnu, children of Aditi, including Indra, Mitra, Rudra, Tvashtar, Varuna and Vishnu.

Aeneas The son of Anchises and the goddess Aphrodite, reared by a nymph. He led the Dardanian troops in the Trojan War According to legend, he became the founder of Rome.

Aengus Óg Son of Dagda and Boann (a woman said to have given the Boyne river its name), Aengus is the Irish god of love whose stronghold is reputed to have been at New Grange. The famous tale 'Dream of Aengus' tells of how he fell in love with a maiden he had dreamt of. He eventually discovered that she was to be found at the Lake of the Dragon's Mouth in Co. Tipperary, but that she lived every alternate year in the form of a swan. Aengus plunges into the lake transforming himself also into the shape of a swan. Then the two fly back together to his palace on the Boyne where they live out their days as guardians of would-be lovers.

Aesir Northern gods who made their home in Asgard; there are twelve in number.

Afrásiyáb Son of Poshang, king of Túrán, who led an army against the ruling shah Nauder. Afrásiyáb became ruler of Persia on defeating Nauder.

Afterlife Life after death or paradise, reached only by the process of preserving the body from decay through embalming and preparing it for reincarnation.

Agamemnon A famous King of Mycenae. He married Helen of Sparta's sister Clytemnestra. When Paris abducted Helen, beginning the Trojan War, Menelaus called on Agamemnon to raise the Greek troops. He had to sacrifice his daughter Iphigenia in order to get a fair wind to travel to Troy.

Agastya A rishi (sage). Leads hermits to Rama.

Agemo (Yoruba) A chameleon who aided Olorun in outwitting Olokun, who was angry at him for letting Obatala create life on her lands without her permission. Agemo outwitted Olokun by changing colour, letting her think that he and Olorun were better cloth dyers than she was. She admitted defeat and there was peace between the gods once again.

Aghasur A dragon sent by Kans to destroy Krishna.

Aghríras Son of Poshang and brother of Afrásiyáb, who was killed by his brother.

Agni The god of fire.

Agora Greek marketplace.

Ahura-Mazda Supreme god of the Persians, god of the sky. Similar to the Hindu god Varuna.

Ajax Ajax of Locris was another warrior at Troy. When Troy was captured, he committed the ultimate sacrilege by seizing Cassandra from her sanctuary with the Palladium.

Ajax Ajax the Greater was the bravest, after Achilles, of all warriors at Troy, fighting Hector in single combat and distinguishing himself in the Battle of the Ships. He was not chosen as the bravest warrior and eventually went mad.

Aje (Igbo) Goddess of the earth and the underworld.

Aje (Yoruba) Goddess of the River Niger, daughter of Yemoja.

Akhet Season of the year when the River Nile traditionally flooded.

Akkadian Person of the first Mesopotamian empire, centred in Akkad.

Akwán Diw An evil spirit who appeared as a wild ass in the court of Kai-khosráu. Rustem fought and defeated the demon, presenting its head to Kai-khosráu.

Alba Irish word for Scotland.

Alberich King of the dwarfs.

Alcinous King of the Phaeacians.

Alf-heim Home of the elves, ruled by Frey.

All Hallowmass All Saints' Day.

Allfather Another name for Odin; Yggdrasill was created by Allfather.

Alsvider Steed of the moon (Mani) chariot.

Alsvin Steed of the sun (Sol) chariot.

Amado Outer panelling of a dwelling, usually made of wood.

Ama-no-uzume Goddess of the dawn, meditation and the arts, who showed courage when faced with a giant who scared the other deities, including Ninigi. Also known as Uzume.

Amaterasu Goddess of the sun and daughter of Izanagi after Izanami's death; she became ruler of the High Plains of Heaven on her father's withdrawal from the world. Sister of Tsuki-yomi and Susanoo.

Ambalika Daughter of the king of Benares.

Ambika Daughter of the king of Benares.

Ambrosia Food of the gods.

Amemet Eater of the dead, monster who devoured the souls of the unworthy.

Amen Original creator deity.

Amen-Ra A being created from the fusion of Ra and Osiris. He champions the poor and those in trouble. Similar to the Greek god Zeus.

Ananda Disciple of Buddha.

Anansi One of the most popular African animal myths, Anansi the spider is a clever and shrewd character who outwits his fellow animals to get his own way. He is an entertaining but morally dubious character. Many African countries tell Anansi stories.

Ananta Thousand-headed snake that sprang from Balarama's mouth, Vishnu's attendant, serpent of infinite time.

Andhrímnir Cook at Valhalla.

Andvaranaut Ring of Andvari, the King of the dwarfs.

Angada Son of Vali, one of the monkey host.

Anger-Chamber Room designated for an angry queen.

Angurboda Loki's first wife, and the mother of Hel, Fenris and Jormungander.

Aniruddha Son of Pradyumna.

Anjana Mother of Hanuman.

Anunnaki Great spirits or gods of Earth.

Ansar God of the sky and father of Ea and Anu. Brother-husband to Kishar. Also known as Anshar or Asshur.

Anshumat A mighty chariot fighter.

Anu God of the sky and lord of heaven, son of Ansar and Kishar.

Anubis Guider of souls and ruler of the underworld before Osiris;

he was one of the divinities who brought Osiris back to life. He is portrayed as a canid, African wolf or jackal.

Apep Serpent and emblem of chaos.

Apollo One of the twelve Olympian gods, son of Zeus and Leto. He is attributed with being the god of plague, music, song and prophecy.

Apsaras Dancing girls of Indra's court and heavenly nymphs.

Apsu Primeval domain of fresh water, originally part of Tiawath with whom he mated to have Mummu. The term is also used for the abyss from which creation came.

Aquila The divine eagle.

Arachne A Lydian woman with great skill in weaving. She was challenged in a competition by the jealous Athene who destroyed her work and when she killed herself, turned her into a spider destined to weave until eternity.

Aralu Goddess of the underworld, also known as Eres-ki-Gal. Married to Nergal.

Ares God of War, 'gold-changer of corpses', and the son of Zeus and Hera.

Argonauts Heroes who sailed with Jason on the ship Argo to fetch the golden fleece from Colchis.

Ariki A high chief, a leader, a master, a lord.

Arjuna The third of the Pandavas.

Aroha Affection, love.

Artemis The virgin goddess of the chase, attributed with being the moon goddess and the primitive mother-goddess. She was daughter of Zeus and Leto.

Arundhati The Northern Crown.

Asamanja Son of Sagara.

Asclepius God of healing who often took the form of a snake. He is the son of Apollo by Coronis.

Asgard Home of the gods, at one root of Yggdrasill.

Ashvatthaman Son of Drona.

Ashvins Twin horsemen, sons of the sun, benevolent gods and related to the divine.

Ashwapati Uncle of Bharata and Satrughna.

Asipû Wizard.

Asopus The god of the River Asopus.

Assagai Spear, usually made from hardwood tipped with iron and used in battle.

Astrolabe Instrument for making astronomical measurements.

Asuras Titans, demons, and enemies of the gods possessing magical powers.

Atef crown White crown made up of the Hedjet, the white crown of Upper Egypt, and red feathers.

Atem The first creator-deity, he is also thought to be the finisher of the world. Also known as Tem.

Athene Virgin warrior-goddess, born from the forehead of Zeus when he swallowed his wife Metis. Plays a key role in the travels of Odysseus, and Perseus.

Atlatl Spear-thrower.

Atua A supernatural being, a god.

Atua-toko A small carved stick, the symbol of the god whom it represents. It was stuck in the ground whilst holding incantations to its presiding god.

Augeas King of Elis, one of the Argonauts.

Augsburg Tyr's city.

Avalon Legendary island where Excalibur was created and where Arthur went to recover from his wounds. It is said he will return from Avalon one day to reclaim his kingdom.

Ba Dead person or soul. Also known as ka.

Bairn Little child, also called bairnie.

Balarama Brother of Krishna.

Balder Son of Frigga; his murder causes Ragnarok. Also spelled as Baldur.

Bali Brother of Sugriva and one of the five great monkeys in the Ramayana.

Balor The evil, one-eyed King of the Fomorians and also grandfather of Lugh of the Long Arm. It was prophesied that Balor would one day be slain by his own grandson so he locked his daughter away on a remote island where he intended that she would never fall pregnant. But Cian, father of Lugh, managed to reach the island disguised as a woman, and Balor's daughter eventually bore him a child. During the second battle of Mag Tured (or Moytura), Balor was killed by Lugh who slung a stone into his giant eye.

Ban King of Benwick, father of Lancelot and brother of King Bors.

Bannock Flat loaf of bread, typically of oat or barley, usually cooked on a griddle.

Banshee Mythical spirit, usually female, who bears tales of imminent death. They often deliver the news by wailing or keening outside homes. Also known as bean sí.

Bard Traditionally a storyteller, poet or music composer whose work often focused on legends.

Barû Seer.

Basswood Any of several North American linden trees with a soft light-coloured wood.

Bastet Goddess of love, fertility and sex and a solar deity. She is often portrayed with the head of a cat.

Bateta (Yoruba) The first human, created alongside Hanna by the Toad and reshaped into human form by the Moon.

Bau Goddess of humankind and the sick, and known as the 'divine physician'. Daughter of Anu.

Bawn Fortified enclosure surrounding a castle.

Beaver Largest rodent in the United States of America, held in high esteem by the native American people. Although a land mammal, it spends a great deal of time in water and has a dense waterproof fur coat to protect it from harsh weather conditions.

Behula Daughter of Saha.

Bel Name for the god En-lil, the word Is also used as a title meaning 'lord'.

Belus Deity who helped form the heavens and earth and created animals and celestial beings. Similar to Zeus in Greek mythology.

Benten Goddess of the sea and one of the Seven Divinities of Luck. Also referred to as the goddess of love, beauty and eloquence and as being the personification of wisdom.

Bere Barley.

Berossus Priest of Bel who wrote a history of Babylon.

Berserker Norse warrior who fights with a frenzied rage.

Bestla Giant mother of Aesir's mortal element.

Bhadra A mighty elephant.

Bhagavati Shiva's wife, also known as Parvati.

Bhagiratha Son of Dilipa.

Bharadhwaja Father of Drona and a hermit.

Bharata One of Dasharatha's four sons.

Bhaumasur A demon, slain by Krishna.

Bhima The second of the Pandavas.

Bhimasha King of Rajagriha and disciple of Buddha.

Bier Frame on which a coffin or dead body is placed before being carried to the grave.

Bifrost Rainbow bridge presided over by Heimdall.

Big-Belly One of Ravana's monsters.

Bilskirnir Thor's palace.

Bodach The term means 'old man'. The Highlanders believed that the Bodach crept down chimneys in order to steal naughty children. In other territories, he was a spirit who warned of death.

Bodkin Large, blunt needle used for threading strips of cloth or tape through cloth; short pointed dagger or blade.

Boer Person of Dutch origin who settled in southern Africa in the late seventeenth century. The term means 'farmer'. Boer people are often called Afrikaners.

Bogle Ghost or phantom; goblin-like creature.

Boliaun Ragwort, a weed with ragged leaves.

Book of the Dead Book for the dead, thought to be written by Thoth, texts from which were written on papyrus and buried with the dead, or carved on the walls of tombs, pyramids or sarcophagi.

Bors King of Gaul and brother of King Ban.

Bothy Small cottage or hut.

Brahma Creator of the world, mythical origin of colour (caste).

Brahmadatta King of Benares.

Brahman Member of the highest Hindu caste, traditionally a priest.

Bran In Scottish legend, Bran is the great hunting hound of Fionn Mac Chumail. In Irish mythology, he is a great hero.

Branstock Giant oak tree in the Volsung's hall; Odin placed a sword in it and challenged the guests of a wedding to withdraw it.

Brave Young warrior of native American descent, sometimes also referred to as a 'buck'.

Bree Thin broth or soup.

Breidablik Balder's palace.

Brigit Scottish saint or spirit associated with the coming of spring.

Brisingamen Freyia's necklace.

Britomartis A Cretan goddess, also known as Dictynna.

Brocéliande Legendary enchanted forest and the supposed burial place of Merlin.

Brokki Dwarf who makes a deal with Loki, and who makes Miolnir, Draupnir and Gulinbursti.

Brollachan A shapeless spirit of unknown origin. One of the most frightening in Scottish mythology, it spoke only two words, 'Myself' and 'Thyself', taking the shape of whatever it sat upon.

Brownie A household spirit or creature which took the form of a small man (usually hideously ugly) who undertakes household chores, and mill or farm work, in exchange for a bowl of milk.

Brugh Borough or town.

Brunhilde A Valkyrie found by Sigurd.

Buddha Founder of buddhism, Gautama, avatar of Vishnu in Hinduism.

Buddhism Buddhism arrived in China in the first century BC via the silk trading route from India and Central Asia. Its founder was Guatama Siddhartha (the Buddha), a religious teacher in northern India. Buddhist doctrine declared that by destroying the causes of all suffering, mankind could attain perfect enlightenment. The religion encouraged a new respect for all living things and brought with it the idea of reincarnation; i.e. that the soul returns to the earth after death in another form, dictated by the individual's behaviour in his previous life. By the fourth century, Buddhism was the dominant religion in China, retaining its powerful influence over the nation until the mid-ninth century.

Buffalo A type of wild ox, once widely scattered over the Great Plains of North America. Also known as a 'bison', the buffalo was an important food source for the Indian tribes and its hide was also used in the construction of tepees and to make clothing. The buffalo was also sometimes revered as a totem animal, i.e. venerated as a direct ancestor of the tribesmen, and its skull used in ceremonial fashion.

Bull of Apis Sacred bull, thought to be the son of Hathor.

Bulu Sacrificial rite.

Bundles, sacred These bundles contained various venerated objects of the tribe, believed to have supernatural powers. Custody or ownership of the bundle was never lightly entered upon, but involved the learning of endless songs and ritual dances.

Bushel Unit of measurement, usually used for agricultural products or food.

Bushi Warrior.

Byre Barn for keeping cattle.

Byrny Coat of mail.

Cacique King or prince.

Cailleach Bheur A witch with a blue face who represents winter. When she is reborn each autumn, snow falls. She is mother of the god of youth (Angus mac Og).

Calabash Gourd from the calabash tree, commonly used as a bottle.

Calchas The seer of Mycenae who accompanied the Greek fleet to Troy. It was his prophecy which stated that Troy would never be taken without the aid of Achilles.

Calpulli Village house, or group or clan of families.

Calumet Ceremonial pipe used by the north American Indians.

Calypso A nymph who lived on the island of Ogygia.

Camaxtli Tlascalan god of war and the chase, similar to Huitzilopochtli.

Camelot King Arthur's castle and centre of his realm.

Caoineag A banshee.

Caravanserai Traveller's inn, traditionally found in Asia or North Africa.

Carle Term for a man, often old; peasant.

Cat A black cat has great mythological significance, is often the bearer of bad luck, a symbol of black magic, and the familiar of a witch. Cats were also the totem for many tribes.

Cath Sith A fairy cat who was believed to be a witch transformed.

Cazi Magical person or influence.

Ceasg A Scottish mermaid with the body of a maiden and the tail of a salmon.

Ceilidh Party.

Cerberus The three-headed dog who guarded the entrance to the Underworld.

Chalchiuhtlicue Goddess of water and the sick or newborn, and wife of Tlaloc. She is often symbolized as a small frog.

Changeling A fairy substitute-child left by fairies in place of a human child they have stolen.

Channa Guatama's charioteer.

Chaos A state from which the universe was created – caused by fire and ice meeting.

Charon The ferryman of the dead who carries souls across the River Styx to Hades.

Charybdis See Scylla and Charybdis.

Chicomecohuatl Chief goddess of maize and one of a group of deities called Centeotl, who care for all aspects of agriculture.

Chicomoztoc Legendary mountain and place of origin of the Aztecs. The name means 'seven caves'.

Chinawezi Primordial serpent.

Chinvat Bridge Bridge of the Gatherer, which the souls of the righteous cross to reach Mount Alborz or the world of the dead. Unworthy beings who try to cross Chinvat Bridge fall or are dragged into a place of eternal punishment.

Chitambaram Sacred city of Shiva's dance.

Chrysaor Son of Poseidon and Medusa, born from the severed neck of Medusa when Perseus beheaded her.

Chryseis Daughter of Chryses who was taken by Agamemnon in the battle of Troy.

Chullasubhadda Wife of Buddha-elect (Sumedha).

Chunda A good smith who entertains Buddha.

Churl Mean or unkind person.

Circe An enchantress and the daughter of Helius. She lived on the island of Aeaea with the power to change men to beasts.

Citlalpol The Mexican name for Venus, or the Great Star, and one of the only stars they worshipped. Also known as Tlauizcalpantecutli, or Lord of the Dawn.

Cleobis and Biton Two men of Argos who dragged the wagon carrying their mother, priestess of Hera, from Argos to the sanctuary.

Clio Muse of history and prophecy.

Clytemnestra Daughter of Tyndareus, sister of Helen, who married Agamemnon but deserted him when he sacrificed Iphigenia, their daughter, at the beginning of the Trojan War.

Coatepetl Mythical mountain, known as the 'serpent mountain'.

Coatl Serpent.

Coatlicue Earth mother and celestial goddess, she gave birth to Huitzilopochtli and his sister, Coyolxauhqui, and the moon and stars.

Codex Ancient book, often a list with pages folded into a zigzag pattern.

Confucius (Kong Fuzi) Regarded as China's greatest sage and ethical teacher, Confucius (551–479 BC) was not especially revered during his lifetime and had a small following of some three thousand people. After the Burning of the Books in 213 BC, interest in his philosophies became widespread. Confucius believed that mankind was essentially good, but argued for a highly structured society, presided over by a strong central government which would set the highest moral standards. The individual's sense of duty and obligation, he argued, would play a vital role in maintaining a well-run state.

Coracle Small, round boat, similar to a canoe. Also known as curragh or currach.

Coyolxauhqui Goddess of the moon and sister to Huitzilopochtli, she was decapitated by her brother after trying to kill their mother.

Creel Large basket made of wicker, usually used for fish.

Crodhmara Fairy cattle.

Cronan Musical humming, thought to resemble a cat purring or the drone of bagpipes.

Crow Usually associated with battle and death, but many mythological figures take this form.

Cu Sith A great fairy dog, usually green and oversized.

Cubit Ancient measurement, equal to the approximate length of a forearm.

Cuculain Irish warrior and hero. Also known as Cuchulainn.

Cutty Girl.

Cyclopes One-eyed giants who were imprisoned in Tartarus by Uranus and Cronus, but released by Zeus, for whom they made thunderbolts. Also a tribe of pastoralists who live without laws, and on, whenever possible, human flesh.

Daedalus Descendant of the Athenian King Erechtheus and son of Eupalamus. He killed his nephew and apprentice. Famed for constructing the labyrinth to house the Minotaur, in which he was later imprisoned. He constructed wings for himself and his son to make their escape.

Dagda One of the principal gods of the Tuatha De Danann, the father and chief, the Celtic equivalent of Zeus. He was the god reputed to have led the People of Dana in their successful conquest of the Fir Bolg.

Dagon God of fish and fertility; he is sometimes described as a sea-monster or chthonic god.

Daikoku God of wealth and one of the gods of luck.

Daimyō Powerful lord or magnate.

Daksha The chief Prajapati.

Dana Also known as Danu, a goddess worshipped from antiquity by the Celts and considered to be the ancestor of the Tuatha De Danann.

Danae Daughter of Acrisius, King of Argos. Acrisius trapped her in a cave when he was warned that his grandson would be the cause of his ultimate death. Zeus came to her and Perseus was born.

Danaids The fifty daughters of Danaus of Argos, by ten mothers.

Daoine Sidhe The people of the Hollow Hills, or Otherworld.

Dardanus Son of Zeus and Electra, daughter of Atlas.

Dasharatha A Manu amongst men, King of Koshala, father of Santa.

Deianeira Daughter of Oeneus, who married Heracles after he won her in a battle with the River Achelous.

Deirdre A beautiful woman doomed to cause the deaths of three Irish heroes and bring war to the whole country. After a soothsayer prophesied her fate, Deidre's father hid her away from the world to prevent it. However, fate finds its way and the events come to pass before Deidre eventually commits suicide to remain with her love.

Demeter Goddess of agriculture and nutrition, whose name means earth mother. She is the mother of Persephone.

Demophoon Son of King Celeus of Eleusis, who was nursed by Demeter and then dropped in the fire when she tried to make him immortal.

Dervish Member of a religious order, often Sufi, known for their wild dancing and whirling.

Desire The god of love.

Deva A god other than the supreme God.

Devadatta Buddha's cousin, plots evil against Buddha.

Dhrishtadyumna Twin brother of Draupadi, slays Drona.

Dibarra God of plague. Also a demonic character or evil spirit.

Dik-dik Dwarf antelope native to eastern and southern Africa.

Dilipa Son of Anshumat, father of Bhagiratha.

Dionysus The god of wine, vegetation and the life force, and of ecstasy. He was considered to be outside the Greek pantheon, and generally thought to have begun life as a mortal.

Dioscuri Castor and Polydeuces, the twin sons of Zeus and Leda, who are important deities.

Distaff Tool used when spinning which holds the wool or flax and keeps the fibres from tangling.

Divan Privy council.

Divots Turfs.

Dog The dog is a symbol of humanity, and usually has a role helping the hero of the myth or legend. Fionn's Bran and Grey Dog are two examples of wild beasts transformed to become invaluable servants.

Dōshin Government official.

Dossal Ornamental altar cloth.

Doughty Persistent and brave person.

Dragon Important animal in Japanese culture, symbolizing power, wealth, luck and success.

Draiglin' Hogney Ogre.

Draupadi Daughter of Drupada.

Draupnir Odin's famous ring, fashioned by Brokki.

Drona A Brahma, son of the great sage Bharadwaja.

Druid An ancient order of Celtic priests held in high esteem who flourished in the pre-Christian era. The word 'druid' is derived from an ancient Celtic one meaning 'very knowledgeable'. These individuals were believed to have mystical powers and in ancient Irish literature possess the ability to conjure up magical charms, to create tempests, to curse and debilitate their enemies and to perform as soothsayers to the royal courts.

Drupada King of the Panchalas.

Dryads Nymphs of the trees.

Dun A stronghold or royal abode surrounded by an earthen wall.

Durga Goddess, wife of Shiva.

Durk Knife. Also spelled as dirk.

Duryodhana One of Drona's pupils.

Dvalin Dwarf visited by Loki; also the name for the stag on Yggdrasill.

Dwarfie Stone Prehistoric tomb or boulder.

Dwarfs Fairies and black elves are called dwarfs.

Dwarkanath The Lord of Dwaraka; Krishna.

Dyumatsena King of the Shalwas and father of Satyavan.

Ea God of water, light and wisdom, and one of the creator deities. He brought arts and civilization to humankind. Also known as Oannes and Nudimmud.

Eabani Hero originally created by Aruru to defeat Gilgamesh, the two became friends and destroyed Khumbaba together. He personifies the natural world.

Each Uisge The mythical water-horse which haunts lochs and appears in various forms.

Ebisu One of the gods of luck. He is also the god of labour and fishermen.

Echo A nymph who was punished by Hera for her endless stories told to distract Hera from Zeus's infidelity.

Ector King Arthur's foster father, who raised Arthur to protect him.

Edda Collection of prose and poetic myths and stories from the Norsemen.

Eight Immortals Three of these are reputed to be historical: Han Chung-li, born in Shaanxi, who rose to become a Marshal of the Empire in 21 BC. Chang Kuo-Lao, who lived in the seventh to eighth century AD, and Lü Tung-pin, who was born in AD 755.

Einheriear Odin's guests at Valhalla.

Eisa Loki' daughter.

Ekake (Ibani) Person of great intelligence, which means 'tortoise'. Also known as Mbai (Igbo).

Ekalavya Son of the king of the Nishadas.

Electra Daughter of Agamemnon and Clytemnestra.

Eleusis A town in which the cult of Demeter is centred.

Elf Sigmund is buried by an elf; there are light and dark elves (the latter called dwarfs).

Elokos (Central African) Imps of dwarf-demons who eat human flesh.

Elpenor The youngest of Odysseus's crew who fell from the roof of Circe's house on Aeaea and visited with Odysseus at Hades.

Elysium The home of the blessed dead.

Emain Macha The capital of ancient Ulster.

Emma Dai-o King of hell and judge of the dead.

En-lil God of the lower world, storms and mist, who held sway over the ghostly animistic spirits, which at his bidding might pose as the friends or enemies of men. Also known as Bel.

Eos Goddess of the dawn and sister of the sun and moon.

Erichthonius A child born of the semen spilled when Hephaestus tried to rape Athene on the Acropolis.

Eridu The home of Ea and one of the two major cities of Babylonian civilization.

Erin Term for Ireland, originally spelled Éirinn.

Erirogho Magical mixture made from the ashes of the dead.

Eros God of Love, the son of Aphrodite.

Erpa Hereditary chief.

Erysichthon A Thessalian who cut down a grove sacred to Demeter, who punished him with eternal hunger.

Eshu (Yoruba) God of mischief. He also tests people's characters and controls law enforcement.

Eteocles Son of Oedipus.

Eumaeus Swineherd of Odysseus's family at Ithaca.

Euphemus A son of Poseidon who could walk on water. He sailed with the Argonauts.

Europa Daughter of King Agenor of Tyre, who was taken by Zeus to Crete.

Eurydice A Thracian nymph married to Orpheus.

Excalibur The magical sword given to Arthur by the Lady of the Lake. In some versions of the myths, Excalibur is also the sword that the young Arthur pulls from the stone to become king.

Fabulist Person who composes or tells fables.

Fafnir Shape-changer who kills his father and becomes a dragon to guard the family jewels. Slain by Sigurd.

Fairy The word is derived from 'Fays' which means Fates. They are immortal, with the gift of prophecy and of music, and their role changes according to the origin of the myth. They were often considered to be little people, with enormous propensity for mischief, but they are central to many myths and legends, with important powers.

Faro (Mali, Guinea) God of the sky.

Fates In Greek mythology, daughters of Zeus and Themis, who spin the thread of a mortal's life and cut it when his time is due. Called Norns in Viking mythology.

Fenris A wild wolf, who is the son of Loki. He roams the earth after Ragnarok.

Ferhad Sculptor who fell in love with Shireen, the wife of Khosru, and undertook a seemingly impossible task to clear a passage through the mountain of Beysitoun and join the rivers in return for winning Shireen's hand.

Fialar Red cock of Valhalla.

Fianna/Fenians The word 'fianna' was used in early times to describe young warrior-hunters. These youths evolved under the leadership of Finn Mac Cumaill as a highly skilled band of military men who took up service with various kings throughout Ireland.

Filheim Land of mist, at the end of one of Yggdrasill's roots.

Fingal Another name for Fionn Mac Chumail, used after MacPherson's Ossian in the eighteenth century.

Fionn Mac Chumail Irish and Scottish warrior, with great powers of fairness and wisdom. He is known not for physical strength but for knowledge, sense of justice, generosity and canny instinct. He had two hounds, which were later discovered to be his nephews transformed. He became head of the Fianna, or Féinn, fighting the enemies of Ireland and Scotland. He was the father of Oisin (also called Ossian, or other derivatives), and father or grandfather of Osgar.

Fir Bolg One of the ancient, pre-Gaelic peoples of Ireland who were reputed to have worshipped the god Bulga, meaning god of lighting. They are thought to have colonized Ireland around 1970 BC, after the death of Nemed and to have reigned for a short period of thirty-seven years before their defeat by the Tuatha De Danann.

Fir Chlis Nimble men or merry dancers, who are the souls of fallen angels.

Flitch Side of salted and cured bacon.

Folkvang Freyia's palace.

Fomorians A race of monstrous beings, popularly conceived as sea-pirates with some supernatural characteristics who opposed the earliest settlers in Ireland, including the Nemedians and the Tuatha De Danann.

Frey Comes to Asgard with Freyia as a hostage following the war between the Aesir and the Vanir.

Freyia Comes to Asgard with Frey as a hostage following the war between the Aesir and the Vanir. Goddess of beauty and love.

Frigga Odin's wife and mother of gods; she is goddess of the earth.

Fuath Evil spirits which lived in or near the water.

Fulla Frigga's maidservant.

Furies Creatures born from the blood of Cronus, guarding the greatest sinners of the Underworld. Their power lay in their ability to drive mortals mad. Snakes writhed in their hair and around their waists.

Furoshiki Cloths used to wrap things.

Gae Bolg Cuchulainn alone learned the use of this weapon from the woman-warrior, Scathach and with it he slew his own son Connla and his closest friend, Ferdia. Gae Bolg translates as 'harpoon-like javelin' and the deadly weapon was reported to have been created by Bulga, the god of lighting.

Gaea Goddess of Earth, born from Chaos, and the mother of Uranus and Pontus. Also spelled as Gaia.

Gage Object of value presented to a challenger to symbolize good faith.

Galahad Knight of the Round Table, who took up the search for the Holy Grail. Son of Lancelot, Galahad is considered the purest and most perfect knight.

Galatea Daughter of Nereus and Doris, a sea-nymph loved by Polyphemus, the Cyclops.

Gandhari Mother of Duryodhana.

Gandharvas Demi-gods and musicians.

Gandjharva Musical ministrants of the upper air.

Ganesha Elephant-headed god of scribes and son of Shiva.

Ganges Sacred river personified by the goddess Ganga, wife of Shiva and daughter of the mount Himalaya.

Gareth of Orkney King Arthur's nephew and knight of the Round Table.

Garm Hel's hound.

Garuda King of the birds and mount Vishnu, the divine bird, attendant of Narayana.

Gautama Son of Suddhodana and also known as Siddhartha.

Gawain Nephew of King Arthur and knight of the Round Table, he is best known for his adventure with the Green Knight, who challenges one of Arthur's knights to cut off his head, but only if he agrees to be beheaded in turn in a year and a day, if the Green Knight survives. Gawain beheads the Green Knight, who simply replaces his head. At the appointed time, they meet, and the Green Knight swings his axe but merely nicks Gawain's skin instead of beheading him.

Geisha Performance artist or entertainer, usually female.

Geri Odin's wolf.

Ghommid (Yoruba) Term for mythological creatures such as goblins or ogres.

Giallar Bridge in Filheim.

Giallarhorn Heimdall's trumpet – the final call signifies Ragnarok.

Giants In Greek mythology, a race of beings born from Gaea, grown from the blood that dropped from the castrated Uranus. Usually represent evil in Viking mythology.

Gilgamesh King of Erech known as a half-human, half-god hero similar to the Greek Heracles, and often listed with the gods. He is the personification of the sun and is protected by the god Shamash, who in some texts is described as his father. He is also portrayed as an evil tyrant at times.

Gillie Someone who works for a Scottish chief, usually as an attendant or servant; guide for fishing or hunting parties.

Gladheim Where the twelve deities of Asgard hold their thrones. Also called Gladsheim.

Gled Bird of prey.

Golden Fleece Fleece of the ram sent by Poseidon to substitute for Phrixus when his father was going to sacrifice him. The Argonauts went in search of the fleece.

Goodman Man of the house.

Goodwife Woman of the house.

Gopis Lovers of the young Krishna and milkmaids.

Gorgon One of the three sisters, including Medusa, whose frightening looks could turn mortals to stone.

Graces Daughters of Aphrodite by Zeus.

Gramercy Expression of surprise or strong feeling.

Great Head The Iroquois Indians believed in the existence of a curious being known as Great Head, a creature with an enormous head poised on slender legs.

Great Spirit The name given to the Creator of all life, as well as the term used to describe the omnipotent force of the Creator existing in every living thing.

Great-Flank One of Ravana's monsters.

Green Knight A knight dressed all in green and with green hair and skin who challenged one of Arthur's knights to strike him a blow with an axe and that, if he survived, he would return to behead the knight in a year and a day. He turned out to be Lord Bertilak and was under an enchantment cast by Morgan le Fay to test Arthur's knights.

Gruagach Mythical creature, often a giant or ogre similar to a wild man of the woods. The term can also refer to other mythical creatures such as brownies or fairies. As a brownie, he is usually dressed in red or green as opposed to the traditional brown. He has great power to enchant the hapless, or to help mortals who are worthy (usually heroes). He often appears to challenge a boy-hero, during his period of education.

Gudea High priest of Lagash, known to be a patron of the arts and a writer himself.

Guebre Religion founded by Zoroaster, the Persian prophet.

Gugumatz Creator god who, with Huracan, formed the sky, earth and everything on it.

Guha King of Nishadha.

Guidewife Woman.

Guinevere Wife of King Arthur; she is often portrayed as a virtuous lady and wife, but is perhaps best known for having a love affair with Lancelot, one of Arthur's friends and knights of the Round Table. Her name is also spelled Guenever.

Gulistan *Rose Garden*, written by the poet Sa'di

Gungnir Odin's spear, made of Yggdrasill wood, and the tip fashioned by Dvalin.

Gylfi A wandering king to whom the Eddas are narrated.

Haab Mayan solar calendar that consisted of eighteen twenty-day months.

Hades One of the three sons of Cronus; brother of Poseidon and Zeus. Hades is King of the Underworld, which is also known as the House of Hades.

Haere-mai Maori phrase meaning 'come here, welcome.'

Haere-mai-ra, me o tatou mate Maori phrase meaning 'come here, that I may sorrow with you.'

Haere-ra Maori phrase meaning 'goodbye, go, farewell.'

Haji Muslim pilgrim who has been to Mecca.

Hakama Traditional Japanese clothing, worn on the bottom half of the body.

Hanuman General of the monkey people.

Harakiri Suicide, usually by cutting or stabbing the abdomen. Also known as seppuku.

Hari-Hara Shiva and Vishnu as one god.

Harmonia Daughter of Ares and Aphrodite, wife of Cadmus.

Hatamoto High-ranking samurai.

Hathor Great cosmic mother and patroness of lovers. She is portrayed as a cow.

Hati The wolf who pursues the sun and moon.

Hatshepsut Second female pharaoh.

Hauberk Armour to protect the neck and shoulders, sometimes a full-length coat of mail.

Hector Eldest son of King Priam who defended Troy from the Greeks. He was killed by Achilles.

Hecuba The second wife of Priam, King of Troy. She was turned into a dog after Troy was lost.

Heimdall White god who guards the Bifrost bridge.

Hel Goddess of death and Loki's daughter. Also known as Hela.

Helen Daughter of Leda and Tyndareus, King of Sparta, and the most beautiful woman in the world. She was responsible for starting the Trojan War.

Heliopolis City in modern-day Cairo, known as the City of the Sun and the central place of worship of Ra. Also known as Anu.

Helius The sun, son of Hyperion and Theia.

Henwife Witch.

Hephaestus or **Hephaistos** The Smith of Heaven.

Hera A Mycenaean palace goddess, married to Zeus.

Heracles An important Greek hero, the son of Zeus and Alcmena. His name means 'Glory of Hera'. He performed twelve labours for King Eurystheus, and later became a god.

Hermes The conductor of souls of the dead to Hades, and god of trickery and of trade. He acts as messenger to the gods.

Hermod Son of Frigga and Odin who travelled to see Hel in order to reclaim Balder for Asgard.

Hero and Leander Hero was a priestess of Aphrodite, loved by Leander, a young man of Abydos. He drowned trying to see her.

Hestia Goddess of the hearth, daughter of Cronus and Rhea.

Hieroglyphs Type of writing that combines symbols and pictures, usually cut into tombs or rocks, or written on papyrus.

Himalaya Great mountain and range, father of Parvati.

Hiordis Wife of Sigmund and mother of Sigurd.

Hoderi A fisher and son of Okuninushi.

Hodur Balder's blind twin; known as the personification of darkness.

Hoenir Also called Vili; produced the first humans with Odin and Loki, and was one of the triad responsible for the creation of the world.

Hōichi the Earless A biwa hōshi, a blind storyteller who played the biwa or lute. Also a priest.

Holger Danske Legendary Viking warrior who is thought to never die. He sleeps until he is needed by his people and then he will rise to protect them.

Homayi Phoenix.

Hoodie Mythical creature which often appears as a crow.

Hoori A hunter and son of Okuninushi.

Horus God of the sky and kinship, son of Isis and Osiris. He captained the boat that carried Ra across the sky. He is depicted with the head of a falcon.

Hotei One of the gods of luck. He also personifies humour and contentment.

Houlet Owl.

Houri Beautiful virgin from paradise.

Hrim-faxi Steed of the night.

Hubris Presumptuous behaviour which causes the wrath of the gods to be brought on to mortals.

Hueytozoztli Festival dedicated to Tlaloc and, at times, Chicomecohuatl or other deities. Also the fourth month of the Aztec calendar.

Hugin Odin's raven.

Huitzilopochtli   God of war and the sun, also connected with the summer and crops; one of the principal Aztec deities. He was born a full-grown adult to save his mother, Coatlicue, from the jealousy of his sister, Coyolxauhqui, who tried to kill Coatlicue. The Mars of the Aztec gods. In some origin stories he is one of four offspring of Ometeotl and Omecihuatl.

Hurley   A traditional Irish game played with sticks and balls, quite similar to hockey.

Hurons   A tribe of Iroquois stock, originally one people with the Iroquois.

Huveane   (Pedi, Venda) Creator of humankind, who made a baby from clay into which he breathed life. He is known as the High God or Great God. He is also known as a trickster god.

Hymir   Giant who fishes with Thor and is drowned by him.

Iambe   Daughter of Pan and Echo, servant to King Celeus of Eleusis and Metaeira.

Icarus   Son of Daedalus, who plunged to his death after escaping from the labyrinth.

Ichneumon   Mongoose.

Idunn   Guardian of the youth-giving apples.

Ifa   (Yoruba) God of wisdom and divination. Also the term for a Yoruban religion.

Ife   (Yoruba) The place Obatala first arrived on Earth and took for his home.

Igigi   Great spirits or gods of Heaven and the sky.

Igraine   Wife of the duke of Tintagel, enemy of Uther Pendragon, who marries Uther when her first husband dies. She is King Arthur's mother.

Ile (Yoruba) Goddess of the earth.

Imhetep High priest and wise sage. He is sometimes thought to be the son of Ptah.

Imam Person who leads prayers in a mosque.

Imana (Banyarwanda) Creator or sky god.

In The male principle who, joined with Yo, the female side, brought about creation and the first gods. In and Yo correspond to the Chinese Yang and Yin.

Inari God of rice, fertility, agriculture and, later, the fox god. Inari has both good and evil attributes but is often presented as an evil trickster.

Indra The King of Heaven.

Indrajit Son of Ravana.

Indrasen Daughter of Nala and Damayanti.

Indrasena Son of Nala and Damayanti.

Inundation Annual flooding of the River Nile.

Iphigenia The eldest daughter of Agamemnon and Clytemnestra who was sacrificed to appease Artemis and obtain a fair wind for Troy.

Iris Messenger of the gods who took the form of a rainbow.

Iseult Princess of Ireland and niece of the Morholt. She falls in love with Tristan after consuming a love potion but is forced to marry King Mark of Cornwall.

Ishtar Goddess of love, beauty, justice and war, especially in Ninevah, and earth mother who symbolizes fertility. Married to Tammuz, she is similar to the Greek goddess Aphrodite. Ishtar is sometimes known as Innana or Irnina.

Isis Goddess of the Nile and the moon, sister-wife of Osiris. She and her son, Horus, are sometimes thought of in a similar way to Mary and Jesus. She was one of the most worshipped female

Egyptian deities and was instrumental in returning Osiris to life after he was killed by his brother, Set.

Istakbál Deputation of warriors.

Izanagi Deity and brother-husband to Izanami, who together created the Japanese islands from the Floating Bridge of Heaven. Their offspring populated Japan.

Izanami Deity and sister-wife of Izanagi, creator of Japan. Their children include Amaterasu, Tsuki-yomi and Susanoo.

Jade It was believed that jade emerged from the mountains as a liquid which then solidified after ten thousand years to become a precious hard stone, green in colour. If the correct herbs were added to it, it could return to its liquid state and when swallowed increase the individual's chances of immortality.

Jambavan A noble monkey.

Jason Son of Aeson, King of Iolcus and leader of the voyage of the Argonauts.

Jatayu King of all the eagle-tribes.

Jesseraunt Flexible coat of armour or mail.

Jimmo Legendary first emperor of Japan. He is thought to be descended from Hoori, while other tales claim him to be descended from Amaterasu through her grandson, Ninigi.

Jizo God of little children and the god who calms the troubled sea.

Jord Daughter of Nott; wife of Odin.

Jormungander The world serpent; son of Loki. Legends tell that when his tail is removed from his mouth, Ragnarok has arrived.

Jorō Geisha who also worked as a prostitute.

Jotunheim Home of the giants.

Ju Ju tree Deciduous tree that produces edible fruit.

Jurasindhu A rakshasa, father-in-law of Kans.

Jyeshtha Goddess of bad luck.

Ka Life power or soul. Also known as ba.

Kai-káús Son of Kai-kobád. He led an army to invade Mázinderán, home of the demon-sorcerers, after being persuaded by a demon. Known for his ambitious schemes, he later tried to reach Heaven by trapping eagles to fly him there on his throne.

Kaikeyi Mother of Bharata, one of Dasharatha's three wives.

Kai-khosrau Son of Saiawúsh, who killed Afrásiyáb in revenge for the death of his father.

Kai-kobád Descendant of Feridún, he was selected by Zál to lead an army against Afrásiyáb. Their powerful army, led by Zál and Rustem, drove back Afrásiyáb's army, who then agreed to peace.

Kailyard Kitchen garden or small plot, usually used for growing vegetables.

Kali The Black, wife of Shiva.

Kalindi Daughter of the sun, wife of Krishna.

Kaliya A poisonous hydra that lived in the jamna.

Kalki Incarnation of Vishnu yet to come.

Kalnagini Serpent who kills Lakshmindara.

Kal-Purush The Time-man, Bengali name for Orion.

Kaluda A disciple of Buddha.

Kalunga-ngombe (Mbundu) Death, also depicted as the king of the netherworld.

Kama God of desire.

Kamadeva Desire, the god of love.

Kami Spirits, deities or forces of nature.

Kamund Lasso.

Kans King of Mathura, son of Ugrasena and Pavandrekha.

Kanva Father of Shakuntala.

Kappa River goblin with the body of a tortoise and the head of an ape. Kappa love to challenge human beings to single combat.

Karakia Invocation, ceremony, prayer.

Karna Pupil of Drona.

Kaross Blanket or rug, also worn as a traditional garment. It is often made from the skins of animals which have been sewn together.

Kasbu A period of twenty-four hours.

Kashyapa One of Dasharatha's counsellors.

Kauravas or Kurus Sons of Dhritarashtra, pupils of Drona.

Kaushalya Mother of Rama, one of Dasharatha's three wives.

Kay Son of Ector and adopted brother to King Arthur, he becomes one of Arthur's knights of the Round Table.

Keb God of the earth and father of Osiris and Isis, married to Nut. Keb is identified with Kronos, the Greek god of time.

Kehua Spirit, ghost.

Kelpie Another word for each uisge, the water-horse.

Ken Know.

Keres Black-winged demons or daughters of the night.

Keshini Wife of Sagara.

Khalif Leader.

Khara Younger brother of Ravana.

Khepera God who represents the rising sun. He is portrayed as a scarab. Also known as Nebertcher.

Kher-heb Priest and magician who officiated over rituals and ceremonies.

Khnemu God of the source of the Nile and one of the original Egyptian deities. He is thought to be the creator of children and of other gods. He is portrayed as a ram.

Khosru King and husband to Shireen, daughter of Maurice, the Greek Emperor. He was murdered by his own son, who wanted his kingdom and his wife.

Khumbaba Monster and guardian of the goddess Irnina, a form of the goddess Ishtar. Khumbaba is likened to the Greek gorgon.

Kia-ora Welcome, good luck. A greeting.

Kiboko Hippopotamus.

Kikinu Soul.

Kimbanda (Mbundu) Doctor.

Kimono Traditional Japanese clothing, similar to a robe.

King Arthur Legendary king of Britain who plucked the magical sword from the stone, marking him as the heir of Uther Pendragon and 'true king' of Britain. He and his knights of the Round Table defended Britain from the Saxons and had many adventures, including searching for the Holy Grail. Finally wounded in battle, he left Britain for the mythical Avalon, vowing to one day return to reclaim his kingdom.

Kingu Tiawath's husband, a god and warrior who she promised would rule Heaven once he helped her defeat the 'gods of light'. He was killed by Merodach who used his blood to make clay, from which he formed the first humans. In some tales, Kingu is Tiawath's son as well as her consort.

Kinnaras Human birds with musical instruments under their wings.

Kinyamkela (Zaramo) Ghost of a child.

Kirk Church, usually a term for Church of Scotland churches.

Kirtle One-piece garment, similar to a tunic, which was worn by men or women.

Kis Solar deity, usually depicted as an eagle.

Kishar Earth mother and sister-wife to Anshar.

Kist Trunk or large chest.

Kitamba (Mbundu) Chief who made his whole village go into mourning when his head-wife, Queen Muhongo, died. He also pledged that no one should speak or eat until she was returned to him.

Knowe Knoll or hillock.

Kojiki One of two myth-histories of Japan, along with the *Nihon Shoki*.

Ko-no-Hana Goddess of Mount Fuji, princess and wife of Ninigi.

Kore 'Maiden', another name for Persephone.

Kraal Traditional rural African village, usually consisting of huts surrounded by a fence or wall. Also an animal enclosure.

Krishna The Dark one, worshipped as an incarnation of Vishnu.

Kui-see Edible root.

Kumara Son of Shiva and Paravati, slays demon Taraka.

Kumbha-karna Ravana's brother.

Kunti Mother of the Pandavas.

Kura Red. The sacred colour of the Maori.

Kusha or Kusi One of Sita's two sons.

Kvasir Clever warrior and colleague of Odin. He was responsible for finally outwitting Loki.

Kwannon Goddess of mercy.

Labyrinth A prison built at Knossos for the Minotaur by Daedalus.

Lady of the Lake Enchantress who presents Arthur with Excalibur.

Laertes King of Ithaca and father of Odysseus.

Laestrygonians Savage giants encountered by Odysseus on his travels.

Laili In love with Majnun but unable to marry him, she was given to the prince, Ibn Salam, to marry. When he died, she escaped and found Majnun, but they could not be legally married. The couple died of grief and were buried together. Also known as Laila.

Laird Person who owns a significant estate in Scotland.

Lakshmana Brother of Rama and his companion in exile.

Lakshmi Consort of Vishnu and a goddess of beauty and good fortune.

Lakshmindara Son of Chand resurrected by Manasa Devi.

Lancelot Knight of the Round Table. Lancelot was raised by the Lady of the Lake. While he went on many quests, he is perhaps best known for his affair with Guinevere, King Arthur's wife.

Land of Light One of the names for the realm of the fairies. If a piece of metal welded by human hands is put in the doorway to their land, the door cannot close. The door to this realm is only open at night, and usually at a full moon.

Lang syne The days of old.

Lao Tzu (Laozi) The ancient Taoist philosopher thought to have been born in 571 BC a contemporary of Confucius with whom, it is said, he discussed the tenets of Tao. Lao Tzu was an advocate of simple rural existence and looked to the Yellow Emperor and Shun as models of efficient government. His philosophies were recorded in the Tao Te Ching. Legends surrounding his birth suggest that he emerged from the left-hand side of his mother's body, with white hair and a long white beard, after a confinement lasting eighty years.

Laocoon A Trojan wiseman who predicted that the wooden horse contained Greek soldiers.

Laomedon The King of Troy who hired Apollo and Poseidon to build the impregnable walls of Troy.

Lava Son of Sita.

Leda Daughter of the King of Aetolia, who married Tyndareus. Helen and Clytemnestra were her daughters.

Legba (Dahomey) Youngest offspring of Mawu-Lisa. He was given the gift of all languages. It was through him that humans could converse with the gods.

Leman Lover.

Leprechaun Mythical creature from Irish folk tales who often appears as a mischievous and sometimes drunken old man.

Lethe One of the four rivers of the Underworld, also called the River of Forgetfulness.

Lif The female survivor of Ragnarok.

Lifthrasir The male survivor of Ragnarok.

Lil Demon.

Liongo (Swahili) Warrior and hero.

Lofty mountain Home of Ahura-Mazda.

Logi Utgard-loki's cook.

Loki God of fire and mischief-maker of Asgard; he eventually brings about Ragnarok. Also spelled as Loptur.

Lotus-Eaters A race of people who live a dazed, drugged existence, the result of eating the lotus flower.

Ma'at State of order meaning truth, order or justice. Personified by the goddess Ma'at, who was Thoth's consort.

Macha There are thought to be several different Machas who appear in quite a number of ancient Irish stories. For the purposes of this book, however, the Macha referred to is the wife of Crunnchu. The story unfolds that after her husband had boasted of her great athletic ability to the King, she was subsequently forced to run against his horses in spite of the fact that she was heavily pregnant. Macha died giving birth to her twin babies and with her dying breath she cursed Ulster for nine generations, proclaiming that it would suffer the weakness of a woman in childbirth in times of great stress. This curse had its most disastrous effect when Medb of Connacht invaded Ulster with her great army.

Machi-bugyō Senior official or magistrate, usually samurai.

Macuilxochitl God of art, dance and games, and the patron of luck in gaming. His name means 'source of flowers' or 'prince of flowers'. Also known as Xochipilli, meaning 'five-flower'.

Madake Weapon used for whipping, made of bamboo.

Maduma Taro tuber.

Mag Muirthemne Cuchulainn's inheritance. A plain extending from River Boyne to the mountain range of Cualgne, close to Emain Macha in Ulster.

Magni Thor's son.

Mahaparshwa One of Ravana's generals.

Maharaksha Son of Khara, slain at Lanka.

Mahasubhadda Wife of Buddha-select (Sumedha).

Majnun Son of a chief, who fell in love with Laili and followed her tribe through the desert, becoming mad with love until they were briefly reunited before dying.

Makaras Mythical fish-reptiles of the sea.

Makoma (Senna) Folk hero who defeated five mighty giants.

Mana Power, authority, prestige, influence, sanctity, luck.

Manasa Devi Goddess of snakes, daughter of Shiva by a mortal woman.

Manasha Goddess of snakes.

Mandavya Daughter of Kushadhwaja.

Man-Devourer One of Ravana's monsters.

Mandodari Wife of Ravana.

Mandrake Poisonous plant from the nightshade family which has hallucinogenic and hypnotic qualities if ingested. Its roots resemble the human form and it has supposedly magical qualities.

Mani The moon.

Manitto Broad term used to describe the supernatural or a potent spirit among the Algonquins, the Iroquois and the Sioux.

Man-Slayer One of Ravana's counsellors.

Manthara Kaikeyi's evil nurse, who plots Rama's ruin.

Mantle Cloak or shawl.

Manu Lawgiver.

Manu Mythical mountain on which the sun sets.

Mara The evil one, tempts Gautama.

Markandeya One of Dasharatha's counsellors.

Mashu Mountain of the Sunset, which lies between Earth and the underworld. Guarded by scorpion-men.

Matali Sakra's charioteer.

Mawu-Lisa (Dahomey) Twin offspring of Nana Baluka. Mawu (female) and Lisa (male) are often joined to form one being. Their own offspring populated the world.

Mbai (Igbo) Person of great intelligence, also known as Ekake (Ibani), which means 'tortoise'.

Medea Witch and priestess of Hecate, daughter of Aeetes and sister of Circe. She helped Jason in his quest for the Golden Fleece.

Medusa One of the three Gorgons whose head had the power to turn onlookers to stone.

Melpomene One of the muses, and mother of the Sirens.

Menaka One of the most beautiful dancers in Heaven.

Menat Amulet, usually worn for protection.

Mendicant Beggar.

Menelaus King of Sparta, brother of Agamemnon. Married Helen and called war against Troy when she eloped with Paris.

Menthu Lord of Thebes and god of war. He is portrayed as a hawk or falcon.

Mere-pounamu A native weapon made of a rare green stone.

Merlin Wizard and advisor to King Arthur. He is thought to be the son of a human female and an incubus (male demon). He brought about Arthur's birth and ascension to king, then acted as his mentor.

Merodach God who battled Tiawath and defeated her by cutting out her heart and dividing her corpse into two pieces. He used these pieces to divide the upper and lower waters once controlled by Tiawath, making a dwelling for the gods of light. He also created humankind. Also known as Marduk.

Merrow Mythical mermaid-like creature, often depicted with an enchanted cap called a cohuleen driuth which allows it to travel between land and the depths of the sea. Also known as murúch.

Metaneira Wife of Celeus, King of Eleusis, who hired Demeter in disguise as her nurse.

Metztli Goddess of the moon, her name means 'lady of the night'. Also known as Yohualtictl.

Michabo Also known as Manobozho, or the Great Hare, the principal deity of the Algonquins, maker and preserver of the earth, sun and moon.

Mictlan God of the dead and ruler of the underworld. He was married to Mictecaciuatl and is often represented as a bat. He is also the Aztec lord of Hades. Also known as Mictlantecutli. Mictlan is also the name for the underworld.

Midgard Dwelling place of humans (Earth).

Midsummer A time when fairies dance and claim human victims.

Mihrab Father of Rúdábeh and descendant of Zohák, the serpent-king.

Milesians A group of iron-age invaders led by the sons of Mil, who arrived in Ireland from Spain around 500 BC and overcame the Tuatha De Danann.

Mimir God of the ocean. His head guards a well; reincarnated after Ragnarok.

Minos King of Crete, son of Zeus and Europa. He was considered to have been the ruler of a sea empire.

Minotaur A creature born of the union between Pasiphae and a Cretan Bull.

Minúchihr King who lives to be one hundred and twenty years old. Father of Nauder.

Miolnir *See* Mjolnir.

Mithra God of the sun and light in Iran, protector of truth and guardian of pastures and cattle. Alo known as Mitra in Hindu mythology and Mithras in Roman mythology.

Mixcoatl God of the chase or the hunt. Sometimes depicted as the god of air and thunder, he introduced fire to humankind. His name means 'cloud serpent'.

Mjolnir Hammer belonging to the Norse god of thunder, which is used as a fearsome weapon which always returns to Thor's hand, and as an instrument of consecration.

Mnoatia Forest spirits.

Moccasins One-piece shoes made of soft leather, especially deerskin.

Modi Thor's son.

Moly A magical plant given to Odysseus by Hermes as protection against Circe's powers.

Montezuma Great emperor who consolidated the Aztec Empire.

Mordred Bastard son of King Arthur and Morgawse, Queen of Orkney, who, unknown to Arthur, was his half-sister. Mordred becomes one of King Arthur's knights of the Round Table before betraying and fatally wounding Arthur, causing him to leave Britain for Avalon.

Morgan le Fay Enchantress and half-sister to King Arthur, Morgan was an apprentice of Merlin's. She is generally depicted as benevolent, yet did pit herself against Arthur and his knights on occasion. She escorts Arthur on his final journey to Avalon. Also known as Morgain le Fay.

Morholt The Knight sent to Cornwall to force King Mark to pay tribute to Ireland. He is killed by Tristan.

Morongoe the brave (Lesotho) Man who was turned into a snake by evil spirits because Tau was jealous that he had married the beautiful Mokete, the chief's daughter. Morongoe was returned to human form after his son, Tsietse, returned him to their family.

Mosima (Bapedi) The underworld or abyss.

Mount Fuji Highest mountain in Japan, on the island of Honshū.

Mount Kunlun This mountain features in many Chinese legends as the home of the great emperors on Earth. It is written in the *Shanghaijing* (*The Classic of Mountains and Seas*) that this towering structure measured no less than 3300 miles in circumference and 4000 miles in height. It acted both as a central pillar to support the heavens, and as a gateway between Heaven and Earth.

Moving Finger Expression for taking responsibility for one's life and actions, which cannot be undone.

Moytura Translated as the 'Plain of Weeping', Mag Tured, or Moytura, was where the Tuatha De Danann fought two of their most significant battles.

Mua An old-time Polynesian god.

Muezzin Person who performs the Muslim call to prayer.

Mugalana A disciple of Buddha.

Muilearteach The Cailleach Bheur of the water, who appears as a witch or a sea-serpent. On land she grew larger and stronger by fire.

Mul-lil God of Nippur, who took the form of a gazelle.

Muloyi Sorcerer, also called mulaki, murozi, ndozi or ndoki.

Mummu Son of Tiawath and Apsu. He formed a trinity with them to battle the gods. Also known as Moumis. In some tales, Mummu is also Merodach, who eventually destroyed Tiawath.

Munin Odin's raven.

Murile (Chaga) Man who dug up a taro tuber that resembled his baby brother, which turned into a living boy. His mother killed the baby when she saw Murile was starving himself to feed it.

Murtough Mac Erca King who ruled Ireland when many of its people – including his wife and family – were converting to Christianity. He remained a pagan.

Muses Goddesses of poetry and song, daughters of Zeus and Mnemosyne.

Musha Expression, often of surprise.

Muskrat North American beaver-like, amphibious rodent.

Muspell Home of fire, and the fire-giants.

Mwidzilo Taboo which, if broken, can cause death.

Nabu God of writing and wisdom. Also known as Nebo. Thought to be the son of Merodach.

Nahua Ancient Mexicans.

Nakula Pandava twin skilled in horsemanship.

Nala One of the monkey host, son of Vishvakarma.

Nana Baluka (Dahomey) Mother of all creation. She gave birth to an androgynous being with two faces. The female face was Mawu, who controlled the night and lands to the west. The male face was Lisa and he controlled the day and the east.

Nanahuatl Also known as Nanauatzin. Presided over skin diseases and known as Leprous, which in Nahua meant 'divine'.

Nandi Shiva's bull.

Nanna Balder's wife.

Nannar God of the moon and patron of the city of Ur.

Naram-Sin Son or ancestor of Sargon and king of the Four Zones or Quarters of Babylon.

Narcissus Son of the River Cephisus. He fell in love with himself and died as a result.

Narve Son of Loki.

Nataraja Manifestation of Shiva, Lord of the Dance.

Natron Preservative used in embalming, mined from the Natron Valley in Egypt.

Nauder Son of Minúchihr, who became king on his death and was tyrannical and hated until Sám begged him to follow in the footsteps of his ancestors.

Nausicaa Daughter of Alcinous, King of Phaeacia, who fell in love with Odysseus.

Nebuchadnezzar Famous king of Babylon. Also known as Nebuchadrezzar.

Necromancy Communicating with the dead.

Nectar Drink of the gods.

Neith Goddess of hunting, fate and war. Neith is sometimes known as the creator of the universe.

Nemesis Goddess of retribution and daughter of night.

Neoptolemus Son of Achilles and Deidameia, he came to Troy at the end of the war to wear his father's armour. He sacrificed Polyxena at the tomb of Achilles.

Nephthys Goddess of the air, night and the dead. Sister of Isis and sister-wife to Seth, she is also the mother of Anubis.

Nereids Sea-nymphs who are the daughters of Nereus and Doris. Thetis, mother of Achilles, was a Nereid.

Nergal God of death and patron god of Cuthah, which was often known as a burial place. He is also known as the god of fire. Married to Aralu, the goddess of the underworld.

Nestor Wise King of Pylus, who led the ships to Troy with Agamemnon and Menelaus.

Neta Daughter of Shiva, friend of Manasa.

Ngai (Gikuyu) Creator god.

Ngaka (Lesotho) Witch doctor.

Niflheim The underworld In Norse mythology, ruled over by Hel.

Night Daughter of Norvi.

Nikumbha One of Ravana's generals.

Nila One of the monkey host, son of Agni.

Nin-Girsu God of fertility and war, patron god of Girsu. Also known as Shul-gur.

Ninigi Grandson of Amaterasu, Ninigi came to Earth bringing rice and order to found the Imperial family. He is known as the August Grandchild.

Niord God of the sea; marries Skadi.

Nippur The home of En-lil and one of the two major cities of Babylonian civilization.

Nirig God of war and storms, and son of Bel. Also known as Enu-Restu.

Nirvana Transcendent state and the final goal of Buddhism.

Nis Mythological creature, similar to a brownie or goblin, usually harmless or even friendly, but can be easily offended. They are often associated with Christmas or the winter solstice.

Noatun Niord's home.

Noisy-Throat One of Ravana's counsellors.

Noondah (Zanzibar) Cannibalistic cat which attacked and killed animals and humans.

Norns The fates and protectors of Yggdrasill. Many believe them to be the same as the Valkyries.

Norvi Father of the night.

Nott Goddess of night.

Nsasak bird Small bird who became chief of all small birds after winning a competition to go without food for seven days. The

Nsasak bird beat the Odudu bird by sneaking out of his home to feed.

Nü Wa The Goddess Nü Wa, who in some versions of the Creation myths is the sole creator of mankind, and in other tales is associated with the God Fu Xi, also a great benefactor of the human race. Some accounts represent Fu Xi as the brother of Nü Wa, but others describe the pair as lovers who lie together to create the very first human beings. Fu Xi is also considered to be the first of the Chinese emperors of mythical times who reigned from 2953 to 2838 BC.

Nuada The first king of the Tuatha De Danann in Ireland, who lost an arm in the first battle of Moytura against the Fomorians. He became known as 'Nuada of the Silver Hand' when Diancecht, the great physician of the Tuatha De Danann, replaced his hand with a silver one after the battle.

Nunda (Swahili, East Africa) Slayer that took the form of a cat and grew so big that it consumed everyone in the town except the sultan's wife, who locked herself away. Her son, Mohammed, killed Nunda and cut open its leg, setting free everyone Nunda had eaten.

Nut Goddess of the sky, stars and astronomy. Sister-wife of Keb and mother of Osiris, Isis, Set and Nephthys. She often appears in the form of a cow.

Nyame (Ashanti) God of the sky, who sees and knows everything.

Nymphs Minor female deities associated with particular parts of the land and sea.

Obassi Osaw (Ekoi) Creator god with his twin, Obassi Nsi. Originally, Obassi Osaw ruled the skies while Obassi Nsi ruled the Earth.

Obatala (Yoruba) Creator of humankind. He climbed down a golden chain from the sky to the earth, then a watery abyss, and formed land and humankind. When Olorun heard of his success, he created the sun for Obatala and his creations.

Oberon Fairy king.

Odin Allfather and king of all gods, he is known for travelling the nine worlds in disguise and recognized only by his single eye; dies at Ragnarok.

Oduduwa (Yoruba) Divine king of Ile-Ife, the holy city of Yoruba.

Odur Freyia's husband.

Odysseus Greek hero, son of Laertes and Anticleia, who was renowned for his cunning, the master behind the victory at Troy, and known for his long voyage home.

Oedipus Son of Leius, King of Thebes and Jocasta. Became King of Thebes and married his mother.

Ogdoad Group of eight deities who were formed into four male-female couples who joined to create the gods and the world.

Ogham One of the earliest known forms of Irish writing, originally used to inscribe upright pillar stones.

Oiran Courtesan.

Oisin Also called Ossian (particularly by James Macpherson who wrote a set of Gaelic Romances about this character, supposedly garnered from oral tradition). Ossian was the son of Fionn and Sadbh, and had various brothers, according to different legends. He was a man of great wisdom, became immortal for many centuries, but in the end he became mad.

Ojibwe Another name for the Chippewa, a tribe of Algonquin stock.

Okuninushi Deity and descendant of Susanoo, who married Suseri-hime, Susanoo's daughter, without his consent. Susanoo tried to kill him many times but did not succeed and eventually forgave Okuninushi. He is sometimes thought to be the son or grandson of Susanoo.

Olokun (Yoruba) Most powerful goddess who ruled the seas and marshes. When Obatala created Earth in her domain, other gods began to divide it up between them. Angered at their presumption, she caused a great flood to destroy the land.

Olorun (Yoruba) Supreme god and ruler of the sky. He sees and controls everything, but others, such as Obatala, carry out the work for him. Also known as Olodumare.

Olympia Zeus's home in Elis.

Olympus The highest mountain in Greece and the ancient home of the gods.

Omecihuatl Female half of the first being, combined with Ometeotl. Together they are the lords of duality or lords of the two sexes. Also known as Ometecutli and Omeciuatl or Tonacatecutli and Tonacaciuatl. Their offspring were Xipe Totec, Huitzilopochtli, Quetzalcoatl and Tezcatlipoca.

Ometeotl Male half of the first being, combined with Omecihuatl.

Ometochtli Collective name for the pulque-gods or drink-gods. These gods were often associated with rabbits as they were thought to be senseless creatures.

Onygate Anyway.

Opening the Mouth Ceremony in which mummies or statues were prayed over and anointed with incense before their mouths were opened, allowing them to eat and drink in the afterlife.

Oracle The response of a god or priest to a request for advice – also a prophecy; the place where such advice was sought; the person or thing from whom such advice was sought.

Oranyan (Yoruba) Youngest grandson of King Oduduwa, who later became king himself.

Orestes Son of Agamemnon and Clytemnestra who escaped following Agamemnon's murder to King Strophius. He later returned to Argos to murder his mother and avenge the death of his father.

Orpheus Thracian singer and poet, son of Oeagrus and a Muse. Married Eurydice and when she died tried to retrieve her from the Underworld.

Orunmila (Yoruba) Eldest son of Olorun, he helped Obatala create land and humanity, which he then rescued after Olokun flooded the lands. He has the power to see the future.

Osiris God of fertility, the afterlife and death. Thought to be the first of the pharaohs. He was murdered by his brother, Set, after which he was conjured back to life by Isis, Anubis and others before becoming lord of the afterworld. Married to Isis, who was also his sister.

Otherworld The world of deities and spirits, also known as the Land of Promise, or the Land of Eternal Youth, a place of everlasting life where all earthly dreams come to be fulfilled.

Owuo (Krachi, West Africa) Giant who personifies death. He causes a person to die every time he blinks his eye.

Palamedes Hero of Nauplia, believed to have created part of the ancient Greek alphabet. He tricked Odysseus into joining the fleet setting out for Troy by placing the infant Telemachus in the path of his plough.

Palermo Stone Stone carved with hieroglyphs, which came from the Royal Annals of ancient Egypt and contains a list of the kings of Egypt from the first to the early fifth dynasties.

Palfrey Docile and light horse, often used by women.

Palladium Wooden image of Athene, created by her as a monument to her friend Pallas who she accidentally killed. While in Troy it protected the city from invaders.

Pallas Athene's best friend, whom she killed.

Pan   God of Arcadia, half-goat and half-man. Son of Hermes. He is connected with fertility, masturbation and sexual drive. He is also associated with music, particularly his pipes, and with laughter.

Pan Gu   Some ancient writers suggest that this God is the offspring of the opposing forces of nature, the yin and the yang. The yin (female) is associated with the cold and darkness of the earth, while the yang (male) is associated with the sun and the warmth of the heavens. 'Pan' means 'shell of an egg' and 'Gu' means 'to secure' or 'to achieve'. Pan Gu came into existence so that he might create order from chaos.

Pandareus   Cretan King killed by the gods for stealing the shrine of Zeus.

Pandavas   Alternative name for sons of Pandu, pupils of Drona.

Pandora   The first woman, created by the gods, to punish man for Prometheus's theft of fire. Her dowry was a box full of powerful evil.

Papyrus   Paper-like material made from the pith of the papyrus plant, first manufactured in Egypt. Used as a type of paper as well as for making mats, rope and sandals.

Paramahamsa   The supreme swan.

Parashurama   Human incarnation of Vishnu, 'Rama with an axe'.

Paris   Handsome son of Priam and Hecuba of Troy, who was left for dead on Mount Ida but raised by shepherds. Was reclaimed by his family, then brought them shame and caused the Trojan War by eloping with Helen.

Parsa   Holy man. Also known as a zahid.

Parvati   Consort of Shiva and daughter of Himalaya.

Passion   Wife of desire.

Pavanarekha   Wife of Ugrasena, mother of Kans.

Peerie Folk Fairy or little folk.

Pegasus The winged horse born from the severed neck of Medusa.

Peggin Wooden vessel with a handle, often shaped like a tub and used for drinking.

Peleus Father of Achilles. He married Antigone, caused her death, and then became King of Phthia. Saved from death himself by Jason and the Argonauts. Married Thetis, a sea nymph.

Penelope The long-suffering but equally clever wife of Odysseus who managed to keep at bay suitors who longed for Ithaca while Odysseus was at the Trojan War and on his ten-year voyage home.

Pentangle Pentagram or five-pointed star.

Pentecost Christian festival held on the seventh Sunday after Easter. It celebrates the holy spirit descending on the disciples after Jesus's ascension.

Percivale Knight of the Round Table and original seeker of the Holy Grail.

Persephone Daughter of Zeus and Demeter who was raped by Hades and forced to live in the Underworld as his queen for three months of every year.

Perseus Son of Danae, who was made pregnant by Zeus. He fought the Gorgons and brought home the head of Medusa. He eventually founded the city of Mycenae and married Andromeda.

Pesh Kef Spooned blade used in the Opening the Mouth ceremony.

Phaeacia The Kingdom of Alcinous on which Odysseus landed after a shipwreck which claimed the last of his men as he left Calypso's island.

Pharaoh King or ruler of Egypt.

Philoctetes Malian hero, son of Poeas, received Heracles's bow and arrows as a gift when he lit the great hero's pyre on Mount Oeta. He was involved in the last part of the Trojan War, killing Paris.

Philtre Magic potion, usually a love potion.

Pibroch Bagpipe music.

Pintura Native manuscript or painting.

Pipiltin Noble class of the Aztecs.

Pismire Ant.

Piu-piu Short mat made from flax leaves and neatly decorated.

Po Gloom, darkness, the lower world.

Polyphemus A Cyclops, but a son of Poseidon. He fell in love with Galatea, but she spurned him. He was blinded by Odysseus.

Polyxena Daughter of Priam and Hecuba of Troy. She was sacrificed on the grave of Achilles by Neoptolemus.

Pooka Mythical creature with the ability to shapeshift. Often appears as a horse, but also as a bull, dog or in human form, and has the ability to talk. Also known as púca.

Popol Vuh Sacred 'book of counsel' of the Quiché or K'iche' Maya people.

Poseidon God of the sea, and of sweet waters. Also the god of earthquakes. His is brother to Zeus and Hades, who divided the earth between them.

Pradyumna Son of Krishna and Rukmini.

Prahasta (Long-Hand) One of Ravana's generals.

Prajapati Creator of the universe, father of the gods, demons and all creatures, later known as Brahma.

Priam King of Troy, married to Hecuba, who bore him Hector, Paris, Helenus, Cassandra, Polyxena, Deiphobus and Troilus. He was murdered by Neoptolemus.

Pritha Mother of Karna and of the Pandavas.

Prithivi Consort of Dyaus and goddess of the earth.

Proetus King of Argos, son of Abas.

Prometheus A Titan, son of Iapetus and Themus. He was champion of mortal men, which he created from clay. He stole fire from the gods and was universally hated by them.

Prose Edda Collection of Norse myths and poems, thought to have been compiled in the 1200s by Icelandic historian Snorri Sturluson.

Proteus The old man of the sea who watched Poseidon's seals.

Psyche A beautiful nymph who was the secret wife of Eros, against the wishes of his mother Aphrodite, who sent Psyche to perform many tasks in hope of causing her death. She eventually married Eros and was allowed to become partly immortal.

Ptah Creator god and deity of Memphis who was married to Sekhmet. Ptah built the boats to carry the souls of the dead to the afterlife.

Puddock Frog.

Pulque Alcoholic drink made from fermented agave.

Purusha The cosmic man, he was sacrificed and his dismembered body became all the parts of the cosmos, including the four classes of society.

Purvey To provide or supply.

Pushkara Nala's brother.

Pushpaka Rama's chariot.

Putana A rakshasi.

Pygmalion A sculptor who was so lonely he carved a statue of a beautiful woman, and eventually fell in love with it. Aphrodite brought the image to life.

Quauhtli Eagle.

Quern Hand mill used for grinding corn.

Quetzalcoatl Deity and god of wind. He is represented as a feathered or plumed serpent and is usually a wise and benevolent god. Offspring of Ometeotl and Omecihuatl, he is also known as Kukulkan.

Ra God of the sun, ruling male deity of Egypt whose name means 'sole creator'.

Radha The principal mistress of Krishna.

Ragnarok The end of the world.

Rahula Son of Siddhartha and Yashodhara.

Raiden God of thunder. He traditionally has a fierce and demonic appearance.

Rakshasas Demons and devils.

Ram of Mendes Sacred symbol of fatherhood and fertility.

Rama or **Ramachandra** A prince and hero of the Ramayana, worshipped as an incarnation of Vishnu.

Ra-Molo (Lesotho) Father of fire, a chief who ruled by fear. When trying to kill his brother, Tau the lion, he was turned into a monster with the head of a sheep and the body of a snake.

Rangatira Chief, warrior, gentleman.

Regin A blacksmith who educated Sigurd.

Reinga The spirit land, the home of the dead.

Reservations Tracts of land allocated to the native American people by the United States Government with the purpose of bringing the many separate tribes under state control.

Rewati Daughter of Raja, marries Balarama.

Rhadha Wife of Adiratha, a gopi of Brindaban and lover of Krishna.

Rhea Mother of the Olympian gods. Cronus ate each of her children, but she concealed Zeus and gave Cronus a swaddled rock in his place.

Rill Small stream.

Rimu (Chaga) Monster known to feed off human flesh, which sometimes takes the form of a werewolf.

Rishis Sacrificial priests associated with the devas in Swarga.

Rituparna King of Ayodhya.

Rohini The wife of Vasudeva, mother of Balarama and Subhadra, and carer of the young Krishna. Another Rohini is a goddess and consort of Chandra.

Rōnin Samurai whose master had died or fallen out of favour.

Rubáiyát Collection of poems written by Omar Khayyám.

Rúdábeh Wife of Zál and mother of Rustem.

Rudra Lord of Beasts and disease, later evolved into Shiva.

Rukma Rukmini's eldest brother.

Rustem Son of Zál and Rúdábeh, he was a brave and mighty warrior who undertook seven labours to travel to Mázinderán to rescue Kai-káús. Once there, he defeated the White Demon and rescued Kai-káús. He rode the fabled stallion Rakhsh and is also known as Rustam.

Ryō Traditional gold currency.

Sabdh Mother of Ossian, or Oisin.

Sabitu Goddess of the sea.

Sagara King of Ayodhya.

Sahadeva Pandava twin skilled in swordsmanship.

Sahib diwan Lord high treasurer or chief royal executive.

Saiawúsh Son of Kai-káús, who was put through trial by fire when Sudaveh, Kai-káús's wife, told him that Saiawúsh had taken advantage of her. His innocence was proven when the fire did not harm him. He was eventually killed by Afrásiyáb.

Saithe Blessed.

Sajara (Mali) God of rainbows. He takes the form of a multi-coloured serpent.

Sake Japanese rice wine.

Sakuni Cousin of Duryodhana.

Salam Greeting or salutation.

Saláman Son of the Shah of Yunan, who fell in love with Absál, his nurse. She died after they had a brief love affair and he returned to his father.

Salmali tree Cotton tree.

Salmon A symbol of great wisdom, around which many Scottish legends revolve.

Sám Mighty warrior who fought and won many battles. Father of Zál and grandfather to Rustem.

Sambu Son of Krishna.

Sampati Elder brother of Jatayu.

Samurai Noblemen who were part of the military in medieval Japan.

Sanehat Member of the royal bodyguard.

Sango (Yoruba) God of war and thunder.

Sangu (Mozambique) Goddess who protects pregnant women, depicted as a hippopotamus.

Santa Daughter of Dasharatha.

Sarapis Composite deity of Apis and Osiris, sometimes known as Serapis. Thought to be created to unify Greek and Egyptian citizens under the Greek pharaoh Ptolemy.

Sarasvati The tongue of Rama.

Sarcophagus Stone coffin.

Sargon of Akkad Raised by Akki, a husbandman, after being hidden at birth. Sargon became King of Assyria and a great hero. He founded the first library in Babylon. Similar to King Arthur or Perseus.

Sarsar Harsh, whistling wind.

Sasabonsam (Ashanti) Forest ogre.

Sassun Scottish word for England.

Sati Daughter of Daksha and Prasuti, first wife of Shiva.

Satrughna One of Dasharatha's four sons.

Satyavan Truth speaker, husband of Savitri.

Satyavati A fisher-maid, wife of Bhishma's father, Shamtanu.

Satyrs Elemental spirits which took great pleasure in chasing nymphs. They had horns, a hairy body and cloven hooves.

Saumanasa A mighty elephant.

Scamander River running across the Trojan plain, and father of Teucer.

Scarab Dung beetle, often used as a symbol of the immortal human soul and regeneration.

Scylla and Charybdis Scylla was a monster who lived on a rock of the same name in the Straits of Messina, devouring sailors. Charybdis was a whirlpool in the Straits which was supposedly inhabited by the hateful daughter of Poseidon.

Seal Often believed that seals were fallen angels. Many families are descended from seals, some of which had webbed hands or feet. Some seals were the children of sea-kings who had become enchanted (selkies).

Seelie-Court The court of the Fairies, who travelled around their realm. They were usually fair to humans, doling out punishment that was morally sound, but they were quick to avenge insults to fairies.

Segu (Swahili, East Africa) Guide who informs humans where honey can be found.

Sekhmet Solar deity who led the pharaohs in war. She is goddess of healing and was sent by Ra to destroy humanity when people turned against the sun god. She is portrayed with the head of a lion.

Selene Moon-goddess, daughter of Hyperion and Theia. She was seduced by Pan, but loved Endymion.

Selkie Mythical creature which is seal-like when in water but can shed its skin to take on human form when on land.

Seneschal Steward of a royal or noble household.

Sensei Teacher.

Seriyut A disciple of Buddha.

Sessrymnir Freyia's home.

Set God of chaos and evil, brother of Osiris, who killed him by tricking him into getting into a chest, which he then threw in the Nile, before cutting Osiris's body into fourteen separate pieces. Also known as Seth.

Sgeulachd Stories.

Shah Nameh *The Book of Kings* written by Ferdowski, one of the world's longest epic poems, which describes the mythology and history of the Persian Empire.

Shaikh Respected religious man.

Shaivas or Shaivites Worshippers of Shiva.

Shakti Power or wife of a god and Shiva's consort as his feminine aspect.

Shaman Also known as the 'Medicine Men' of Indian tribes, it was the shaman's role to cultivate communication with the spirit world. They were endowed with knowledge of all healing herbs, and learned to diagnose and cure disease. They could foretell the future, find lost property and had power over animals, plants and stones.

Shamash God of the sun and protector of Gilgamesh, the great Babylonian hero. Known as the son of Sin, the moon god, he is also portrayed as a judge of good and evil.

Shamtanu Father of Bhishma.

Shankara A great magician, friend of Chand Sadagar.

Shashti The Sixth, goddess who protects children and women in childbirth.

Sheen Beautiful and enchanted woman who casts a spell on Murtough, King of Ireland, causing him to fall in love with her and cast out his family. He dies at her hands, half burned and half drowned, but she then dies of grief as she returns his love. Sheen is known by many names, including Storm, Sigh and Rough Wind.

Shesh A serpent that takes human birth through Devaki.

Shi-en Fairy dwelling.

Shinto Indigenous religion of Japan, from the pre-sixth century to the present day.

Shireen Married to Khosru. Her beauty meant that she was desired by many, including Khosru's own son by his previous marriage. She killed herself rather than give in to her stepson.

Shitala The Cool One and goddess of smallpox.

Shiva One of the two great gods of post-Vedic Hinduism with Vishnu.

Shogun Military ruler or overlord.

Shoji Sliding door, usually a lattice screen of paper.

Shu God of the air and half of the first divine couple created by Atem. Brother and husband to Tefnut, father to Keb and Nut.

Shubistán Household.

Shudra One of the four fundamental colours (caste).

Shuttle Part of a machine used for spinning cloth, used for passing weft threads between warp threads.

Siddhas Musical ministrants of the upper air.

Sif Thor's wife; known for her beautiful hair.

Sigi Son of Odin.

Sigmund Warrior able to pull the sword from Branstock in the Volsung's hall.

Signy Volsung's daughter.

Sigurd Son of Sigmund, and bearer of his sword. Slays Fafnir the dragon.

Sigyn Loki's faithful wife.

Símúrgh Griffin, an animal with the body of a lion and the head and wings of an eagle. Known to hold great wisdom. Also called a symurgh.

Sin God of the moon, worshipped primarily in Ur.

Sindri Dwarf who worked with Brokki to fashion gifts for the gods; commissioned by Loki.

Sirens Sea nymphs who are half-bird, half-woman, whose song lures hapless sailors to their death.

Sisyphus King of Ephrya and a trickster who outwitted Autolycus. He was one of the greatest sinners in Hades.

Sita Daughter of the earth, adopted by Janaka, wife of Rama.

Skadi Goddess of winter and the wife of Niord for a short time.

Skanda Six-headed son of Shiva and a warrior god.

Skraeling Person native to Canada and Greenland. The name was given to them by Viking settlers and can be translated as 'barbarian'.

Skrymir Giant who battled against Thor.

Sleipnir Odin's steed.

Sluagh The host of the dead, seen fighting in the sky and heard by mortals.

Smote Struck with a heavy blow.

Sohráb Son of Rustem and Tahmineh, Sohráb was slain in battle by his own father, who killed him by mistake.

Sol The sun-maiden.

Soma A god and a drug, the elixir of life.

Somerled Lord of the Isles, and legendary ancestor of the Clan MacDonald.

Soothsayer Someone with the ability to predict or see the future, by the use of magic, special knowledge or intuition. Known as seanagal in Scottish myths.

Squaw North American Indian married woman.

Squint-Eye One of Ramana's monsters.

Squire Shield- or armour-bearer of a knight.

Srutakirti Daughter of Kushadhwaja.

Stirabout Porridge made by stirring oatmeal into boiling milk or water.

Stone Giants A malignant race of stone beings whom the Iroquois believed invaded Indian territory, threatening the Confederation of the Five Nations. These fierce and hostile creatures lived off human flesh and were intent on exterminating the human race.

Stoorworm A great water monster which frequented lochs. When it thrust its great body from the sea, it could engulf islands and whole ships. Its appearance prophesied devastation.

Stot Bullock.

Styx River in Arcadia and one of the four rivers in the Underworld. Charon ferried dead souls across it into Hades, and Achilles was dipped into it to make him immortal.

Subrahmanian Son of Shiva, a mountain deity.

Sugriva The chief of the five great monkeys in the Ramayana.

Sukanya The wife of Chyavana.

Suman Son of Asamanja.

Sumantra A noble Brahman.

Sumati Wife of Sagara.

Sumedha A righteous Brahman who dwelt in the city of Amara.

Sumitra One of Dasharatha's three wives, mother of Lakshmana and Satrughna.

Suniti Mother of Dhruva.

Suparshwa One of Ravana's counsellors.

Supranakha A rakshasi, sister of Ravana.

Surabhi The wish-bestowing cow.

Surcoat Loose robe, traditionally worn over armour.

Surtr Fire-giant who eventually destroys the world at Ragnarok.

Surya God of the sun.

Susanoo God of the storm. He is depicted as a contradictory character with both good and bad characteristics. He was banished from Heaven after trying to kill his sister, Amaterasu.

Sushena A monkey chief.

Svasud Father of summer.

Swarga An Olympian paradise, where all wishes and desires are gratified.

Sweating A ritual customarily associated with spiritual purification and prayer practised by most tribes throughout North America prior to sacred ceremonies or vision quests. Steam was produced within a 'sweat lodge', a low, dome-shaped hut, by sprinkling water on heated stones.

Syrinx An Arcadian nymph who was the object of Pan's love.

Tablet of Destinies Cuneiform clay tablet on which the fates were written. Tiawath had given this to Kingu, but it was taken by Merodach when he defeated them. The storm god Zu later stole it for himself.

Taiaha A weapon made of wood.

Tailtiu One of the most famous royal residences of ancient Ireland. Possibly also a goddess linked to this site.

Tall One of Ravana's counsellors.

Tammuz Solar deity of Eridu who, with Gishzida, guards the gates of Heaven. Protector of Anu.

Tamsil Example or guidance.

Tangi Funeral, dirge. Assembly to cry over the dead.

Taniwha Sea monster, water spirit.

Tantalus Son of Zeus who told the secrets of the gods to mortals and stole their nectar and ambrosia. He was condemned to eternal torture in Hades, where he was tempted by food and water but allowed to partake of neither.

Taoism Taoism (or Daoism) came into being at roughly the same time as Confucianism, although its tenets were radically different and were largely founded on the philosophies of Lao Tzu (Laozi). While Confucius argued for a system of state discipline, Taoism strongly favoured self-discipline and looked upon nature as the architect of essential laws. A newer form of Taoism evolved after the Burning of the Books, placing great emphasis on spirit worship and pacification of the gods.

Tapu Sacred, supernatural possession of power. Involves spiritual rules and restrictions.

Tara Also known as Temair, the Hill of Tara was the popular seat of the ancient High-Kings of Ireland from the earliest times to the sixth century. Located in Co. Meath, it was also the place where great noblemen and chieftains congregated during wartime, or for significant events.

Tara Sugriva's wife.

Tartarus Dark region, below Hades.

Tau (Lesotho) Brother to Ra-Molo, depicted as a lion.

Taua War party.

Tefnut Goddess of water and rain. Married to Shu, who was also her brother. She, like Sekhmet, is portrayed with the head of a lion. Also known as Tefenet.

Telegonus Son of Odysseus and Circe. He was allegedly responsible for his father's death.

Telemachus Son of Odysseus and Penelope who was aided by Athene in helping his mother to keep away the suitors in Odysseus's absence.

Temu The evening form of Ra, the Sun God.

Tengu Goblin or gnome, often depicted as bird-like. A powerful fighter with weapons.

Tenochtitlán Capital city of the Aztecs, founded around AD 1350 and the site of the 'Great Temple'. Now Mexico City.

Teo-Amoxtli Divine book.

Teocalli Great temple built in Tenochtitlán, now Mexico City.

Teotleco Festival of the Coming of the Gods; also the twelfth month of the Aztec calendar.

Tepee A conical-shaped dwelling constructed of buffalo hide stretched over lodge-poles. Mostly used by native American tribes living on the plains.

Tepeyollotl God of caves, desert places and earthquakes, whose name means 'heart of the mountain'. He is depicted as a jaguar, often leaping at the sun. Also known as Tepeolotlec.

Tepitoton Household gods.

Tereus King of Daulis who married Procne, daughter of Pandion King of Athens. He fell in love with Philomela, raped her and cut out her tongue.

Tezcatlipoca Supreme deity and Lord of the Smoking Mirror. He was also patron of royalty and warriors. Invented human sacrifice to the gods. Offspring of Ometeotl and Omecihuatl, he is known as the Jupiter of the Aztec gods.

Thalia Muse of pastoral poetry and comedy.

Theia Goddess of many names, and mother of the sun.

Theseus Son of King Aegeus of Athens. A cycle of legends has been woven around his travels and life.

Thetis Chief of the Nereids loved by both Zeus and Poseidon. They married her to a mortal, Peleus, and their child was Achilles. She tried to make him immortal by dipping him in the River Styx.

Thialfi Thor's servant, taken when his peasant father unwittingly harms Thor's goat.

Thiassi Giant and father of Skadi, he tricked Loki into bringing Idunn to him. Thrymheim is his kingdom.

Thomas the Rhymer Also called 'True Thomas', he was Thomas of Ercledoune, who lived in the thirteenth century. He met with the Queen of Elfland, and visited her country, was given clothes and a tongue that could tell no lie. He was also given the gift of prophecy, and many of his predictions were proven true.

Thor God of thunder and of war (with Tyr). Known for his huge size, and red hair and beard. Carries the hammer Miolnir. Slays Jormungander at Ragnarok.

Thoth God of the moon. Invented the arts and sciences and regulated the seasons. He is portrayed with the head of an ibis or a baboon.

Three-Heads One of Ravana's monsters.

Thrud Thor's daughter.

Thrudheim Thor's realm. Also called Thrudvang.

Thunder-Tooth Leader of the rakshasas at the siege of Lanka.

Tiawath Primeval dark ocean or abyss, Tiawath is also a monster and evil deity of the deep. She took the form of a dragon or sea serpent and battled the gods of light for supremacy over all living beings. She was eventually defeated by Merodach, who used her body to create Heaven and Earth.

Tiglath-Pileser I King of Assyria, who made it a leading power for centuries.

Tiki First man created, a figure carved of wood, or other representation of man.

Tirawa The name given to the Great Creator (**see** Great Spirit) by the Pawnee tribe who believed that four direct paths led from his house in the sky to the four semi-cardinal points: north-east, north-west, south-east and south-west.

Tiresias A Theban who was given the gift of prophecy by Zeus. He was blinded for seeing Athene bathing. He continued to use his prophetic talents after his death, advising Odysseus.

Tirfing Sword made by dwarves which was cursed to kill every time it was drawn, be the cause of three great atrocities, and kill Suaforlami (Odin's grandson), for whom it was made.

Tisamenus Son of Orestes, who inherited the Kingdom of Argos and Sparta.

Titania Queen of the fairies.

Tlaloc God of rain and fertility, so important to the people, because he ensured a good harvest, that the Aztec heaven or paradise was named Tlalocan in his honour.

Tlazolteotl Goddess of ordure, filth and vice. Also known as the earth-goddess or Tlaelquani, meaning 'filth-eater'. She acted as a confessor of sins or wrongdoings.

Tohu-mate Omen of death.

Tohunga A priest; a possessor of supernatural powers.

Toltec Civilization that preceded the Aztecs.

Tomahawk Hatchet with a stone or iron head used in war or hunting.

Tonalamatl Record of the Aztec calendar, which was recorded in books made from bark paper.

Tonalpohualli Aztec calendar composed of twenty thirteen-day weeks called trecenas.

Totec Solar deity known as Our Great Chief.

Totemism System of belief in which people share a relationship with a spirit animal or natural being with whom they interact. Examples include Ea, who is represented by a fish.

Toxilmolpilia The binding up of the years.

Tristan Nephew of King Mark of Cornwall, who travels to Ireland to bring Iseult back to marry his uncle. On the way, he and Iseult consume a love potion and fall madly in love before their story ends tragically.

Triton A sea-god, and son of Poseidon and Amphitrite. He led the Argonauts to the sea from Lake Tritonis.

Trojan War War waged by the Greeks against Troy, in order to reclaim Menelaus's wife Helen, who had eloped with the Trojan prince Paris. Many important heroes took part, and form the basis of many legends and myths.

Troll Unfriendly mythological creature of varying size and strength. Usually dwells in mountainous areas, among rocks or caves.

Truage Tribute or pledge of peace or truth, usually made on payment of a tax.

Tsuki-yomi God of the moon, brother of Amaterasu and Susanoo.

Tuat The other world or land of the dead.

Tupuna Ancestor.

Tvashtar Craftsman of the gods.

Tyndareus King of Sparta, perhaps the son of Perseus's daughter Grogphone. Expelled from Sparta but restored by Heracles. Married Leda and fathered Helen and Clytemnestra, among others.

Tyr Son of Frigga and the god of war (with Thor). Eventually kills Garm at Ragnarok.

Tzompantli Pyramid of Skulls.

Uayeb The five unlucky days of the Mayan calendar, which were believed to be when demons from the underworld could reach Earth. People would often avoid leaving their houses on uayeb days.

Ubaaner Magician, whose name meant 'splitter of stones', who created a wax crocodile that came to life to swallow up the man who was trying to seduce his wife.

Uile Bheist Mythical creature, usually some form of wild beast.

Uisneach A hill formation between Mullingar and Athlone said to mark the centre of Ireland.

uKqili (Zulu) Creator god.

Uller God of winter, whom Skadi eventually marries.

Ulster Cycle Compilation of folk tales and legends telling of the Ulaids, people from the northeast of Ireland, now named Ulster. Also known as the *Uliad Cycle*, it is one of four Irish cycles of mythology.

Unseelie Court An unholy court comprising a kind of fairies, antagonistic to humans. They took the form of a kind of Sluagh, and shot humans and animals with elf-shots.

Urd One of the Norns.

Urien King of Gore, husband of Morgan le Fey and father to Yvain.

Urmila Second daughter of Janaka.

Usha Wife of Aniruddha, daughter of Vanasur.

Ushas Goddess of the dawn.

Utgard-loki King of the giants. Tricked Thor.

Uther Pendragon King of England in sub-Roman Britain; father of King Arthur.

Utixo (Hottentot) Creator god.

Ut-Napishtim Ancestor of Gilgamesh, whom Gilgamesh sought out to discover how to prevent death. Similar to Noah in that he was sent a vision warning him of a great deluge. He built an ark in seven days, filling it with his family, possessions and all kinds of animals.

Uz Deity symbolized by a goat.

Vach Goddess of speech.

Vajrahanu One of Ravana's generals.

Vala Another name for Norns.

Valfreya Another name for Freyia.

Valhalla Odin's hall for the celebrated dead warriors chosen by the Valkyries.

Vali The cruel brother of Sugriva, dethroned by Rama.

Valkyries Odin's attendants, led by Freyia. Chose dead warriors to live at Valhalla. Also spelled as Valkyrs.

Vamadeva One of Dasharatha's priests.

Vanaheim Home of the Vanir.

Vanir Race of gods in conflict with the Aesir; they are gods of the sea and wind.

Varuna Ancient god of the sky and cosmos, later, god of the waters.

Vasishtha One of Dasharatha's priests.

Vassal Person under the protection of a feudal lord.

Vasudev Descendant of Yadu, husband of Rohini and Devaki, father of Krishna.

Vasudeva A name of Narayana or Vishnu.

Vavasor Vassal or tenant of a baron or lord who himself has vassals.

Vedic Mantras, hymns.

Vernandi One of the Norns.

Vichitravirya Bhishma's half-brother.

Vidar Slays Fenris.

Vidura Friend of the Pandavas.

Vigrid The plain where the final battle is held.

Vijaya Karna's bow.

Vikramaditya A king identified with Chandragupta II.

Vintail Moveable front of a helmet.

Virabhadra A demon that sprang from Shiva's lock of hair.

Viradha A fierce rakshasa, seizes Sita, slain by Rama.

Virupaksha The elephant who bears the whole world.

Vishnu The Preserver, Vedic sun-god and one of the two great gods of post-Vedic Hinduism.

Vision Quest A sacred ceremony undergone by Native Americans to establish communication with the spirit set to direct them in life. The quest lasted up to four days and nights and was preceded by a period of solitary fasting and prayer.

Vivasvat The sun.

Vizier High-ranking official or adviser. Also known as vizir or vazir.

Volsung Family of great warriors about whom a great saga was spun.

Vrishadarbha King of Benares.

Vrishasena Son of Karna, slain by Arjuna.

Vyasa Chief of the royal chaplains.

Wairua Spirit, soul.

Wanjiru (Kikuyu) Maiden who was sacrificed by her village to appease the gods and make it rain after years of drought.

Weighing of the heart Procedure carried out after death to assess whether the deceased was free from sin. If the deceased's heart weighed less than the feather of Ma'at, they would join Osiris in the Fields of Peace.

Whare Hut made of fern stems tied together with flax and vines, and roofed in with raupo (reeds).

White Demon Protector of Mázinderán. He prevented Kai-káús and his army from invading.

Withy Thin twig or branch which is very flexible and strong.

Wolverine Large mammal of the musteline family with dark, very thick, water-resistant fur, inhabiting the forests of North America and Eurasia.

Wroth Angry.

Wyrd One of the Norns.

Xanthus & Balius Horses of Achilles, immortal offspring of Zephyrus the west wind. A gift to Achilles's father Peleus.

Xipe Totec High priest and son of Ometeotl and Omecihuatl. Also known as the god of the seasons.

Xiupohualli Solar year, composed of eighteen twenty-day months. Also spelt Xiuhpōhualli.

Yadu A prince of the Lunar dynasty.

Yakshas Same as rakshasas.

Yakunin Government official.

Yama God of Death, king of the dead and son of the sun.

Yamato Take Legendary warrior and prince. Also known as Yamato Takeru.

Yashiki Residence or estate, usually of a daimyō.

Yasoda Wife of Nand.

Yemaya (Yoruba) Wife of Obatala.

Yemoja (Yoruba) Goddess of water and protector of women.

Yggdrasill The World Ash, holding up the Nine Worlds. Does not fall at Ragnarok.

Ymir Giant created from fire and ice; his body created the world.

Yo The female principle who, joined with In, the male side, brought about creation and the first gods. In and Yo correspond to the Chinese Yang and Yin.

Yomi The underworld.

Yudhishthira The eldest of the Pandavas, a great soldier.

Yuki-Onna The Snow-Bride or Lady of the Snow, who represents death.

Yvain Son of Morgan le Fay and knight of the Round Table, who goes on chivalric quests with a lion he rescued from a dragon.

Zahid Holy man.

Zál Son of Sám, who was born with pure white hair. Sám abandoned Zál, who was raised by the Símúrgh, or griffins. Zal became a great warrior, second only to his son, Rustem. Also known as Ním-rúz and Dustán.

Zephyr Gentle breeze.

Zeus King of gods, god of sky, weather, thunder, lightning, home, hearth and hospitality. He plays an important role as the voice of justice, arbitrator between man and gods, and among them. Married to Hera, but lover of dozens of others.

Zohák Serpent-king and figure of evil. Father of Mihrab.

Zu God of the storm, who took the form of a huge bird. Similar to the Persian símúrgh.

Zukin Head covering.

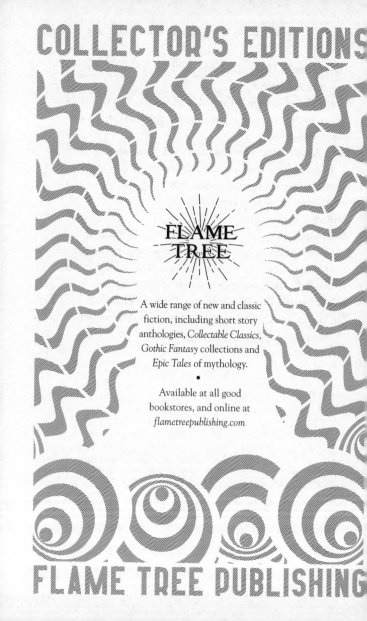